In the Clear

STEVE LOPEZ

In the Clear

HARCOURT, INC.

New York   San Diego   London

www.HarcourtBooks.com

Library of Congress Cataloging-in-Publication Data
Lopez, Steve.
In the clear/Steve Lopez.—1st ed.
p.   cm.
ISBN 0-15-100284-3
1. Casinos—Fiction. 2. Sheriffs—Fiction. 3. Ex-police officers—Fiction.
4. New Jersey—Fiction.   I. Title
PS3562.O673   I6   2002
813'.54—dc21   2001006068

Designed by Linda Lockowitz
Text set in Bulmer

Printed in the United States of America

First edition
K J I H G F E D C B A

For Alison, again.

And for David Tucker.

My thanks to Walter Bode and David Black, a pair of aces.

And to Arthur Abraham, the best plumber and finest man in six states.

Also to the memory of Thelma's Luncheonette, and to those who fought to save their homes from the wrecking ball in Atlantic City.

In the American consciousness, there is no confusing the Jersey shore with, say, Hilton Head. Any mention of it is likely to conjure up images of medical waste bobbing in mucky brown surf and body parts washing ashore in dreary towns with Superfund sites. It could also be said that a short-lived rebate offer during a particularly wretched summer of coliform bacteria infestation—"If the water smells, it's free motels"—was somewhat counterproductive. But the stereotypes were mostly just that, and despite the endless abuse from unoriginal comics and other professional hacks, the Jersey shore did not have to be sold to anyone within two hundred miles of the Atlantic. Memorial Day to Labor Day, the forty-mile strip of south Jersey shoreline from Atlantic City to Cape May was transfused and repopulated as a sort of Row House Riviera. Half of Greater Philadelphia packed up and clocked in, chasing relief from all that boiling asphalt and the flat rhythms of summer in the city. Some parked their pasty winter-fed bodies in front of the slots and never saw the sun; others nursed flaming sunburns in oceanfront joints that all had happy hour pub cuisine of the jalapeño poppers variety and Top 40 cover bands that swung unashamedly from "Proud Mary" to "Livin' La Vida Loca."

But mostly a Jersey shore summer was a family one, and a throwback one at that. People had rented the same houses for thirty years and staked out the same spots on the beach year after year, setting up playpens for their sunblocked toddlers and big lazy umbrellas to shade the grandparents. At night, balmy breezes pushed a tonic of sea salt, Noxema, and fried fat over the gathered hordes. Kids ran wild on the boardwalks in Ocean City and Wildwood and adults strolled in shorts and bleached sweaters, picking fudge samples from trays held out by the mushroom-skinned Irish kids who came over every summer in the exchange program. The air was scented for three solid months with coconut oil, cotton candy, roasted peanuts, and funnel cakes. It was the last place in the country without pretense, the proud miniature golf capital of planet Earth, unashamedly tacky in a uniquely wholesome, Americana sort of way. Wildwood alone, with its grand endless boardwalk and the nightly neon inferno of its infinite motel signs—Tiki Winds, Caspian Sea, Arabian Nights—put off enough light to be used as a beacon in intergalactic travel. But vacationers didn't have to go for the glitz of Atlantic City or the excess of Wildwood and Ocean City. There were options in south Jersey, and the quietest and smallest of them was the town of Harbor Light. Too quiet and perhaps too small, some believed, to survive.

FRIDAY, APRIL 4
HARBOR LIGHT, NEW JERSEY

"I can't arrest him, Pop. It's not a crime to sell wholesale."

"The way they do it, it should be. It's immoral, so it should be illegal."

"And how's that?"

"They buy a load of crap, and then undercut me on price. You see this hammer in my hand, son? It'll last you until you're my age."

"It looks like the same hammer Bargain Acres sells for two dollars less."

"The fact that you can say that, Albert, just shows."

"Shows what?"

"That you should build something from time to time, so you'd know the difference between a quality tool and a piece of junk."

"Pop, I really gotta go. Anyway, I think I might have heard this speech before."

"They're destroying our way of life, Albert. They're destroying this town, and somebody should bring them to justice."

"You're right, Pop. I'll get on my radio right away and notify the FBI. See you later."

"And you call yourself a cop? Dinner on Friday, don't forget. And bring Rickie, so I can talk to somebody who understands we can't let these bastards get away with this."

Outside Albert's office, a silver Ferrari coupe sharked in alongside the rusted-out truck from Manny's Bait Bucket and Oscar Price stepped out in a thousand-dollar suit. Albert, with twenty-eight years of law enforcement training, suspected he wasn't here to buy worms. He closed the newspaper, stubbed out his cigar, and asked himself the obvious question. What business would a billionaire casino mogul have with the Harbor County Sheriff's Department?

"Excuse me, sir," Georgianna brayed into the intercom, "but Mr. Price from the casino is out here. He has no appointment."

"I think we can squeeze him in, Georgianna. Send him on back."

Georgianna sat just on the other side of the coatroom. They were no more than twelve feet apart, and if he leaned forward he could see her stationed behind that PT boat of a desk, looking for all the world like Ernest Borgnine in a wig. But she had always considered it more professional to buzz him on the intercom than to simply call out to him. The coatroom, with a sofa that smelled like it had once been a nesting ground for some unspecified form of wildlife, separated Albert's office from the reception area. He was grateful that Harlan Wayans, who passed out on that sofa two or three times a week after leaving Mo's Tavern, hadn't stumbled in yet for his nap. Albert glanced around his cluttered office, wishing it were a little more professional-looking. But how often did he have this kind of company?

"Sheriff LaRosa, good to see you," Oscar Price chirped, extending a hand that folded into nothing when Albert took hold of it. Albert grabbed a folding chair with Knights of Columbus stenciled onto it, flicking off a pile of fishing and boating magazines. They thudded onto the AstroTurf carpeting—still there from the days when this office and the two adjoining ones were part of an indoor Putt-Putt golf course that ultimately tanked—and raised a small cloud of dust that both of them noticed.

Price wore a navy blue double-breasted with a crisp shirt that was so white Albert feared retinal damage. He was coming up on sixty, BB-eyed and birdlike, with thinning light brown hair cut short and spiky. Every time Albert saw him he was reminded of quail-hunting trips he and Creed James had taken in the Pine Barrens as boys.

"Can I get you some coffee?" Albert asked, raising his own cup, which bore the name of an Atlantic City bail bondsman.

"You don't happen to have tea," Price said.

"Can't say that I do," Albert said flatly. What was he running, a cafeteria? He offered a cigarette-size cigar, which Price declined politely. "You mind?" Albert asked, lighting one for himself. Albert recalled seeing him in khakis and a work shirt on Cannery Way a time or two over the last couple of months, flitting in and out of shops like he was just another local yokel. Albert couldn't remember ever seeing him in civvies otherwise, doing nonbillionaire things like running errands and breathing the same air as the local fish eaters.

Price took in the room as if something about it surprised him. Maybe it was the cache of deadly assault weapons Albert had confiscated over the years: kitchen knives, lamps, flowerpots, shoes, cookware of every type, all tossed into the cubbyhole shelving Albert snagged from the second-grade classroom when Lighthouse Primary closed. Another curiosity was the eight-foot-square holding cell back in the corner. Albert took a Polaroid of everyone who'd spent time in there, and pushpinned the photos to the back wall.

"I didn't realize you detained people here," Price said.

"We're full-service. They call the job resident deputy," Albert said. "It's sort of like having my own sheriff's department."

Oscar Price looked genuinely interested in that little piece of information, which made Albert all the more curious about what he was doing here. He had better things to do than come hear the history of a one-man cop shop. Maybe he was here to complain about the trespassers again. Price had bought the old Sisters of Mercy retreat house at the southeast corner of the island a few years ago and poured millions into it, turning the place into a seaside villa that made the cover of one of those dental office magazines. Price had called once about people schlepping right past the Private Beach signs, like there was something Albert could do about it if he didn't catch them in the act. But Price didn't look like someone who was going to tell him how to do his job, a look Albert had seen a few times, and the few hundred bucks Albert had on Evolution's line of credit wouldn't buy the silk tie Price was wearing, so he couldn't be here to collect. "So tell me," Price said. "How long exactly have you been here?"

Albert looked out to the marina, where a forty-footer was chugging in with a catch of flounder or maybe bluefish. "Feels like about a hundred fifty years," he said. "I've never lived anywhere else except a few years in Philadelphia."

"The job," Oscar Dan said. "What I mean to ask is, how long have you been sheriff?"

"Twenty-three years, six months, three weeks, and almost four and a half days," Albert said.

Oscar Price smiled, to the extent that a man with no lips can smile. "Going for twenty-five?" he asked.

Albert sipped his coffee, peering at his visitor over the top of his cup. He puffed on his cigar and politely blew the smoke toward Georgianna, who was trying her best to listen in. Probably as mystified by this visit as Albert was. "I put in five years in Philadelphia, Twenty-fourth District, before that. A whole different job. Different world altogether. But I should have stuck it out and I'd have my feet up now, going through my investment portfolio."

He meant it as a joke, but Price nodded as if everyone had an investment portfolio. With an ex-wife still drawing alimony, Albert was not exactly piling it up.

"I imagine it must be a handful. You're it for the entire island, am I right?"

"Theoretically there's backup nights and weekends, but I can't get any help out here. People call me at home anyway or come by the house. It takes a certain touch, you know? A way with people." Albert had no idea why he was suddenly defending his honor, but if Price was asking about when he planned to give up his job, maybe he was here to offer him a different one. Lots of cops had made soft landings in A.C. after retirement, working security jobs that paid more than they'd ever earned on the street for half the hassle. Albert had considered going that way himself. The thing was, a casino boss would never get involved in hiring at that level.

"I've never heard anything but the most flattering words about the job you do. But is a job worth holding on to once you start counting the days? Life's too short, you know? With your experience, your reputation, you must have passed up a lot of opportunities."

Albert felt the heat climb the cigar for his fingers. He took another drag before losing any skin and snuffed it out in the oyster shell ashtray. Of course he'd had opportunities, and other cops had told him he should have jumped at the chance to get off the Andy Griffith beat here on Slow Poke Island. But they didn't know the whole story. Why he left Philadelphia. Why he hung on in Harbor Light.

Georgianna buzzed him just then.

"Would you please hold the calls?" Albert said with irritation.

"I wouldn't have bothered you," Georgianna said. "But it sounds rather urgent."

"This won't take a minute," Albert told Price, reaching for another smoke when he realized who it was.

"There's no way," Albert said. "Look, I'm going to have to call you back later. But there's no way I can raise that, Ramon. Are you kidding me? Listen, I'm in the middle of something, so I'll . . . hello?"

Albert dropped the receiver.

"Is there a problem?" Price asked.

Albert shook his head no.

"Just a friend in Philadelphia who needs some help."

"A friend from your days on the police force there?"

"You might say that. Now where were we?"

"I was just wondering why you're still wearing a badge if you had chances to move on to something better," Price said.

"Right. Well it was never the right deal. What can I tell you?" Albert said, looking at his holstered service revolver atop the desk. He hated the weight of it hanging off of him, hated sitting down or getting in and out of the patrol car with all that hipped baggage. "Plus, you'd have to start all over with benefits, seniority, all that. Here, if you hold out for twenty-five years, they give you three-fifths of your salary and benefits for life. That's the plan, anyway, then I'd maybe pick up something else so I've got two checks coming in. After a couple of years of that, it's looking pretty good, you know? Puts me pretty close to where I'm in the clear."

Price nodded, and Albert thought: Yeah, sure. Must be fascinating stuff. Maybe he ought to tell him he was putting away twenty dollars a month in the Christmas club. That'd knock him out. Evolution was, and had been, the hottest casino on the Boardwalk. It turned profits and brought back customers at rates the competition only dreamed about. And Price had a reputation for doing whatever it took to stay out front of the pack. Whatever it took.

Price came up in his seat now and the fixed smile was gone. Whatever dance he was doing, it was time for work. He shot a glance toward Georgianna as if to make sure this was a private conversation. Albert went over and closed the door. He could honestly say—much to his frustration, because you still had to have some pride as a detective, even if the bulk of the job was pulling people over for driving too slow—he had no earthly idea what was about to come out of Oscar Dan's mouth.

"I was wondering, Albert—can I call you Albert?—this is frankly none of my business, and if you think I'm out of line, tell me so and I'll be on my way. But don't you think maybe you're underestimating yourself?"

Albert didn't answer right away. This *was* a job offer. What kind of job, and why, he couldn't say. For Price to come in person, all this secrecy about it, it had to be something big. Or maybe something shady.

"What I mean is, you're a young man," Price went on. "What are you, barely fifty?"

"Forty-nine as we speak."

"That leaves plenty of time for a second career. And I happen to have a business proposal that's going to put a bigger pop in your pistol."

Albert sat dead still.

"Is there any way you can break away from here for half an hour?"

Albert wondered how much it would take to make him do business with a man he didn't trust. He was figuring high six figures.

Oscar Price insisted they take his Ferrari. The doors closed with a quiet, expensive whoosh, raising the scent of new upholstery. Price ground out of the gravel lot, dropped the car into gear, and cruised north on Waterman in the direction of Atlantic City. The platinum sky before them was bright with morning burn-off, and the back bay, brushed by a five-knot westerly, shone like a bed of nickels. An egret stood still as a lawn ornament in the ripe green fringe of the marshland shallows. Albert wasn't exactly a car head, but it all looked a little prettier from the cockpit of a Ferrari.

Harbor Light was flat as the sea and shaped like a clamshell, straight and true along the oceanfront and bowed on its western edge along the marshy back-bay shore. The town was named for the lighthouse that had once guided fishermen home through fog and roiling seas, but commercial fishing had dried up for the most part and the candle had been dark for years. The island, home to forty-five hundred year-round residents, was small enough that you could walk its perimeter in under an hour. It was separated from Atlantic City by a one-hundred-fifty-foot inlet that flushed boats into the marina and out to sea. As a boy, Albert had explored every square inch of the island. As a cop, nothing happened that he didn't know about. That was the best thing about his job, and the worst thing, too.

"This won't take but a few minutes," Oscar Price said as they highballed around the bend, past the neat little craftsmen in the Western Addition. The speed was deceiving what with the noise-free glide. Albert couldn't help but sneak a peek at the speedometer. Fifty-two in a thirty-five zone. Price caught him peeking, but something told Albert to keep his mouth shut until he found out what kind of adventure he was on. "Rides real nice," he said, and Price stared straight ahead, poker-faced.

Price had the whole island talking three years ago when he moved his family out of a six-million-dollar A.C. penthouse and settled in little old Harbor Light. Albert knew from the Rubio real estate family that he'd paid around a million for the abandoned retreat house, which had become a giant oceanfront pigeon coop. By some accounts Price had sunk another ten million into the rehab and an engineering job to turn erosion around and put a little more beach at his feet. To some, it was a source of pride that anyone would think the island worthy of such an investment. But others talked, the way folks do in small towns, about how it was the beginning of the end. The whole place was going to go upscale, they hyperventilated, and they'd be priced out of their own homes. They worried over ulterior motives, too, none of which anyone could make a strong case for. You heard a lot of yacking about tax shelters, as if anyone understood the ins and outs of managing an empire that made it into the Top 10 on the Fortune 500 list.

"Looks like it's going to warm up nice today," Albert said. "Another two months and it starts already. Can you believe it?"

"That's right. Memorial Day's right around the corner. You realize the summer trade in Harbor Light has dropped at least five percent a year the last three years?" Price asked. "I was talking to Mayor Joe about it. Seems the island isn't holding its own against the rest of the shore."

"No Boardwalk here, it gets harder every year," Albert said. "These kids are conditioned nowadays that they expect something every minute of the day or they don't know what to do with themselves."

"Exactly," Price said approvingly.

Albert hit the window button and reached into his shirt pocket for a cigar, showing it to Price to make sure it was okay.

"Do me a favor," Price said. "Pop the glove box."

It opened to a gold-colored box of Monte Cristo No. 2s, made in Havana.

"Would you prefer one of those?" Price asked, winking as he did, either because you couldn't find a better cigar or because they were illegal, Albert wasn't sure which. Albert was in most cases entirely respectful of the law, and believed in principle that there was no such thing as a little bit of bad in an otherwise good cop. One toe over the line, and you might as well jump to the other side. But this one wasn't hard to figure. Stupid law, good cigar.

"Don't mind if I do," Albert said, taking two and offering one to Price. When Price declined, Albert put the extra in his shirt pocket. The cigar was perfect to the touch. Like clay. "I noticed you down on Cannery Way a couple times recently," Albert said, flicking his lighter and twisting the Monte Cristo for a nice even burn. "For the life of me, I can't remember exactly when or where."

"Phelps Drugs, maybe. Or your father's store, it might have been. What a classic, that place. There's just something about an old-fashioned hardware store that takes you back, you know what I mean?"

Albert nodded. His father hadn't changed a thing in LaRosa's Hardware for fifty years and never would. Every once in a while, Albert's sister Sam came down from New York and told him he ought to try this or that to keep up with the times. What a waste of time. Like he was going to dress the front window or redo housewares with items that had been manufactured in the last quarter century. Just like when she tried to coax him into retirement. Sam knew as well as Albert that there was only one way the old man would leave that store.

"You might say he's a little on the stubborn side, my old man. A lot of pride there about holding on, especially with Bargain Acres and the rest of them putting the squeeze on the little guy." Albert drew on the cigar, rolled the taste around in his mouth and throat, and then let it fly out the window. Pain in the ass was another way to describe his father, but he didn't know Price well enough to get into it.

"God bless him that," Oscar Price said.

They were coming up on the old Sea-Fruit Cannery, which had sat abandoned for a good twenty-five years. The thirty-foot-tall fiberglass mascot, Betty the Blue Crab, was decaying atop the boxy, four-story brick building, and there'd been talk for years of relocating her onto the beach as a tourist attraction. Yeah, Albert thought, they'd come flocking in for that. The old-timers on the island were full of big dreams that never panned out.

"But I wonder how your father's business is doing, to tell you the truth," Price said. "Your father, the drugstore, Nuba's Pie Shop, all the others. It's not like it used to be down there, is it?"

"They manage to hang on somehow," Albert said. "I thought they were done in when the Bargain Acres came in up on the Parkway. They took a hit, for sure. What little town hasn't? It's a different game today in retail. The whole world's changing."

"They could use a little more help from the city, if you ask me. Those trees used to get trimmed every year as I understand, and you wouldn't have seen the bricks coming up on Cannery Way sidewalks. No good for business, any of that. The bike shop didn't make it, or the haberdashery, for that matter. And Mayor Joe tells me he's going to call it quits, too. It used to be that people would resole their shoes two or three times. But now they'll just take that ten bucks and it practically pays for a new pair of shoes at Bargain Acres. I like Joe, you know? I like the way he thinks."

Albert knew only one thing. If he had Price's wallet in his

pocket, he wouldn't lose any sleep over the state of tree trimming or the price of shoe repair.

Price crossed over Kip Slough Road and pulled around the back side of the cannery, where it nudged up to the edge of the slough. He parked facing Atlantic City, and the hotel-casino towers rose before them like columns on a financial growth chart. It used to be that half of Harbor Light worked in fishing. Now the jobs were in Atlantic City. You dealt cards, poured liquor, waited tables. Price killed the engine and turned to Albert.

"I want this to be between just the two of us for now," he said.

Albert didn't give him anything more than a noncommittal nod.

"I see a fresh start for this town. I see a way to get it back on track. This cannery here? I've had an engineering company take a look, and they tell me it's solid as a rock. Of course, I'd have to make a few structural changes here and there, but the point is to maintain the integrity of the building. Maintain a nautical theme, too."

Price got out of the car and Albert followed him to the edge of Kip Slough, fifty yards of black water that separated two different worlds. A bridge had been started twenty years ago from the Atlantic City side, but the project was stalled when a gang of foaming-at-the-mouth Harbor Light preservationists, led by Albert's father, sued the county. With Memorial Bridge on the south side of the island, they argued, a bridge on the northern end would turn Harbor Light into a highway linking Atlantic City and Ocean City, destroying the very essence of the place. And so the bridge ended in midair, a quarter of the way across the slough, a lasting monument to small-town fight and to the

Olympic stubbornness of Joaquin LaRosa. Mayor Joe Salvatore
tried for at least a decade to get Evel Knievel interested in making a jump, but a Knievel scout had issued a pronouncement that
was strung across page one of the *Harbor Light Beacon* one day.

It's No Royal Gorge

The tide was coming in now and the water climbed the
banks below them, the smell of the sea wafting up. Against his
father's warnings, Albert had swum across the slough many
times as a boy, pulling as hard as he could against the wicked
tides. It was a small miracle he was drawing breath today.
Price's eye followed the water out toward the sea, out to where
Peg's As You Like It diner pushed out to the edge of the inlet.
If you needed to find someone in a hurry in Harbor Light,
there were two places to look. The marina or the As You Like
It. Albert's girlfriend Rickie ran the diner with her aunt Rose.

Price took a deep breath. Looking back at the cannery, he
said: "This old cannery is about to have a second life, Albert.
I'm reopening it as a destination property, accessible by car
and ferry, the boats leaving every twenty minutes from the Atlantic City marina. Small-scale paddle wheels with entertainment aboard, green-visored dealers at the tables. There'll be
nothing like it anywhere, and right here next to the casino, for
the kids, an indoor/outdoor marine park. It's going to knock
your socks off, and it's going to revive this town. I guarantee it.
You're looking at my new dream, Albert. What do you think?"

Albert didn't know how to begin to respond. Gazing up at
the hulk of the old fish-processing plant and looking out over
what was left of the rusted-out loading docks, it was hard to
imagine a casino.

"I thought the Rubio family bought the property," Albert said. "As far as I knew, they were turning it into condos and lofts, with their own little marina. Boat slips and all."

"There's a snag in the deal," Price said matter-of-factly.

Albert had never known the Rubios—who owned half the commercial property on Harbor Light and handled about two-thirds of the summer rentals—to have anything fall through on them. They were wired, with friends in all the right places. But Price had higher voltage wires.

The haze was all but gone now, and the A.C. casinos grew bolder against the far sky. Albert took a puff and blew a cloud of Cuban gold at all those stacks of money.

"I know what you're thinking," Price said. "You're wondering how we'd get state sanction for gambling outside of Atlantic City."

"That thought did occur," Albert said. "Among others."

"Let's just say I've already inspected the landscape and have a healthy degree of optimism. It'll be put to an advisory vote here in Harbor Light before we go to the statewide ballot, and that's partly where you come in."

Albert turned to face him, but Price's gaze was lost on the cannery.

"The way I do business," he said, "is to surround myself in key positions not just with technically qualified people, but with people I can trust. You've got twenty-eight years of trust in your personnel file, Albert, and you've also got standing in the community. That's going to help us both out when you start talking this place up around town. There's going to be opposition. I've already gotten a hint of it. Who knows? Your father is a likely candidate to get in the way as much as he can.

You always get a few, and I want someone they trust who can reassure them this will benefit everyone in Harbor Light. My employees are like ambassadors, Albert. They're people I know I can count on in a pinch."

Albert looked down toward the diner, where Rickie was getting ready for the lunch crowd. Price had sworn him to secrecy, but how was he going to be able to keep this from her?

"A question," Albert said.

"Go ahead."

"I'm a little hazy on the ambassador part of it. What exactly would my job be?"

"This is a few weeks off, but what I'd like to do is bring you up to Atlantic City for a few months, and also have my pilot fly you out to Vegas so you can have a look at our operation there. Not that there's a heck of a lot we can teach somebody with your experience, outside of a few industry tricks. When this casino opens here in Harbor Light, you're my chief of security. You'll have a staff of fifty reporting to you, and you'll report directly to my operations director."

Before Albert could respond, Price left him standing there and walked back to the Ferrari. He opened the passenger door and came back with the box of Cubans.

"If you're worrying about those eighteen months you need for a sixty percent retirement, I've already set up a trust that will take care of that, and you'll be able to draw on it after five years on my payroll. Doesn't sound too hard to take, does it? You'll be retiring to a life of luxury before you're fifty-five, if that's the decision you make. They tell me you've topped out at forty-eight thousand in this job, is that right?"

"Right around there," Albert said. "We work on a scale."

"My scale starts a little higher, Albert. You'll have to come up to Evolution in the next week or so and look at the contract I've had my law department draft. You'll be starting at a hundred thousand."

Albert suspected a true professional, with fifty underlings reporting to him, wouldn't jump, scream, or wet his pants, so he controlled each and every one of those urges and just stood there with a look of dumb luck. And, to be honest, a few dozen doubts. He trusted no one with money for the simple reason that he had never had any.

"You asking for a decision right now?" he asked.

"I wouldn't insult you that way. I'll admit to a bit of a self-serving motive in presuming you'd want to leave law enforcement. Give it some thought. Sleep on it. But these cigars are yours. Later on, if you decide to come aboard, there'll be a nice little signing bonus that will include a trip to Vegas for you and Rickie. You are still seeing her, am I right?"

"We've been known to get together," Albert said.

"Lovely woman," Price said. "You're a lucky man."

He turned once more to the cannery, so Albert did, too, seeing himself up there in a fine three-piece suit, his staff dropping by his office for daily assignments. He'd always loved the jazzed-up feeling he got when he walked into a casino. White light on green velvet, the clatter of risk, the smell of chance.

"One thing you'll always be able to count on," Oscar Price said. "I take care of my people. You'll earn those six figures, believe me. But you'll be taken care of from the start. Is there another way to do business?"

Albert didn't trust him for a minute, but that wasn't the scary part. The scary part was, he was ready to sign up.

Six figures. A hundred grand. One hundred thousand dollars. Ten spins around the island, and Albert still couldn't believe it. He banked the police cruiser in counterclockwise victory laps, grinning like a thief. Past the marina, up the beach, down the backstretch along the bay, which caught a break of light and looked practically Caribbean.

Not that he was some kind of rube. Albert LaRosa realized that in the new economy, a hundred thousand dollars wasn't what it used to be. Complete morons who grew up staring into computer screens raked in millions of dollars making things you couldn't see, smell, or hold in your hands, and even bigger morons made millions of dollars buying and selling it, whatever it was. The whole economy was vapor. But for a guy who grew up slaving in his old man's hardware store in a fishpacking town, and then wore a badge his entire adult life, a hundred thousand dollars was shinier boots and smoother whiskey. A hundred grand was gold.

Back at the office, Albert said not a word to Georgianna, who would probably get down on her knees and thank the Lord Jesus she was rid of him. When he walked in, she was on the phone with her twin sister, Lu, who worked at the *Beacon*.

They were no doubt cranking up the rumor mill about his mysterious little drive with Oscar Price.

Harlan Wayans was asleep in the coatroom cave, laid out like a hibernating bear and blowing tuba blasts of flammable breath. A whiff of rotten bait was coming through the walls from Manny's, too, and dizzying drafts of Georgianna's lavender-scented toilet water filled out the bouquet. It was no wonder the ceiling paint was curling off and falling like scabs.

What was he doing here? It's not as if there was any pressing business this morning, and he felt as though he'd already outgrown the place.

It was a little early for a drink, but Albert intended to break as many rules as he could today. He tiptoed past Georgianna and swaggered easily across Waterman Highway under a towering sun, soaking up the glory of the day. Maybe he should just clock out for the rest of his shift and have them cover out of Rag Harbor if anything came up. Oscar Price could have hired anyone for this job, and he'd picked Albert. He had to have a quick one to mark the occasion.

A light westerly blew briny drifts off the bay, and Mo's Tavern, an unseaworthy, shingled houseboat, rocked and creaked in the marina. Crossing the gravel lot, Albert caught his reflection in the rain-spotted mirror of Mo's pickup and stopped for a closer look.

What he saw were the ravages of his own predictability. He was tired around the eyes. He was gray at the edges. He had the terrifyingly complacent look of a man who'd played it safe for far too long. Wore the same khaki uniform every morning, ate the same bacon and egg sandwich, went to the same stifling office and answered nuisance calls from the same cast of lunatics.

Albert's play-it-safe instinct was to trust his doubts about Oscar Price, finish out his days, and collect that guaranteed pension. Price could turn out to be a real prick to work for. He could end up starting a civil war in Harbor Light with this casino, and he'd already made it clear that Albert's job would be to run interference, even if it meant taking on his own father.

But the truth of it was, he desperately wanted out. He should have left law enforcement altogether two decades ago. Should have turned in his badge the night of the call at Ramon's house in Philadelphia and run for the hills, is what he should have done.

This was his chance. If it didn't work out for some reason, so what? What had he lost but a few bucks a month out of a lousy pension?

"Forget where you're headed, Sheriff?"

Albert turned to find Red Miller on a floating sidewalk. He was on Slip D, filling up the Rubio family's forty-two-foot yacht. *Mint Condition, Ocean View.*

Albert decided he didn't need a drink at Mo's after all. He needed to start his new life.

"Hey Red, you know if Sonny D. sold his boat yet?"

Red Miller, closing in on ninety, had been the harbormaster since the days when Harbor Light actually needed one. He had fought in two world wars and wore a legionnaire's hat on his march to and from work every day, replacing it with a blue harbormaster cap on the job. No one had had the heart to let him go when he hit mandatory retirement age, especially after his wife, Arlene, passed. So he'd stayed on another twenty years at half salary. Hanging on made sense for Red. He was happy just to have something to do.

"Not that I recall," Red said, looking across to Slip B. Sonny DiMaggio, a pit boss up at Harrah's, had just gotten wiped out in divorce court after his wife discovered that all that overtime had been spent outside the pits. Albert had seen the waitress, who moonlighted as an A-list escort for high rollers. No disrespect to Sonny or the waitress, but Albert would rather have the boat, which was suddenly a real consideration now that he was a six-figure man. The money he'd be making, he could get Ramon out of the jam he was in, too. Another good reason to take Price up on his offer.

Sonny's boat was a thirty-two-foot Tiara Pursuit, good-size cabin, swivel up front, twin Chrysler 450 inboards. Mayor Joe's boat, a beat-up old trawler, looked like a floating potato next to Sonny's dream boat. "You got the same look as forty years ago, when I used to see you in front of the penny candy at Phelps Drugs with two nickels burning a hole in your britches," Red Miller said.

"I still got that sweet tooth, Red. Do me a favor, will you? You see Sonny down here, tell him I'll take it. Don't let anybody else set foot on it, and then you and me, we'll take a spin off the shelf and see if we don't come back with dinner for a month."

"You just rob a bank?" Red called up.

"Yeah," Albert said, reading the name on the back of Sonny's boat. *Double Down.* He'd have to change that, soon as he got a chance. "Something like that."

Albert turned onto Cannery Way, a quaint little four-block stretch of two-story brick storefronts shaded by mulberry, poplar, and ash. He waved to Lu, who was leaving Nuba's Pie

Shop holding a cakebox by the strings. Albert suspected Nuba would have been in bankruptcy long ago if not for George and Lu, whose idea of dieting was to skip dinner and go straight to the dessert.

Oscar Price was right. Cannery wasn't what it once was. When Albert was a boy, and spent his days running up and down this street and in and out of shops, Cannery Way was bustling. But that was when Harbor Light served all the fishermen, mill workers, and truck drivers who lived with their families in flattop bungalows west of the town limits, beyond the back bay and across the Garden State Parkway. They had their own stores out there now, and the Bargain Acres, which opened less than a year ago, advertising itself as the largest retail space under one roof in North America. Chance's, the last family-owned department store in New Jersey and the Cannery Way anchor, hung on for six months beyond the grand opening of Bargain Acres. Now it had a big For Rent, Sale or Lease sign in the window where Lester Chance climbed into the Barcalounger one morning, held a gun to his head, and pulled the trigger.

Sure, Albert's father would probably grab his musket and lead the charge against the casino. But so what? Albert knew just how to handle it. Let him alone. Let the old man rant. You'd need a muzzle and shackles to keep him down, anyway. In his world, it was still 1950. Walk into his store and what did you see? A Beta video display. Beta! The old man had laid his chips on Beta when VCRs first came out, and he was letting it ride. The dust on those movie boxes was so thick, you needed a miner's pick and a headlamp to see the titles. That's how hard his helmet was.

Albert could see his father in there now through the picture window, kibitzing with Drugstore Max Phelps from down
the street. Talking up some new marketing strategy for Cannery Way, no doubt. They never stopped. Albert and his sister
Sam had practically been raised in that store, and his earliest
memories were of his parents planting him in a playpen (as an
advertisement for the playpen) right there in the display window, where the sign, freshly repainted each year, said LaRosa's
Hardware & More, Service With Pride Since 1950. Now
the window showed off rakes and hoes suspended from the
ceiling in a jazzy little clamor, stacks of fertilizer and plant food
assembled to create a path for a life-size cutout of a happy
homeowner waging some sort of chemical warfare on his lawn,
which was depicted by a green shag carpet.

Still, the old man knew exactly who he was, which was
more than you could say for a lot of people. The navy blue
LaRosa delivery wagon, with its twice-rebuilt engine and a
rooftop sandwich board guaranteeing the lowest prices on the
Jersey shore, was parked diagonally out front. Joaquin LaRosa
and Max Phelps had come up with the diagonal parking con-
cept just over a year ago because it added six parking spaces on
Cannery. Their way of competing with Bargain Acres, where
the parking lot was roughly the size of an aircraft carrier.

Jack, Rickie's son, was cleaning the front windows from inside the store. People said about Jack that he hadn't found
himself yet, but what did they expect of a kid twenty years old?
He did just fine, splitting his workday between the hardware
store and Peg's As You Like It, where he washed dishes. He
drove Rickie crazy on occasion, the way he picked up and left
every now and then without a hint as to where he was going.

Why not? He was too good-looking and too smart to be tied down. To Albert, the bigger surprise was that he always came back.

Albert thought of his relationship with Jack as a near-perfect deal. He got the companionship without the responsibility, and if anything went wrong, he simply told him exactly what he thought—he didn't have to lose sleep over it the way a parent would. Strangely enough it seemed to work better than if he had, and Jack took to it with an easy companionability that seemed just right for the both of them. Also strangely enough, Albert loved him like a son. He wished he could tell him where he was headed right now, but Jack would know soon enough. Everyone else would, too. There were no secrets in Harbor Light.

Albert parked in front of Addie's Jewel Box, three doors down from LaRosa's Hardware, and went inside. The last time his sister Sam was in town, Albert had gone with her to get a battery for her watch. While they waited, Sam pointed to a simple silver band in the display case. "Not that she'd say yes, but if you ever decide to propose," Sam had said, "that'd be the ring for Rickie." Sam was Rickie's number one fan.

A boat. A ring. A new van for Ramon. What next? Albert had no idea he could be this dangerous with money in his pocket.

"Bravo-thirty-four, Bravo-thirty-four. Do you copy, Bravo-thirty-four?"

What now? Georgianna's voice was infused with more than the usual amount of hysteria. Albert picked up the receiver and gave his location.

"I have Sheriff Caster on a landline. Stand by and I'll patch him through," Georgianna said.

It was a little unusual for the boss himself to call. Had he read Albert's mind on the subject of bailing out?

For all of her efficiency, using modern technology was not a strength of Georgianna's. She cut Fitch off twice before making the connection.

"Albert, you ever pick up anything on the creep who re-decorated your Bargain Acres?"

Someone had broken a few windows and spray-painted a half dozen skull-and-crossbones symbols on the front walls of the store four days ago.

"Zilch. I contacted the store manager but didn't get much further than that."

"Well you better take another run over there and poke around."

Technically speaking, the Parkway was just outside Albert's beat. But they were shorthanded (they were always shorthanded), and Albert often got stuck with nickel-and-dime stuff like shoplifting or smash-and-grab thefts from cars. Fitch wouldn't get involved, though, for such a minor offense.

"What have you got?" Albert asked.

"I don't know if it's related to the vandalism," Fitch said. "But some nut-job just called in a bomb threat."

Albert wasted a good forty-five minutes standing around at Bargain Acres. The store had already been evacuated by the time he got there, and some nimrod lieutenant from the county bomb squad had him on peon detail, jotting down license plates in the parking lot.

Albert figured the threat might have come from some disgruntled employee. But when he suggested looking up a manager to ask about personnel problems, the jar-headed lieutenant ordered him to leave it for two dicks who were on their way out from Rag Harbor.

This was exactly what he was talking about. He finally gets something halfway interesting, and someone pulls rank and treats him like a rookie. Albert begged off the detail and headed back into town, where he had more important matters to tend to. Maybe he'd circle back to Bargain Acres later, when all the brass were gone.

Peg's As You Like It, banked up against the inlet at the northern end of Fifth Street, looked like a railroad car that had lost its engine. Named for Rickie's mother, it had been the unofficial town hall for forty years. Copper-skinned fishermen with barracuda teeth gathered here before and after their runs to sip coffee and trade tales. Kids scrambled up to the horseshoe counter after school and all summer long to buy milk shakes and sundaes with coins dug from pocket lint. Pit bosses, dealers, bartenders, and waitresses came in to have their white-toast sandwiches and menthol cigarettes before clocking in on the swing shift in Atlantic City. Marriages had ended here, affairs had begun, deals of every variety had been cooked. From 6 A.M. to 3 o'clock, when Rickie and Aunt Rose shut the doors and walked home to their old Victorian on Third, the As You Like It was filled with rumor and smoke. The food wasn't bad, either.

Aunt Rose's twenty-five-year-old Cadillac, polished once a week by Albert's old pal Creed James for fifteen dollars cash, was parked along the inlet like a pink taffy whale, its great gleaming grille smiling on the sea. Harlan Wayans, the very Harlan Wayans who had been asleep in Albert's office only a few hours ago, and who had an unexplainable talent for being everywhere on the island at all times, had parked his 1978 Chevy pickup six feet from the door. Albert idled out to Aunt Rose's Cadillac and looked upriver to the cannery. Maybe he should ring Fitch back and call it quits right now. It's not like he was going to be able to concentrate on anything. He dropped the ring into his shirt pocket and set off to begin the rest of his life.

Like every other guy on the island, Albert had always had a thing for Rickie going back to school days. The red hair, green eyes. The way she was built. The wild child reputation. As insecure adolescent goobers, it wasn't an attraction any of them had the courage to act on. How could they, the way she was? All the way back to junior high, she scared people around her. An opinion about everything, and interests way beyond anything they knew about. So they cut her up behind her back, the know-it-all with the attitude. Who could ever be with her?

No one was surprised when, two weeks after high school graduation, she moved to another planet. Her parents had socked every spare dollar away for years, slaving at the diner so they could save enough for their only child to go to college. But after two years at UC Berkeley she dropped out, breaking their hearts. And people nodded in a self-satisfied way. Same old Rickie.

You heard things about her occasionally after that, most of it made up or embellished, the way small-town people have of creating characters that fit the story they need to hear. Albert knew part, but not all, of the truth. Became an amateur Buddhist, lived on a marijuana farm in Humboldt County, married a fellow flower child while chained to a tree, got arrested for running naked through a wetlands protection hearing in Eureka, got pregnant by someone who was out of the picture before Jack was born. If Albert had a type, she was the farthest thing from it. But the longer she was away, the more he thought about her. And then one night seven years ago, he was the one who called her on Whidbey Island, off Seattle, where she managed a little deli, ran kayak tours, and led harangues against greedy developers who were transforming the island. Aunt Rose, too distraught, had given the number to Albert, who was calling to tell her that her parents had been killed.

Everyone from Atlantic City to Cape May Point had known Eddie and Margaret Davenport. They'd worked side by side at the diner, along with Aunt Rose, for thirty-five years. Every Saturday night, they drove down to Cape May for dinner at the Pilot House, their one weekly reward to each other. They were on their way back one night when a life insurance salesman with a blood-alcohol level of .21 barreled the wrong way out of the Parkway rest stop in Wildwood. Rickie's parents swerved head-on into a tree and were gone in an instant.

Albert was the one who had answered the call, a scene he still flashed on, and he was the one who picked up Rickie and Jack at the airport in Philadelphia. The moment he saw her, first time in twenty years, his marriage was done. It hadn't been much to begin with, and he didn't even have to push hard.

When he sat Diane down and started to tell her he wanted a divorce, she finished his sentence for him.

Albert got out of the car and marched toward the diner. He walked as if he were on one of those playground suspension bridges, every step a little creaky. The knees, banged up in high school football, were partly to blame, but mostly it was just the way he was limbed together, big and rangy, like his Sicilian mother had been. At six-four, he was a walking set of hinges, long limbs swinging in wide arcs. He had his mother's good looks, olive-skinned and dark-eyed, with his father's square jaw and thick wavy hair. Rickie liked to tell him he was lucky he was so good-looking, because she sure wasn't interested in him for his money. He smiled at that thought now, head down, his dusty cowboy boots plotting his course across the parking lot. He tapped his shirt pocket at the bottom of the stairs, feeling for the ring. A little nervous, maybe. But still smiling as he threw open the door of the diner.

You always got hit with a blast of cigarette smoke, bacon, and maple syrup, the scent Rickie brought home in her hair and skin. Aunt Rose was behind the counter, packing a lunch bag for Albert's father. The two of them had been dating for going on two years.

"A little late today, aren't we?" Aunt Rose asked without looking at him.

"Crime keeps no schedule," Albert said, scanning the restaurant for Rickie. "Some anarchist threatened to blow Bargain Acres to kingdom come, but it was a hoax."

"That's a shame," Aunt Rose said.

"Yeah, some psycho."

"No," Aunt Rose said. "I meant it's a shame it was a hoax."

Harlan Wayans was at the counter, boring through a mushy mound of creamed chipped beef on toast. Eight or ten fishermen held down two booths, lingering over coffee.

"She's on the horn in back, having it out with the roofers," Aunt Rose said proudly. They were two of a kind, Rickie and her mother's sister.

"What now?" Albert asked.

Aunt Rose put her hand on the hip of her pink uniform. Her frost-white perm, fire-glazed in the shape of a deep-sea diving helmet, was a marvel of geometric symmetry. Albert had once seen her bull across Cannery Way in a hurricane, angled at forty-five degrees, not one hair out of place.

"They're two weeks behind schedule, six hundred dollars over estimate, and the bathroom took on water like the *Titanic* when it rained Tuesday. I gotta go deliver this to the LaRosa with the looks, so do me a favor and check for a pulse on these sailors every few minutes. I slipped Viagra into their coffee to double my tip, so the whole gang could go into cardiac arrest any minute."

Albert went behind the counter to pour himself some coffee.

"You can warm me up if you don't mind," Harlan said, tapping his cup with his fork. He had slept off his drunk and was coming around, just like he did every day about this time. Albert gave him a withering glance, but he had a soft spot for Harlan, going back a ways.

Harlan had made his living on the sea for thirty-five years, same as his father before him, refusing to give up the family business and hook up with one of the conglomerates that took over the fishing trade, squeezing out most of the independents who had made Harbor Light their home base for three generations. One day eight or ten years ago Harlan put out a Mayday six miles offshore and the Coast Guard scooped him up off the hull of his trawler moments before it bubbled and glubbed under. With the insurance settlement, he remodeled the kitchen for Jeanie and sent the youngest of their six off to college, the first Wayans to graduate high school let alone attend a university.

The insurance company snoops were all over him from the day the boat went down, rifling through bank records, interviewing fishermen who'd been in the area, and knocking on Harlan's door at all hours with the smiles of undertakers. If he'd stuck to his story, he'd have gotten away with it. All you had to do was stick to your story. But Harlan didn't have the stones for it. He walked the streets at night, studied the rearview mirror all day, and finally caved. He'd been in hock ever since, working two and three jobs, and wearing out his welcome just about everywhere because of the bottle problem.

"How's Jeanie been?" Albert asked after pouring Harlan some coffee.

"She's a good egg," said Harlan, who could be annoyingly sentimental when he wasn't half bagged. "When you finally decide to settle down, get yourself a woman with a good heart. You think you can grab me that salt and pepper while you're back there?"

Albert went over and topped off the others and chatted awhile with Mayor Joe Salvatore, who'd just popped in. Joe had the face of a prosthetic hook, a mug that had been at the front of every parade down Cannery and into Legion Park the last quarter of a century. If Albert knew Joe the way he thought he did, Joe was going to wet himself at the prospect of a casino coming to town. He'd been a cobbler on Cannery Way the last thirty-five years, but he wasn't the hardheaded traditionalist Joaquin LaRosa was. Joe had put one grand scheme after another on the table, and all of them failed. He wanted to turn the cannery into an Italian American museum and indoor bocce stadium, a scheme that fell apart when death threats were made in a row over the financial involvement of an Atlantic City mafioso who wanted his name on the building. Next, Joe wanted to have the Wallenda family walk a high wire from the cannery to the lighthouse one year for Columbus Day festivities, but that one fell apart over insurance considerations. And he was the one who'd tried to plant a riverboat casino in Harbor Light, bringing Joaquin LaRosa to the brink of a stroke.

It might actually have worked if not for the fact that the riverboat, which Joe said he could get a really good deal on, took on water coming up from Lewes, Delaware, for a trial run. It listed like a top-heavy birthday cake as it came into view in rough water. The local militia, Harbor Light's ragtag navy of sea-bitten gnomes, had been rallied by Mayor Joe to meet the riverboat at sea and escort it around to the back bay. But they ended up on a rescue mission instead, fishing crew out of the water as the riverboat broke up in heavy surf and sank to the bottom of the sea. Mayor Joe hadn't been back on the island ten minutes when his heavy brow twitched and trembled the way it always did when he was hatching an idea. "Harbor Light, gateway to an underwater museum of tragedy at sea," he said.

Albert broke free of Mayor Joe when he saw Jack busing dishes from behind the counter.

"What are you doing tomorrow around noon?" he asked.

Jack set the dishes on the counter and shrugged, which often was as close as he got to genuine communication. He'd give you his eyes, take them away. Flash a shy, respectful smile, then disappear into some other world. The boy just needed to get laid a little more regularly and he'd be fine, Albert thought.

"Nothing," Jack said, stroking red chin stubble to fill a pause. "Washing dishes, I guess."

"I may be test-driving Sonny D.'s boat if you want to come along for the ride."

"You're buying Sonny's boat?" Jack asked incredulously.

Albert saw Rickie coming toward them and winked at Jack. "I'll explain later," he said.

She was in a tizzy about the roofers. Classic Rickie. She suffered no wrong, no incivility, without a fight. He offered the appropriate expression of sympathy and moral outrage and directed her to the back booth, where they'd have some privacy. Her green eyes had narrowed and her glorious, cascading strawberry hair was ablaze with the sunlight that poured through the large picture pane behind her. It looked like her head might combust.

"How do these people stay in business treating their customers like this? Now they tell me it's the flushing or the copper something or other, I don't even know what the hell they're talking about. And the guarantee doesn't extend to that. You have any idea what the flushing is?"

"Flashing. It's sort of like weather stripping. You want me to make a call?"

"I want you to lock them up for fraud. I should call the Better Business Bureau about this. Is there a contractor left in the world who shows up when they say they're going to and then actually does the job you pay them to do?"

"These guys are out of where?"

"Ventnor. I knew I should've gone with Connelly Brothers from Stone Harbor, but their estimate was high. The leak in the bathroom soaked through to the storage room and ruined a case of pancake mix, and these crooks are telling me they think they can have someone take a look next week. I'm running a business six days a week and they're going to come by next week to fix a job they screwed up a month ago."

Ron Rubio, the real estate man, was coming through the door with his driver, Joey Tartaglione. Albert wondered if Rubio had gotten word that Oscar Price had beaten him to the punch on the cannery. Rickie started to rise as Rubio settled into a booth near the cash register, but Aunt Rose came in right behind him.

"Let her take this," Albert said. "There's something I wanted to tell you."

"Let me just give her a quick update on the idiot roofers. I'll be right back."

Albert admired her as she huffed away in contempt of the world's incompetence. This was it. He felt a bit of a nervous flutter, but that was part of the adventure—he felt like being a little reckless today. He felt like he'd had two stiff ones before dinner. Not tipsy, just a little softheaded and generous. He took the silver band out of his pocket and looped it over the nipple of the ketchup bottle, wondering how long it would take her to see it.

The six years they'd been together, marriage had come up only once. That was two months into it. He'd taken Rickie to

Philadelphia for the weekend, nice little hotel off Rittenhouse Square. Took her to a couple of restaurants he knew in South Philly, too. One of them, a red gravy Italian, was run by a retired cop he'd worked with years ago and the guy took care of them. Nice romantic corner table, attentive service, a special appetizer that wasn't on the menu. They were on their second carafe of Chianti, deciding whether to go for the cannoli or the tiramisu, when Rickie grabbed him under the table.

"Take me back to the hotel," she said, a deliciously evil look in her eye. "I want to screw all night and get married in the morning."

Albert's throat closed, which was unfortunate because he had just taken a sip of Chianti that rose into his nasal cavity and nearly blasted out through his ears. He recovered neatly enough, sneezing his brains into his napkin a few times. But he just didn't know what to say, and so he said the worst possible thing.

"You sure you don't want dessert?"

The fight started before they left the restaurant, everyone turning to have a look at this miserable couple that couldn't make it through a meal without a mix-up. That was his problem, she said. No surprises. No sense of adventure. No balls.

She had a point. What risks had he ever taken? Didn't go to college because he knew he'd never live up to his sister Sam's success. Gave up on Philadelphia over one shooting that had spooked him ever since. Carped and moaned about his job so many times Rickie was sick of listening.

All of that would end today.

"Ron Rubio, the tightwad," Rickie was saying when she returned. "What's he worth? A million bucks? Five million? He's got ten holes punched on his card so he spins the Free Meal

Wheel. It comes up Italian hoagie and he wants to know if he can switch it to crab cakes. The man's a millionaire and he wants to screw me out of seventy-five cents. Can you believe it?"

"That's how he got to be a millionaire," Albert said, borrowing the line from his father. As he said it, it occurred to him that over the next ten years, he'd earn a million dollars.

"Why I came in is I've got some big news, Rick."

This got her attention, pulling her out of the day's worries. She gave him a quizzical look, those green eyes clear and deep.

"Got a visit this morning from Oscar Dan Price down at the office."

"What's going on with that guy? He's popping up everywhere all of a sudden," Rickie said. "He's come by here two or three times the last couple of weeks. Twice for breakfast that I recall, and maybe one time for lunch. I don't know if he'd ever been in here once before then."

"There's this deal coming up I'm not supposed to talk to anyone about. He asked me not to say a word. I wanted you to be the first to hear it."

She could tell now, by his tone, that whatever he had to say was a big deal. Her body language told him to hurry up and get on with it. Get to the point. But Albert tended to tell stories the way they happened, beginning to end, developing the narrative and building mystery and suspense. It probably had something to do with the fact that no one who called the police with a problem ever started from the beginning. You had to back them up, key on the details. Get them to retell the whole story. He started with the silver Ferrari pulling up outside his office and took Rickie through every twist and turn. At a certain point in the telling of it, the blood drained from her face. But she was without expression, so Albert took it to mean she was stunned, proud, and otherwise thrilled for him.

"You're kidding," she finally said.

"No I'm not."

"You have to be."

He shook his head no. "And guess what the starting salary is." He laughed, giddy at the thought of it, still not catching on. "Six figures. I'm buying the *Double Down*. Sonny's boat? Price is doubling my salary! Can you believe it?"

"I'll tell you what I believe, Albert. I believe you're a moron."

It took him completely by surprise. Rickie turned around and looked in the direction of the cannery. You couldn't see it from here, but her eyes followed the inlet as far as she could, just short of the loading docks. Then she looked across to Atlantic City and kept her focus there for a half minute, as if trying to vaporize it with a laser shot.

"What?" he protested, but she stood without answering and began to leave. Albert hooked her arm as she passed and demanded to know what was wrong.

"Don't touch me," she said, wheeling around to face him.

"I came in here to tell you I'm starting a new career that doubles my salary, and this is the response I get?"

"A new career? You're going to get pressed into action when some ninety-year-old day-tripper from Philadelphia loses a roll of quarters on the bus. You call that a career? You're going to be looking through a hole in the ceiling to see if some greaseball is using loaded dice. Is that what you want to do with your time?"

"You're the one who's been telling me I need to get out of the job I'm in."

"Not to go work in a casino that's going to ruin this island, Albert! I can't even believe it. What do you think a casino's going to do to Harbor Light?"

"I don't know. Bring in a few thousand jobs and a trainload of money? Save it from sinking?"

"They said the same thing about the Bargain Acres as I recall, and what has that done for us? Oscar Price is buying you off, Albert. I can't believe you came so cheap."

She paused for a moment as another element of the betrayal occurred to her.

"That's why he's been in here all of a sudden, the prick. Like he's suddenly one of us. Does he think we're that stupid?"

Now Albert was the one who was boiling. He scowled at the old fishermen who were watching, straining to hear what this was all about. They went back about their business and Albert laid into her.

"I come in here bored to tears with my job, best news I've had in twenty-five years, and your reaction is to piss all over it? I don't believe it."

"I can't believe you expected it any other way. What do you think this is going to do to my restaurant, detective, having a casino next door?"

"I don't know, Rickie. Bring more customers through the door? You got a problem with that, like you've got a problem with everything else in the world?"

"When's the last time you went to Atlantic City to throw away a day's pay and stopped at one of the local restaurants along the way?"

"This is an entirely different situation."

"You're right. Now it's my restaurant that's going to tank. And the last town on the Jersey shore that hasn't been junked up for tourists is going to be turned into Sea World with slot machines. I don't care to live in Sea World, Albert. I'm not a mermaid. It's no wonder he's been coming in here lately. Probably wanted to figure out how long it'll take to bulldoze the place for a parking lot."

"You're overreacting, Rickie. What a surprise."

"Don't tell me I'm overreacting. It's not over- and it's not under-, it's right on the money. And I'll tell you something else, Albert. I understand you're desperate for a change, but this is the wrong one, and I'll go after this billion-dollar bastard with every pot and pan I've got. I'll clear out the kitchen to fight this thing, so you're going to have to make a choice. Do you understand what I'm saying?"

It had to have been temporary insanity. What was he thinking, coming in here with a wedding ring? If anything, this little tantrum made him all the more certain he was doing the right thing in taking the job. Besides, that ring was the price of a whole new set of fishing gear.

When Rickie had stomped away, he grabbed it and ran.

Albert had a phobia about guns. This was not something he would tell anyone, particularly not another cop. He'd rather say he liked to wear panty hose and crochet mittens. But he wished he had a weapon in his hand right now. He'd like to take dead aim and blow about six holes in the telephone, which had been ringing every ten minutes since seven.

He managed to crack open one eye wide enough to see the clock. Half past nine. He was an hour and a half late for work, but no one should have to go to the office on three hours' sleep. The chimes of the phone echoed off the walls inside his head. He couldn't remember much about the night except Mo saying not to worry about it, Rickie would come around. And if not, there were plenty of other women out there. Exactly, Albert kept saying. Who needs her? And then he'd have another drink.

This must be Rickie now. Calling to apologize for being such a red-head. Or Georgianna, calling to tell him how many calls he'd missed. Maybe what he ought to do was swallow half a bottle of aspirin and drive out to Rag Harbor and tell Fitch Caster he was done. No way he was going to be able to keep dragging himself out of bed for forty-eight thousand dollars a year with this new thing lined up. All the vacation and sick time he had stacked up, he should be out on Sonny's boat right now. His boat. Hell with Rickie Davenport.

Albert reached blindly for the phone and held it to his ear.

"This better be about someone dead or dying," he said.

"I'm sorry. Did I wake you?" Albert didn't recognize the voice at first, everything fuzzy. He lay on his back, staring up at the ceiling until it came to him.

Oscar Price.

"No sir, I've been up for hours," Albert said, clearing his throat. He sat up so quickly he almost blacked out. "Had a jog on the beach, got some paperwork cleared at the office, and just ran home to grab a cup of coffee."

"Actually it is about someone dead or dying, in a manner of speaking," Price said. "I got a call here at the office this morning. A man's voice. It was brief and blunt. He said if I enjoyed breathing, I should stay the hell out of Harbor Light."

"He said what?"

"It was a threat," Price said. "In so many words, he threatened to kill me."

"You recognize the voice at all?"

"No. It was all very quick. The whole thing took a minute or two."

"And that's all he said?"

"No. Not exactly."

"You want to tell me what else he said?"

Albert waited, a hammer tapping out a steady beat on the back of his eyeballs. Finally, Price spoke. "He said, 'Tell your buddy the cop to keep the job he's got. If he knows what's good for him.' "

Albert nearly clipped the guardrail on Memorial Bridge, plowing across to Jersey Landing. He stopped at Cuff's Lunch Box for a cup of black coffee and was on his way, shooting out to the Parkway half blinded by ground fog. He was fairly certain there must be some brain swelling, the way his head throbbed. That'd make a nice impression, showing up in Oscar Price's office with an ice bag on his head. But except for that, this new life wasn't all bad, was it? Twenty-four hours ago he was tobogganing down the long, slow slide, the days indistinguishable and uneventful. Now he had no idea what was going to fly up at him next. One minute he was about to get married, the next minute he was back in circulation. One minute no one cared that he existed, now someone was itching to knock him off. He hadn't felt so alive in twenty-five years.

Maybe the competition in A.C. wasn't thrilled to hear that Oscar Price was trying to lure customers out of town with a new operation in Harbor Light. They couldn't even keep up with him in A.C. Ten, twenty years ago, a move like this would have brought the wiseguys flying out of their dugouts. But the Philadelphia-A.C. mob, a stupendously inept band of meatballs with no equals in the history of organized crime, had wiped each other out after years of infighting, bodies turning up in trunks and along riverbanks so often it was like a year-round Easter egg hunt for the feds. Still, Albert couldn't see a tie-in here. The casinos were corporate operations today. They'd screw their own employees and cheat their customers, no qualms, if it looked good on paper. But they wouldn't hire goons to crack heads. At least Albert didn't think so.

Atlantic City lured you in off the expressway like a '70s pimp in a cheap fur, the promise of a good time scrawled across its tawdry skyline with names you could trust to leave you penniless and filled with regret. Bally's, Tropicana, Trump Taj, Harrah's, Caesars, Showboat, Evolution. They ought to just tunnel you straight under the city and into the casinos, because you had to pass through hell to get to the show. Pawnshops, liquor stores, by-the-hour motels. Yeah, Rickie was right about it. But what she didn't remember—what nobody seemed to remember when they trashed the casinos and recited sad homilies to the kind of town A.C. used to be—was that Atlantic City was no Shangri-la in the wretched years before the casinos turned their lights on. It was a ramshackle, filthy, hopelessly bushwhacked Newark-by-the-Sea. At least now you had a few jobs. You had people coming in to see a show, roll the dice, have a good time. Albert scooted up Atlantic and cut across on New York, curving around slow traffic in a blur. Not wanting to keep the new boss waiting. He parked the car himself and made his way to the employee elevator, where an operator named Gus, an old black guy with white sideburns, sat on a stool reading the *Racing Form*.

"Here to see Mr. Price," Albert said.

"Name please?"

"Sheriff LaRosa. Albert LaRosa."

"Yes. He's expecting you. Welcome aboard."

Albert didn't know whether he meant the elevator or the payroll. This wasn't bad, going to work in a chauffeured elevator.

He wondered if he'd ride this thing every day during his so-called training.

The top floor of Evolution floated thirty stories above the beach and Boardwalk, the whole million-dollar view hitting you through floor-to-ceiling windows the second you stepped off the elevator. Albert stumbled into the reception foyer, a little wobbly from the combination of the elevator ride and the corn alcohol he was still burning.

"I don't know how you get anything done up here," he said to the receptionist, a middle-aged woman who had the look of someone trained to smile through discontent. You could make out a half dozen fishing boats through the veil of fog, levitating on the slumbering sea.

"Mr. Price doesn't leave you much of an option in that regard," she said, hitting an intercom button and announcing his arrival.

Price appeared immediately through a set of oversize oak double doors, small and pale in the opening, leading Albert into an office that looked like the lobby of a five-star hotel. Persian carpets, antique French furniture, fireplace with a nice marble mantel. He wasn't buying discount.

"Make yourself comfortable," he said, directing Albert to the sofa.

Albert tiptoed first to the edge of the room, which fell off into the sea. It almost looked like you could drop a line from up here.

"Very nice," he said.

"A little too nice at times," Price said, punching a button on a remote control he picked up off a glass-top coffee table. A shade dropped slowly from the ceiling and Price let it motor halfway down. He hit another button and one wall opened to reveal a full wet bar with coffee and tea service and a silver platter of fresh Danish. Albert wondered if Price had a button on his James Bond clicker that brought dancing girls cartwheeling out of the wall.

Price put the remote down and folded himself onto a highback chair. "What I'm going to tell you has to stay between us," he said.

Lots of "between you and me" with this guy, Albert thought.

"I can't emphasize that too much," Price went on. "There are too many people affected." A photo of his wife sat on his desk. Dark hair, hazel eyes, pretty but maybe a little bored-looking. She struck Albert as one of those southern ladies who came from money and met her friends at monthly luncheons to discuss fund drives for crippled and underprivileged children. Price's three girls were in a separate photo, blond like their dad and cute like their mom. Those were the only photos in the room, which told you something. A guy like Price obviously met a ton of celebrities and dignitaries, but he wasn't the type to stand in front of a camera or hang diplomas and plaques on the wall. He was as private and unreachable as he could be, which had to make it extra uncomfortable to get to the office this morning and take a call like that.

"Someone threatens to kill somebody, that's a crime in itself," Albert said. "I know some people in the Atlantic City P.D., if that's what you're worried about. Guys you can trust to handle it discreetly."

"I'm going to trust one person and that's you," Price said. "You and I both know the Atlantic City Police Department can't do anything about an anonymous phone call. My fear is that if this were made public, it would bring a tone of negativity to the proceedings. Getting the state behind this proposal is going to involve a great deal of public relations positioning, and we don't need anyone wondering what's so horrific about the plan that threats would be made on someone's life."

"So in other words, you're not concerned about someone actually wanting to kill you."

"I don't know, Sheriff. Should I be? I've got to admit I'm not accustomed to death threats."

"Who would you guess made the call?"

Price looked out the window at nothing but empty sky. He was in dark blue again, a gold tie this time. Not quite as crisp as yesterday, but no less invincible. Still looking out at the blue-gray of thinning fog and ocean mist, not at Albert, he said, "Frankly, I am concerned. Not for myself, but for my family."

"Did he threaten them?"

"Not directly."

"Tell me about the call," Albert said.

"A man's voice. No hello, no introduction. He got through by telling my secretary he was one of my lawyers. I pick up, he says, 'Listen to me with both ears.'"

"Listen to me with both ears?"

"And something about greedy little billionaires who can never get enough. And then he says, 'So watch your back, and tell Marshal Dillon to stay put.'"

Marshal Dillon. Terrific, Albert thought. It wasn't enough for someone to threaten him. They had to insult him, too.

"So that's it?" Albert asked. "Did he say anything else?"

Price indicated that he hadn't.

"And did you say anything to him?"

"Well of course I did," Price said. He was coming back into his skin now, more like the Oscar Price who stood out at the cannery yesterday and told Albert the way it was going to be. Not a doubt in his head. "I told him that if he had business to discuss, he should show himself, but if he thought he could intimidate me with a cowardly anonymous phone call, he must not have any idea who he was dealing with. Why are you looking at me like that? You think it was a mistake to be so forthright?"

"I don't know. Considering that we don't know who we're dealing with, I'm not sure confrontation is the best strategy."

"That's how I play the game, Sheriff, and it seems to have worked for me so far. I've never lost at anything."

It got chilly in the room. Albert still didn't trust him entirely, to be honest. Didn't know exactly what he was getting into. After years of utter predictability, it was a thrill.

"Any thoughts on who our prospective killer might be?" Price asked.

"A few. How about you?"

Price looked him levelly in the eye. "I can't think of a mortal soul."

He wasn't going to make it easy. "I need to clarify something first. Am I looking into this as Albert LaRosa, resident sheriff of Harbor Light, Albert LaRosa, private investigator, or Albert LaRosa, Evolution employee?"

"I suppose a little of all three," Price said, going over to his desk for an envelope. "At least until the first of the month."

Albert opened the envelope and perused three pages of legal blather. His contract, with a starting date of May 1. The numbers were all he looked at. One hundred grand the first year, one twenty-five the second, then one fifty. The signing bonus alone—$25,000—would pay for Sonny D.'s boat, if not bail Ramon out of trouble. Albert's hands trembled.

"Everything appear to be satisfactory?" Price asked.

Albert set the contract on his lap and looked out the window. He was taking this job, and Rickie couldn't understand why; he really didn't need to be with her.

"I'm going to have my lawyer take a look at this," Albert said. He didn't have a lawyer, but it sounded like the right thing to say.

"So this threat isn't enough to scare you off?"

"It makes me all the more inclined to say yes," Albert said. "But if you want me to help you out, so that we don't both find ourselves floating up on the beach out there one fine day, you're going to have to answer some questions."

"Ask away, Sheriff. Whatever you need to know."

Albert felt so good he almost wanted to pay his taxes. He lit one of the Cuban cigars Price had given him and strolled the Atlantic City Boardwalk with a watermelon grin. You know what? The hell with Rickie. Yeah, the hell with her. If she couldn't get into this, couldn't stand up and blow a kiss at the clouds and say why the hell not, then screw her. Albert had won. He'd hit the big one. There was no better cure for a hangover than having your life threatened and your salary tripled before your second cup of coffee.

He had a little trouble taking the death threat seriously, but maybe there was enough resentment of Price's success that the idea of him drawing customers out of Atlantic City had pushed someone over the edge. Albert had a mob contact, a kid he went to school with, who might know. Logical choice would be Ron Rubio. The guy had just been screwed out of buying the cannery, and had a reputation for being on the shady side. But regardless, you had to take it as a bluff, and an amateurish one at that. Would anyone really shoot Oscar Price dead over a fish-processing plant that had been abandoned since the Eisenhower administration?

Albert hiked back for his car and rounded out of the garage. Now was as good a time as any to make it official. He'd drive straight out to Rag Harbor and tell Fitch Caster he better start looking for a new deputy in Harbor Light. Albert felt something in his stomach, just a flutter, that hadn't been there since he was a rookie cop in Philadelphia. You couldn't put a price on it, and that's why the money was secondary.

He was coming up on the Bargain Acres strip mall, a collection of the usual chain retailers and eateries. Bargain Acres sat on a property so vast it had a jitney to cart people from the outer acreage of the parking lot to the front door of the McDonald's and the store itself. They called the six-car purple caterpillar tram BART, for Bargain Acres Rapid Transit.

You couldn't even talk about this place to Joaquin LaRosa. Hell, maybe he was the one who'd made the bomb threat. You couldn't even say the words "Bargain Acres" without the loco coming up in those Spanish eyes. He'd twitch and snort and launch into a screed about architectural abomination and the murder of entrepreneurial spirit, and vow never to spend a dime in any of the Parkway chains. Yeah, Albert thought. That'll put them under by Christmas. A hundred and fifty accountants were probably confabbing in Houston, or wherever the hell Bargain Acres took its mail, worrying over what to do about the Joaquin LaRosa problem out in east jackass New Jersey. It was pretty much the same with Rickie, who didn't get worked into quite the lather Joaquin LaRosa did, but could deliver a similar lament, all in italics. To no effect whatever on anything.

It's not that Albert couldn't respect them on principle and even agree with a lot of what they said. What jughead could feel good about himself after eating at a place called Mama Parm's Macaronium or sitting in a caterpillar tram with people who seemed to be enjoying the experience? He didn't particularly enjoy enduring a theme park experience to go pick up a pair of boxers and a tube of toothpaste. But Rickie and his father were fools if they thought there was any percentage in pining for the past and taking on the retail moguls and Oscar Prices of the world. Look at the traffic out here. Parking lots were jammed, exit ramps backed up. The vote was in, and mom and pop had lost. Time to move on.

"So you're giving me two weeks' notice," Sheriff Fitch Caster said. He'd put on about five pounds a year in office and wore it proudly, a great ripe jersey tomato with a shaved head and a permanent case of mumps.

Albert nodded.

"Ready to move on, are you?"

"Chance of a lifetime."

Fitch had been reelected four times and was in his sixties, possibly the most respected figure in Harbor County politics. The deputies loved him, too, partly because of this right here.

The way you could walk in unannounced and sit down with him and not have him act like your boss. He'd been on the street himself, of course, and always gave you the sense that that was where he'd rather be. "And what am I supposed to do in Harbor Light?"

Albert wasn't going to turn over for him. He knew Fitch would do this because he'd done it the other three times Albert had come in over the years to say he was done.

"You know I don't have anyone living there, and I can't afford to cover it three shifts a day. It's always been a resident-sheriff setup."

"So send a car over a couple of times a day, Fitch. Nothing happens there anyway."

"Nothing happens because you're there. Come on, Albert. You think anybody else I send into Harbor Light is going to know how to handle Creed James selling life insurance to ninety-year-old widows, or that pervert Dr. DiMitri charging his customers for free samples and chasing his nurses around the office with cotton swabs? I don't need more paperwork from deputies and phone calls from wet-behind-the-ears prosecutors, Albert. I need someone who can steer that stuff out of the criminal justice system."

"That's what I'm talking about. I'm not a cop, Fitch. I'm a zookeeper."

"I'll make you a lieutenant zookeeper."

"I don't want a promotion."

"How about a raise?"

"I just got one. Oscar Dan Price is doubling my salary, and that's just for starters."

Fitch tapped a pen on his desk and thought about that

awhile. "He got any more openings?" he finally asked with a big warm pumpkin-head grin.

"It's not going to work this time," Albert said.

"Let me tell you what doesn't work, Albert. Your logic. You had that aggravated assault with a croquet mallet a few years ago. You had that old vet who went after his nurse with his cane last Christmas. A half dozen stolen boats, couple of boosted cars, the kid selling dope right out of his lifeguard stand. There's been lots of other stuff, too."

"Yeah. You just can't recall what it might have been."

"Albert, I've got deputies who've been around twenty years and haven't done anything but write tickets."

"Give me a break, Fitch. I put my time in, all right? It's not just that I need to get out of this line of work, either. I'm jazzed about the new job. I feel like a kid about it."

"You're going to be sitting around in a suit all day, never see the light of day. That's what's got you all revved up? You're going to be peeking through a two-way window at some nose picker to see if he's counting cards. That's excitement? The answer is no. I won't accept a letter of resignation. You're a good cop and you're too young to retire. Besides, with this attrition policy they've saddled me with, I can't put another name on the roster just because I scratch yours."

Albert got up to leave. He'd done what he had to do. He'd stop downstairs and pick up the forms and send them back, and that would be it. Fitch was calling his name now, but Albert was at the door. Another step and he'd be on his way. Maybe it wouldn't be a better life, but that wasn't the point.

"Albert LaRosa, don't walk out that door without hearing me out. And that's an order."

Albert couldn't do it. He had too much respect for Fitch, and Fitch was pleading. Not saying a word, but pleading just the same. Albert walked back over and sat down, but it wouldn't be for long. He wasn't going to give any ground here, he was just going to make himself clear.

"Listen, Fitch, I know you're not kidding about the trouble it'll be to cover Harbor Light."

"They're cutting my budget ten percent, Albert. How would you like to try to run this department on a shoestring?"

"Don't take this the wrong way, but that's not my problem."

"Of course it is. You live on that island. Your family lives there. Your girl. You want their well-being left in the hands of some greenhorn who doesn't know his ass from a doughnut?"

Albert took a deep breath and held on to it. He didn't owe Fitch any more of an explanation than he'd already given, so maybe the hangover was clouding his judgment. Or maybe it wasn't for Fitch's sake that he was about to tell him about Ramon. Maybe it was for his own.

"You want to hear a little story, Fitch?"

"I'll listen to anything that keeps me out of the meeting I'm supposed to be in right now."

Albert hesitated a moment, but that's all it was. Bottling it up, as he had done, had certain advantages, same as booze did, but self-pity was too handy a crutch. Fuck that. He was cleaning out the attic, ghosts be damned.

"I was still in training pants in Philly, two years on the street. We got a call one night in the Twenty-fourth. Domestic dispute."

"Worst kind," Fitch said.

"I pull up and get out of the car, the perp inside the house empties a round through the window. I can hear it ring past my ear. I drop, crawl back around the car for cover, and now I hear the wife inside, screaming."

"You radio for backup?"

"Yeah. And my sergeant told me to hold off. But I knew my buddy was on his way. We could read each other's every move after six months working together. I hear another round from inside and the woman screams again, so I make a dash for the house."

"Without clearance?"

"Two years and I'd been shot at three times. It was the wild west in Philadelphia back then. I got numb. I thought I was bulletproof. I'm at the door, announcing. Telling this perp to drop his weapon and open the door. Not a peep. I don't know if this animal's shot himself, I don't know if he's plugged her and she's lying on the floor dying. I don't know who else is in the house."

"So you kicked the door open and went in like a marine."

"Crawled in on the floor like a grunt and couldn't see a thing. I called out, announcing, cursing, threatening. Nothing. The stereo's going full blast, lights off. I can't see a thing, can't hear a thing but this goddamn music. Marvin Gaye at ten thousand decibels, which I haven't been able to listen to since. One of those situations where you don't know ten seconds from ten minutes, and now I hear my partner coming in from the back of the house, identifying."

"He should never have gone in like that."

"Well he did, Fitch. He did. You know it's split decisions out there. He did what he thought he had to do. And this guy, out of the pitch-black, turns on him and rips off two rounds. I can see the flash from the muzzle, that's all I had to go on, and I shot at it. I shot at the flash. You've got to make up your mind not knowing everything, but I knew this guy was trying to kill my partner. I emptied on him. On the flash, anyway, and then got up and moved on him. My partner found a light and he turns it on, and this perp's got one in the hand and one in the back, both mine. He's choking on his blood and the wife's lying next to him with one in the head, right here."

Fitch didn't move. Didn't say a thing.

"My partner gets on the phone and makes the call. I'm working on the wife, mouth-to-mouth, CPR, pounding on her chest, shaking her, praying it's not my bullet that went clear through her brain. My partner takes the stereo and throws it against the wall, and that's all for Marvin. My buddy realizes he's taken one in the leg, not too bad. He's mad and scared more than hurt, and he's kind of fingering the hole, a strange sort of amused look on his face, like it's not real. Take the finger off, it's a geyser. Put it back on, it stops. Off and on. He was in shock."

"You shot your partner," Fitch said.

Albert nodded.

"And with the stereo off we hear this sort of gurgling and moaning and follow the sound into the kitchen."

Albert stopped himself. He always got stuck right here when he played it back to himself. He'd been stuck here over twenty years.

"You okay, Albert?"

"There's a kid on the floor with a slug, lying on his back

and looking up at us with eyes big as Christmas, a look of fear I can still see. And I knew."

"His father shot him, Albert. You didn't shoot that boy."

"I shot him, Fitch."

"I'm saying whoever's bullet it was, his daddy got that boy shot."

That's what his sergeant had told him at the time. That's what his partner had told him, too.

"When you're sitting at home for six weeks on administrative leave, nothing to do but drink and run replays in your head, how you shot your partner, how you shot a three-year-old kid in the back, it gets to where you don't know what you did right or wrong."

"You did right, Albert. That situation, there's no rules to go by."

"I gave it another six months," Albert said. "For a while I thought I was all right. You know, when you're young and all. But then I'd find myself thinking too much, afraid I was going to get somebody hurt. That's when I should have realized I ought to be selling aluminum siding or something. Instead I came home thinking I could pull myself together where it's a little quieter, get back in shape for the front lines. It's a little ridiculous, isn't it? Twenty-odd years of pulling yourself together?"

"You put a badge on, it doesn't matter where, Albert. That's the front lines."

Albert got up to leave and his knees snapped as if to tell him this was the right thing to do. He was way over the hill as a cop.

"I'm done, Fitch."

This was the first time he'd spoken about it, to anyone, in better than twenty years. His father, his ex-wife, Rickie—none of them knew all the details. Albert was at the door when Fitch stopped him.

"I gotta ask this, Albert. Last time you came in here to resign was about five years ago. You were just back from a funeral for a Philly cop who turned a gun on himself."

"You're one hell of a detective, Sheriff. Yeah, my old partner."

"And the kid?"

"Ramon is his name. I'll bring the smokes, and the drinks are on me, too, Fitch. Let's you and I get together one night. You get me drunk enough and I'll tell you the rest of the story."

SPECIAL EDITION
WEDNESDAY, APRIL 9

FISH AND CHIPS!
Battle Lines Drawn on $1 Billion Proposal
For Marine-Theme Casino on Cannery Site

If there had ever been a bigger, bolder headline in the *Beacon,* nobody could remember when. The weekly rag devoted its entire six-page edition to Oscar Price's grand plan to remake the island as a year-round attraction. The tongue-wagging over the news had kept a steady breeze blowing through Peg's As You Like It, which had been jammed out the door and into the parking lot since 7 A.M. "We're sitting on gold mines," Warren Smith was exclaiming, thumbs hooked in his bib overalls and dollar signs dancing in his piggish eyes. He owned two empty acres just a few hundred yards north of the cannery where he raised goats. "You have any idea what Oscar Price is going to have to pony up for the right-of-way property around here? Roadways, parking, bus terminals. He'll need this entire half of the island to make it happen."

Aunt Rose couldn't resist baiting Smith. "Read Joaquin's editorial in the paper, Mr. Green Jeans. It ain't going to happen."

The *Beacon* had pro and con columns by Mayor Joe Salvatore and Joaquin LaRosa stripped down opposite ends of the front page. Their mug shots were turned toward each other as if they were prepped for a shoot-out at high noon.

"You must have missed Joe's editorial," Smith said, and began reading it. "Fifty years we've been waiting for our boat to come in, and this is it! Our dreams have come true!"

"It's another wet dream, is all it is," Aunt Rose said. "You want some duffer in a pair of jackass slacks dragging a half dozen snot-nosed kids through here to go watch seals slapping around with beach balls on their snouts? Between that and the fat old broads waddling in to yank the slots, forget it. I'll marry a Hong Kong Chinaman and raise chickens in Shanghai before I hang around for that. Joaquin laid it all out for you right there in the paper. Fish and chips my ass. This ain't going to happen, hon."

Joaquin LaRosa had not backed into the subject. His first sentence was a bazooka shot.

"Over my dead body."

And that was a mere warm-up in a screed that amounted to a declaration of war against Oscar Price, city hall, "and anyone else who thinks we're going to roll over while they bludgeon history and heritage, destroying the fabric of our community. You want hookers, loan sharks, and drunks strolling down Cannery Way, which is going to be nothing but pawnshops and liquor stores? Is that the kind of town you want, neighbor? Wake up, Harbor Light! Open your eyes before it's too late!"

"You get the feeling we're in a minority?" Aunt Rose asked as Rickie passed her in the crush of bodies, loaded down with breakfast platters. "What do you say we offer half-price eats to the ones on our side?"

Rickie smiled, but the smile didn't mask a growing discomfort. From the moment the doors opened and anxious
townsfolk poured in like a great hundred-footed beast awak-
ened from deep slumber, she had wanted to take a long walk
on the beach or climb a tree and hide from it all. "I just hope
this doesn't turn ugly," she said. "Especially with that lunkhead
Albert in the middle."

The *Beacon* had published an anonymous call that threatened to blow Evolution sky-high if Price didn't back off. Ron
Rubio had filed a hundred-million-dollar suit accusing Price,
the owner of the cannery, and Harbor County officials of col-
luding to sink Rubio's move on the property. Across Kip
Slough, trucks and tractors and building equipment were already rolling into position like tanks on their way to the front.
No more than a half hour ago, a dozen Harbor Light retirees
had stood in Rickie's parking lot, cheering the commotion.

Rickie serviced her table and went back around the
counter to survey the room, momentarily blocking out the
pitch and wail. Jack was quietly eating his eggs like he was in
the kitchen at home, which he was, in a way. "Are you helping
Joaquin out today?" she asked him.

"Yeah. Looks like he's gonna need all the help he can get."

Whatever might come of it, Oscar Price's casino dream
had split the town for good. And it wasn't the splitting that
bothered Rickie so much as the thing they were split over.

"Not that I begrudge anyone a little wager now and then,"
she said. "But there's just something evil in it."

"What do you mean?" Jack asked, squirting a stream of
ketchup onto his eggs.

"I don't know. Something about the for-profit manipulation of human weakness. People lose money in casinos."

"Usually people who don't have it to lose."

"Exactly. Is there a greater scam in American business than pitching the promise of riches to wide-eyed fools even as you slip a hand into their pockets? The devil himself is in on this deal, Jack. I'm sure of it."

So much so that she'd had a dream last night that transported her back to her rebel days. A dream in which she chained herself to a tree, and everyone who zombied in for the kill was wielding a chain saw and looked exactly like Oscar Price. Actually, all but one looked like Price. The one, pretty tall and very good-looking, wore a badge.

Albert pushed open the door of the store, ringing the cowbell that had been clamped to the frame since the beginning of time. "Be right with you," his father said from the neighborhood of Fourth and Maple. He had set up the store with street names for the aisles, based on the downtown grid. If someone came into LaRosa's Hardware asking for a toilet plunger, Joaquin LaRosa would tell them to go down Second, turn left on Willow, and proceed to the intersection of Fourth. Half a century, that's the way it has been, and that's the way it was going to stay. The old man was stubborn as gravity and he could be mean as the August sun, and there was little doubt how he was going to react to his son's first assignment as Oscar Price's goodwill ambassador. For all intents and purposes, Albert was on a suicide mission.

The thing of it was, he loved this store as much as his father did. Loved the space, the history, the smells. The first

scent that always hit you, first foot in the door, was the floor oil
his father sprayed to keep the dust down on twelve-inch planks
sanded silky smooth by years of foot traffic. Then you smelled
the dust itself, thrown by rows of ceiling fans that wobbled like
the propellers of nosediving airplanes. In spring, the store
smelled of bonemeal, bug spray, and fertilizer, and as summer
gave way to fall, the paint began to dominate. If you were in
hardware, you might pick up the sharp metal odor that radi-
ated off the bulk bins of nails, nuts, and bolts and cut straight
through to your sinuses.

But for Albert, the most memorable scent of all in LaRosa's
Hardware, a scent long gone, was the chicken soup. On the
harshest days of winter, his mother made it at home, lugged it
down to the store, and then brought it to a glorious simmer on
a hot plate behind the front counter, fogging the front windows. She scooped it into little wax paper cups and offered it
to customers, and she always made sure to save enough for
when Sam and Albert came in after school. Never from a can,
either. Mom would have stock bubbling in a huge cast-iron pot
every night. The old man didn't believe in the canned.

"Oh, it's you," he said, not with a snarl but with the disappointment of a lost sale. "I thought it was a customer."

He was softer before she died, a hopeful look in his eyes,
not as short-fused and much less distrustful. It was one week
after a physical, the doctor having pronounced her fit and
clean, that Antoinette LaRosa keeled over right there behind
the counter while Nuba Ludwick dug into her purse to pay for
a tin of beeswax and a can of Raid. Fifty-eight years old and out
like a light, no warning, no time for good-byes.

"How do you know I'm not a customer?" Albert asked.

The old man had come running up from the basement when he heard Nuba's screams, and he couldn't even look at his wife. He kept right on going, dashing out the door and into the middle of the street, calling for help, half out of his mind. Out of his mind because he knew she was gone, knew they'd both been cheated, but couldn't even say of what. You work side by side your whole adult life, waiting for the day you can settle into something else, whatever it is. Retirement? A warm-weather condo? They'd been robbed of the chance to even make the plans. To this day, Joaquin LaRosa was looking to get even.

"You? This store pays for your diapers and your fillings and what happens? You run up to Bargain Acres and the rest of those shysters, same as all the other ingrates your mother and I took care of in this town for years. It's bad enough you don't want to take over the business, you don't even give any business."

"You know that's not true, Pop. I always come here for hardware. Besides, what's wrong with being a cop?"

"What does Harbor Light need a cop for?"

"Look Pop, so I'm not smart like Sam, and I'm not pigheaded like you. We've covered this ground already, haven't we?"

"Pigheaded? Look at the pot that's calling the kettle pigheaded!"

His father went around behind the register and leaned forward on his elbows to take a good look at his son. He wore glasses the size of half dollars, rims like gold thread, and he wiped them now on his blue apron. Joaquin LaRosa was shaped more like the bull than the matador. The hair was white as snow now, but still thick and healthy, and cut like the shoe brushes he sold—go down First and turn right on Ash, middle shelf on the left—for six dollars and fifty cents, a tin of Kiwi boot wax thrown in gratis.

"So what brings you in?" his father asked. "You here to arrest me for the bomb threats?"

"You didn't make any bomb threats, Pop."

"Don't be so sure about that," his father said.

Sit him at a table with a jug of wine and the beret he wore in winter months, his eyes like small black olives, and he'd look like he was plotting against Franco. But no. Albert's father was not the kind of man who made bomb threats.

Albert went up to the counter, descending into the creaking valley where the floorboards sagged from half a century of people standing there and sliding money across the counter. "I saw the taillight was smashed on the station wagon out front," he said. "A little dink on the bumper, too."

"I noticed it yesterday myself. Someone must have nicked it outside there. Probably Mrs. Costanza. She came in the other day for some plant food and walked right into the door on her way out. Blind as a bat, and she goes gunning around town like she's in the Cracker Barrel 500."

"What's the deductible on the insurance?"

"Insurance! You know what insurance is?"

Albert had made the unforgivable mistake of opening the Joaquin LaRosa book of quotations, golden nuggets of wisdom hauled up from the caves of blue-collar toil and delivered with a finger-wagging, vein-popping intensity that frightened children and household pets.

"Insurance is where you pay someone to tell you you've got no coverage. That's insurance. They've got it figured out so your deductible leaves you with your thumb up your ass every time."

All these little summaries his father had, no ambiguity in anything. Albert had heard them a thousand times each. *Their job is to put your money in their pocket. Nobody ever went wrong doing business with mom and pop. There's an extra hour of work in a ten-minute nap.* And then there was the old man's all-time favorite. *Never enter a store or restaurant where you can't shake the hand of the owner.*

That was the one that turned an admirable sense of history and nostalgia into a cranky and unrealistic lament. It wasn't the new world that annoyed Joaquin LaRosa, it was the very idea of change. Change of any type was like a call from the grave, time marching on. Albert had never known anyone so afraid of death. You had to plead with him to go to the doctor, and he'd blame it on Antoinette being pronounced healthy as a horse a week before she died. But really it was the fear of bad news.

Albert retreated to a seat on a bed of bagged plant food and turf builder, raising an unpleasant cloud, and wondered if they were all brain-damaged from the chemicals they'd been breathing for years. It would explain so much.

"I can't believe you don't have insurance on the car, Pop. That station wagon is twenty-five years old."

"That's what you came in here for, Albert? To put the cuffs on an old geezer for driving without insurance? What is that, a felony in your book?"

Albert, given his old-country bloodlines, was doomed to love his father with a genuine and deep sense of loyalty while also vowing on occasion to never speak to him again.

"No. I came in here because I saw your battle cry in the *Beacon* today. I wanted to explain why I'm going to work for Oscar Price."

Albert could almost hear his father's pulse quickening.

"Explain? What's there to explain? You're happy to sell the town down the river for a few bucks and I'm ready to sacrifice life and limb for the betterment of mankind. You're happy to take a bite out of the apple, and if I see that reptile come anywhere near my store again, I'll chase him down the street with a garden hoe. You want Rickie and Rose to be out on the street, and I want to eat at Peg's. What more could there be to discuss?"

Albert climbed out of the hole he'd dug in the turf builder and gave right back.

"Take a look outside, will you, Pop? Do you notice anything?"

"What am I supposed to see?"

"It's not 1950. Chance's is closed, the bike shop, Hap's. People get into their cars and they drive out to the big discount houses. You don't like it, I don't like it, but neither one of us is going to change that, and this is exactly what Oscar Price is talking about. That casino is going to put more people on the street. Are you so thick you can't see the logic of it? It's going to put hundreds of people to work, and some of them are going to walk down Cannery Way with money in their pockets. This is the best chance you've got."

"You know how long people have been telling me I'm

dead? Twenty-five years," the old man raged, shaking an iron fist. "And what does that sign on the door say? Open for business, that's what. I've been in business fifty years, and I don't need Oscar Price to tell me what's going to make it work. Who the hell is he? That son of a bitch was born on third base and he's going to tell me how to make it home?"

The old man's eyes looked like a couple of bloodshot ping-pong balls. If blowing off steam were healthy, they'd both be in the Olympics for all the workouts they had. But Albert's whole body ached, and right now it felt like drum practice in his chest.

The door opened with a ring and Jack walked in. He took a look at each of them and started to back out.

"Come on back. I was just leaving," Albert said.

They hadn't spoken since Albert asked him along on a test-drive of Sonny's boat. Jack, like everyone else who mattered, was avoiding him.

"All of a sudden," Albert said, headed for the door, "this is the smallest town in six states."

Sonny DiMaggio's wife was beating him like a runaway dog. Every day, another whack. The car, the house, half his paycheck. If he weren't such a rack of blubber, she'd probably take one leg of every pair of pants for herself, too. Her brother was an attorney and her father a judge, and Sonny didn't stand a chance in a Harbor County court system that was 98 percent who you knew. Albert felt like a thief, writing Sonny a thousand-dollar check to seal the deal on the boat, but he had to train himself to keep from grinning. He'd hand over the rest of the cash when the bonus came through.

"I've been through it," Albert said as he pocketed the keys on the porch of the Western Addition hovel Sonny was renting. He'd be eating beans and tortillas for the next twenty years and every alimony payment would feel like passing a stone, but the most benevolent thing you could do for a man in this situation was lie through your teeth. "You'll be fine."

"I thought about living on the boat," Sonny said with a beggar's eyes, and Albert knew without asking that the mistress had run for her life the minute Sonny's paycheck was garnished. "But my wife'd get her hands on that, too. I'd rather you have it."

Albert slapped Sonny on the back and gave him a buck-up wink. "Whenever you need to get back out on the water, just call," he said. He'd feel a little sorrier for him if he really knew Sonny well, but he didn't, and all Albert could think about was spending the next twenty years riding the swells in high style. What else did a man need? It wasn't even the fishing so much as the being removed from polite indulgence of everyone's misinterpretation of you. There was a point offshore, a point that depended on the weather, at which Albert felt whole. It was the point where he lost sight of land. You didn't have to apologize for wrecking your marriage. You didn't have to replay the day you shot a boy twenty-five years ago in a wretched Philadelphia row house and planted him in a wheelchair for life. Out there, the wind in your face, it smelled like the beginning of time.

Georgianna's voice, a tongue-tied, exasperated shriek, warbled through the car speaker like a cry from a distressed pachyderm.

"Radio alert, repeat, radio alert. Bravo-thirty-four, radio alert. Disturbance at five-oh-two Kip Slough Road. Shots fired. PRC Erica Davenport. Radio alert, Bravo-thirty-four."

Rickie's diner.

Albert's heart flipped. He bonked his skull on the headrest as he jammed the gas and rocketed up Ocean. The surf pounded in great frothy explosions as he searched his brain for explanations other than serious trouble. Backfire from a car. Kids playing with firecrackers. Duck hunters shooting out of season. But why would Rickie have called and reported a disturbance?

The face of the town melted past him as he burned north, siren wailing. A row of a dozen Victorian B&Bs with gingerbread dollops and ocean-view portals sat like fat ladies in crocheted sweaters, even the darker hues sandblasted to salty pastels. The lighthouse—dark for forty years—fingered up at two o'clock. Albert had kissed his first girl out there, Jill Aiello, in sixth grade.

He'd taken Rickie out to the lighthouse, too, a couple of weeks after they started going out. One of the advantages of being sheriff was that he had a key to everything, including the lighthouse tower, and he had gone by earlier that day to sink a bottle of wine into a bucket of ice up in the lantern room. He led her up the spiral stairwell at sunset, right up the shaft, clearing cobwebs and finger-flicking spiders as he blazed a trail for the girl he'd had a crush on since high school. The lantern room was aglow with warm, soft light, and the sky was streaked with cotton candy. Albert held her from behind, peering at the roiling surf through the lantern window and breathing in the scent of her hair and skin. Before they'd gotten halfway through the bottle, they were at each other.

Albert banked up on two wheels at the top of Ocean and fishtailed onto Kip Slough Road. Three blocks away and he could see a crowd in the parking lot and cars overflowing onto Kip and across the street on Fifth. Two blokes appeared to be locked in a scrum out by Aunt Rose's pink Caddy, cheered on by a half-circle of local all-stars. Someone had probably fired a round in the air to get the fight stopped. Rickie was at the top of the stairs screaming at someone down in the crowd, but as far as he could tell she appeared to be in one piece.

In the surest sign yet that it was time to take up another career, no one stopped anything they were doing just because the law had arrived. One window of the diner was busted out, leaving a shark-toothed frame of shards. Albert picked his way through the crowd to where the two brawlers had taken a tumble and were rolling around on the gravel. It was Creed James, Albert's boyhood buddy, and Warren Smith, the pig-faced goat farmer.

"Break it up!" Albert ordered. "Don't make me have to get rough with you two."

"Like your new boss is getting rough with me?" Creed snapped.

"I don't know what the hell you're talking about, Creed, but if you two don't give it a rest I'm going to hurt someone."

Albert reached in to grab Creed by the collar and was nearly bitten by Warren, whose jagged, tobacco-stained choppers snapped like a bear trap.

"All right, that's it," Albert said, whipping out his cuffs and joining Warren's wrists. He dragged him over to his squad car, Warren resisting all the way, and stuffed him into the back seat.

"Get over here," he ordered Creed.

"I'm not getting over anywhere, Albert."

"You'll do as I say or you'll spend a night in the tank. Now get over here and tell me what this is all about."

"I tried to tell you what it's about. Oscar Price is having me evicted out of my own house."

"He's not evicting anybody, Creed. That's bullshit."

"Then come look at what I got in the mail."

They walked over to Creed's truck, and he searched the cab, reached into the glovebox, and looked under the seat.

"It was right here," he said.

"Yeah, I'm sure it was," Albert said, but now he lost interest altogether.

Rickie was coming his way, and Albert's heart turned flips. They hadn't talked in five days, which had felt like five months.

"What happened with these two?" Albert asked.

"What do you think happened? They got into it over the casino. Warren's ready to sell out in a minute and Creed's ready to fight till death. Warren called him a moron and Creed grabbed him by the seat of his pants and tossed him clean through the window, like he was a sack of apples. Warren's gotta go two hundred fifty pounds, and Creed picked him up like he was nothing."

The whole dynamic between them had changed. They were in that horrible breakup phase where you go back to the beginning, suddenly addressing each other like you just met, avoiding steady eye contact, everything sort of perfunctory and

pleasant and completely full of shit. Albert scanned the horizon and followed Kip Slough out to the sea. Cool. Detached.
Doing fine. And then he saw the lighthouse and couldn't help
but ache. She was gazing in that direction, too, pushing
corkscrews of red hair from her face. She was probably looking
nowhere in particular but seemed to be seeing something clear
as day.

"You doing okay?" he asked.

She took a step toward him. One little step filled with so
much anticipation. Albert felt his breathing shallow out and
quicken. She had a tear in her eye and she was about to say
something, or maybe she wasn't. Maybe she didn't need to.
The look said it all, the tear that didn't fall. And then she
turned and walked slowly up toward the diner.

Now was the time to stop her, to share a thought that had
crossed his mind earlier. A compromise. He gave up the new
job, she sold the diner, and they both got the hell out of here
and started over somewhere else. He wanted to say it but knew
that he wouldn't, and he wondered what it was that got you to
these moments, these rare precious moments where you knew
exactly what you had to do, but no amount of logic, no level of
courage or human experience, could make you do it.

The sky had drawn around her, ice blue, and Albert got
only her silhouette burned onto the horizon. She hesitated for
an instant and then continued on, floating away on wasted
time, and Albert was left looking at the lighthouse, way up top
to the lantern room, where once they'd made love.

"Is this towel yours or mine?" Rickie chirped from the bathroom, sounding not nearly as heartbroken as one might have expected.

"Hold on. Let me look through the wall with my X-ray vision," Albert responded from the living room, where he held a stiff drink in one hand and puffed away on a cigarillo with the other, sending up toxic yellow gas bombs. He had his size fourteens up on the steamer trunk coffee table and was half watching a ball game between the wretched Phillies and the insufferable Mets. The Mets were about to pull another win out with an ugly ninth-inning rally that included not one hit that had traveled farther than you could spit.

"It's the green one on the rack," Rickie called again.

"Take it," Albert said, pleasantly numbed for the occasion. He had begun drinking four hours ago, when she left a message saying she might drop by to claim her things. "Take the toothpaste and the dental floss if you like, too. Knock yourself out."

She muttered a response he couldn't make out, but it didn't take a vivid imagination. Albert was no stranger to the dicker and bicker of breakups, and this one was actually a lot easier than his divorce. For one thing, Rickie hadn't actually lived with him. She spent maybe two or three nights a week here for the last five or six years, but she'd kept most of her things in the house she and Aunt Rose shared on Third Street. She liked her independence; he liked his. She liked it a lot, in fact.

Marriage would never have worked. It was so clear to him now, he had to laugh at what a fool he'd been to buy that ring. The gods must have been looking down on him in the diner that day when Rickie blew up before she even knew what he'd gone in there for. He still had to take that thing back to the Jewel Box and get himself some walking-around money to celebrate his return to single life.

Albert jabbed his cigar out and sprung up off the sofa on crackling knees. He was hanging around because of the weak, delusional notion that she was going to walk back in here, take one good look at him, and see something in the history of them together that would make her come to her senses. Pathetic. Nothing was going to happen, and he was not going to sit here another minute, indulging the fantasy.

"Listen, take whatever you need," Albert shouted toward the bedroom as he buckled his holster and grabbed his keys. "Take the washer and dryer, the tomato soup, and half the soda crackers. Get a chain saw and cut everything down the middle if that does it for you. I've got some business to take care of, so I'll see you around."

After he left, Rickie sat in the chair where he'd been. She lit a cigarette and accidentally knocked the ashtray onto the floor. Then she began to cry.

Mo set Albert's second whiskey double in front of him and he admired the soft amber glow in the pale light before holding the medicine in his mouth. It burned a canker sore on the lower left gutter of his mouth, but there was something satisfying about the pain. "And pour one for my buddy Harlan," Albert said. Harlan Wayans, anchored in his usual spot at the end of the bar, never refused such an offer nor did he ever respond in kind. He raised his beer mug in appreciation.

"Just off work, Harlan?"

"On my way as soon as this one goes down. I've hired on as a night watchman with an outfit in Atlantic City. Watching over construction sites and whatnot. You know, so no one runs off with tools or building materials."

Albert shifted on his barstool to pull his lighter out of his pocket. It was his own personal barstool, with a copy of his badge inlaid on the seat and handsomely decoupaged. In conversation with Georgianna, Albert called Mo's Tavern the administrative annex, which sent her over the edge every time. Mo's was moored on the banks north of the marina in violation of virtually every health, business, and maritime code on the books. The place smelled of beer-soaked wood, drunken fishermen, and retold stories. The planked walls were lined with seashells and dusty photos of sailors no one knew, and fishnets hung like military camouflage from rough-hewn ceiling beams. Mo kept a baited line dropped through the window behind the bar, and when she hooked a bass or crappie, she panfried it in a cast-iron skillet and passed it around with fresh lemon wedges and hunks of French bread. On the house. Heaven.

"Your FBI buddy was in here earlier," Mo said.

"Muldoon? Did he confess his love?"

"He's not my type, Albert."

"He talks about you all the time, you know. He'd leave his wife in a second."

"If she were any kind of woman, she'd beat him to it."

Albert took another slug of whiskey and drew on his cigar. "I thought you told me the number one rule of bartending was to stay out of other people's business."

"Here here," said Harlan, who was a little top-heavy when he stood to say good-bye. Albert offered to drive him to work but Harlan insisted he was okay, just a little tired from the double shifts. He said he always caught a couple hours' sleep at work and he was fine.

"You know what I ought to do once I get set up in the new job?" Albert asked. "I ought to sell my place and get the hell out of town. Get a nice little condo or something in Ventnor or Margate. How about one of those places you see coming in off the expressway in A.C. With the boat tie-ups out back?"

Mo didn't hear a word of it. The TV was on. The TV was always on, because Mo was trying to break the international record for the longest-running Brigitte Bardot film festival. A bar in a small town in the south of France had gone 432 days. Mo announced her challenge on the Internet and had just broken 400 days with no intention of slowing down. Mo, short for Maureen, was French Canadian and claimed she'd had an affair with Bardot on a trip to Nice in the 1960s. None of the hardcore regulars believed Brigitte Bardot was capable of a crossover, but Mo kept the illusion alive with Bardot movie posters on every wall and with a grainy three-by-five Polaroid that was framed and propped up on the bar. The photo showed two topless sea nymphs with their arms around each other on a Mediterranean beach. Of that, there was no question. But it was at least twenty years old and it was not clear beyond a reasonable doubt that one was Mo and the other was Bardot. Once every several weeks, Mo settled a bet by lifting her shirt to reveal her boobs, which bore a fantastic resemblance to those in the photo. But Albert wasn't sure whether to believe her. She stood close to six feet tall, with dramatic cheekbones that took on an X-ray glow from the light of the TV. When her favorite scene ended, Mo turned back to Albert and splashed him a refill that climbed to the lip of the glass.

"This one's on the house," Mo said. "You're going to be fine, by the way. It just takes a little time."

There had been nights, after his divorce if not before, when Albert climbed out of his cups and floated away with Mo in his imagination, riding the late-night vapors back to her place in Rio Grande. Right now, though, still hollowed out from the sight of Rickie gathering up her things without the faintest hint of regret or doubt, he needed a bartender more than a sackmate. Besides, the Amazonian bisexual thing scared the snot out of him, and he was certain Mo would have frightening things to confess. Like she had pythons roaming free around the house, or that as a schoolgirl athlete in Canada, she'd once thrown the discus halfway to Gander.

"So when do you start this new job?" Mo asked.

"Not a minute too soon," Albert said as a car pulled up.

Mo leaned out the window behind the bar but couldn't tell who it was. She reeled in to check the bait and dropped the line again. The door opened and a rush of salted marsh air deodorized the room. "My big sister," Albert said with surprise. "How'd you know I was here?"

"It was either here or the library. I took a wild guess."

"Mo, did I mention that my older sister Sam was a smart-ass?"

"Why do you think I like her so much?"

Mo reached for a bottle of Sam's favorite beer, but Sam waved her off. "I've got to drive back up to Long Island," she said. "Can you make it just a soda?"

"Not staying for the big show tonight? You can watch Pops in all his glory."

"I'd actually like to, but I have to get back." Mo set the Coke down and Sam, in her most dramatic tone, said, "Albert, we've got to talk."

Albert grabbed their drinks and led her to a table against the back wall, the floor swaying under them as the houseboat rocked. Albert admired Sam even though she reminded him so much of his father. He had gotten his mother's looks and Sam had drawn the other card, which meant the game was rigged in her favor from the beginning. Pop's little pet. She'd graduated salutatorian from Harbor County Area High School, got that fully loaded scholarship to Villanova, married a doctor, and raised two terrific and adorable girls who were both in Ivy League schools and well on their way to becoming saints or discovering cures for cancer. Albert, on the other hand, left town the day after high school to work on a fishing boat in Key West and spent a year thinking about where to go to school. Never had he seen his father so thoroughly draped in disappointment as the day he returned to Harbor Light and announced that he wasn't going to college after all. He'd met a Philadelphia cop on the boat one day in Florida and got to know him a little bit, and the cop told Albert they were looking for recruits. The old man screamed at Albert for a week and then didn't speak to him for a month.

Sam popped two aspirin and threw them back with a shot of Coke.

"I had a talk with Dr. DiMitri, and I'm worried about Pop," she announced.

She was always worried about Pop, which made for endless opportunities to flog Albert for being the irresponsible child.

"He's fine, Sam."

"What do you mean he's fine? I've had to drive all the way down here because I can't count on you to keep after him. His blood pressure is up, his weight is up, and he's got a box of pastries from Nuba's behind the counter in the store."

"Look, if you'd seen him the other day out at the diner, he was wearing the beret and leading the charge."

"That's what I'm talking about. I'm worried about the way he's getting all worked up over the casino, especially since he's headed for a slaughter. And it doesn't help that you're on the other side of the fence. Do you have any idea how upset he is by that?"

"That's his problem, Sam. I'm looking out for myself."

"No, it's my problem. You should have seen him at the store, telling Jack how he was going to give it to Oscar Price tonight at the meeting. He's too old for this, Albert. I'm begging you. Don't make me have to drive down here once a week to separate the two of you. And I can't believe what you did to Rickie."

"What did I do to Rickie?"

"I stopped in to see her, Albert. She told me everything. There's nothing you need more than to be with her, and you keep sabotaging it because . . ."

"Because what, Sam? What do you get, seventy-five bucks an hour to tell people why they do what they do?"

"A hundred fifty."

"I'll check with Oscar Price tonight and see if head exams are covered under my new plan."

"You won't let anyone near it, Albert, and it has the same effect as pushing people away."

"Oh, so we're back to Philadelphia now, are we?"

"We're not back to it; we've never left it. You ruined a marriage over this and now you're losing the best catch you've ever made. It's been over twenty years, Albert. Rickie's not a gal who's going to wait on a man who still needs his wounds licked twenty years after he fell off his horse."

Suddenly she didn't merely look like his father. She *was* his father. Round-faced and olive-eyed, insufferable, and militantly wrong. Sam knew part of the story, but not all of it. That didn't keep her from concluding with uninhibited arrogance that she knew all the faces and histories of Albert's ghosts.

"I don't need a trite simplification of my life, Sam. And for your information, I don't need my wounds licked."

"No," she said as Albert threw down the rest of his shot and looked desperately toward Mo for a refill. "You just soak them in alcohol."

"This again?"

"You've got a drinking problem, Albert. Do I have to remind you what I do for a living?"

"Do I have to remind you I am not one of your patients?'"

Sam put her hand over his on the table. "I love you dearly and you know it," she said. "But there's not a patient I've had longer than you."

"Thank you, Mr. Price. This council would like to sincerely thank you for your excellent presentation."

Oscar Price took a seat to wild approval as his minions gathered up several slick, multicolored charts and wheeled away a plastic, computer-designed, glass-encased model of the proposed casino and marine park. Mayor Salvatore waited patiently for the applause to die down, but finally had to bring the gavel down to quiet the room.

"Your attention please. Your attention please."

Price, elegantly attired in a navy blue suit, took it upon himself to stand again and bow. He gave a shy wave and then lowered both hands, signaling for quiet.

"Ladies and gentlemen, if we could move ahead now," Mayor Salvatore intoned, drawing electronic feedback that probably had dogs howling in Wildwood. "The council would like to recognize the next speaker. Would you please state your name and address for the record."

The next speaker had no charts, no plastic models, no props of any kind. He did, however, wear his two-button wool sportcoat, circa 1950, and a black beret cocked for revolution. Always a bad sign, Albert thought. Every time his blood ran hot and he took on a cause, he dug that black beret out of the back of the closet and thought he was Che Guevara.

"Name and address? You know who I am, Joe. Everyone in this room knows who I am, and you know where I live."

"It's the rules, Joaquin. Everybody has to do it. This is an official public hearing before the town council of the municipality of Harbor Light, and that's the way it has to be done under statutory law."

"Joaquin LaRosa. That's J-o-a-q-u-i-n L-a-R-o-s-a. Of seven-sixty-four Third Street. T-h-i-r . . ."

"I didn't say spell it, I said state it."

"Well I stated it, and now I'm going to state something else."

The crowd in Assembly Hall, the town's multipurpose room going back to the turn of the century, stirred in anticipation. City Hall and the Post Office were upstairs, and down here they held bake sales, arts and crafts fairs, plays, awards banquets, shuffleboard tournaments. But Albert couldn't remember a swarm like this. Every chair was spoken for and people stood shoulder-to-shoulder across the back of the hall. Two hundred total? Three hundred? Albert could pick out Jack in the front row, as if he were Joaquin's personal appointments secretary. And it wasn't hard to find Rickie's flaming curls. She was whispering to someone Albert didn't recognize, at least not from the back.

"Well folks, we've just heard a moving presentation from Mr. Price here about a project that's going to transform our lives. Trees will be trimmed, sidewalks will be fixed, there'll be jobs aplenty, a chicken in every pot, and candy for all the children. I'm surprised he didn't tell you bald men would grow hair and the lame and bedridden would kick off their woes and dance a jig on Cannery Way. If these kinds of promises ring a bell, they should, because we heard the same thing two years ago when they rammed that Bargain Acres down our throats."

The crowd groaned. Oscar Price had lit a fire, promising things the town had never dreamed possible, and here was Joaquin LaRosa, old, curmudgeonly Joaquin, blowing out the candles.

"There's a hundred fifty jobs at the Bargain Acres!" Mayor Joe retorted, trembling over this insurrection. "It's the same thing with the casino. It's jobs we're looking at. Money in the bank. That's something for all of us."

"Joe, I love you like a brother," Joaquin LaRosa said. "Actually more like an in-law. But who do you know at Bargain Acres that can pay the mortgage and raise a family? Not a solitary soul, that's who. Why is that, you ask? I'll tell you why. Because there's six guys in a tower in Texas and a dozen more on Wall Street, sitting there with fat cigars and fatter smiles because they've got this whole thing figured out. You know what their job is, Joe? Their job is to put your money in their pockets. You're running up there to save two bits on a six-pack of underwear from a clerk who can't afford shoes for her kids. Those tall Texans are laughing all the way to the bank. They're taking home six-million-dollar bonuses while the merchant here on Cannery Way is going belly up. My friends, I have a question for you tonight. Is that the world you want to live in?"

This drew a smattering of applause, but also a few hisses and boos. Joe Salvatore took hold of his gavel again and hammered like a carpenter.

"This hearing, for everyone's information, is not about

Bargain Acres or the Golden Mile out on the Parkway. It's about the casino."

"Mr. Mayor, if I can interject," said Price, who stood in place, upright and reverent as a Boy Scout.

"Why does he get to interject?" Joaquin LaRosa protested. "Did I interrupt him when he yammered on for half the night?"

"The purpose of this hearing is to help this council arrive at the most well-informed decision on the proposal before us," Mayor Salvatore scolded. "Mr. Price, please proceed."

"Thank you, Mr. Mayor. For the record, I'd like to remind everyone that our salaries at Evolution tend to exceed by two to three times the average salaries in the retail industry." He held aloft a six-color chart that was just handed to him by one of his assistants. "And secondly, I'd like to reiterate that we share Mr. LaRosa's sense of community and home rule. We're not based in Texas. I live just a few blocks from here as a matter of personal preference. I also share Mr. LaRosa's commitment to the future of Harbor Light, even if we might have an entirely different sense of the tremendous potential for this unique community. Joaquin's own son, I might add, very much understands our dream. For those who don't already know, we've agreed to terms with Sheriff Albert LaRosa that will make him a key player in the transformation of a blighted building into a destination attraction you'll all be proud of. Sheriff, if you don't mind a wave from the back of the room?"

Albert, who had stumbled in as discreetly as possible toward the end of Price's spiel, acted as if he'd been there all along. He waved to all from the back of the hall and smiled with his lips sealed. He was in full uniform and it probably would be best not to let on that a key player in the transformation of Harbor Light was so tanked that his breath could curl the linoleum. What a lucky break, he thought, getting here just in time to catch the boss's notice. But he realized, seeing his father at the front of the room, that he had sandbagged the old man in the middle of his big moment. The old man bristled, too. Albert could tell, from across the hall, that this affront would be neither forgotten nor forgiven.

"Mr. LaRosa, if you have anything further," Joe Salvatore said impatiently, as if there were a general understanding that he had just been discredited if not totally humiliated.

"As a matter of fact I do," Joaquin said calmly. "I noticed that a couple of things didn't appear on Mr. Price's fancy charts. One was that he promised us he already had all the property he needed, and now we discover Mr. Price has bought two parcels along the Slough and has a dozen offers on the table to buy more. And how, you might ask, has he managed to pull off public projects and land transactions in a fraction of the time it ordinarily takes? Because Mr. Price has money, and money buys friends in all the right places, from the town hall all the way up to the governor's office."

Joe Salvatore banged his gavel like a woodpecker, protesting the inference and threatening to sue for slander. Joaquin LaRosa just spoke louder and faster.

"What did you get out of the deal, Joe? Has he got you in rubber boots, feeding anchovies to dancing dolphins?"

The mayor cracked for order.

"Calm down and let me finish, Joe. He's had this thing greased from day one, when he started hanging around on Cannery Way like he was one of us, and instead of standing up and asking questions, you dummies couldn't wait to line up and bend over."

"Mr. Mayor, if I might . . ." Price interrupted.

"I'm not finished, Mr. Price. I have the floor and I'll hold it until I've had my say. A couple more numbers must have fallen off your charts. There's a little report up at the highway office in Rag Harbor, for everyone's information, that says traffic on the island will increase tenfold. He didn't tell you that little fact, did he? Tenfold! What do you think that's going to do to the way of life here? We'll be a shortcut from Atlantic City to Jersey Landing when this bridge is built. Remind your children to look both ways, because people leave casinos one of two ways—flat broke or stinking drunk. We're about to become a parking lot, too. Do you know how many acres of parking the average casino in Atlantic City has? Enough to cover half this island. This man is taking over, don't you see it? We've got a real community here, a place to raise a family, walk to the store, enjoy a stroll on a beach, and he's turning it into a one-trick company town. He's not just a businessman, he's the new mayor, the chamber of commerce president, the owner, king, and emperor of Harbor Light. Now I may not have his connections or clout, and I know I don't have his money. But if stopping this man means throwing ourselves in front of the bulldozers, you're looking at the first volunteer."

Assembly Hall split in two as Joaquin LaRosa raised his fist in a gesture of defiance. He'd won a fair number of converts with the fury of his unconditional love for the snoring old burg, and the room fissured under the polar forces of yea and nay. Oscar Price was on his feet again, a billionaire among borrowers, trying to turn back the doubt. Mayor Joe banged his gavel and waved his arms, blabbing parliamentary gibberish that morphed into ear-piercing feedback. Above the municipal din came the concussion of an explosion so fearful it drew shrieks, followed by the synchronized drop and cover of a generation schooled in the evils of the red menace and other dark forces.

"We're under attack!" yelled Red Miller, the ninety-some legionnaire.

"Everyone remain calm!" Mayor Joe screeched in the uncalmest of voices.

Albert was the first one, the only one, up the stairs. The heat knocked him back as he stumbled half drunk onto Cannery Way, which was lit by the fire of battle. Albert shielded the furnace with his hands, watching helplessly as Oscar Price's silver Ferrari disappeared in a fireball. The first grenade in the war for Harbor Light had been lobbed, and it was a direct hit.

Albert turned around in front of the crowd that was now beginning to pour out the doors. "Everybody stop right where you are," he shouted, holding both arms up wide. "These other cars catch fire, the whole block could blow. Bob, Harold, get the rest of your volunteers down to the firehouse and get that old truck here. Joe, go grab a phone and tell the watch commander to get hold of Fitch Caster. Tell him we've got a possible car bomb situation here and have him get me some forensics people on the double."

Max Phelps made a dash for his car, which was parked behind Price's, but Albert hooked him by the arm and pulled him back.

"I've got to get my Cadillac out of there," Max protested.

"Let it go," Albert demanded, putting a body on him and pushing him back to the curb. "It's just a car. I don't want you behind the wheel if it should happen to go up like Price's."

Albert shielded his face with his hands and tried to creep closer to Price's Ferrari, but hisses and pops drove him back. A gust blew the acrid black smoke toward the park, giving him a clearing, and Albert tiptoed in again to see if he could determine an ignition point or pick up any kind of forensic footprint. But the wind shifted once more and the heat blasted him back onto his heels.

He turned toward the crowd to look for Oscar Price, and instead he found his father and Warren Smith faced off as if they were about to go at it. Rickie was pushing her way toward them, but if fists started flying, he didn't want her in the middle of it.

Jesus H. And Sam had just told him their pop was gunning for a heart attack. Albert took two steps in their direction before Price cut him off.

"I want to know who did this," he insisted, the light of the fire reflecting in his pale blue eyes.

"I'm working on it," Albert said. "Just give me a little time, and I'll have your answer."

"I want it prosecuted to the fullest," Price said through his teeth.

They were both facing the car when Albert spotted Jack standing alone on the sidewalk across the street, staring at the crackling sedan with a look of wonder. Albert promised Price he'd give the case his full attention and then yelled across to

Jack, who didn't hear him at first. The fire truck was roaring around the curve at Legion Park, siren screaming. Finally Jack came trotting over.

"You need me to do anything?" he asked.

"Yeah. Keep an eye on Pop, will you? He's all wound up over there, like he's ready to trade knuckles with Warren Smith."

Harold Baldwin, who wore bifocals and walked with a severe limp, had trouble tapping the fire hydrant. Albert grabbed the wrench from him and used all his lanky leverage to crank open the valve. As flames flickered dangerously close to overhead power lines, an argument raged between Harold Baldwin and Bob Casey about whether you were supposed to use water or foam on a car fire. Albert saw Price taking it in.

"Just put the goddamn fire out before we lose the whole downtown," Albert ordered. "Use both if you have to. Just get to work, and let's stop looking like complete amateurs."

Albert hustled toward his car to radio for a backup engine company out of Atlantic City, just in case the fire jumped.

"Everybody off the street," he yelled. "I want this area cleared immediately. If that power line catches, you'll all be toast."

He had just gotten off the radio when he heard the sound of breaking glass from up the street. What now?

"That's my store," he heard his father blurt.

Jack took off running toward the sound, Joaquin LaRosa huffing along behind him.

"Pop!" Albert called, but his father kept on. Albert started after them but stopped over the screams of the crowd. The elm nearest Price's car had exploded in flame, and the firefighters aimed the hose on it. Some of the branches brushed against the second floor of City Hall, and Albert grabbed a ladder and an ax off the fire truck. He chopped away until he could barely take another swing, and thankfully the Atlantic City company pulled in to take over.

It took only another ten minutes before the car fire was extinguished and the tree was contained. Albert was soaked with sweat and ready to pass out. He plopped down on the curb to catch his breath, but Joaquin LaRosa was not about to let him have a break.

"He's got a rifle!" someone yelled.

Albert looked down to the next block and saw his father and Aunt Rose in the middle of the street, both of them armed and dangerous. He broke into a trot.

"Jack, you were supposed to be watching out for him!" Albert puffed when he arrived on the scene.

"What do you want me to do?" Jack cracked back. "Some asshole smashed a brick through the front window of the hardware store. I'd have gotten the twenty-two for him if I knew where he kept it."

Aunt Rose was standing next to the old man with her shotgun cocked, and now she was wearing a beret, too. They looked like Basque terrorists who'd just broken out of a retirement home.

A sharp pain clamped down on Albert's shoulder, as if he'd been pinched with a pair of ice tongs. With any luck, maybe it was the start of a massive and fatal coronary.

"Would you drop the goddamn muskets?" he pleaded.

His father completely ignored him and turned in the opposite direction, leveling his aim on the cannery at the end of the block.

"Pop, I'm serious," Albert insisted.

The old man pulled the trigger. On the distant sound of breaking glass, Aunt Rose let out a whoop.

Albert moved in and snatched away their weapons, careful not to end up on the wrong end of a muzzle. "I'm disgusted by both of you," he said. "What the hell is even the point?"

"The point?" his father bellowed. "No one's going to come in here to pillage and plunder without a fight from Joaquin LaRosa. What the hell would you understand? You're the captain of the welcome wagon."

Three hours later, after all the combatants had been separated and the crime lab boys had packed up and left, Albert stopped at Mo's for a nightcap. It turned into three, and while he and Mo traded theories as to what local hero had decided to join an Islamic jihad, the fog advanced on the island. The dreaded Jersey fog. This time of year, it traveled as quickly as milk spilled across a tabletop, blotting out everything in its path. It was too thick, Mo decided, to drive all the way home to Rio Grande in Cape May County. Albert ought to stay at the Tavern, too, she suggested, just to be safe.

Albert was not too tanked to understand the implication of the suggestion. He didn't know the mechanics of it, but when Mo didn't feel like driving home to Rio Grande, she somehow converted the pool table into a bed. He took a long look at the table, imagining the two of them bunked out up there like giant redwoods. He'd like nothing more than a good roll, frankly. It would help take the edge off. But even in this state of inebriation, Albert saw a little more of the M than the F in Mo's hormonal aura, and there was just no way he was chopping wood with Paul Bunyan tonight.

Mo talked him into leaving the police cruiser in the lot, probably a good idea, and Albert started hoofing it home. He'd once swerved off the road and into a ditch after an evening at Mo's, and didn't need his picture in the *Beacon* at this particular juncture. This time of year the fog could hang for days. It could cut to the bone, too, but Albert wasn't feeling much of anything. Unfortunately, his memory was entirely unfazed by the booze, and he couldn't help but reflect on the day's highlights. Let's see, his lover of six years divided up the towels and cleared out for good. His father had done everything but fire a cannon shot in declaring war on Albert's new boss. And someone, he had no idea whom, had blasted Oscar Price's car into the next century. Maybe he should have just gone ahead and plugged Mo after all, put the kibosh on that relationship, too, and call it a grand-slam day. About all he needed now was to have Oscar Price drive by and see him staggering home half cockeyed. The sooner Albert got out of uniform and into the new job the better off he'd be.

Albert turned the corner of Bayview and Jib, a half block from home, reconsidering Mo's offer. Returning to an empty home with a cold bed held no great appeal at the moment. He aped through the screened-in porch, where he spent many a summer evening with a stiff drink and a good smoke, eavesdropping on the wave action two blocks away. With the casino coming in, property values might spike, which would make it all the smarter to sell this shack and take a no-maintenance singles pad in A.C. An entire new life was out there just beyond the clearing, waiting for Albert to toss some baggage overboard and make the leap. He'd call Ron Rubio tomorrow and have them come sink a For Sale sign into the ground. Hell, he had to call him anyway to find out where he was when Oscar Price's car got barbecued. He wasn't in Assembly Hall, Albert was almost certain, so on a short list of suspects, he was near the top.

For the first time, Albert regretted having ignored neighborhood concerns about the upkeep of his property. Several anonymous notes had been left on his porch expressing grave concerns over the general appearance of his weed-spotted rock garden and the rotting, overturned skiff that was the centerpiece of an arrangement he took a certain amount of pride in. The rotting was part of the effect, as was the rusted anchor next to it. In the abstract, it was a mood piece on the aging process and the sense of displacement it brought. But more importantly, it was entirely maintenance-free. He might have to plow a few dollars into the yard now, though, which he'd be sure to get back in the resale.

Albert was fishing his keys out of his pocket, imagining himself idling up to the dock of his new condo in the Tiara Pursuit, when an odd sensation came over him and a tickle crawled up his spine. He heard not a thing, but felt as though he wasn't alone. He looked over his shoulder and onto the street. No movement, no strange vehicles, nothing in the picture disturbed. Surely he was imagining things. Never should have sucked down those last three drinks. That's what it was. He could smell it on his own skin, the alcohol leaching through his pores. Better swallow some aspirin now or he'd wake up in the morning with a head of glass. Albert raised the key and as he went for the lock, he realized the door was ajar.

Rickie wouldn't have left it open when she cleared out her things earlier. She was annoyingly vigilant about locking and latching. On this thought, Albert brightened. Maybe she'd come back. Maybe she had come across a washcloth or pillowcase of indeterminate ownership and wanted to get a final determination from him. Or maybe she had realized on reconsideration, just in the nick of time, that nothing on the planet meant more to her than the cold comfort of his spacious humor and humanity—not to mention his intellect—and that her meager existence without him had become emotionally unbearable. He was more than willing, however, to settle for a disputed pillowcase.

Albert eased the door open, stuck his nose in, and listened. All he could hear was the slow thunder and swoosh of the breakers echoing through the house. He took one step inside and saw first that someone had smashed his crystal collection and second, that a light was on in his bedroom. It occurred to him now that if it weren't Rickie, the possibilities included the caller who had threatened his and Oscar Price's life, as well as the person who had just overhauled Price's Ferrari.

One hand on his gun, Albert tiptoed toward the room, stopping just short of the half-open door. Light flickered from inside and Albert smelled a candle burning. He unholstered his gun, set the muzzle against the door, and pushed.

On his bed was an envelope, addressed to Creed James from the State of New Jersey.

Albert opened it and unfolded Creed's eviction notice.

———

Joaquin LaRosa was waiting up for Jack in the kitchen when he got home from visiting friends in Ocean City.

"Almost midnight. I thought you'd be upstairs by now," Jack said.

"I'm too wound up after a night like this. How can I sleep?"

Jack grabbed the remains of a three-day-old pizza out of the refrigerator and joined Mr. LaRosa, filling their glasses with jug wine. This wasn't a bad deal he had, working for Mr. LaRosa four or five mornings a week before pulling the lunch shift at his mother's diner. The two jobs put a few bucks in his pocket, and Mr. LaRosa liked having company in his big empty house, so room and board were free. Jack still kept some things at the place his mother shared with Aunt Rose, and he stayed there now and then. But he preferred this setup. It was like having a grandfather who was half guardian and half shit-kicker.

"You see the look on his face when he first came up on the street?" Jack asked.

"Did I see his look? Are you kiddin' me? That putz comes running up the stairs, and there's his fancy sports car, toasted like a campfire marshmallow. Glory be, I wish I'd had a camera."

Kentucky bourbon was such a lie. All that romancing and all you ended up with was a half-empty bed and the sound of the Confederate army marching through your head. Albert worked the phone to see if the crime lab had come up with anything, and he called his buddy Mike Muldoon, retired FBI, to pick his brain. Still groggy, he showered and dressed, and then sat on the front porch with a cup of coffee and a smoke. Arthur Abraham, the Drain Surgeon, was getting into his plumbing truck when he saw Albert and came hurrying across the street.

"Oscar Price's people came by my place yesterday," Arthur said, grinning like he'd just picked the winning horse in the Kentucky Derby. "He wants to put me on retainer for emergency plumbing jobs at the new casino."

He was no amateur, Oscar Price. He'd now knocked on the doors of a dozen businesses, getting his ducks in a line. You could call it payola if you were so inclined. But it was business, and he was a businessman. That was how the world worked, regardless of the sentimental, nostalgic rumblings of the sadly misguided army of the People's Republic of Harbor Light.

"How about that," Albert said, welcoming the company. Arthur Abraham was a hardworking, sensible, decent man who happened to appreciate the economic realities of the time. Arthur had a son and daughter to put through college, not to mention a tax load that pushed him to the edge of the cliff. If not for the summer trade, when those fat-assed tourists from Northeast Philly and Queens waddled into town and crapped out the sewage system, Arthur would be in the tank. "I'm on my way to see him now," Albert went on. "Were you at the meeting last night?"

"No, my grandson had a soccer game in Ocean City. But I heard all about it. A little scary, don't you think? That kind of thing happening in Harbor Light?"

"I wouldn't worry about it," Albert said.

"I don't know. Sounds to me like we got us a nut on the loose. Any idea who?"

"I'm working on it, Arthur. You'll be the first to know."

Albert's car was still at Mo's, so he walked over to retrieve it, whipped over Memorial Bridge, and dashed up the Parkway to Atlantic City. The Golden Mile was already overrun with eight billion or so ravenous consumers or Albert would have ducked into Tortilla Gulch for the huevos rancheros and a Bloody Mary, get his equilibrium back up and running. Of course after last night he might end up hanging his head over the side of BART, the ridiculous purple caterpillar jitney, puking his guts out in full uniform. Give kids a look at the exciting possibilities in a law enforcement career.

Gus was still operating the employee elevator at Evolution and still reading the *Racing Form*. Albert asked if he had any good tips and Gus said, "Yes. A horse would never bet on a person."

Okay. A philosopher running the dumbwaiter. Albert was

dumped out on the thirtieth floor and gathered his bearing. This was twice now that he'd wobbled in here straight off a drunk. The receptionist was on the phone, the Atlantic painted behind her like it was the border of her portrait. She held a finger up and smiled an indulgence, and Albert danced back politely on his heels and noticed for the first time a motto spelled out in one-thousand-dollar Evolution chips on the wall next to the elevator.

BAD LUCK IS FEAR OF RISK

Here, here. A much better notion than BEWARE OF FALSE PROPHETS, which Georgianna had on a plaque next to her desk.

Price had a closed circuit unit so he could monitor the lobby from his office, and he was through the door before the receptionist could extricate herself from the phone call.

"Good to see you," he said, extending a hand, and Albert thought he saw him give the receptionist a subtle, unspoken scolding for making a guest wait. "Come on in."

They set up in their regular spots—Price on his Napoleonic throne, Albert on the sofa that didn't show up anywhere in the IKEA catalog. Price clearly didn't have the time or desire to talk about the weather, so Albert launched right in.

"We won't know anything conclusively until the lab report comes in, but I talked to the arson investigator and a guy I know at the county crime lab," Albert said. "There's no question it was some type of explosive device as opposed to an electrical short or any other natural cause, so to speak. He threw out C4 and TNT as possibilities. Maybe even a grenade, the way the door on the driver side ended up across the street and through the window of the pawnshop, which I didn't notice until after you were gone and the smoke had cleared. All this is speculative for now, but the point is it didn't look like a gas tank explosion from an electronic or mechanical malfunction."

"Someone wanted the car blown to bits, simple as that," Price said. His face was as pale as a dollar bill gone through the wash in your back pocket, but it wasn't dread; it was his normal skin tone. If anything, he was more pinched than ever, as if last night's strike had made him all the more committed to the cause.

"I'm afraid so. I went door-to-door after the meeting. A two-, three-block area. Asking if anyone saw anything or anyone on Cannery Way."

"Nothing?"

Albert shook his head in disappointment. He'd wanted to find something—anything—to offer up, no matter how small. Just to reward Price's trust in him.

"You parked there at what time, would you say?" Albert asked.

"It had to be around seven."

"Well, the explosion was at seven forty-three."

"Which tells us what?"

Albert fidgeted for a response and Price did a very poor job of hiding disappointment. Just get the job done, his look said. Same as with the receptionist a moment ago. Just get the job done, honey.

"I've got a buddy, retired FBI. He tells me any amateur can build a timing device. It could have been planted on the car right here in Atlantic City, earlier in the day. It could have been set to go off . . ."

"As I drove home after the meeting?" Price interrupted. A conversation was like chess for him. He tried to stay a step ahead.

"I suppose it's a possibility, but it's too soon to jump to conclusions."

"My concern is not for myself, Sheriff. It's for my family. I've got a wife and three children, and I shudder to think of the possibilities had I left that meeting, gone home, and had the thing explode where it might have harmed one of them."

Price kind of drifted off for a moment, his eyes turning inward.

"I can certainly appreciate that, sir," Albert said.

"Well, detective, I suppose that brings us to the sixty-four-thousand-dollar question, now, doesn't it?"

"Yes, I suppose it does. Who's our bomber? And is it our friend from the other day? 'Listen to me with both ears.'"

"Precisely."

Albert had fallen asleep last night trying to answer that question.

"Well Ron Rubio, as you know, feels as though he got cheated out of the cannery property. I can tell you from experience that he's always been a little on the shady side, so there's that possibility. He's in a position to know some people. His driver, in fact, comes out of South Philadelphia."

"I want it checked out," Price said flatly, sounding for all the world like just another boss, and for the first time Albert realized this new adventure, this sweetheart deal, would not be a free ride. You could be deceived by Price, get the idea he enjoyed giving money away. But he wasn't running the March of Dimes. The things you heard about him, the shrewdest man in

Atlantic City, were true. He was generous with his employees but he expected a lot in return. All of which was perfectly acceptable to Albert. It's not like he was sixty-three and looking for a way to coast down the last stretch of road. He was taking this job precisely because of the new challenges it presented.

"Of course," Albert said cheerfully. "The other possibility that comes to mind, and we've been over this, is that one of your competitors would just as soon not have you drawing potential customers out of town. I've got some contacts here, including someone in what's left of the local mob. If there were any of that kind of involvement, I'll know about it before the day is out. Meantime, I'd also like to start checking on employees who might have left here on bad terms. And I'll start digging out the pyros in the area, see what they're doing with their time."

"Pyros?"

"Pyromaniacs."

"Then let's get on it," Price said, slapping his knees as he began to stand.

"One more thing, sir. I've turned in my notice with the county, just so you know. And to tell you the truth, I'm ready to start that training here in Atlantic City and out in Vegas. I mean, whenever you say the word, I'm yours."

"It's a little soon for that," Price said immediately. "I think you're of more use to us in Harbor Light for the time being, don't you?"

This was not what Albert had hoped to hear. Mentally, he'd already changed jobs and moved off the island. He could already see himself in his new bachelor pad on the back bay in A.C.

"Do you really think so?" he asked. "Because if I make the switch now, I'll have no distractions."

"I'm certain of it," Price said. "I like the idea of you being in uniform a while longer on the island, where you can be of more use to us than if you were here in Atlantic City all day. That'll give you a chance to work on your father and some of the others. Understandably, he swings some weight with a certain element in town, judging by the reaction last night, and I'm concerned about public sentiment building on the other side. He's a powerful presenter, your father."

Powerful presenter? He was Paul Revere on a horse. If Albert had had the slightest chance of bringing his father around, it was lost when Oscar Price asked him to give that gay little wave last night from the back of Assembly Hall. Thank god he was impaired at the time, or he might not have been able to pull it off. His father, he was certain, would never forgive him.

"So you want me to work on him, you say?"

"Help them understand I'm on his side. That's all."

"I don't think you under . . ."

"You know the thing that escapes me?"

Yes. Albert knew exactly what escaped him. That there was a better chance of Yasir Arafat becoming camp counselor at a kibbutz than of Joaquin LaRosa falling in line for the casino.

"The very logic of your father's argument. And I mean no offense by that, but every study we've commissioned at least doubles the amount of foot traffic on Cannery Way. The city profits because we grow the tax base, the merchants see a doubling of sales, residents get far better services and many more options. Everybody wins," Price said, getting up and heading over to his desk. "And I trust that you won't pay attention to the rumors that are circulating. This nonsense that I'm throwing people out of their houses?"

Albert thought of Creed, and the mysterious appearance of the eviction notice in his bedroom last night.

"You know as well as I do that that bridge has been in the county highway plans for twenty years, and from the beginning it called for some right-of-way clearance. And furthermore, I'm paying above market value out of my own pocket to the few people who have to be relocated. It's a windfall for them. You always get a few harmless resisters who hold out for something more, but that's going to be worked out to everyone's satisfaction. I guarantee it. And you, as my ambassador, can help set the record straight."

Among the dream jobs Albert had imagined over the course of his life, an ambassadorship to Harbor Light was not one of them. Maybe he ought to make it crystal clear right now that he was far more interested in the security end of the deal. Albert took a hard swallow.

"The first time you and I talked," Price said, speaking before Albert could get going, "I told you about that aspect of the job. That's all I'm getting at. Letting people know there's no limit to the opportunities this project will create. There's something for everyone who wants to be a part of it."

He came back across the room and handed Albert a white envelope.

"Go ahead. Open it."

Albert had no idea what he might find in here. He klutzed at the envelope, which appeared to have been sealed by a blowtorch, and took a nasty little paper cut. Finally, he clawed his way in and drew out the contents.

A check for twenty-five thousand dollars.

"Your signing bonus," Price said matter-of-factly. "Go out and treat yourself to something fantastic."

On the other hand, the very idea of an ambassadorship was quite flattering, wouldn't you say? Albert had never held twenty-five thousand dollars in his hands. Nothing even close. He felt a little disingenuous, because there was no way he could deliver his father. Not now, not ever. But he could see Ramon tooling around Philadelphia in a spiffy new van. And as he looked through the window and out to sea, he could see himself on the Tiara Pursuit. The image was so real, he heard the sound of an engine growing louder, louder, louder, until he realized it wasn't his imagination but an approaching plane hauling an ad along behind it.

"What in God's name is this?" Price asked, moving over to the window as Creed James sputtered down the beach in his crop duster. The plane veered inland—its engine stuttering and spitting—and for a split second looked like it might lop off the top floor of the Evolution tower on a kamikaze mission. Oscar Price hit the floor before Creed banked left and nearly brushed the windows with the sign he was hauling.

SAVE HARBOR LIGHT
BOYKOTT EVOLUTOIN

Albert fingered the check he'd just been handed and wondered if twenty-five thousand dollars was enough of a bonus. "That's one of the harmless resisters," he said, watching as Creed cleared the Boardwalk and throttled hard for Harbor Light.

The sirens woke him.

The first one pried one eye half open, but he fell back asleep.

The second one lifted his head off the pillow to check the clock. Four in the morning.

Albert grumbled and mumbled and cursed. He put on his trousers and searched for his keys and went out into the chill. From his front lawn he followed the sound of the sirens to the west, where the not-so-distant sky was lit by a comet. Albert ran for his car.

Black smoke spiraled into the brightening night, and as Albert cannonballed toward Bargain Acres he saw two arcs of water disappear into an orange glow. It took a good while to cover the distance of the parking lot, which was big enough to handle a space shuttle landing. Engine Company Twenty-eight had gotten the first call out of Jersey Landing and a hook and ladder company answered the second alarm out of Atlantic City. Albert maneuvered around the rigs and into the riot of flame and heat.

The face of the store was ablaze, and under it, the caterpillar jitney looked like smoldering roadkill. Jim Gervac, the lieutenant from Atlantic City, came over when he saw Albert.

Gervac had been on the scene the night before when Price's car went up.

"Sorry to interrupt your beauty sleep," Gervac said.

"What's it look like?" Albert asked.

"It looks like the forces of evil are on the loose in Harbor Light."

"Come on, Jim. Tell me it's an electrical short. Tell me someone left a burner on in the employee lounge."

"Sorry, Albert. I wouldn't bet my job on it just yet, but my guess is that your bomber has struck again."

Albert had just lit a smoke when Georgianna buzzed him on the intercom.

"Sheriff Caster on line one."

"I'm not here, Georgianna."

Fitch had called twice already this morning, wondering if perhaps the IRA was conducting paramilitary training in Harbor Light. Albert simply didn't have anything to tell him yet, and he'd rather wait until he did than stammer through another pointless conversation in which they both wracked their brains for possible perps and wondered if there was a connection between the job on Oscar Price's car and the blast at Bargain Acres. The only person Albert could remotely link to both cases motivewise was his father, and the very idea of it was a complete absurdity.

"You must not have heard me, sir. I said it's Sheriff Caster."

"No, I heard you the first time, George. There's nothing new to report, partly because I can't do my job if he's going to be calling here every ten minutes. Tell him I got hit by a car, will you? Tell him I'm being held hostage by terrorists. I don't care."

Albert could hear her blood pressure rising through the phone line.

"I must refuse your request," she finally said in mortal fear of God's wrath. "I will not under any circumstances deceive the commander in chief of this department."

No, of course not. Fitch could call every ninety seconds to ask what time it was, and she'd put the calls through because it wasn't her place to wonder why. Albert scooped his keys off the desk and blew past Georgianna and out the door. He stopped there and tossed an order back through the screen.

"Tell him I'm not here now and it won't be a lie. If he's just absolutely got to know, I'm meeting Mike Muldoon at Bargain Acres to see what I can find out."

On that night in Philadelphia, Albert's duty sergeant was a former navy SEAL with a tough constitution and a reputation for always backing up his squad. His name was Mike Muldoon, and most of his patrol unit, Albert included, idolized him. A decorated Vietnam vet, he was known for fearlessly and calmly inserting himself into live situations. Shoot-outs, barricade jobs, hostage negotiation, prison riots. A few of the old-timers in the district said he was bomb-rattled and more than a little reckless, but the younger officers didn't see it that way. To them, he was living proof that they were all invincible.

Albert puffed on a smoke and watched Muldoon drive toward him across the Bargain Acres parking lot. He had left the Philadelphia Police Department for the FBI two years after

Albert's shoot-out, and now he was with G-Tech, a private Virginia-based squad of elite former FBI, Secret Service, and CIA agents who did high-power security and investigation all over the world. Bargain Acres's corporate office, understandably nervous about what was happening in Harbor Light, had hired G-Tech to look into the bombing. Muldoon drew the case, partly because he lived in North Cape May but mostly because he had worked both the 1993 World Trade Center and Oklahoma City bombings and spent most of his time at the FBI in the domestic terrorism unit.

Muldoon, a forty-eight long who had an inch heightwise on Albert, lurched around the car with a world-weary expression, sizing up the scene as if he were deep in forensic analysis. The hair was still full and mostly dark, but he had a couple of sand traps now on either side of the fairway. "This guy didn't do a bad job for an amateur," Muldoon said. Damage was estimated at one million dollars and the store would be closed up to a month for repairs. The scarred, sooty entrance was trussed up with stalks of lumber, and the barbecued jitney, dragged off to the side to make way for construction crews, looked about like Oscar Price's Ferrari.

"I know where you can get a good deal on a golf cart," Albert said, looking at the melted glob that used to be the engine of the jitney.

"Yeah. That thing looks like a skunk caught in a forest fire."

"Anything out of the G-Tech lab yet?"

"Chemical fire bottle straight out of the Anarchist's Cookbook, my friend. A little sulfuric acid, some potassium chlorate, add a dash of sugar, and light the candles. Sort of a high-grade

Molotov cocktail. And then you've got your common pipe bomb with homemade gunpowder and possibly a cigarette delay. It doesn't take a genius. An eight-year-old can put this stuff together from instructions off the Internet."

"The Internet's going to kill us all, isn't it?"

"You can't knock the porn," Muldoon said, and Albert was sure he wasn't kidding.

"What's with this cigarette delay you're talking about?"

"Ordinarily you take a cigarette, cut half the filter off, and punch a clean hole down to the tobacco. Are you with me? You light the cigarette, then stick the fuse of the pipe bomb into the hole. He probably tossed the cocktail, set the cigarette delay, and was ordering his first beer when the pipe bomb blew this caterpillar's head off. Cigarette delay."

Albert handed Muldoon a small cigar and flicked his lighter. One crew of hard hats was exiting the store as another went in. The arched entrance, with its sooty smear, resembled a singed eyebrow.

"You hear any more about whether the FBI's going to have a look?" Albert asked.

Muldoon exhaled and scrunched his big dog features into a dismissive Who cares? It didn't take much to get him going about how the FBI had screwed him over. He called it quits a year ago, taking early retirement at fifty-five after getting passed over for a promotion. Depending on his mood, he either trashed the agency as the most incompetent band of boobs ever assembled, or, if he wanted to convey the full import of his meteoric rise in law enforcement, he could make it sound as if it were the most elite squad of freedom fighters in the history of man, but for a few imbeciles at the top.

Although Bargain Acres wasn't part of Albert's turf, Fitch wanted him to stick with the case until they knew for sure there was no connection to Oscar Price's car. Muldoon, a gracious gent despite the healthy ego, was more than happy to share notes. Especially since he knew Albert was no slouch, and might help him as much as he helped Albert. Muldoon had faxed him a list of employees who might conceivably have grievances with management, but Albert hadn't found a strong suspect among them, so he was casting a wider net now.

"We've got about half a dozen known pyros on the books in the county, but four are locked up and the other two have airtight alibis," Albert said. "Took me a while to nail it down, but neither one of them could have been within fifty miles when this thing blew."

"What about the rest of the employees?" Muldoon asked. "If I had to work here, I know I'd be itching to blow the place up. I'll have someone in their headquarters office in Texas fax you a list of names and addresses and you can start in."

"So you still don't see a tie-in with Oscar Price's car?" Albert asked.

"I didn't say that. What I said was I'm not getting paid to figure out what happened to Oscar Price's car. Once you get something concrete from the crime lab on that job, show me what you've got and we'll see what it tells us."

"I like one of Ron Rubio's people for the car," Albert said. "But I can't see what he'd have to gain by shutting down Bargain Acres."

"Maybe this one was just practice," Muldoon said. "Or maybe it's just a misdirection play. Listen, you got time to go for a ride?"

"I'm kind of swamped, and there's no cover back on the is-land. Why, where you headed?"

"Cherry Hill Bargain Acres," Muldoon said with a smile Albert recalled from his rookie days a quarter of a century ago. A smile that said he was working a good mystery and he loved doing this more than anything, and, above all else, that he'd get his man in the end. "I got a call on the mobile as I was pulling up. A bomb threat evacuated the store this morning. Plot thick-ens, Albert. Some psychopath's got it in for discount retail."

Jack went home for some cold pizza on his lunch break, choked it down, then decided to take a quick stroll on the beach promenade. He lit a cigarette and watched a fishing boat chug out of Jersey Landing, the sound of its tubercular putter traveling unfiltered across the flat mercury sea.

Sarah Keener came jogging up the beach and Jack waved, but she pretended she didn't see him. That was one problem on the island. Not enough girls. And the ones who grew up here came in only two types. Those who couldn't wait to get out, and those who thought you were going to marry them and have six kids just because you'd banged them a couple of times. Sarah Keener fell into the latter group, but Jack had a steady in Philadelphia now anyway. It took barely an hour to get there, and he could hang out with her in the city when he wanted a little more of a scene than Harbor Light offered.

Sometimes he wished he'd grown up in a town like this, where at least you could understand what people were talking about, whether it was fishing or the competition between the old-fashioned downtown businesses and the new box stores up on the Parkway. Not like in California and Washington state, where his mother and her spacey friends got together and blabbed until the wine bottles were empty and the candles burned themselves out. It's like they were speaking in code half the time, crazy gibberish about self-realization and about men who were terrified of one thing or another.

Then his mother would break up with another guy just as Jack was getting to know him, and when he asked what happened to so-and-so his mother always had the same response. Jack was too young to understand. Like he was an infant, or some kind of idiot. Finally, she meets the right guy back home in Harbor Light, of all places, and now that had fallen apart, too. No thanks to Albert, the fool, and this ridiculous job he just had to have. But Jack wondered if his mother was the one who was afraid of something this time.

Halfway to the lighthouse, he heard a horn behind him and looked over his shoulder to see Albert pulling up in the squad car.

"What did I tell you?"

"I still don't believe it."

"I'm telling you I bought the boat."

"You couldn't have. Oscar Price is paying you that much?"

"Have I ever lied to you, Jack? Tell me that. Have I ever lied to you about anything?"

"How would I know?"

"I haven't. That's the point, is I've never lied to you."

"I don't know, Albert."

"You don't know what?"

"I don't know. It just feels kind of weird for me to go out there with you. I mean, with everything that's going on."

"Would you look at me, Jack? This isn't about your mother and me, all right? It's two guys on a boat playing hooky in the middle of the day while the rest of the world's at work. Just because your mom and I have a little problem doesn't mean there's got to be anything different between you and me."

Albert led Jack down the gangway on Slip B. The day sparkled under the noon sun, and Albert was determined to spend the lunch hour on the water with Jack, who was wearing his Rage Against the Machine T-shirt. Either he had seven of them, or this thing went through the wash a few times a week. Or didn't.

Albert hadn't shared this with Muldoon two hours ago at Bargain Acres, because it was a little too early to tip anyone as to his darkest fears, but a betting man who liked long shots might have put a couple of dollars on one of the local preservationists doing a number on both Price's car and Bargain Acres. If so, maybe Mr. Rage Against the Machine would know something. Georgianna happened to mention she had seen Jack and Creed James together this morning out at Kip Slough, watching over the bridge construction. And Jack was acting rather reluctant for someone who loved being out on the water as much as he did. Could it all be attributed to the awkwardness of the breakup?

"I don't really have the time," Jack protested. "My mom gave me the day off because your father needs some help at the store."

"Yeah, I'll bet he does, now that he's blown up Bargain Acres. I'm surprised he didn't think of this sooner, aren't you?"

Jack had not inherited Rickie's penchant for wearing every emotion. He had the same fires burning, Albert suspected, but he was more the type to quietly suffer internal bleeding than let out a yell the way his mother would. Albert's little joke about his father drew a twenty-year-old's grin, but who past forty could read anything on the faces of these kids?

"Sometimes I wonder about you, Jack."

"What do you mean?"

"Look at you. Smart. Handsome. You ought to be in New York or Philadelphia spending money like you're the only one who has any. You ought to be trying on girls in every size and color and grinning like the devil. Harbor Light has never had anyone between eighteen and thirty years old in it, ever. Are you aware of that, Jack? Never. They all run like hell as soon as they know the score, because it isn't hard to see that they'll end up picking their noses at the diner into their nineties. So what keeps you here? Are you listening to me, Jack? What makes a young turk like you decide to bunk with a cranky old coot and wash dishes at the greasy spoon when you're not hauling sacks of cow dung up from the basement at the hardware store?"

Jack shrugged. He had that sweet, defensive, confused expression of his, a look that served as a sort of buffer between him and the world everyone else lived in. He really was a handsome kid, with a feathery pile of mahogany hair pushed back off a face he must have gotten from his father, whoever the asshole might be. He'd left nothing behind but the look of abandonment that crept into Jack's eyes sometimes when you tried talking to him and he was off in his own dreamworld.

"Are you even listening to me, Jack? You look like you're a million miles away."

"What's not to like? I can work when I want, fish when I

want, go hang out in the city when I want. But as long as I'm sort of based here, I can watch out for my mom."

It was an idea that had never really occurred to Albert. Maybe, being the adult, he'd only seen it one way. Rickie worrying over Jack. He'd run out on his mother now and then since they moved onto the island, scaring holy hell out of her the way he'd drift, reappear, then drift again. For reasons so obvious, in retrospect.

"You remember much about your grandparents?" Albert asked.

"Course I do. My mom sent me out here a few summers to spend a couple weeks at a time with them. Those were some of the best times I had as a kid. I loved coming to Harbor Light and hated having to go back out to California or Washington or wherever."

"I remember that. I remember you sitting up at the counter in the diner with a mountain of ice cream bigger than you."

He remembered not just because Jack was such a cute tyke, but because he was the flesh and blood of the high school love interest Albert had never gotten out of his head.

"It still gets to her, you know?" Jack said. "Them getting killed and all. She doesn't talk about it much, but that's how I know."

"Yeah," Albert said. "I know. So what do you say, Jack? We going to take this boat ride, you and me?"

"I feel a little funny about it," Jack said as they stood in the blinding white glare of the boat, with its big DOUBLE DOWN lettering on the bow. Maybe Jack could help him come up with a new name.

"What's to feel funny about?" Albert asked.

"I just don't understand," Jack said. "That's all."

"Don't understand what?"

"You. You and my mother. I can't believe you just left her like that. If it was so you could take this stupid job, I don't get it."

"I didn't leave her, Jack. Look, it's more complicated than that."

Red Miller called over to them from Slip D just then. "If you're taking her out, she's on empty," he said.

"Albert turned back to Jack, who was gazing past Memorial Bridge toward open sea.

"Look, you can't tell me you wouldn't give your left nut to be out on a Tiara Pursuit on a killer day like this," Albert said. "I'm not asking you to choose sides, Jack. I respect your loyalty to her, and I'm sorry it's gotten a little icy between your mother and me. But that doesn't mean I'm out of your life unless you want it that way."

Jack's pose was defiant, his gaze still fixed on the sea. As if against his better judgment, he put his hand out. "Give me the key," he said. "I'll drive it around and you can fill it up."

"I've always wanted to try that," Rickie said. She was standing at a window at Wanamaker, Goldman & Suggs, watching teams of scullers row down the Schuylkill toward downtown Philadelphia.

"Maybe we should move this meeting out onto the river," said H. Dewitt Nelson, a senior partner.

"What, you have a boat?"

"Spent my whole life on the water. I was raised by crayfish

and then rowed for Penn once those Yankees found out that's
all I knew how to do. Weekends, I coach some of the good
young stock from Saint Joe's Prep."

He was narrow-waisted and nicely tapered, now that he
mentioned it, and much mellower in person. He was short on
the phone, and Rickie felt like she could hear the meter running.

"So tell me what the trouble is in Harbor Light. Nice little
town, by the way."

"You've been there?"

"I've got a house down at Cape May Point. I'm from the
south, which you might have picked up on? Harbor Light re-
minds me a little of the towns along the Outer Banks in North
Carolina, if you've ever been down that way."

"It's as if that's a different ocean. Something a little dreamier
and more dangerous about it. I had a friend in Topsail I used
to visit."

H. Dewitt Nelson tapped a yellow legal pad with a pen
point and looked at her as if they were birds of a feather.

"My family's summer home's in Topsail," he said with surprise. "Well I do hope for the sake of southern hospitality and
my family's honor that someone down there told you you have
a fetching smile."

Rickie blushed and there was an awkward pause that H.
Dewitt Nelson finally rescued her from.

"Well maybe we ought to get down to business. You say
you own this restaurant with your aunt?"

"The deed to the property is in my aunt's name, but the
business license is both of ours," Rickie said. "We're together
on this, though. I mean, we both want to save the restaurant."

"I'm just curious," he said. "How did you happen to find out about me?"

"The Atlantic City case."

"Right, where the state came in and threw a dozen people out of their houses so Steve Wynn would have a shortcut to his new casino. That was a nice one, wasn't it?"

"I remember you saying they were flyspecks on his windshield. And something about how *eminent domain* must be Latin for 'you're up a creek if you don't have the money and clout to buy off the right people around here.'"

"Well I do admit it sounds like the sort of unrefined thing I might say in a moment of distress. But what makes you think we're looking at the same situation there in Harbor Light?"

"I have a friend with a connection at the law firm Oscar Dan Price uses. It also happens to be where state senator Croydon is a partner. As I understand it, Price is maneuvering to take over the entire northern half of Harbor Light, with this Croydon character helping to clear the way. I wouldn't be surprised if down the road, he tries turning the whole island into his own private resort."

Nelson rocked up and back, his hands steepled together in contemplation. Rickie had wondered if she could even afford his time, and the trappings of the place didn't exactly put her at ease. The marbled lobby and gold-trimmed elevators, the formal secretaries with their executive-elite coiffures, the HDN monogram on the Eucharist-crisp pocket of Nelson's shirt. He had a calming, reassuring manner, though with a little smile that said "Trust me." But then, didn't every lawyer?

He laid his pen down and leaned forward as if to signal it was time to stop doodling and get to work.

"I want you to understand something," he said, looking at her as if he were about to share his deepest secrets. "I'm a straight shooter. I tell my clients where they stand, not what they want to hear. And I have to tell you you're up against some powerful interests. I know Oscar Price. He runs hard at you, and I don't think it's an exaggeration to say he owns the New Jersey state legislature, the governor, the gaming commission, Boardwalk, Park Place, and half of Christmas. Do you see what I'm getting at? Because that's the way the game is played, through political connections, and that ol' boy's got more bed-fellows than a dog has fleas."

"I think I get the picture, Mr. Nelson. He's got the whole thing wired."

"Oh yes ma'am. He is frightful good at it."

"But that's why I came to see you. Are you telling me that I can't win, or that I can't afford you?"

Nelson grinned so wide his ears moved. "I'm telling you that if it turns out you're right, and he comes after your restaurant with a bulldozer, I'd be happy to put up a few roadblocks. But it ain't going to be easy."

"I'm just wondering what . . ."

"Don't worry about what it's going to cost. We'll be able to work that out on some type of contingency arrangement."

"I just wanted to make something clear," Rickie said. "With the Atlantic City case, some of those people who held out got twice as much as the original offer."

Nelson smiled proudly. "With two of them, we called Steve Wynn's bluff long enough to darn near triple the offer."

"Right. Well, I'm not holding out for double, triple, or quadruple the offer. I'm in it to keep my restaurant right where it is. So as far as your contingency arrangement, I'm not looking at this as a moneymaking deal."

"Ms. Davenport, I must say I admire your style," Nelson said, looking at his watch. "If you'd be so kind as to indulge a weakness for slow walks in glorious sunshine, I'd like to suggest we continue this discussion at a favorite lunch spot of mine."

"I really should get back to the diner, actually. I left Aunt Rose with a handful."

"We could take a cab to lunch if you're in a hurry," he said.

Rickie looked out the window at clear blue sky. The words were almost out of her mouth—maybe another time. But she hesitated and then was almost surprised by what she said.

"I enjoy a good walk myself."

Jack stood tall and straight in the cockpit at full throttle, the wave blown out of his hair. He had a cigarette going and the smoke curled back as if from the top of a refinery smokestack on a windy day. Albert sat toward the rear of the boat but could see by Jack's jawline that he had a smile from Manasquan to Cape Henlopen. Albert threw his head back, knowing what the feeling was like. Even as a boy, the water had been magic to him.

Jack cut the gas a mile or so from a Norwegian tanker that was steaming north. He turned her around to face the shoreline and came back to sit with Albert, and they bobbed on three-foot swells.

"That's a dangerous habit," Albert said as he lit his own smoke and heard Muldoon's words again.

Cigarette delay.

The hotel casinos in Atlantic City were like matchsticks from out here. Over in Harbor Light, you saw the lighthouse and could barely make out Betty the Blue Crab atop the old Sea-Fruit that was on its way to becoming a casino.

"Hope to hell Fitch Caster doesn't find out where I am," Albert said.

"Why not? You're a short-timer, what can he do?"

"Cars and buildings blowing up. People getting death threats. I'm supposed to be out there on the trail, tracking down this psycho. And here I am with you."

Jack, a young man of few words, wasn't letting go of any. But Albert needed to know some things, and they weren't going back ashore before he asked a few questions. He was next to certain that Creed wasn't at the meeting when Price's car was blown to kingdom come, and he knew Creed and Jack were buddies, in a way. Albert had been trying to talk himself out of the possibility all morning, but who knew? Before he could get his first question out, Jack broke his silence.

"Can I tell you something, Albert?"

Albert took a deep hit and blew a puff of smoke.

"No one knows this, and don't tell my mother," Jack said. "All right?"

Albert could feel his pulse. "You can trust ol' Uncle Albert," he said.

"I got into a little bit of a jam in Philadelphia a year or so ago. Not a big deal. I was hanging out with some people I shouldn't have, which I knew at the time. But they gave me some community service as part of my sentence, and they put me in this recreation program. They had me referee these games in the rec league."

"What kind of trouble were you in?"

"It was no big deal, and that's not the point. The league was for guys in wheelchairs."

He paused there, and Albert flinched.

"So I got to know some of them after a few games, and one of them, when I said I was from Harbor Light, he said he knew a cop there."

Albert was speechless. What were the chances of Jack meeting up with Ramon? And now Jack knew. He knew that Albert's bullet had put a kid in a wheelchair for life. A kid not much older than Jack.

"Anyway, he told me what you've been doing for him all these years."

"Look, Jack. It's amazing to me that you happened to come across him. But it's something I just don't like to talk about."

"I know it's your thing, the two of you. It's none of my business. But I just wanted to say that . . ."

"You wanted to say what?"

"I don't know. I don't really know what I wanted to say."

Albert put a hand on Jack's shoulder. "It was a long time ago," Albert said.

A fish jumped off the starboard side but was gone before they could see what it was. Albert couldn't even get to his questions. Not now. He was almost afraid of how Jack would answer.

Insomnia, which never had been a problem for Albert, was visiting him regularly of late. He was neither awake nor asleep when the phone rang, and upon opening his eyes, knew he'd heard something other than the phone. A thump, a bang, a concussive thud. It was soft around the edges, though. Muffled. And then Albert remembered the fog.

"Hello. Yes. No, that's all right. What time? That's all you know? I'm on my way."

Dispatch calling with a report of an explosion up by Kip Slough. Albert was out the door in three minutes.

When was this going to end?

Fog usually advanced on Harbor Light a little at a time, as if it weren't sure it should bother. Last night was different. Albert had seen it gathering offshore like the edge of a storm, waiting to make its move as if it were in on some conspiracy. And then all at once it lay across the town—a white sheet over an outstretched body. The damp chill penetrated Albert's khaki uniform as he hurried across the rock garden, nearly tripping over the new For Sale sign Ron Rubio had just sunk. The fog had erased the other side of the street, and Albert knew he'd be a blind man out at U-Boat Slough, where it would hang over the water like drapery.

Nine times out of ten, a call like this was nothing. People imagined all sorts of things, especially at night. But Albert thought maybe he'd heard something himself in his half-conscious state. Maybe a car fire and explosion on the Atlantic City side.

Albert had to negotiate Ocean by the broken line on the roadway. He rounded the bend at Kip Slough Road and sniffed something—something burnt—when he hit Second Street. He leaped out of the car just before Peg's diner and the smell was overpowering. He grabbed the flashlight from the glove box and held it at arm's length, following the funnel of light along the shoulder of the road. The vacant land just south of Peg's was puddled up, but it hadn't rained in three days. Albert knelt and shone the light on the water, touched it, sniffed his fingers.

Closer to the slough he found a spray of rock. He squatted and palmed one chunk the size of a golf ball. Concrete. There was more of it at the water's edge. Albert slid down the bank, falling on his left hip and bouncing back up, skidding toward the water. He shot a beam of light across the rippled black surface and something rose in his chest.

Now the bomber had taken out the bridge.

Albert had seen a crane up top the bridge in daylight, and it was in the water now, half submerged and still bubbling as it went down. Albert toed his way back up the bank, a nervous tickle running down his back. Tie off Kip to traffic, he thought. Call A.C. police and have them seal off the other side of the slough. Get a crew out here from the sheriff's marine unit.

Albert made a quick pass up the shore before leaving the scene. He slogged through puddles all the way up to the cannery, struggling with the fog and the darkness. On the way back he saw something on the surface of the water but gave it only a glance. All sorts of debris washed through here. But something drew him back for a second look at this thing. The contour, the color, the weightless suspension. Albert shone the light and saw it bobbing just below the surface. He grabbed a knotty limb that had washed ashore and reached across the water, poking and raking. Now it was gone, sinking out of sight. Albert was ready to move on when he saw it rising again, a gray sphere slowly rotating so that when it broke the surface, an open eye was staring up at him. It appeared that Albert's last case as a cop would be his first-ever murder investigation.

The farther west you traveled in Harbor Light, the less expensive the houses. The neighborhood known as the Western Addition, nearest the back bay, ran from Twenty-third Street all the way out to Waterman's Highway. Except for a few Craftsmans, the houses were basic two- and three-bedroom clapboards with concrete porches the size of doormats and lunch-pail mailbox stands on the sidewalk. A lot of fishermen had bought out here and it was kind of a nice neighborhood before the industry went corporate, squeezing out the small-timers. Albert parked in front of the last address on Twenty-eighth, just before Anchorage, and wondered how Harlan and Jeanie Wayans had managed to raise six kids in this toolbox of a house without daily 911 panic calls.

A scattering of toys served as lawn and walkway ornaments. Albert remembered Harlan saying that four of his grandchildren were staying with them temporarily along with one, two, or three of their offspring. Albert could never keep track, but it took neither a shrink nor an artist to imagine why Harlan had been the town drunk for a good twenty years. A couple of those grandchildren were wailing when Albert knocked. There was a poodle in there, too, or half poodle, rather, that Albert occasionally saw ratting around the front yard. One of those good-for-nothing little mutts with the vital organs of a hummingbird and hair in its eyes all the time.

Jeanie answered Albert's knock wearing a housedress, her hair wrapped in a towel. Her eyes sank when she saw him.

"Another DUI?" she asked.

"Can I come in, Jeanie?"

The dog came for him the minute he set foot on the carpet. It was too dumb a beast to pick up Harlan's scent on Albert.

"Toto, no!" Jeanie yelled. "Back, girl. Toto!"

One of the grandchildren appeared then, a naked cherub, the top of her head at Albert's knee. She looked up at him as if he were the jolly green giant, considered him briefly, and then wailed like Ethel Merman. Jeanie's daughter was in a robe, too. Everyone in the house was naked or in a robe. She came for the kid, grabbed an arm, and dragged her down the hall and into one of the dreary caves at the back of the house.

Jeanie slid the miserable Toto out the side door in the kitchen. "You want coffee?" she asked, trying to light a cigarette. She knew it was something bad, of course. Albert did not make social calls here. Her hands shook, and she had aged ten years in the five since Albert had seen her. Since Harlan got caught in that insurance scam, sinking his boat and calling Mayday, she'd retreated into this house and looked now as if she hadn't seen daylight in thirty years. Her skin was gray as Harlan's had been just moments ago.

Albert took her cigarette, lit it himself, and gave it back. He realized now that his hands were caked with dry mud from the bank of the slough, and there was blood on his knuckles. Harlan's or his own, he couldn't be sure. He looked around the kitchen, which didn't go at all with the rest of the house. The kitchen they'd fixed with the dirty insurance money. Albert remembered that day in the diner now. Harlan saying Jeanie was a good egg, and telling Albert to find himself a woman with a good heart.

"Jeanie, I've got bad news," Albert said. "Harlan's not coming home this morning."

The fog had lifted but the sky was milky with burnoff as Albert sped down Waterman's Highway, his thoughts like tangled fishing line. The world had changed for everyone, not just fishermen, but those old-timers had a harder time adjusting. Fishermen knew fishing, that was it. The relationship with the sea was primal, and when it was done, they were lost. Albert had had a half dozen suicides over the years, all of them fishermen, which was one reason he'd tried to watch out for Harlan and let him sleep off a drunk now and then in the office.

There was no way of knowing whether the bomber had waited for Harlan to drink himself into his nightly coma before moving in or if he had any idea Harlan was up there at all. Either way, the law called it murder. It wouldn't actually be Albert's first homicide, but it was the first one that qualified as a genuine whodunit. About fifteen years ago, a housewife from Ocean City pulled up outside Mo's Tavern one night and waited for her sap of a husband to saunter out with his concubine on his arm. Her first shot with the pearl-handled twenty-two, a direct hit, didn't kill him, but it effectively ended the affair. Then she stood over her target and plugged him twice more, one in the knee and then the money shot, a dart in the chest, and as he squibbed and twitched on the ground, the Mrs.

booted him down the bank and into the bay like a bucket of chum. Albert arrested her at her house, where she was sitting on the porch, waiting, and on the way to the tank in Rag Harbor, she begged him to stop at a motel and ravage her. Sort of like kicking dirt in the face of her dead old man. Albert almost went for it, too, but having just pulled her husband out of the drink with a bullet through the whistle, he wasn't sure he could handle this firecracker.

So now he had a real murder, and three explosions in three nights, which was the exact number of all the whodunits and all the explosions over the last five thousand years in Harbor Light. Condolences to Harlan's family aside, Albert felt a rush of adrenaline, or maybe it was just plain fear. Half the people on his list of most likely suspects were practically family.

Albert squealed around the bend, past Mo's Tavern, and jammed the brakes as soon as his office came into view. Two TV news vans were in the lot, and both crews were doing business. Channel Six was getting the lowdown from Manny of Manny's Bait Bucket, and Dr. DiMitri, who was a hundred and twelve, was filling in Channel Three.

For fuck's sake. Did they have no better sense than to talk to TV reporters? Had they never watched an episode of the evening news? Albert believed millions of people, particularly the elderly, watched the evening news in absolute terror, convinced beyond all doubt that if a nor'easter didn't sweep them off the face of the continent and out to sea, famine or pestilence would come for them.

Both cameramen, who looked like they had alligators slung over their shoulders, abandoned their subjects and came for Albert the instant he lumbered out of his car. The reporters led the charge, a woman who was almost nonexistent behind a good half bucket of makeup and a young guy you could tell was after an acting career. They came like piranha and Albert crossed his arms as if he were performing an exorcism.

"Sheriff, you've had three explosions in three nights in a sleepy little town, and now a killer is on the loose," the little brunette intoned with pitch-perfect dread. "Can you give residents any assurance that their lives are not in danger?"

Albert knew he would live to regret this, but he couldn't help himself. Besides, he was on his way out, so what did he have to lose?

"No, as a matter of fact, I can't. If it's not a crazed killer that gets us, it'll be the next hurricane. Either way, I suggest that residents get to the supermarket as soon as humanly possible, stock up on bottled water and canned goods, and lock themselves in their basements until further notice."

It was fair to say she was knocked off stride. She was in brain stall, mouth open, and a line of perspiration ran like maple ice cream down her face. The other reporter piped in to save her.

"Sheriff, our sources tell us there has been a threat on the life of Oscar Price, the owner of Evolution Hotel and Casino in Atlantic City, and a threat on the life of a sheriff's deputy as well. Are you that deputy, and what precautionary steps have you taken for your own safety?"

"Are any suspects in custody?" the other one broke in, fully recovered from her paralysis. "We understand the FBI is now taking a look at the case and a possible link to the other bombings. Can you confirm that at this juncture?"

"No, as a matter of fact, I can't. I'll wait until the next juncture." Actually, he wasn't going to confirm anything of any sort at this or any other juncture. He was a little ticked off about the death threat being leaked and couldn't figure out where they would have gotten that. But what really bothered him now was the FBI coming in, if it were true. He certainly wasn't going to trust this twit's reporting. But Harlan's fish eye had looked up at no one else but him. As his last act in law enforcement, he now wanted desperately to be the one who cracked this case.

"A man has been killed this morning," Albert said. "We don't know any more than that at this point, and it would be irresponsible for me to speculate. Now if you'll excuse me, I've got work to do."

Georgianna was on the telephone reading Robert Frost's death march to her sister, Lu, when Albert walked in. She closed with, "*And miles to go before I sleep.* Talk to you later, Lu. I'll bring home a pork roast tonight." She was wearing black and her eyes were red as radishes. This took Albert somewhat by surprise, since Georgianna was irritated to the point of occasionally breaking out in hives over Harlan's drunken woodcutting in the coatroom.

"Do I smell something burning?" Albert asked.

"I didn't think you'd mind, sir. I've set up a candlelight vigil in Harlan's room."

Albert peeked in and saw six candles burning around a small bouquet of flowers. He suspected it might be a fumigation project as much as a memorial, but he was going to give Georgianna the benefit of the doubt. He turned back to compliment her and found her staring at his pants and boots in obvious grief. He glanced down to see a mud stain the color of red clay from his hip all the way to his boot. The other leg was smudged, too, and he still had saltwater in his boots.

"Did he appear to have suffered much pain?" Georgianna sobbed.

"I don't think he knew what hit him, George. I couldn't have gotten there fifteen minutes after it happened, and he was already a goner. Could you do me a favor and check on Jeanie in a couple of hours? Tell her if she needs anything, feel free to call me at home tonight, too."

Georgianna nodded gravely and assured him she would.

"As you might imagine, it's been mayhem in here, sir. Sheriff Caster wants a briefing at your earliest opportunity, and Mr. Price's secretary has called several times. At least a dozen news reporters have been ringing as well."

"I'm not talking to any of those parasites, George. Tell them to call Rag Harbor and harass somebody in the public information office."

Albert thought he heard a knocking sound coming from his office and queried Georgianna with a look.

"Oh my goodness, I almost forgot. Mr. Muldoon is in your office waiting for you."

Muldoon didn't even hear Albert enter. He was lost in concentration as he lined up a putt on the worn AstroTurf, bent over the thing like a question mark. Nice easy backswing and *ping*. The line was good but Muldoon had given it a little too much steam. The orange ball—an original from the Putt-Putt course—sailed right over the eighteenth hole and under the door of the holding cell, clunking against the back wall. Manny knocked back twice from the bait shop.

"I see your game is picking up," Albert said.

"I hate everything about this sport, Albert. I played the Cricket Club in Philadelphia last week. Did I tell you this? One guy in our foursome crapped out on us so this buddy of mine brings his wife along. Can you imagine? I mean, the whole idea is for the guys to get together out there amongst each other, you know? So you don't have to watch what you say."

"So let me guess," Albert said, sliding behind his desk. "She beats you by what, six strokes?"

"Four strokes, Albert. Four! I hadn't played in three weeks. I was doing fine until I triple-bogeyed a par four dogleg. I was so flummoxed I wrapped my five iron around a ball washer. The damn club looked like a corkscrew."

"I'd have called it a day and headed to the clubhouse for a drink," Albert said, poring over two dozen messages. He assumed Muldoon was here with an update on his Bargain Acres investigation, but Albert's priorities had shifted now. "Listen, I've got to make a couple of quick phone calls. How are you on time?"

Muldoon set the putter against the holding cell and came over.

"Wait," he said. "Before you do, I've got something important."

"I've got a murder on my hands, Sarge. You heard about Harlan Wayans, didn't you?"

"Yeah, but this is more important."

Albert looked up from his messages. "What could be more important than an active murder investigation?"

"I saw Rickie last night," Muldoon said.

"You saw her where?"

"I went to the Ugly Mug for a beer, and she's in there with this guy. I thought the two of you were still together."

"We kind of hit the skids," Albert said. "What do you mean she was with a guy?"

"Like a date. That's what I mean."

"Well who was he? It couldn't have been a date. Not this soon. She was just over my place picking up some of her things."

"Well what does that tell you, pal? Listen to me, Albert. I may not know much, but I know women," said Muldoon, whose favorite subject, after golf and the glory of police work, was the possibility that Mo could be cured of her bisexuality. "This was a date. They were eating, drinking, laughing, having a grand time. She didn't look like she was exactly suffering through the breakup. So this guy goes to the bathroom for the second or third time—he's got the bladder of a goat—and I make a pass by the table and ask how she's been. You know, feel her out a little bit. See what's going on, because not knowing the two of you are split, I figure she's stepping out on you. And listen to this: She tells me she and her attorney are going over some things regarding Oscar Price, in case he tries to move her out of the restaurant."

"So it was a meeting, in other words."

"As a friend, Albert, I'm telling you this was more than a meeting."

"What'd he look like, this lawyer?"

"I don't know what he looked like, Albert."

"What do you mean you don't know what he looked like? You're a career cop, one of the best snoops the FBI ever had, and you can't provide a description of a man you saw in a restaurant twelve hours ago?"

"He was the kind of guy where I suppose some women would say he's suave, sophisticated, good-looking. Like it's a big deal that a guy works out and he's got a full head of hair and he wears some nice clothes."

"Yeah, that's a bad look, isn't it?" Albert said, his throat closing and a sudden wave of flu-like symptoms rippling through him.

"He had a southern accent. You know. Southern gentleman. A charmer."

"I think I get the picture, Mike. First you couldn't describe him, and now he's Paul Newman in *Cat on a Hot Tin Roof.*"

"She introduced him to me when he came back."

"You remember his name?"

"No. Big fancy law firm in Philadelphia, though. Wanamaker, Goldman and Suggs, maybe. I'm telling you as a friend who's walked a beat with you. This guy's making a move for her, so you better keep an eye on him. Why the hell'd you break up with her, anyway?"

"It's too long a story to go into," Albert said.

"You're throwing away a winner, pal. Looks, smarts, spirit. She's got the big three, and you're sitting here pullin' your pud while she's cracking Beer Nuts with Ted Turner at the Ugly Mug. If there's still time, you might want to think this one through, Albert. Rickie's a real beauty."

One of the attractions, Albert would admit, had always been that side of her that he just couldn't get to. The part of herself she held back. Especially after his first marriage, which was like a summer book. Once you'd read it, did you really need to keep it around?

"It doesn't figure," Albert said. "She's not the type to walk right out of one relationship and into another like it was a simple stroll across the block, no worries, no looking back. We were about to get engaged."

"Well maybe she had other ideas longer than you knew." Muldoon looked back down at the putting green. "So, you seeing somebody yourself?"

"I'm seeing two packs of cigarillos a day is what I'm seeing, and I'm cleaning out the bourbon section at Quicker Liquor. And I've got to tell you, Sarge, it may be early, but I could use a drink right about now." He pulled a bottle out of his desk drawer and splashed a stream into a cup with a stain of dried coffee on the bottom. Muldoon declined his offer to join the party. "I got no sleep last night. I pulled a dead man out of the mud before sunup. I just went and told Jeanie Wayans she was a widow. And now you're telling me my girl is living it up with some hotshot. You got any more good news?"

"I didn't mean to upset you, Albert. As a friend, I thought you should know."

The whiskey tasted like floor polish, quite frankly. It was a cheapo brand to begin with, and that was no Kahlúa at the bottom of the cup. Albert winced and poured himself another.

"It doesn't matter anyway," he said. "We broke up, that's that."

Albert looked around his office at the cluttered sum of his career, an assortment of confiscated junk gathering dust in schoolhouse cubbyholes. Across the room, this stale and claustrophobic, highly flammable pigeon coop of a room, was the window. His life was out there, he told himself. Out there with the new. And he wasn't trading it for anything.

"She can see whoever she wants. I'm not going to sit

around worrying about it," Albert said with such finality it approached believability. "I've got a terrific new job that's going to triple my salary, and in the meantime, I've got a murder investigation to take care of."

"Well I hope you're making more progress than I am. So far the employee check is a bust."

"How about the bomb threat at the Cherry Hill store yesterday? Any leads there?"

"Nothing. The perp calls, gets the assistant manager who was about to open the store, tells him to run for his life because there's a bomb on the premises. Fuckin' store is the size of Seattle. Took forever to search the place and they lost a full day of sales. You should see the bonus babies Bargain Acres flew in from the home office in Texas, Albert. A couple of vice presidents. One looks like Ross Perot and the other sounds like him, like he's had his adenoids removed with a pair of pliers. These cowpokes took home about eight million apiece last year in bonuses alone, and they were so distraught over a few lost sales in Harbor Light and Cherry Hill, I almost had to give them grief counseling on the spot."

"That's all the caller said? Get out before the place blows?"

"We're dealing with a drama major here, Albert. The assistant manager picks up the phone and this guy says, 'Listen to me with both ears.'"

Albert froze.

There was no question now. The same person who threatened Price's life was the Bargain Acres terrorist. And, most likely, Harlan Wayans's murderer.

"Listen to me with both ears?" Albert asked.

"Yeah. Like he's watched too many *Godfather* movies or something."

"Sounds like it."

Muldoon put away his putter and took a seat. He trained his eyes on Albert until Albert met his glance.

"You wouldn't happen to be holding out on your old sergeant now, would you?" Muldoon asked.

"What are you talking about?"

"Come on, Albert. I didn't admit it earlier, but everything points toward someone in this town, and you know this place better than anybody. Come on, give."

"I'm insulted. If I knew anything, you'd be the first one I'd tell. Ron Rubio got screwed out of the cannery and he's not happy about it, Mike. That much you know. Why Rubio would be interested in reducing Bargain Acres to a pile of ash is something I haven't figured out yet, but with his mob pals and all the real estate shenanigans he's pulled over the years, I'm not ruling him out. 'Listen to me with both ears' is precisely the kind of primary grunt you'd hear out of Joey Tartaglione, that ripe little meatball who ferries Rubio around like he's the fucking pope. Aside from that crew, I don't know. But there is one local nut-job that could be a possibility."

"You son of a bitch," Muldoon said. "I knew you were holding back."

"I'm not holding anything back, Mike. There's more than a few local yokels who crossed my mind, but none of them seem sophisticated enough to get caught up in this kind of intrigue. One guy in particular."

"Who is he?"

"You must have seen him once or twice in Mo's. Creed James."

"Tell me more."

"Best way I can describe him is he's in a middle ground somewhere between mild retardation and lifelong eccentricity."

"Been like this all his life?"

"When we were kids, we had a little accident at the cannery. We used to wander over to the loading docks and watch the fishing boats unload their hauls onto the absolute coolest-looking quarter-scale boxcars. They ran on a rail from the water's edge up through the face of the cannery on the third floor. We didn't even have to talk about it, we just knew we had to do it.

"So one Fourth of July—we couldn't have been more than this high—we sneak away from the Zambelli Internationale fireworks show in Legion Park and head for the back of the cannery. Hennepin Merriwether, the town drunk before Harlan inherited the job, had already finished the bottle of sloe gin Creed had swiped from an older cousin and which we left for him there."

"Planning ahead. That's good."

"Hennepin was down at the loading docks and it looked like he was wrestling a bear. Turned out to be Nuba Ludwick, married to Sid Ludwick, who was working the barbecue back at the picnic. Hennepin had his pants around his ankles, drunk as a skunk, and we snuck right past them. I didn't want to do it at first—that slope toward Kip Slough looked like an Alpine cliff all of a sudden—but Creed said we were going to do it together or not at all."

"So which of you is the retarded one?"

"The cable gives, and we fly down that ramp a hundred miles an hour. I'm saying a prayer we don't sail off the end of that thing and sink to the bottom of Kip Slough. Instead we slam into the restraint at the bottom of the rail and I knock my front tooth right through my lip. But Creed gets the worst of it. He gongs his head into the iron wall, knocks himself out cold, and gets pulled out by paramedics with both ears bleeding. Lots of people say he never was the same after that."

"And this is the guy you think is blowing up the eastern seaboard?"

"Well, he's unpredictable, and he gets these ideas in his head and they don't get out. And he loves the *Godfather* movies."

"I'd put him on the short list," Muldoon said.

"Yeah. Somewhere near the top."

Those who couldn't find parking at Peg's diner, which overflowed with gossip, drove down Cannery Way to see what trouble they could get into. Some were even on their way to do the shopping they ordinarily did at Bargain Acres, and Albert fell into line behind them, inching along the four-block business district. Every last parking space had been nabbed, and there were ant trails in and out of Phelps Drugs, Nuba's Pie Shop, Renati Florist, Mario's Barbershop, and LaRosa's Hardware, among others. It was an absolute renaissance. A small group of locals yacked outside Nuba's and full-blown meetings were in session outside the Town Hall and Post Office. Harbor Light was just not accustomed to making headlines every day.

Albert's father was playing traffic cop out front of the hardware store in his blue apron and combat beret, directing contractors who normally bought their supplies at Bargain Acres. "Cut hard right and ease her back now. That's it, now come straight in. Keep coming, keep coming, keep coming. Hold it!" Meanwhile, Jack was coming through the door pushing a cart loaded down with concrete mix, redwood fence posts, and sacks of topsoil.

Joaquin LaRosa saw Albert, mentioned the Bargain Acres fire, and asked, "Why the hell didn't I think of this before?" Jack had begun loading supplies onto the truck and paused to see Albert's reaction.

"Is that Creed inside the store?" Albert asked as he idled past.

"Everybody's inside the store," his father said. "Business is booming."

Albert tanked the cruiser into a narrow space. Warren Smith was coming out of the Post Office and Albert tried to duck, but he was too late.

"I'm hearing Harlan had two bullets in his back, Albert. It's gettin' out of hand around here. I got a twelve-gauge and a nine-millimeter semiautomatic in my truck, loaded and ready for bear. You give the word if you need to deputize a local militia and put these terrorists down. I got me a fat handsome offer on my land from Oscar Price, and I won't let no lunatic get in the way of my payday."

"First of all, Warren, Harlan Wayans didn't have two bullets in his back. And second, you know damn well it's illegal to carry loaded weapons. You go straight home and put them up, or I swear to God I'll run you in. You got that?"

Smith spit a wad of chewing tobacco in disgust and huffed away. Albert headed for the hardware store, but didn't get half a block before Mrs. Costanza cornered him.

"I saw you on television a half hour ago," she said. "My sister-in-law called me from Voorhees and said we were under attack. I'm a widow, Albert. You know Hank's been gone seven and a half years. With the kind of taxes I pay, I expect some protection here."

"Everything's under control, Mrs. Costanza. I might have overreacted a little, but there's nothing to worry about."

"Well I certainly hope not. A lot of us are senior citizens around here, Albert, and we don't like the idea of having a killer on the loose."

Albert kept his head down the rest of the way. This idea of selling his house and moving to Atlantic City had never sounded better.

A Temporary Help Wanted sign was in the window, and Creed James was at the checkout counter inside with enough materials to build an ark, should the next bomb obliterate the entire island.

"You sure you can get the sandbags to me by sundown?" Creed was asking Jack.

"He'll get them to you, don't worry about it," said Joaquin LaRosa, who was tapping the cash register like a pianist. "This kid is the most reliable employee I've ever had. Present company included."

"Yeah, good afternoon to you, too," Albert said. "Creed, you mind telling me what you plan to build with all this?"

"A bunker."

"What do you mean, a bunker?"

"Your boss's boys called this morning. Harlan's body wasn't cold yet, and they were telling me the bulldozer's coming in tomorrow if I don't settle by six o'clock tonight."

"What the hell are you talking about?" Albert asked, but Creed had turned his attention back to Jack and Joaquin.

"You wanna give me eight boxes of those shotgun shells, Joaquin? They come for me, they've got trouble. And if you come for me, Albert, you've got trouble. I'm sorry about Harlan, but Price is the one who declared war, and there's going to be casualties on both sides before this is over."

"All right, this is officially getting out of hand now," Albert said. He was a small-town boy himself, and he could respect the spirit of this little underdog rebellion. No one wanted to be jerked out of comfortable routine after they'd spent a lifetime perfecting the art of easy repetition. You didn't want your town to be transformed or your house to be carted away on the back of a dump truck any more than you wanted to get old and grow a belly.

"This makes no sense, Creed. Why would they need to put you out of your house way down there on Third Street?"

"Good question. Why don't you ask the guy who'll be signing your fat checks."

"There are certain realities everyone has to face up to, but..."

"There are some realities you're going to have to face up to, *Sheriff,* and one of 'em is that nobody's going to touch my house."

Getting through to Creed was useless, so Albert tried working his father.

"You can't be serious, Pop. You're going to sell ammunition to this guy so he can go to jail for shooting innocent people?"

"Innocent people? The state of New Jersey is about to run a backhoe through this man's living room so they can drop trained seals into a swimming pool and sell tickets to the show. Don't tell me about innocent people, you sellout!"

"He's going to get killed!"

"Well he won't be alone, I can tell you that," Joaquin LaRosa volunteered. "I'm going to be standing right next to Creed when they come for him. We'll die with our pride intact, at least. And the blood will be on your hands."

"I'll be right there with them," Jack chimed in.

"No you won't be, Jack. And I can't believe they'd drag you into this with them. If you're out there pointing guns, you're all going to be run off to jail. I promise you that."

"I make my own decisions," Jack said, standing up to Albert for the first time.

"Not with these dingbats brainwashing you with all this propaganda, you can't."

"What do you mean, dingbats?" Joaquin LaRosa demanded. "We're fighting for a principle here. They're coming out to flatten the house of your lifelong buddy here, and you're going to give them an escort. What principle are you fighting for?"

"Jack, can't you see they've lost all sanity and perspective? They look like they're ready to feed on nuts and berries and creep through the trenches with canteens clipped to their belts. Pretty soon you'll all be wearing these ridiculous berets and marching in step."

Albert reached for Jack's arm—he had to get him the hell out of here. But Creed stepped between them and knocked Albert back with a mighty shove. Albert found his feet and cocked his arm, but stopped himself. Blood boiling, he looked across the street to the knot of people outside Nuba's, where suspicion swirled over the identity of Harlan's killer. He took in these three rebels once more and suppressed a scream of frustration. Without a word, he wheeled away and heel-toed out of the store, leaving a trail of dried mud from the banks where Harlan Wayans kissed this town good-bye. Friend, family, whoever it was, Albert was going to arrest the man who killed him.

Albert worked into the night, hunting clues out by Kip Slough and reconstructing the whereabouts of certain people in the hours before the blast. The phone was ringing when he got home just before midnight. Fitch Caster calling with news from the autopsy. Harlan had survived the blast that launched him off the bridge, where he died by drowning. The pathologist said he had taken a good bump on the head, most likely from a projectile or from landing on bridge debris, but it was difficult to determine whether he was unconscious when he drowned. Albert hoped to hell he was. The image of Harlan thrashing around out there was particularly unpleasant. In that fog, middle of the night, he might have died from not knowing the way to shore.

That wasn't all Fitch had to report. The county crime lab had concluded that the same type of device had been used on the caterpillar jitney as on Oscar Price's car. Your basic homemade pipe bomb. The final piece of forensic news was that a slightly more sophisticated device had been used on the bridge, or at least that was the preliminary indication. Fitch said they were doing some tests to determine whether it was standard dynamite or something in more of a designer line, like C4.

"The FBI has two guys on it now, Albert, and I'd sure love to beat them at their own game."

"Let me remind you that this is my swan song, Fitch. I intend to leave here making both of us look like we know what we're doing."

"Well lean on Muldoon if you have to."

Albert said he would do whatever it took.

"This report tell you anything?" Fitch asked.

"Yeah, Fitch. Tells me I won't be sleeping the next few nights. And listen, I know you're short, but I need someone to keep an eye on Oscar Price's house, which might be the next thing to blow. And I need some backup units out here tomorrow. The bulldozer's headed for Creed James's house, and the local militia's loading up for a face-off. It could get messy."

Feeling like death, Albert went out to the porch with a cigar and a bottle. He took a pad and pen, too, to scribble some notes regarding the pathologist's report. At one point, fading fast, he looked down to see that without knowing it, he'd written the first four digits of Rickie's phone number.

"Do not," he said, "under any circumstances, call Rickie." First of all, it was too late. Second of all, whatever she was up to was her business. And third, notwithstanding roughly a dozen cruises past her house earlier this evening, what did he care? A good long swallow of whiskey and a fresh hot shot of tar and nicotine sharpened his outlook—they always did—and he dialed his sister Sam in Long Island to torment her with a family update.

"I'm sorry," he said. "I thought you might still be up."

"I was up at six this morning, Albert, going all day. And tomorrow is pure hell for me."

"Then you're going to be glad your much younger little brother called to save you from all that. You've got to come down here tomorrow, Sam. If you don't, your father could get seriously hurt and it'll be on your conscience till the day you die."

He told her the details and she did exactly what he expected she'd do. She screamed at him loudly enough to wake half of Long Island. Albert was certain beyond a shred of doubt that a college degree conferred no guarantee of intelligence on a person.

"Don't yell at me, Sam. I'm not the one who's going to grab a musket and muddle off to Creed's bunker to fire pellets at state employees. You want to yell, you ought to call old bricks and mortar and empty your lungs on him. Besides, you're the only one he'll listen to."

"There is absolutely and unconditionally no way I can physically be in Harbor Light tomorrow, Albert. I have to be in court, for god's sake!"

"Not even for your own father?"

"He's *your* father, too!"

"No way, huh?"

"Absolutely no way."

"Well, I'm sure there'll be visiting hours."

"Albert, are you talking about what I think you're talking about?"

"Yes. I plan to have him arrested," he said.

"Don't you dare."

"What option do I have? I'm going to have my hands full out there, Sam, and if he intends to hunker down in that bunker and start shooting, arresting him is about the safest thing I can do for him and the rest of the town."

"I want you to try talking him out of this again in the morning, Albert, and call me at the office to let me know what's going on."

"I won't have a chance, Sam. I'll be in Atlantic City tomorrow morning with Oscar Price."

"Doing what?"

"Trying to hold on to my job. Price called today and wanted to know when exactly I intend to figure out who's blowing everything up in the town I police. In particular, he wanted to know if I'd considered anyone in my family or immediate circle as a suspect."

"Have you?"

"Are you kidding me? Of course I have."

"What about Rickie?"

"As a suspect?"

"No. Maybe she can get Pop off the front lines."

"Of course she can't."

"How do you know? Have you called her?"

"No, I haven't called her. She's been busy. She's keeping the diner open extra hours."

"How do you know?"

"Well, I have to patrol there."

"Right."

"Anyway, I'm over her. I'm moving on. I'm looking around."

"Looking around where? Mo's?"

"Are you kidding? I'm about to become a six-figure executive, Sam, with a small army of underlings reporting to me. A man like that doesn't troll dive bars for dates. Every woman in Mo's is wearing a pink T-shirt from Cancún and she's got her hair doing things you only see in Jersey and possibly among the Aborigines. I'm not going to find a venture capitalist in there. I'm not going to find a doctor or lawyer."

"Why would you want to meet a lawyer? I thought you hated lawyers, like all good cops."

"Never mind that. I'm just tired."

"Albert, you have to call her."

"Call whom?"

"You know exactly who I'm talking about."

"No can do."

"Of course you can."

"Sam, tell me something. Just where were you when the bridge was blown up?"

"I'm going to bed, Albert. Don't arrest Daddy. Call Rickie."

"How about a prescription for some Jim Beam, doctor?"

"Go to bed, Albert."

By even the most generous standard of judgment, it was probably fair to say that in his job as the new casino's ambassador to Harbor Light, Albert was out of the running for a Nobel Prize. It was now evident that the post could not be parlayed into an ambassadorship to France, say, or Monaco. If Price had any remaining doubt about Albert's skills as a mediator, it would most likely be erased when Joaquin LaRosa marched out to Creed's place with a sauce pot on his head and a rifle strapped over his shoulder and took up a position behind a wall of sandbags and cannonballs. So naturally, Albert was not relishing this particular trip to the principal's office, and did not even make an effort at small talk with Gus the elevator man. Oddly enough, Gus wasn't in the mood, either. It was almost as if he knew Albert was coming in for a whipping.

Albert noticed this time that the receptionist wore no wedding ring, no engagement ring, no ring of any type. She wasn't bad-looking, either. But he supposed he was on precarious enough ground without asking the boss's secretary out. The point was, he had to start keeping his eyes open.

"He's expecting you," she said, waving him in, and this time Price apparently wasn't secretly monitoring foyer movement on infrared. He didn't bound out of his office, in other words, and Albert knocked to make sure it was okay to enter.

Price motioned him over to the sofa without looking at him. He was working off a pile of papers and doing a finger dance on a calculator, banging on that thing like he was clocking himself to beat yesterday's time. Albert sat down and didn't feel so hot. He never felt so hot when he wasn't drinking, and out of pure exhaustion last night, he'd only managed to lift a couple of drinks. But sitting there, watching Price race through numbers, he caught a spark of inspiration. He was going to take charge. That's the kind of thing a guy like Price looked for in his staff. Look at him bang the holy abacus out of that poor calculator. This guy didn't sit around waiting for someone else to take the lead. So when Price finally shut down his operation and stepped around the desk wringing the cramps out of his overworked digits, Albert opened fire right away.

"Sir, I'm going to have to cut this meeting pretty short. I've set up a get-together with an organized crime figure who's going to be able to point us in the right direction."

Not bad. This could work. Price sat down, crossed his legs, and considered the information.

"An organized crime figure?"

"I think you'll understand when I tell you I can't divulge his name. My meeting with him is not taking place, if you know what I mean. If the psychopath we're after isn't hooked up with Ron Rubio or organized crime in some way, I'll know soon enough. And if not, then we can draw back and focus on a few other people."

"Albert, do you understand that the longer this goes on, the easier it is for certain opportunists to take advantage of the situation? To stir up unnecessary controversy over this project?"

"Exactly. That's why I'm working double shifts, Mr. Price."

"Did you see the *Beacon* yesterday? Over sixty-five percent of the island is in favor of this project, according to their poll. My own pollsters put the numbers a little higher, but be that as it may, whoever it is that's out to get us is subverting the will of the people."

"I'm in hourly contact with a decorated FBI agent who happens to be one of my closest friends. I'm as frustrated as you are, but I have no doubt we'll get it cleared soon. And I've gotten Sheriff Caster to free a unit for round-the-clock security at your place in Harbor Light."

"Well I do appreciate that. My family's safety has been my primary concern all along."

Albert got up to leave. Short and sweet. Just one last thing.

"In terms of negative publicity and controversy, sir, a couple of loose cannons are building a fortification in front of Creed James's house, and it could get nasty if that bulldozer closes in today. I'm just suggesting that if there's any way to avoid it, that might be wise."

Price led Albert to the door and put his hand on his shoulder.

"Albert, I have no power to compel the state to desist from its business. If they feel it's time to start work on that causeway, there's nothing I can do. And don't let them fool you out there. These people were notified months ago as to the state's right-of-way plans. They've simply ignored every entreaty."

"I see."

"I'm not sure you do. Do you have any idea how many of my employees get signing bonuses and three-year contracts that begin at six figures? I can count them on one hand. And why are you up there? Not just because of your quarter of a century in law enforcement, to be honest, and not simply because I know you'll make a fine chief of security once the casino opens. I'm a businessman, Albert. Quite frankly I hired you because no one else was capable of doing the job I needed done. The FBI can't talk to these people. They can't persuade the Joaquin LaRosas or Rickie Davenports as to the merits of this project. Whoever is behind these acts of terrorism, I want an end to it, and I want it soon. And one way to accomplish that is to make it clear that no amount of interference—not a threat on my life, not a car bomb, not the cowardly murder of that poor man on the bridge—can serve as a deterrent. If the house has to go, for the greater good, that's the state's business, Albert. I don't call those shots."

"That does clarify things, sir."

"But just to prove I'm not the heartless bastard I've been portrayed as, I've got an idea. What would you say Mr. James makes in a year?"

"Creed? It's mostly seasonal. The fishing, the cocktail cruises. He does the aerial advertising, but he keeps losing jobs for bad spelling. I'd say he's in the thirty grand range."

"Well here's what you do. When we build the docks in Harbor Light and start ferrying gamblers in from Atlantic City, I'm going to need some experienced help. So why don't you tell Creed I'm going to make him captain of the fleet and double his salary. I'm bending over backwards, Albert. A year from now, people are going to look back in wonder at what we've accomplished."

Victor Ianicci and Albert went all the way back to Saint Peter Martyr grade school together. They caught their ride to Jersey Landing at the bus stop in front of Chance's Department Store and traded lunches on the way to school, Albert's veal parm sandwich for Victor's chicken cutlet with hot peppers. To Albert and others, Victor was just another kid on the bus until the week his father washed ashore in two sections, the upper torso and head in Atlantic City on a Tuesday and the rest of the body in Jersey Landing on Good Friday.

"Take a seat right here," a Ristorante Victor waiter told Albert. "He's on the phone in the back. He'll be right out."

Victor was one of the smarter members of what had been the Cacciatore crew in Philadelphia and Atlantic City, but *smart* was a relative term, and it was not hard to shine in that clubhouse. If you put a sack of sourdough biscuits in the chair next to Momo Cacciatore, the biscuits could get into NYU. But as inept as that crew was, to the point of bringing about their own demise by taking target practice on each other's heads, Albert owed Victor Ianicci his right arm or at least his first offspring for helping to squelch crime in Harbor Light. Victor's mother still lived there, and at the first sign of trouble, one phone call brought a small army of gorillas bounding into the streets with heavy lumber.

Albert grabbed at the Italian bread that had been laid in front of him, dipping it in olive oil. Victor no doubt used this restaurant to launder proceeds from loan-sharking, prostitution, and other business interests in the family tradition. Under their agreement, it was none of Albert's business, nor was this his jurisdiction, and so it never came up in conversation. The one or two times a year they ran into each other, they were much more likely to talk about the glory days of Harbor County High football, senior year, with Albert at quarterback and Victor as his center. What a year it was. The Harbor High Flounder made it all the way to the Taylor Pork Roll Schoolboy Championships at the Meadowlands, where quaint underdog spirit was finally trampled by the only thing in football more insurmountable than the ignorance of unwarranted optimism. Beef and talent. The Flounder fell, 48–7, to Cherry Hill High. After the game, Coach Cadenaso made the big moral victory speech—that was when Albert first suspected there was no such thing—and they wailed like toddlers all the way home.

"QB," Victor said, wrapping his arms around Albert to check for a wire. "Sorry for the delay. I got another shipment of imported anchovy coming in from New York, fresh off the boat from Sicily. Teresa? Teresa, bring out some of the calamari for Albert here, will you? We got this nice little clam out of New Zealand, too. You'll love this, Albert. A little linguine, squirt of lemon, some olive oil. There's a nice tilapia that came in, too. How about a glass of wine for the QB here, Teresa?"

As much as Albert would love to roll up his sleeves and celebrate the feast of the seven fishes, he explained that he was on a tight schedule and had to get down to business. Victor assured Albert that not only was there no involvement whatsoever by any gangsters or known wanna-bes, but that he and a few colleagues were just as anxious to find the son of a bitch responsible for daily phone calls from a quaking Mrs. Ianicci, who had been rattled into a state of terror.

"I thought it was Rubio myself," Victor said. "That guy's a shady character, if you know what I mean. Like there's more than meets the eye."

Unlike, say, Victor himself. In the parlance, this meant that Victor had a beef with Rubio. Albert did know for a fact that Rubio was one of several developers being looked at in a grand jury investigation into kickbacks to Atlantic City councilmen over building contracts and permits. According to Albert's A.C. police contacts, Victor was angry about being cut out of the deal, and was giving Ron Rubio the option of A) paying up, B) being ratted out, or C) having his testicles fed to his cat.

"But we couldn't find a thing, Albert. Tory and my cousin Vince snooped around his operation a little bit and he came up clean."

Translation: Tory and cousin Vince dropped by and informed Rubio that if he was holding back any knowledge about the bombings, and they found out about it later, they would return and take batting practice on his head.

Just then, Joey Tartaglione came through the door and apologized for being late. Albert didn't even know he was supposed to be here, but obviously Victor still held rank over him dating back to when the old gang was up and running. They were bookends, these two, jowls like hams and hairlines that came within a half inch of their eyebrows. You could bowl them down the street and send the high-rises kicking like tenpins.

"Tell him, Joey. Tell him what you told me."

"You got us all mixed up, Albert. Rubio's got no beef with Oscar Price. He yanked the lawsuit over the cannery two days ago. What should happen but he finds out one of his associates gave him three acres of land about ten years ago to settle a debt. He's got so much fucking property he forgot he even had this. Three acres just south of the cannery. With a casino coming in, that's prime. This is no Mameluke, Albert. The last thing Ron Rubio wants is to stand in the way of Oscar Price."

If Joey Tartaglione told Albert it was twelve o'clock on a Sunday, Albert would check a clock first and a calendar second. As a general rule of thumb, Albert trusted no one who always sat with his back to a wall. Victor Ianicci, on the other hand, despite having never held an honest job in his life, had never once given Albert a reason to doubt him. And so he drove back to Harbor Light with a fist of dread in the pit of his stomach. If not Rubio, then whom?

Maybe he was too close to it, with too many loyalties and biases to honor. If Albert were to sit down with Fitch Caster and Mike Muldoon and tell them everything he knew, they'd naturally suspect Creed, maybe even the old man, and possibly even Rickie and Jack. But he couldn't imagine that Creed was clever enough to pull off one job after another without giving himself up. Albert's father had more fight in him than any of the others, but he was simply too old to be running all over the island planting bombs. Rickie might just be the biggest rebel of them all, and she had spent her youth running around the world with the *Communist Manifesto* in her back pocket. But she's the one who was going the legal route now, hiring this fuckwad lawyer to do her fighting for her.

And Jack? Despite the kid's having taken sides this morning at the hardware store, Albert refused to believe it could be Jack. He was too young and aloof to be passionate about small-town politics, for one thing. For another, Albert had gone by his father's house after the bridge explosion. If Jack had driven up to Atlantic City in his truck to plant that bomb, he hadn't taken his truck. The engine was cold to the touch. That didn't mean Jack didn't know something about who was responsible, and Albert suspected he could get Jack to talk if he leaned on him heavily enough. But Albert didn't want to be told who his bomber was. As a matter of pride, he wanted to find out on his own.

On his way to Creed's Albert saw Creed's truck in the lot at Peg's. He'd been trying to avoid the diner, but he had a job to do. And as if the tension in town weren't ratcheted up high enough, Aunt Rose had propped a sandwich board atop her pink Caddy in the parking lot.

RAPE IN PROGRESS
SEND GUNS AND AMMO

Just what Albert needed. A few more crackpots to enter the fray. As it was, Albert was having a little trouble shaking the image of Creed at his father's store, stocking up on birdshot with Joaquin and Jack cheering him on.

Albert pushed through the door and saw him seated in the second booth. Any hope that Creed might have moderated his views vanished when Albert saw that he was wearing military fatigues and maneuvering salt and pepper shakers as if they were battlefield pieces. At the first table, four old-timers were in the process of solving the case for Albert. James Parsons, who wore an American Legion cap and tried year-round to sell you those little white canes, asked Albert if the rumors were true.

"I heard there's more than one body," he said. "And there's other bombs set to go off all around town. What kind of crazy nut is this, Albert?"

Before Albert could set him straight, Drugstore Max Phelps offered this little nugget of international goodwill: "There's Arabs involved in them A.C. casinos nowadays. I say it's the rag heads trying to keep the competition in line. Kill the enemy and that's a ticket to heaven is how they think. They'll stop at nothing."

All right, so this was part of the deal. If you chose to live in a place where a lost mitten would be found on the street and returned to its owner, a place where the *Beacon* ran a weekly neighbor-of-the-week column, and where the whole town pitched dollars into a coffee can at Mario's Barbershop when someone had a run of bad luck, you had to take this kind of thing along with it. But Albert had run out of patience.

"There's no more bodies, there's no more bombs set to go off, and there's no Arabs killing anyone. This isn't the Gaza Strip, boys, it's New Jersey. But I appreciate all the suggestions."

Albert moved on to the next table. "Creed, can I talk to you a minute?"

"You bring your handcuffs?"

"Don't make this difficult, Creed." Albert looked around the room for Rickie but saw no sign of her. Usually, after lunch, she'd be here right till quitting time. Aunt Rose was behind the counter, and Albert would love to kill his curiosity, but he could tell by the glance she shot him that she'd just abuse him for one thing or another if he started a conversation. Instead he walked Creed to the back of the restaurant and the two of them stood at the window, looking out on Kip Slough.

Across the water and just to the south, a tractor was scooping up debris from the blown bridge and plopping it onto a dump truck, the clatter as heavy as the pounding of the surf. There were enough hard hats in and around the construction village to build the Roman Colosseum. The crane and cockpit Harlan had ridden to his death were long gone now. It was as if the explosion had been a mere hiccup, a throat clearing, and then it was on with the show, the transformation of Harbor Light moving apace, advancing of its own momentum.

"They say Oscar Price has been on the phone with the governor, cracking the whip to keep this thing moving," Creed said.

"They? Who's they, Creed?"

Creed looked at him with wonder and disdain. "He raised close to half a million dollars for that man's campaign last time around, Albert. What is it you think is going on here? This bridge is bought and paid for, no matter who gets screwed."

Albert drew their attention upstream to the cannery docks where they'd played as kids. Against their parents' warnings, and probably because of them, they used to swim across the slough, risking their lives against tide and current for the sake of getting to the other side. His whole life, Albert suspected, he had been trying to escape the island without knowing it.

"Creed, I'm going to ask you something I'm pretty sure I know the answer to already."

"You're sounding more like Oscar Price every day, Albert."

Albert grit his teeth and laid out Oscar Price's job offer. He'd never seen him more insulted. "Well if that don't beat everything, you coming over here like Oscar Dan Price's water boy and ask me to be his poodle."

"Creed, I'm not asking you to be anything except law-abiding. And I need you to know something, Creed. The last thing I'm going to do as a deputy is find out who blew up the bridge and killed Harlan. And when I do, it doesn't matter who he is, or whether he's one of the best friends I ever had, he's going away. The last job I do, I'm doing right."

"Why you telling this to me, Albert?"

"So you know."

"You'd send your own buddy to prison for trying to save his house from the wrecking ball?"

"I would and you know it, Creed. I never loved this job, but I did it fair and pretty much by the book. You start making different rules for different people, it comes back and bites you in the ass."

"How about that night in Philadelphia, Albert? Was that by the book, or you got different rules for yourself?"

"What do you know about Philadelphia?"

"I know what you told me one night when you were so drunk I carried you home from Mo's. The night you came back from your partner's funeral."

"I never told anyone a thing."

"Well either you were too sauced to remember, or a little bird put it in my ear."

"I'm not here to talk about something that happened

twenty-five years ago, Creed. You mind telling me where you were the night of the town council meeting?"

"Yeah. I do mind. But I'll tell you anyway. I was getting laid in Atlantic City."

"Sandy's brothel again? Because I know Sandy, Creed. If I ask, she'll tell me the truth."

"Then go ahead and ask."

"How about last night? You have one of Sandy's girls wrapped around you last night, too? Because your truck wasn't at your place after the bridge blew."

"Check my freezer and you'll find out where I was. I was six miles out, catching dinner. I brought home twice my limit, if you want to run me in for that. That'd be by the book, wouldn't it?"

A car pulled into the lot then, and Albert knew exactly who it was even before Rickie got out of the passenger side. The attorney met her at the back of the car and they spoke for half a minute. It was not the way you talked business. The posture was all wrong, the distance between them too short. It was breaking up now and from this angle it was hard to tell, but it looked as if Rickie touched him. Not a casual tap on the arm but a more familiar, intimate gesture. Albert was losing everything. Just now, he was not inclined to try and retrieve any of it.

The last thing Albert wanted to do, given the possibility of World War III being fought in Harbor Light with his father filling in for General Patton, was get called off the island, but that was exactly what happened. A four-car, two-fatality bang-up on the Parkway between Mama Parm's Macaronium and Tortilla Gulch blocked southbound lanes for two hours, and Albert helped paramedics pry two criticals out of the wreckage. He finally begged off when he heard the call on a disturbance at Third and Kip in Harbor Light. It was early, if this was what he thought it was. The bulldozer was supposed to be two hours off. Maybe someone had decided on a sneak attack.

"Bravo-thirty-four to Delta-two. Do you copy?"

The deputy who was sitting on Price's house was a lot closer to Creed's than Albert was.

"I'm pulling up now," the deputy called back. "Jesus, there's some crazy old loon out here with a .22 and a beret."

"That's my father," Albert said. "Just so you know. I'm two minutes out."

The Sea-Fruit Cannery and the lighthouse were pink-gray etchings as he gunned it toward Creed's. The bulldozer's wheels were up on the sidewalk, advancing like a German panzer toward the immaculate white craftsman Creed had lived in his entire life and dutifully maintained in tribute to his deceased parents. The porch was already gone, the living room was now open-air, and the tractor was traversing the crushed bunker Creed had built, boring in to take another bite out of the house. The demolition had begun.

Twenty people huddled on Third Street and more were hustling around the bend at Cannery Way to watch this culmination of promises and threats. Two squad cars were already on the scene and Albert saw, to his relief, that both Creed and his father were disarmed. Creed was cuffed and trying to break free of a deputy who put him down hard and kept him there with a boot to his neck. Jack was on the scene, too, jawing with the deputy who was shoving Albert's father into the back of his cruiser.

Albert rammed the curb and flew up on the front yard, wedging the nose of his cruiser in between the tractor and the porch. The driver side of his car crumpled and he had to climb out the passenger side. The minute he did, a lawyer from the state attorney general's office was standing before him.

"This is a copy of the court ruling on the injunction," he said. "He lost his last appeal and we warned him to stand clear. Nobody wanted it to come to this, but he's had more than enough notice. He refused to even get his things out of the house, so he's left us no choice."

Albert nodded and went over to the deputy. "Could you let him up a minute so I can talk to him?" Creed pushed himself to his feet, dusting off his arms.

"Look, Creed, I'm sure I could get these guys to let you take your stuff. Far as they're concerned, they're just doing a job."

"Like you, huh, Albert?"

Albert felt a sharp pain in his ribs from the collision. He studied Creed, looked at the house, and then back at his father, still struggling to get out of the cruiser. "I never meant for this to happen," he said. Creed's eyes got very big and then very small, and he lunged again when the tractor restarted and maneuvered around Albert's car. The deputy put him back down. And then came the crunching, ripping, screaming birth of a new day in Harbor Light. Albert shivered at the sound, wondering at the cost. Too late to turn back now.

Albert was deep in boozy hibernation, sleeping the sleep of burrowing animals, when the smoke curled into the room, clocked straight up his nose, and penetrated his brain. He opened his eyes and stared at the ceiling, trying to distinguish between dream and reality. He looked at the alarm. Three in the morning. And then came the gunshot, a finite puncture that could have been a balloon popping or a bindered book slammed shut, except that a bullet came zinging through his bedroom with a *phhht-phhht* penetration of the walls.

Albert rolled off the bed and onto the floor, reaching up to the nightstand for his gun. Ordinarily he was slow to rise, but waking to a gunshot and the smell of a house fire was the perfect cure. He lay perfectly still for a few anxious seconds, trying to gather his wits. And then he bellied over to the bedroom door and peered into the living room to see that his porch was going up like kindling.

Albert crab-walked to the front of the house, gun at the ready. There was no way out through the front door. It breathed smoke. He raised his head high enough to look out the living room window and into the front yard, and when he saw no one there, he picked up a chair and crashed it through the window. He left a quarter pound of flesh on the shards as he vaulted out and tumbled into the yard in his skivvies, but he felt nothing as he ran into the street and looked in every direction. When he was sure the coast was clear he ran for the garden hose and aimed an arc at the flames. Arthur Abraham, the Drain Surgeon, was flying across the street in his long johns. He was lugging a little kitchen fire extinguisher, screaming words that meant nothing to Albert. Together, they had the flames snuffed in less than a minute.

"Are you all right?" Arthur Abraham asked, inspecting Albert's wounds like a battlefield comrade.

No, he wasn't all right. He was standing in the cold in his shorts, impotent and useless and miserable, unable to solve a mystery that deepened by the day. He had rejected the woman he loved and betrayed a friend. But proving himself right meant sticking with the plan. It meant finding the bomber— even if it were Creed, even if it were Jack.

A month ago, Albert would have insisted it was impossible for anyone to do anything on this island that he didn't know about. It was a place so incapable of conspiracy that if someone kicked a small dog or yelled at his wife, he knew about it. Albert's ear had always been tuned to Harbor Light's rhythms. Even as a kid, he'd had a knack for it. He'd sit up in that lifeguard stand as a teenager and see things before they happened. An upswell, a rip, a subtle change in the texture of the water. He'd literally saved lives by seeing what to most was entirely invisible. It was almost as if the town, in retaliation for his indifference to it, had decided the deal was off. It was withholding all secrets from him until further notice.

He stepped onto the flooded, charred front porch and ran his finger over a small bullet hole about head high on his front door. A .22, he guessed. He opened the door and followed the path into the smoky house, to another hole on the wall of his bedroom. At the back of the bedroom, the bullet was buried in the wall above his bed. This guy had accomplished at least one of his goals. Albert was listening with both ears.

"You're bleeding like a pig," Arthur said, coming in from the kitchen with a dish towel. "You sure you're not shot? The gunshot's what woke me."

"I'm fine," Albert said, dabbing at the streams of blood under his eye and on his arms and legs. "I think I just cut myself jumping out the window."

"It looks pretty bad. Let me call for an ambulance."

"I'm fine, Arthur. Thanks. You didn't happen to see anyone when you came out of your house, did you? A car? Anything?"

"I might have seen someone running, but I'm not sure. You see how dark it is out here. I went for the fire extinguisher and there was no one out here when I came out of my house. Someone tried to kill you, Albert. What the hell is going on in this town?"

"You're asking the wrong guy," Albert said. "I'm just the sheriff."

When Arthur was gone, Albert went out to his car and retrieved the flyer that was pinned to his windshield. He'd seen it earlier, but didn't want to draw any attention to it while Arthur was there. Letters were cut from newspapers and magazines, in the style of psychopaths, and glued to a plain white sheet of paper.

> Listen to me with both ears
> Lie down with dogs
> Get up with fleas

Not a single word misspelled. That told you something right there.

Dr. DiMitri, eighty-six years old, had delivered Albert nearly a half century ago. Many islanders still swore by him, but it was only fair to wonder if a man who used a white cane to negotiate Cannery Way should still be looking down throats and into ear canals. "You look like you took third place in a hatchet fight," Dr. DiMitri said.

Albert could have used a stiff drink, or at least a smoke, while Dr. DiMitri yanked window out of his face with a tool that looked like something from a Civil War museum. When he was done excavating, he went for the needle and thread. A disconcerting sight under any circumstances, but particularly so in the case of a doctor old enough to have gotten the call when Abraham Lincoln was shot. The cut on his cheekbone took seventeen stitches to close, and Albert needed some knitting on his left arm and right leg, too. But that wasn't his biggest worry. He had banged against the steering wheel when he jammed the curb and skidded to a halt in Creed's front yard yesterday, and it felt like he'd been stabbed in the lungs with an ice pick. Dr. DiMitri pushed here and there, and Albert screamed like a schoolgirl.

"I think you cracked the same rib you broke in high

school," Dr. DiMitri said. "You're going to need pictures of your insides down at County, and then I want you to go home, pour a drink, and tell that wife of yours to go easy on you. You and Rickie are married by now, aren't you?"

Fitch Caster was pulling up as Albert hobbled next door to his office, and Albert knew instantly that this wasn't a get-well visit.

"What's the other guy look like?" Fitch asked.

"I'm fine, boss. Never felt better. What brings you to the West Bank so early in the morning?"

"One of my deputies gets shot at, I take it personally. Invite me inside and offer me a cup of coffee, will you?"

Georgianna leaped to attention and practically saluted when she saw the boss waddle through the door.

"That's how she greets me every day, too," Albert said. "Don't let it go to your head."

Georgianna brought Fitch a cup of coffee with four sugars and offered to run out for anything else he might need. He thanked her and when she was gone, Albert whispered that Georgianna seemed to have a crush on him. "Seriously," he said, "she deserves a raise, Fitch. I don't care what the pay schedule says. She's half deputy, half office manager, and she's had to put up with me. Take care of her when I'm gone."

"Well since you brought it up, that's what I came to see you about, Albert."

It sounded bad, but Albert had no idea. Fitch squirmed, stammered, and then got himself going.

"I don't think it's such a terrific idea for you to stay on the case any longer."

"What are you talking about?"

"You're one of the targets, Albert. That's number one. It sets up certain conflicts."

"It gives me certain advantages is what it does. Forget it, Fitch. You can't boot me off this thing. Not now."

"I'm asking you to do the professional thing, Albert. The FBI has been squawking and I'm tired of running interference. They think we're a bunch of backwater hicks, letting a deputy work a case with leads that run right through his front porch. Come on, Albert. They got their eye on Creed James and know the two of you go back to grade school together. They got their eye on Jack Davenport, and they're not too sure your old man isn't the leader of the Three Musketeers. I know how you feel. But now that you're banged up, maybe this is the time to take a walk."

"Are you saying you want me out of here altogether?" Fitch looked down and cleared his throat. "This isn't you, is it? It's somebody breathing down your back. Let me guess. Attorney general's office? That's who the FBI would run to."

Fitch wiped his brow with his sleeve. His face, with enough broken blood vessels to look like a road map, was as round and red as the planet Mars. "You were the one who came into my office begging to turn your badge in. Do you remember that?"

"Yeah, and I remember you begging me to stay. Now that there's some honest police work to be done, you're pushing me out the door? You've got to go to bat for me here, Fitch. As a boss, as a friend. I can't walk out on this thing now."

"You don't know the heat I've been taking on this, Albert."

"I'm asking two weeks. That's all. Give me two weeks and I'll be gone. I'll drive down to Rag Harbor and give you my badge, my gun, and the car keys. Two weeks for a man to settle his debts. Is that too much to ask after twenty-odd years?"

It came to Albert in the middle of the night and dragged him out of sleep. The FBI was going on the assumption that the bridge bomber moved in from the Atlantic City side and waded into the shallows of Kip Slough to set the explosives against the bridge foundation. But it was coming up on high tide at the time of the blast, and an offshore storm had raised the water level another two to four feet. Unless the bomber was an eight-foot Masai warrior, he didn't wade out there. He sailed out, and the boat had come from the Harbor Light marina. In that fog, it couldn't have come from anywhere else.

It was three o'clock. Albert turned on the night-light and dialed information. The smell of rain washed in through his window.

"Rio Grande," he said. "Maureen Chevereaux."

There was no answer at Mo's. Albert looked out the window and saw a wall of mist and low fog, so he dressed and drove to the tavern to see if she'd spent the night there.

Mo didn't answer on the first or second knocks, but the boat started rocking with the third and she opened the door wearing men's pajamas and a crew cut. If it wasn't the most frightening moment in Albert's adult life, it was in the top five. Did she just get her head shaved, or was the pile of feathers she usually fashioned a wig? Between the hair and men's pajamas, complete with button fly, Albert didn't know quite what to say, but Mo didn't seem the least bit self-conscious about it.

"You're either a little late or a lot early," Mo said. "I'm closed."

"Yeah, I know you're closed. I'm sorry about this, Mo, but I have to ask you something. The night Harlan got killed, the fog was too thick to drive in. You must have stayed here that night, am I right?"

"As I recall. What about it? Am I a suspect now?"

"No. Just think back on that night a minute. Did you hear a boat come out of the marina? Do you remember hearing anything?"

Mo opened the door and turned on a beer sign to give them a little bit of light. Albert looked at the pool table, which had a foam pad over it as a mattress. The window behind the bar, the one that looked out onto the water, was open.

"You always sleep with the window open?"

"Now you're getting personal. Yeah, usually."

"If a boat was puttering out of the marina, you must have heard it."

"I'm not a light sleeper," Mo said. "But come to think of it, yeah, I think I did hear something that night. But I didn't remember it as a boat."

"It would have been right about now. Same time of night."

"I remember something, but I'm just not sure if it was that same night. I remember something waking me, but it was a motorcycle, not a boat."

"You heard a motorcycle?"

"I was half asleep, Albert. I didn't look out the window or get a flashlight and go investigate, but I do remember that it woke me, or half woke me. I'm pretty sure it was that night. I wondered who would be driving around in Harbor Light on a motorcycle at three or four in the morning, all that fog, unless it was someone coming home from work in Atlantic City."

Albert apologized and told Mo to go back to sleep. He paced over to the marina and sat in the cabin of his boat with a smoke, trying to make sense of it. Albert knew of a couple of scooters on the island, but no motorcycles. If Mo really heard one, it couldn't have had anything to do with the bridge. Not unless someone drove to the marina by motorcycle, boarded a boat, and then sailed down Kip Slough to bomb the bridge. But if that were the case, wouldn't Mo have heard a boat engine a few minutes after the motorcycle?

"You have two visitors, sir."

"I'm not here, Georgianna."

"I'm afraid they're here in the lobby, Sheriff. They say they're with the FBI."

Right away they had an attitude. Without a word between them, Albert could tell they'd be talking about him and his low-rent operation when they left. The shorter of the two, a workout fanatic who was busting out of his suit and had a waist you could put your hands around, was the type who didn't say he was with the FBI. If he met someone on the street and they asked what he did, he'd say special agent, like he spent his days investigating an international conspiracy to start World War III. And the other one, you could tell this guy was going to be elbowing other agents about the junior cadet working in an office that used to be a miniature golf course. They introduced themselves and Albert said he was busy but he'd give them a couple of minutes.

"We just thought we'd introduce ourselves as a courtesy,"

said the tall one. "We kind of heard you got banged up a little bit."

"I'm okay. Geez, I hope you boys didn't lose any sleep worrying about my well-being."

"Ballistics says that was a twenty-two, probably fired from a rifle, they dug out of your bedroom wall. You have any ideas who'd come after you like you were an eight-point buck?"

"Yeah. Ex-wife comes to mind."

The tall one smiled. The short one looked like he stood in front of the mirror a lot. Marine buzz. Muscles in his ears. You'd need a pair of pliers to get a smile out of him. He looked like being here was beneath him, but that was the funny part. They wouldn't have come by if they had anything going on. They were stumped. They wouldn't admit to it with guns to their heads, but they didn't have a clue. Why would they be in here sweating him if they knew something?

"No one left a calling card?" the tall one asked. He was the talker to the other guy's mute. Did they really think they could pull a good-cop/bad-cop routine on him? "Any contact of any type from anyone?"

If they knew he'd scooped that note off his windshield, and he said no, they'd have something on him. But how could they know? Albert hadn't even told Fitch Caster. If you didn't know things no one else knew, you weren't doing your job.

"Nothing," Albert said. "Whatever's going on here, they've got me stumped. What about you guys? You got any ideas?"

The short one was walking around the room like he was in the law enforcement wing of Ripley's Believe It or Not. He inspected the holding cell and paused over a cue Creed had used to crack Warren Smith over the head in a brawl at Mo's. Maybe once every couple of years he took the mask off and let himself breathe.

"Atlantic City part of your jurisdiction?" the marine asked now, joining the conversation.

"Not that anyone told me."

"So then that was a social visit when you had lunch with Victor Ianicci? What is he, a buddy of yours?"

This was pathetic. Couple of big-timers parachute in to save the day, and what were they doing? They were tailing Albert. That's how lost they were. This was a shot in the arm, he had to admit. If it didn't hurt like a motherfucker to breathe, he'd have puffed his chest.

"It stands to reason those guys might have an interest in whether there's a casino outside Atlantic City," Albert said. "So you spread nets, right? Everyone a suspect."

"Everyone including your buddy Creed James?" the marine asked.

"Top of the list," Albert said.

"What do you know about Jack Davenport?"

"I know he's a nice kid who likes to fish."

"You do understand that if you withhold anything, we're going to have you brought up for obstruction of justice and accessory to murder."

"I'd expect nothing less from a couple of pros. If I stumble onto anything, you'll be the first to know. And by the way, if I were you guys, I'd keep playing the A.C. connections. It's amazing how much you can find out if you know who to talk to."

The instructions on the painkillers were fairly explicit. Do not mix with alcohol. Don't get completely tanked is what they must mean. If you were in enough pain to be taking these horse pills, of course you were going to have a couple of drinks to take the edge off. Albert had two refreshments at Mo's, two more on the porch, and hadn't felt this good since he hit that three-run homer in the donkey baseball game last year, when the sheriff's department beat the post office in a fund-raiser for muscular dystrophy. And in this state of chemical-induced euphoria, he was thinking of calling an old girlfriend.

Reason number one he should just go ahead and call Rickie: A sufficient amount of time had passed since she cleared her things out of his house. There were rules about these things. The first forty-eight hours were off-limits without qualification or exception. No self-respecting man would pick up the phone the first two days. But after that, the psychology of it changed. She had to be wondering what was up. She had to be sitting in the dark thinking, Seven years with this guy, and I don't mean any more to him than that?

Reason number two to just go ahead and do it: He had not met any other women. In an act of admitted desperation, he called Oscar Price's secretary. The one with the glasses and the turned-up nose. And what did she say to his entreaty, the ungrateful sow? She didn't think so. She didn't think so? What the hell kind of answer was that? You said you were seeing someone, or you didn't date in the office, or you'd donated your genitals to science. You gave some kind of explanation, anything, just out of human decency. Hell, Albert thought. Am I so hideous that you can't give me the courtesy of a simple lie?

Reason number three. Nothing to lose. Not a damn thing. He called her up and said honest to god, Rickie, I've had a few doubts here. Nothing to turn him around, exactly. He still wanted the job. But he saw her side of it, too, and maybe there was a compromise.

What had gotten him thinking, for the first time, that there was an outside chance, somewhere between minuscule and microscopic, that he was on the wrong side of the fence? Creed's house. It was a good thing Creed couldn't look at Albert, because you know what? Albert couldn't look at Creed. He couldn't look into those catfish eyes, the poor fucked-up, grammatically challenged bastard, without feeling like the creep of the year. Creed had nursed both his parents in that house, refusing to send them off to some sunset manor where they'd drool on themselves and reek of urine all day. Creed fed them, bathed them, and clothed them because that was their home and they were his parents. And Albert, his best friend all through school, watched a deputy pin him down like a roped calf while the state bulldozed his house into oblivion.

Albert poured himself another drink. Every time a wave crashed, he pushed back on the rocker and closed his eyes and the planet was a bubble in a glass of champagne. Snug in this universe of infinite reasons to call Rickie on the phone, he didn't want to think about the one that really counted.

Reason number 4. Her son was a suspect in a murder investigation.

Rickie answered on the second ring and told him to come on over.

One January, when he was about eighteen, Albert got drunk and jumped off Memorial Bridge on a dare. Next to that, this was the fastest he'd ever sobered up. Aunt Rose had already gone to bed, and Albert and Rickie sat on the front porch, riding the swing chair. She looked at him without judgment and then she stared out into the dark and quiet street. She looked beat. And beautiful.

"There's something I've got to say," Albert said after summoning the nerve. "I don't know how you feel, but I think it's ridiculous that we let a casino come between us."

"It didn't. That was just an excuse. We took each other for granted, Albert. That was the problem, and it happened awhile ago. I was the part of you who wanted to run away from this place, and you were the part of me that wanted to stay. It worked fine for a while. Made for terrific sex, anyway."

"Are you kidding me? Wild monkey sex."

"But we got crossed up after a while. I don't know. Really, though, I don't care to talk about it. Not now."

Albert didn't know what that meant. What were they supposed to talk about if not that? Earned income credits? High deductibles? There was nothing else to talk about, as far as he was concerned. But she must have something in mind or she wouldn't have called him over here. "You mean you don't want to talk about what went wrong, or what went right, or you don't want to talk just a little more about the sex? Because I can talk about the sex for a couple of hours if you want. I'm flexible on that."

Now she gave him her entire open, irresistible face. She still cast spells over him. A look was all it took and he was gone, full of desire that was only half physical. The rest of it, the mystery of her, was always the best part.

"I'd like you to tell me about that night in Philadelphia. What it was like."

She'd asked before. Twice that he could remember. And he

didn't feel any differently about the subject now. Not even with a potentially lethal combination of medicine and alcohol surfing his veins.

"I don't like to talk about it, Rickie. You know that."

"Why? Because you did something wrong?"

"Because it happened in that house, and I'd like to keep it there."

"It happened in your life, Albert. Your life goes beyond the rooms of that house."

"But the story doesn't have to."

"I'm not trying to force you, you know?"

"It just sort of diminishes everything. I can't tell the story without feeling like I sound like the victim, and I wasn't. You know, a woman died in there. A boy lost both his parents and ended up paralyzed for life. How do you talk about any of that?"

"Tell me about him."

"About whom?"

"The boy. How often do you see him?"

Jack. Jack had told her everything.

"About once a month. I go see him in Philadelphia."

"And what do you do, the two of you?"

"We go places. See a movie, sit in the park, go get something to eat."

"And what do you talk about? Does he ever talk about it?"

Albert took a cigar out of his shirt pocket and lit it. He blew a long stream of smoke and watched it move beyond the light of the porch and disappear.

"He's asked me to kill him," Albert said.

"You mean literally?"

"Finish the job I started and put him out of his misery. Are you beginning to see why I don't like to talk about it?"

"Yes," she said, and she reached for his hand.

They sat without speaking for two or three minutes, and Albert felt like he wanted to leave now.

"I'll tell you the rest of it, Rick. Another night, I promise I'll tell you. But just answer a question for me, will you?"

"It depends."

"Do you know what's going on? You know who left the bomb that killed Harlan?"

"I was going to ask you the same thing."

"Don't play coy with me, Rickie. An innocent man's dead, and everything is crazy. Everything is off."

"What if I were to tell you I was the one? If I were to tell you I firebombed Oscar Price's car and the Bargain Acres and the bridge, too. What would you think about that? I do have a past, you know. Maybe it's kind of a return to action for me."

"I don't think so."

"What *do* you think?"

"I think I'd like to know more about Jack."

Now it was her turn to look uncomfortable. "You know all there is to know about Jack. He's a sweet, screwy kid whose hardheaded mother ran from the cops when she was his age and never thought he needed a traditional home or a father figure. Not until she hooked up with this handsome sheriff back in her old hometown. I think Jack's going to be fine, but I realize he needs something I can't give him. He never had a father and could have used one. But I always . . ." She looked like she was going to completely break down now, that perfect lower lip trembling, and her eyes starting to cloud up.

"Rickie, there's something else I'd like to know."

"What's that?"

"I need to know if you feel something for this attorney of yours."

She smiled a little hesitantly, and watched a breeze rustle leaves and shake shadows over the street. Albert figured he could find out about Jack some other way.

"I don't know," she said honestly, and Albert's heart sank and rose and didn't know what to do. "But I sure know I need an attorney. The state is going to officially condemn the restaurant tomorrow."

Oscar Dan Price was beginning to compromise Albert in ways he hadn't imagined. First Creed's house, and now Rickie's restaurant was slated to be scraped off the face of the town like a wart. A few people might have to be relocated, that was what he'd said. He didn't mention anyone by name. He sure as hell didn't mention Peg's As You Like It diner. So Albert's plan was to drive to Atlantic City before Harlan's funeral and find out whether Price intended to leave anything standing. There was just one problem.

Someone had stolen his car. He stood in the middle of Jib looking at the empty space in front of his house. Albert had walked around the block three times and he wasn't doing it again. He had schlepped all the way over to Mo's Tavern and to his office, still feeling like he'd been trampled in the running of the bulls because of the stitches and the cracked rib. No sign of the car. Was he losing his mind?

"It's an emergency situation," Albert said to the dispatcher in Rag Harbor. "Can't you get him on the radio?"

"He's not answering."

"Did you leave him my message?"

Yes. They'd left Fitch Caster his message half an hour ago,

and his response at the time was all they had to go on. Fitch was tied up, and if the garage manager said there were no cars available, there were no cars available. Fitch was a sheriff, not a magician.

Albert slammed the phone down and tumbled back outside. A construction crew was rebuilding his porch and Albert was fighting with the insurance company over the deductible. It was fair to say the day was not starting out all sunshine and sea breezes. He replayed the evening's events again, backing up the reel in his head. After work he'd gone to Mo's for a couple, then home for a couple more, then over to Rickie's and back. Sure, he had swallowed enough liquor and Percodan to have visited a parallel dimension, but he was next to certain that he'd rounded the corner in good shape, turned right, and parked on the opposite side of the street behind Arthur Abraham's backup van. He'd had blackouts before. He kind of liked them, in fact. If you were so bad off that you involuntarily removed data from your brain, it had to be for your own protection. Mother Nature knew what she was doing.

But he couldn't think of anything more humiliating than having to call and report his own car stolen. Maybe losing your gun would be worse, but at least you could get in the car and go look for the prick who stole it. Clearly, someone was getting the best of him in every way. Making sport of it. But if they were trying to wear him down, it would never happen. He was resourceful. He was smart. And he was tired of being made to feel so desperately incompetent.

Albert lugged his lacerations and calamities across Jib to Arthur's and rapped on the door. Arthur never used the second van until the season heated up and the sewer lines were overwhelmed with the work of those double-wide Philadelphians. Albert had never seen anyone eat like Philadelphia ate. You had to love the counterintuitiveness of it. The entire rest of the country was on a diet, but with Philadelphians there was no slimming down for summer. The majority of the population had no work to speak of. Their job was to eat, smoke, and go to the store for more food and cigarettes. Then from July to August, they moved the show to the Jersey shore, where their gastronomic breeding ran toward pizza, ice cream, and saltwater taffy—don't forget the cigarettes—and Arthur Abraham didn't sleep a wink.

He wouldn't be home now, but Patsy would be in there doing whatever it was she did. Stuffing envelopes or making phone calls. One of those jobs you saw in cryptic ads that guaranteed you'd be on easy street without ever leaving the comforts of the family room, slippers on your feet and moisturizing mask on your face, a bag of Fritos within reach. She answered the door in a housecoat and a wig the color of the snub-nosed mutt that moused around the house and yipped its head off now. The first time Albert had seen that thing out front, he thought they had gophers. Although the door was open only a foot, enough cigarette smoke escaped from the house to spread emphysema into Newfoundland.

"Hey, Albert," Patsy said, and here's when Albert knew it had been a little too long since he'd been with a woman. She looked okay. Not terrific, but under the right circumstances, who was to say?

"Listen, Patsy. I'm in a bit of a jam here. Someone stole my car, and I was wondering if Arthur would mind my borrowing his buggy. It's kind of an emergency. A police emergency."

Patsy disappeared into the smoke and returned eagerly a half minute later with the keys. He thanked her and said he'd explain the whole thing to Arthur later.

It took forever for the motor to catch and the van smelled like the inside of a septic tank. Albert lit a minicigar to freshen the air, then dropped the van into gear and pulled out herky-jerky, the truck sputtering so violently he nearly swallowed his butt. Rounding the corner at Kip, a tool cabinet swung open and emptied its contents onto the ribbed metal floor, and it sounded like he was like driving a tambourine. The engine conked altogether after he made the turn. "Don't disappoint me," he coaxed, thumbing the starter. "Come on. That's it, now you're talking, here we go. On top and still climbing."

Albert gassed up in Jersey Landing and pumped some life into the sad tires, and then the truck wouldn't turn over. It was too late to get to Atlantic City before the funeral or, for that matter, to join the procession to the cemetery. Albert got hold of Jack by phone and asked him to fill in as pallbearer until he got there. Ed Deacon, who had replaced or rebuilt every part in Arthur's van over the years, poked around the carburetor and finally got it going, and Albert drove straight to the cemetery on a little rise out near the Parkway. He used to visit once a month to take flowers to his mother's grave, up under the reach of an ancient oak. But he'd gotten out of the habit and hated himself for it now as he tackled the incline, the first to arrive.

"You been taking care of Mrs. LaRosa?" Albert asked the chief of the crew that was preparing Harlan's grave.

"You know I have, Albert. She looked after me all those years."

Nelson Crowell, who came up a few years after Albert, still lived with his parents in the Western Addition.

"I used to hate going into the store for pickups the times my dad couldn't pay. She kind of made it all right, though. She'd put it on the ledger and pat me on the head. She'd give me some of that chicken soup."

"So you're the bastard," Albert said. "Half the time I went in there for mine, it was gone."

The caravan was coming up from town now, a long train of cars led by the black hearse from Canciamilla's Funeral Home. The day hung low and hazy and a little touch of summer blew up the hill, a hint of dogwoods in the balmy, salted air. In the distance, the meager skyline was engraved on the tinplate sea like a page from the town's history book. Looking north, the next chapter was in the works. The crane rose and levered like a prehistoric grasshopper at work, the new bridge coming along on pace to replace the one Harlan spent his last night on.

The hearse stopped short of the top of the hill, as was the burial custom in Harbor Light. No one could explain with any authority the origin of the rite, but as legend had it, the Indians who lived on the land believed the dead passed their strength on to others, and they honored the inheritance by muscling the body up the hill. And so the back door of the hearse swung open and the six white-gloved pallbearers, led by Joaquin LaRosa and Jack Davenport, took hold of Harlan Wayans's memory and marched in lockstep, lugging the shining ebony casket past the time-smoothed stones of the earliest settlers and up through the centuries.

It still hurt when Albert breathed, and he decided to leave Jack to the job of lugging Harlan up the hill. Watching him now, he realized that he had never known Jack beyond the superficial things anyone knows about anyone else. He couldn't say what he did in his spare time, where he went, or who he hung out with. He was mostly decent and respectful on the outside, but maybe that was a teenage pose constructed for the adults around him. Even so, how would he know about putting a bomb together? And why would he do it in the first place? Why would he care that much about Harbor Light, past or future? And if he was capable of planting the bomb that killed Harlan, was he also capable of carrying Harlan's body up the hill? Albert shook his head. Let it be anyone but Jack. Albert's instinct, from the day he met him as a scrawny, dazed teenager seven years ago, had been to protect him.

Jeanie and the brood followed behind the coffin. The six kids and eight or ten grandchildren, some of them trampling graves and stopping to pluck flowers from vases. One boy, about eight, had raced up ahead of the casket to peer down into the hole his grandfather was going to be dropped into. Then came the town. Mario the barber and Drugstore Max Phelps, Nuba Ludwick and Buzz Dexter of the *Beacon*. Georgianna and her twin sister, Lu. Car doors were still slamming shut and hobbled old fishermen with weatherized faces were joining in the procession. Albert couldn't recall a turnout like this. Not even when Coach Cadenaso fell off the roof of his house on Fifth Street and broke his neck trying to rotate the antenna so he could pick up a blacked-out Eagles game.

It wasn't just a few dozen people, it was at least a hundred, a hundred fifty. Everyone knew Harlan, sure, but only a few could say they had any relationship with him. This was simple respect, that's what it was. You didn't have to know Harlan well to realize his problems stemmed primarily from the consequences of trying too hard to provide for his family. These were people turning out to say that a man who lived with regret had nothing to be ashamed of in death. They were here, as well, because they knew that whether the casino happened now or not, this was a memorial service for a time and place as much as a funeral for Harlan.

Rickie was weeping as she came up the hill, and Albert took a step toward her as she approached. But she went past him and stood alone under the big oak, near where Albert's mother was buried. He found it odd that she was so broken up about Harlan, but figured her tears might have more to do with her own parents, who were buried farther down the hill.

Albert's father had not worn this gabardine suit since burying Albert's mother. He couldn't button the jacket now, and struggled with the weight of the casket and the heat of the day but plowed ahead as if leading the charge to take the mount. Jack's head was bowed respectfully. They set the casket down next to the grave and the mourners arranged themselves in a half circle on the rise above it, forming an amphitheater, and there was a hushed moment before Father Sal from Saint Peter Martyr in Jersey Landing began the service.

"We stand together here today in solemn observance, but in celebration, as well, of a life lived. We stand together here today as a community of one . . ."

Father Sal was not a minute into it, standing as straight and true as a tabernacle choirmaster against a drape of sea and sky, when the buzz of an approaching airplane forced him to pause, turn, and look skyward along with everyone else. Creed tipped his wings as he passed, trailing a sign that kept his record intact.

HELL NO!!!!
TO CASENO
SO LONG, HARLIN

Rickie came over to have a look at him when it started to break up. She touched the butterfly bandages on his face and he pulled back.

"It looks like the stitches might have come loose," she said, her eyes still wet, and red with exhaustion, too. "You're bleeding."

"I'm fine. Listen, you wouldn't happen to have seen my patrol car out and about, have you?"

"No, why?"

"Because someone stole it, that's why."

"Well what's the big deal? You're leaving anyway."

"I haven't left yet, Rickie. I'm working a murder investigation, and I'm not leaving until the job's done."

Albert's father was talking to Jack ten feet away, telling him to hurry back down to the store, because he was expecting a shipment from one of his suppliers. Albert watched Jack stand over Harlan's gravesite before he left, and then the old man came their way, head down.

"Harlan came to me after he had his trouble with the boat," Joaquin LaRosa said. "He needed a break and asked if I had anything he could do around the store."

"You can't run a charity," Rickie said, seeing his guilt.

"No. I guess not."

They watched Jeanie and the kids head off down the hill. When they got into the hearse, Albert's father turned to him.

"By the way. I called Rag Harbor about my rifle, which that son of a bitch deputy confiscated out at Creed's house. They told me they didn't have it."

"No, Pop. He gave it to me."

"Well I want the flipping thing back. Where is it?"

Where was it? Good question. Albert had left it on his porch. The porch that burned the night someone fired two rounds into the house.

From the ocean side of the casino, the facade of Evolution was a take on the classic sequence of man emerging, first on all fours, then Neanderthaling up through time. The last figure was man pulling the arm of a slot machine. A sad but fairly accurate commentary on human development, to Albert's mind. Any ape could see the odds were better in roulette.

He had now walked all the way up to the Boardwalk museum and back, still feeling like one big zipper but beginning to mend. He was not otherwise in the best of shape, though. Aside from having developed a bleeding ulcer overnight, regarding the apparent plan to demolish Rickie's restaurant, he was blindsided by the news, carried in this morning's *Beacon,* that Price planned to build a three-acre indoor amphitheater and performance pool for dolphins and whales, with a retractable roof for summer months. Not only that, he was going to call his new casino the Polynesian Princess.

Was he kidding?

Albert looked toward the entrance for Price, who was supposed to meet him out here so they could stroll the Boardwalk, take advantage of the weather. He wanted to make it
clear that he didn't care to be part of the dismantling of Harbor Light, and he was beginning to wonder just how far Price
intended to go in clearing space for the project. And as for the
Polynesian Princess, if Price expected Albert to run out there
every time some snot-nosed kid threw cotton candy into the
fish tank, he had another thing coming. It was time to put his
foot down, and to make Price see that if he didn't ease up on
the strong-arm tactics, his supporters in Harbor Light might
reconsider.

Albert was so lost in rehearsing what he intended to say, he
didn't see Price approaching. Suddenly he was on him, ac-
companied by possibly the most attractive female Albert had
seen since he didn't know when. A Rubenesque brunette of
about forty, Mediterranean looking, with the most captivating,
luminous brown eyes.

"Albert, I'd like you to meet Gina Fiorentino, my personnel director."

A flutter rose from Albert's stomach to his chest.

"Pleasure to meet you. I'm half Italian myself."

He thought he must have sounded like a moron, but Price
seemed to get a kick out of it and Gina was still smiling.

"I've heard so much about you," she said. "I just wanted to
introduce myself and say how happy we are to have you aboard.
I'd like to set something up with you in the next couple of days
if you get a chance. We just need to get some paperwork going
for your medical benefits and some of the executive relocation

perks. You can reach me pretty much twenty-four hours at this number."

She handed him a business card. Albert glanced at it and thanked her, and Gina excused herself to swish back toward the casino and into whatever painting she'd come out of. She looked like she should be surrounded by baskets of ripe fruit and lush sea delicacies.

"She seems nice," Albert said dumbly.

"Oh, she's the best. Had kind of a rough time for a while with a divorce, but she's coming out of it nicely. I think you're going to like her a great deal, Albert."

They started north, the sun at their backs, and Albert was thinking about the fact that suddenly, the last thing he wanted to do was sabotage this job. Let's not forget that Rickie had hooked up with someone roughly eight seconds after dumping him.

"It sounded urgent, Albert. Are there developments?"

"Developments? Well that's not exactly why I came. I saw Rickie last night and she told me the restaurant was being condemned. I hadn't heard anything, and I wanted to see what I could do for her if it's true."

"I just got off the phone with her attorney. H. Dewitt Nelson. She's hired the best, I'll give her credit there. This guy's got a terrific reputation, but I don't know if he'll be able to do anything for her, I'm afraid."

"You mean it's a done deal? They're bulldozing her place?"

"As I've explained, I'm not in the business of exercising the right of eminent domain, Albert. That's the prerogative of the state, and they seem to think they need that property as right-of-way. What I've done, entirely voluntarily, I might add, is offer to buy the old Moose Lodge out by the marina and lease that property to Rickie and her aunt at one dollar a year. They'd get paid the value of the restaurant they're in, I'd pick up the tab on the relocation costs, and they'd be back in business at what is arguably a better location and a better space."

Albert groaned inwardly. Price could offer to carve her a diner out of gold bullion and build her a castle to live in next door, and Rickie would tell Price to take a flying leap.

"It's principle with her," Albert said. "There's no way she'll go for it."

"Well they have sued, you know, and they lost. This goes back nearly a year, to when they were first notified and the courts tossed it out. They sued the state, the county, the city, and now they've reintroduced it, adding me as a defendant."

"They were told at the time that there was nothing to worry about," Albert said. "They were told for years that the state had no intention of spending that much money on a bridge, and even if it did, their property wouldn't necessarily be needed for right-of-way. They were suspicious all along, but they figured it was a moot point until this. And now they think you've pulled strings, if I can be blunt about it. I mean, if you want me to keep you posted on how the town is reacting, there are some who think you had a hand in this going back a year or more, when they first got their condemnation notices."

"Your job, if you've forgotten, is not to keep me posted on how the town is reacting or what they think of me. It's to talk sense into the handful of resisters, so they don't get others caught up in their misguided little crusade. Did I not make that clear from day one?"

Keep your cool, Albert told himself. Keep your cool, but don't give in.

"Maybe it's not my place, but I'm asking a favor," he said. "I'm asking that if there's any way to save that property, and if you can use your influence to get it done, I'd appreciate it. It would mean a lot to me personally. But as a practical matter, it's going to benefit you in the long run, too. If that restaurant goes down, you've got trouble you haven't even imagined yet. I can guarantee it."

Albert was stuck at a light on Pacific on the way out of town, in front of a motel with rooms by the hour, when a man in a turban stepped out of the office and trotted over.

"You got a minute?"

Of course he didn't have a minute. He had about a zillion things in his head and work to get to. In fact, he was thinking of blowing this light, but he asked the guy what was up.

"Toilet plugged in number six," he said.

It took Albert a moment to remember what he was driving.

"Do you see this badge right here?" he asked.

The man nodded.

"Do you know a lot of plumbers who wear badges and carry guns?" he asked, and he hit the gas.

Back at the office in Harbor Light, there was no word on his stolen cruiser. No word from Fitch on finding him another car either. He did have a message from Arthur Abraham, though, saying feel free to use the backup Drain Surgeon van as long as you like, no problem.

There was also a message from Frank Sindone, a crime lab pal Albert had given the greeting card that was left on his windshield—*Lie Down With Dogs, Get Up With Fleas.* Albert gave him a call.

"Any luck?"

"Well some of the letters were clipped from magazines, and it's usually easier to pull a print off that kind of glossy paper than newsprint. But this guy must have been using gloves."

Albert ground his teeth.

"But if it's any help, judging by typefaces, it looks like the letters were from *Time* magazine, the *Atlantic City Press,* the *Los Angeles Times, National Geographic,* and *Playboy.*"

The *Los Angeles Times?* Who the hell reads the *Los Angeles Times* in New Jersey? Albert called Georgianna in and asked her to see if she could find the nearest newsstand that sold the *Los Angeles Times,* and he asked her to call L.A., too, and see if she could get anyone to tell her whether they had any subscribers in New Jersey. He spent the next hour behind his desk with a list of the seventeen motorcycle owners who lived in a five-mile radius. Of the seventeen, three had records, but nothing that suggested the profile of a low-rent suburban terrorist. One, Jervis Hatton, DOB 6-12-64, lived in Harbor Light and Albert didn't know him well, but he knew he worked as a bartender in Atlantic City. The prior was possession for sale in Florida. Albert was about to call the casino, find out what Jervis Hatton's schedule was the night of the blast, when he thought of a much better idea. He thought of Gina Fiorentino, and he reached into his shirt pocket and removed her business card. Why the hell not?

He ID'ed himself and a secretary put him through.

"Albert LaRosa. No, the pleasure was mine, believe me. Listen, I wonder if you wouldn't mind telling me who your counterpart is over at the Trop. I'm investigating a murder, as you might know, and I need to ask a few questions of someone who works there."

Gina Fiorentino put the phone down to look for a number. He wasn't going to make the same mistake twice after Oscar Price's receptionist snubbed him. He wasn't going to just out of the blue ask her out and get turned down. He'd go see her in a day or two, fill out these forms she was talking about, and play it kind of cool.

She was back on the phone now, giving him a name and number, and then she said, "Albert, a client just canceled a dinner meeting on me."

"That's too bad," Albert said.

"I'm sorry it's such short notice, but since I've got a hole in my schedule, maybe we can get together."

"Tonight? Oh, you mean tonight tonight? Give me a second here, let me see what I've got on the docket. No you're right, it would be nice to get the paperwork started. I never start any paperwork without opening a bottle of wine, myself. Bear with me now, I'm running a surveillance operation this afternoon, interrogating a suspect at six, briefing the FBI. You know what? I could just blow off the FBI. Sure, I think I can clear a couple of things. Tonight at eight then. Perfect. See you then."

Albert set the phone down, leaned back slowly in his rocker, and threw his feet up on the desk. He reached for a whiff, gave his lighter a flick, and blew a self-satisfied flute of smoke. Business meeting my ass. She was interested. Had to be. The way he leered at her this afternoon on the Boardwalk, she couldn't have had any doubt what was on his mind. Come on. You don't invite a pervert like him to dinner to discuss the pension plan.

Georgianna buzzed him then with a report of a car off the road and into Kip Slough.

"Whereabouts, George?"

"Out near the cannery. It's Rose from the diner, and she says it's bobbing along like a dead sea turtle, headed downriver."

Up Ocean, west on Kip Slough, and what does he see?

"Creed, you mind telling me what the hell is going on?"

Creed looked up from the vacant lot where his house had been. He looked up just long enough to try figuring out what Albert was doing in the Drain Surgeon van. Then he went back to lugging building blocks off his truck and placing them in a square the same dimensions as the foundation of his house.

"Creed!"

"I'm not talking to you, Albert."

"Either you're talking to me or I'm running you in. Technically it's not your property anymore."

"I'm building a house," he said. "I went and found where they dumped the materials, and the same damn house is going back up on the same damn lot. If they knock it down, I'll start over again. I don't care who it is. Oscar Price, Senator Croydon, the governor. I'll outlast every one of them."

Albert just didn't have the patience right now. He hit the gas and the van labored and choked like an emphysemic hog. The whole gang was out in the parking lot at Peg's, standing by the edge of the water looking at something. Aunt Rose, Jack, a dozen fishermen, Drugstore Max Phelps, Rickie, and loverboy, suspenders and all. There was something very sly about this prick. Lawyers didn't do fieldwork. They didn't leave the office except to go to court or to sit with their pals over twenty-dollar lunch entrées.

Albert parked his jalopy and joined them, and here it came. The grille surfaced now and then, the headlights showing like the eyes of a fish. You'd think the car would sink, but it was apparently being kept afloat on the power of the air bags. The car rotated on the wake of a passing boat and the stenciled door surfaced briefly.

SERVICE, PROTECTION, HONOR

"Looks like you got transferred to the marine unit there, Albert. You bring your flippers?"

Albert glared at Aunt Rose. What do you say? You're completely at the mercy of someone who's stealing your car, shooting at you, burning your house, stumping you at every turn, and you pull up in a shithouse buggy to see your girl standing next to her new beau. If there were a line appropriate to the situation, something clever or angry enough, Albert sure as hell didn't know what it might be. He glared at Jack, who held his ground. He didn't glare back, didn't look away. He didn't give up a thing, and he was beginning to really piss Albert off.

"Why aren't you at the hardware store?" Albert asked.

"It was kind of quiet. I came over to help my mom out."

Albert tapped Rickie on the arm and nodded for her to come take a walk. The attorney started to come along, too, and Albert stopped dead and gave him a wicked eye.

"I need to talk to her for a minute about her property, if you don't mind," he said.

"Well I'm her attorney. Who exactly are you?"

Very nice. She hadn't told this jerk a thing about him.

"Who does it look like I am?" Albert asked.

"There's no need for hostility. I frankly don't know if you're the forest ranger or the Roto-Rooter man, but this is my client and if it involves the property, I'm going to hear what it's about."

Rickie excused him with a little push on the chest and walked up toward the diner with Albert.

"What an asshole," Albert said, encouraging a like response that wasn't forthcoming.

"So what is it?" she asked impatiently, and he realized instantly that there'd been a transformation. She was a different woman. Cold, distant. Unbelievable. She'd slept with the guy. He could tell by the way she held herself, arms crossed, like she was fencing herself off from him.

"I gave it my best," he said. "I asked Price to do what he could to save the restaurant, and he's going to give it a shot. Worst case, he moves you just up the street to the Moose Lodge."

He felt horrible just saying it, but if Rickie were judging him, she didn't reveal it. She dismissed him with a thanks and turned to walk away. He couldn't explain her anymore. She was scaring him.

The name sort of rolled off the tongue, didn't it?

Gina Fiorentino.

All you had to do was say those two words and you spoke Italian. It was like a little vacation to the isle of Capri, lunch under an umbrella, the sea and the sun too beautiful for words. Albert got out of the bed, still naked, and walked to the window.

"This is a hell of a view you've got here, Gina Fiorentino."

It was no Mediterranean, but the sun coming up on the cinnamon-colored beach in Atlantic City was a nice enough sight if you pretended you couldn't see the giant eggbeater amusements on the Boardwalk and that damn mall. If you enjoyed blowing things up, the Ocean One shopping center, which was supposed to resemble a docked ship, deserved serious consideration. It looked like the *Love Boat* had run aground and collided with the Gap.

"I can't hear you," Gina called from the bathroom.

He could hear the shower running and thought about darting in there to prove he was younger than she might think.

Yes, he was a shallow boy, his sagging spirits hoisted by the voluptuous pleasures of a woman's body. But what in life is more lasting and profound than that, than the unexplained force of animal attraction? Doesn't the rest of the ride pale in comparison to the mere anticipation of pure physical pleasure?

Things had begun innocently enough at Girasol. Nice Italian dinner to celebrate their ancestral commonality, a bottle of red to toast his new job-to-be. Oscar Price was very impressed with him, Gina Fiorentino gushed, and eager to wing him out to Vegas on the private jet for two or three months of training. Casino security had gone super high-tech, she said, from surveillance of gamblers and employees to the sorting and transport of up to a million dollars a day in take. He'd have to get up to snuff on all of that, but Price considered him a fast learner and a self-starter, two labels Albert had never been assigned previously. The idea that Price was so taken with him came as something of a surprise, considering the fact that since they'd joined hands, Harbor Light had become roughly as stable as a Balkan state. But self-deprecation and near-total failure aside, Gina made him understand that he had an air of vigorous capability and professional verve—the crook's worst enemies— even if he hadn't yet cracked the case. "Sounds to me like you're closing in fast," she said with confidence.

Talking to Gina about the business, about anything, was easy. He asked for a bite of her buffalo mozzarella, and she picked up a piece with her fingers and put it into his mouth. Albert was relatively certain that nice personnel directors didn't do things like that. Then she told him he looked kind of sexy with a zipper under his eye and a starburst of flesh the color of antifreeze. "Battle scars," she called them. That was when he knew, no slowpoke he, that he might be coming off the shelf. He drove her back to her place, this swanky condo tower on the beach, and she asked him up for a drink. It started in the elevator, and they were half naked by the time they reached her door.

He was nearly fifty, and this was the first time in his life he'd slept with a woman on the first spin of the merry-go-round. It was also the first time he'd ripped out stitches during relations, and the first time he'd picked up a date in a plumbing truck. He was going to go with a story about an undercover operation, but something told him he could just be straight with her. Gina Fiorentino. It meant flower, he suspected. Or was it fire?

For days, a loose thought had been floating free at the fringes of Albert's consciousness, just out of reach. On the way back to Harbor Light, he reeled it in. His dreaded annual appearance at Harbor County High School's Career Day. The timing couldn't be worse. He'd planned to spend most of the day snooping into Jack's comings and goings, and find out exactly what kind of trouble he'd gotten into in Philadelphia. Albert would love to blow this thing off, especially the way kids were today. But then he wouldn't be able to face Mrs. Camarera, who had been teaching so long, Albert had her for eleventh-grade English.

Pulling into the lot, Albert flashed on a scene involving Jack several years ago, right here in this very spot. Jack was about fourteen at the time, he'd just lost his grandparents, and he was still adjusting to the cross-country relocation he and Rickie were in the midst of. Bobby Leonard and Damian Reinhardt, among others, took him in. Kids Albert had chased around the island regularly with their beer-soaked pranks and harebrained stunts. Albert could never prove it, but that whole crew, Jack included, had a nice one going for about three months one winter, setting fire to nativity crèches up and down the shore.

The prank Albert had in mind, though, involved Nuba Ludwick. In a flurry of entrepreneurial creativity, Nuba had come up with a role for pure cane sugar in the war against drugs. She printed up hundreds of bumper stickers that said:

SAY NO TO DRUGS
YES TO NUBA'S PIES

Couldn't you just imagine a gang of teens sneaking off to the woods after school to pass around slices of cherry pie? As the town's only law enforcement officer, Albert had no choice but to support the notion of a drug-free planet, so he dutifully pasted one of the bumper stickers to his police cruiser and pretty much forgot about it. Then came a succession of double takes and odd reactions from people as he passed them on the street. People would point and guffaw, and Albert got so ticked off one day, he flipped off a construction crew that was resurfacing Memorial Bridge. He couldn't figure out what was going on until the day he drove out to the high school for a Career Day presentation and saw Jack with a half dozen other delinquents spitting on themselves with laughter as he approached. Walking away from his car, he looked back and finally saw what the big joke was. Jack and his pals had taken an X-Acto knife and edited Nuba's work somewhat, and the town's only cop had been driving around for three days with a bumper sticker that said:

SAY YES TO DRUGS

Yes, the more you thought about it, Jack did have a bit of a streak. He was such a quiet kid, turned in on some interior world, you didn't notice it that much. But it was there. Demons at play just beneath the surface. The thing of it was, he seemed to enjoy getting caught and having Albert threaten a good whipping if he didn't stop hanging out with the class clowns. It was around the time that Albert and Rickie were getting serious.

"Boys and girls, please quiet down. Can you boys in the back two rows please pay attention? Thank you. Before we get started, several of you have not picked up your tickets for the graduation ceremony, so remember to stop by Mr. Danilovich's office before Wednesday. And also, please remember to bring in your money and permission slips for next week's field trip to Ellis Island. Very well. Our next Career Day speaker is Mr. Albert LaRosa, who, as you all know, is the sheriff of Harbor Light, not to mention a former student here and star football player for the Flounder. Let's all give Sheriff LaRosa a hand for taking time out of his busy day to come and tell us about the exciting and challenging life of a law enforcement officer."

Mrs. Camarera was about a hundred and forty-eight, and Albert didn't know how she did it. Out of thirty kids, maybe a half dozen appeared to be in the same time zone as she was. Albert took off his hat and shuffled to the front and center of room 310. In twenty years of doing this, the first two questions had always been the same, and this year was no different. One of the valedictorians in the back of the room wanted to know if Albert had ever shot anyone and then another asked if he'd ever been shot himself.

Albert lied. He said he'd never shot anyone, because he certainly wasn't going to get into it here. Some of these kids already knew plenty about the life of a cop, anyway. He'd chased them around the island the last few years, mostly for drinking and typical teenage carrying-on. He'd arrested one of those two geniuses in the back of the room, he couldn't remember which, for feeding marijuana to Al Smith's goats. One of the goats attacked a group of preschoolers at Al's petting zoo, nipping off a small piece of one child's ear.

"Any more questions, class? This is an extra-credit option for anyone who would like to do a five-hundred-word report on Sheriff LaRosa's visit," Mrs. Camarera prodded after Albert's dissertation on the cop's life seemed to lull the class into an even deeper trance. "There we go. Sheriff, we have a question over by the chalkboard."

Albert looked over to see an athletic-looking girl with a pretty face and a terrific smile. He didn't recognize her, so she was probably from the other side of the Parkway or one of the southern communities that had been carved into the district since the population drain in Harbor Light.

"I was wondering if you could tell me why you became a cop," she said, pen and notebook at the ready. "If there was a particular incident that gave you the idea."

This girl might just be the hope of her generation.

"Are you thinking of going into law enforcement?" Albert asked.

"I was thinking of starting with that and then going into the Secret Service or the FBI."

A few of the kids snickered derisively, and Albert shushed them. He looked again at this sweet little freckle-faced girl waiting on his answer and couldn't imagine her in uniform. But he felt he owed her an honest answer.

"I became a cop because my father didn't want me to. He wanted me to do something else, and I was a stubborn young man who just wanted to do his own thing. I'm not telling you you should do the opposite of what your parents want, especially at your age. But I'd been a lifeguard here in Harbor Light and I think that was probably where the seed was planted. I took it seriously as a lifeguard and then as a cop—the idea that I was in a job where I might be able to help someone in trouble."

The room was quiet until the same girl spoke up.

"Did you ever save someone's life?" she asked.

Albert was back in the house in Philadelphia, crawling across the floor in the dark, bullets flying.

"It's not that easy a thing to do," he said. "But if this is the work you want to do, do it. You look to me like you could save a lot of lives."

Jack's truck wasn't at the diner, so Albert stopped by the hardware store.

"Pop, is Jack around?"

"Well I'm sure he's doing something useful, but it's not here, even though the business is going strong and frankly I could use the help. He said he had to take care of something in Philadelphia and would be back tomorrow to help out."

Maybe it was the community service Jack had told Albert about, or maybe it wasn't. One way or another, the time had come to zero in on Jack. Albert was headed back to his office to call the police department in Philadelphia and get the dope on Jack's run-in with the law when he saw Muldoon's car at Mo's Tavern.

Mo was watching a Brigitte Bardot movie, still chasing the film festival record, and Muldoon was watching Mo, still chasing his fantasies. Mo broke away long enough to draw Albert a draft and Muldoon took him over to a corner table for some privacy.

"Just get off the golf course?" Albert asked.

"I'm four over with three holes to go, and what happens? I shank a six iron into the pond and quadruple-bogey sixteen," Muldoon said with the drama of someone who's just been burglarized. For years, he'd spoken to Albert as if he were a golfer and might have genuine compassion for these collapses Muldoon suffered every time out.

"Sixteen is a killer," Albert said, not knowing sixteen from nine. He actually loved to golf, but only at driving ranges. They put a big basket of balls in front of you and you could chop away like a banshee, get a few problems off your chest, and never think twice about where the thing might land. That was the way to go. "What were you doing on the golf course, anyway? Bargain Acres decide they couldn't afford you? I haven't seen you around for a couple of days."

"Yeah, actually. The pricks. We're kind of on standby if something else happens, but other than that they're counting on the FBI to do the job for free."

He said this with a thinly veiled lack of faith.

"I had a couple of agents come around to tell me I needed a hall pass to leave my office."

"Yeah, Mutt and Jeff. I just bumped into them at Peg's."

"They know who you are, don't they?"

"They might, I don't know. I was already gone when they moved into the Philadelphia office. A couple of putzes. I don't think either one of these guys could find his ass with both hands, what I hear."

"What do you hear, exactly?"

"Between you and me? The one guy is all over Ianicci and that crowd, working the angle pretty hard. A waste of time if you ask me."

"There's nothing there," Albert said. "I checked the wiseguy angle myself, and it's clean."

"Well the other goofball is still knocking around here in town. What my guy told me, they talked to Creed yesterday and they're looking for Jack now. Jack Davenport."

It wasn't a surprise, but Albert felt a shiver anyway.

"They got anything you know of?"

Muldoon shook his head dismissively.

"These guys? They don't have a lot of friends in that field office. Both of them think they're going to run the entire department in five years, you know the type. They came up together six weeks ago and already bumped someone off this job, so they've got a little juice in Washington. Probably polished the boss's shoes down there. But as far as experience, they're kids."

Albert had heard enough. He was not going to leave law enforcement getting beat on his own turf.

"Just so you know, I was defending you at the diner," Muldoon said. "Someone had unkind things to say and I tried straightening her out."

"Aunt Rose? Ever since the breakup with Rickie, she's been busting me a little bit."

"No, Rickie. The state left a condemnation notice on the front door of the diner and she ripped it off, balled it up, and set fire to it. I told her you might be able to help out, since you've got a line to Oscar Price, and she flipped out on me."

"What do you mean she flipped out?"

"You know, kind of slammed my food down on the table. Said she didn't need anyone's help fending for herself. I told her I've known you twenty-five years, which is four times as long as she has, and you've always held yourself with dignity."

"I'm sure she was impressed."

"She still seeing this asshole I saw her with in Cape May?"

"Far as I know," Albert said, a little less broken up about it now that he'd gone through orientation with Gina Fiorentino.

"Well she said you can judge a person by the company they keep. Lie down with dogs, get up with fleas."

Albert nearly swallowed his tongue. That's the greeting that was left on his windshield the night someone dropped by to fire a couple of rounds through his bedroom.

"That what she said?"

"She's got on her battle face, Albert."

"Those were her words, or yours? Lie down with dogs."

"I quote verbatim, pal. Lie down with dogs, get up with fleas."

Muldoon saw the color drain from Albert's face. "Jeez," he said. "You don't have to take it to heart."

Yes he did. If Rickie were involved in this somehow, how could he not take it to heart? If Rickie were involved, how could he begin to make sense of the last seven years of his life?

"Lie down with dogs, get up with fleas" was not a phrase Albert had heard Rickie toss around. But it sure sounded like her.

You go to bed with a person, wake up with her, drink wine with her, explore every square inch of her flesh, know where she left her glasses, memorize her smile and fear her wrath, find out there are no fewer than a dozen hair care products that must be balanced on the rim of the bathtub at all times in the war against split ends, but what do you really know? Nothing. That's the answer. You don't know a thing, because whatever it was that shaped her happened in another time. It happened in another place, too. The '60s didn't come to the south Jersey shore. Missed it altogether. That was one of the things Albert found intriguing about Rickie. It was like having a foreign exchange student in town. She read Burroughs, Ginsberg, and Kerouac when he was reading the Ocean City High 4–3–4 defense. She knew things about the other world and she went out to discover more, and he would have chased after her if he weren't so certain she'd find him pathetic and send him home on a Greyhound. He was in love with her all the more after she left, and certain there was never a chance for them, particularly since he'd never had the courage to express his feelings while she was still around. He imagined her running through clouds of tear gas in San Francisco and Berkeley, and where was he? In Philadelphia. A cop. He'd gone the other way all the way, maybe to spare himself the torture of thinking he could ever be with her.

What did she say when he picked her and Jack up in the police cruiser for her parents' funeral? She said she'd always respected the way he helped out at his parents' hardware store even as she refused to work in her parents' diner. She was even more stunning, having grown into her looks. Her hair, her face, those green knowing eyes filled with the pain of having lost her parents before making the apologies she thought she owed them. He told her they were proud of her independence, they'd told him so on a dozen occasions when he went into the diner to ask about her. He confessed he had read the books she had read, trying to find out something about her world of differentness. And she made him feel okay, sort of cool, even, by saying that sometimes there's no greater conformity than non-conformity for its own sake. And he felt even better when she said she was glad to be home.

Now, was this someone who could be involved in the local crime of the century? No, it was a thoughtful, passionate, rational person, albeit one capable of the occasional meltdown, complete with flying saucepans and other selected cookware. But Albert, sitting in the privacy of his office with the door locked and an order that Georgianna not buzz him with any calls under any circumstances, was jotting down a list of the things he couldn't explain away.

She had a short fuse.

She had as good a motive as anyone.

She wept nearly as much as Harlan's wife at his funeral.

She'd asked Albert what he would do if she told him she were the one.

She subscribed to *Time* magazine at the restaurant and *National Geographic* at home. Unless there was something about her he didn't know, she didn't read *Playboy,* but that didn't prove anything.

It was all fairly incriminating, but still, there were things about it that didn't add up. She wouldn't have shot a hole in his front door and set the porch on fire. He wasn't that big of an asshole, and neither was she. He couldn't imagine her sitting down to cut letters out of newspapers and magazines either. Psycho stuff. And it was a man who had called Price and Bargain Acres to say "Listen to me with both ears."

If Rickie was involved, it was to cover for Jack. Albert couldn't see it any other way. Or didn't want to. He began working the phone and got hold of a detective who'd been in the Humboldt County Sheriff's Department going back twenty-five years. Rickie was still talked about, he said, for having run naked through that wetlands hearing, and the photos of her arrest were passed around now and then on slow days. Beyond that, she'd been arrested once for possession of marijuana, but that was it.

On Whidbey Island, where Rickie had spent five years before moving back home when her parents died, he found an old-timer in the Island County sheriff's office. Rickie hadn't registered on their radar screen, but there was one Davenport whose name came up. A juvenile.

"Jack?"

"Bingo. Jack Davenport, 10-16-80. Let's see what the computer tells us. Okay, it's coming up now. Let me double-check the code on this. Grand theft auto is what it says, but that doesn't tell you anything, does it?"

More than he knew.

"We just computerized our files. If you can hold on a second, I'll see if I can call up the details."

Albert flicked his lighter and watched the flame dance and shimmy. He'd like to set a few fires himself right about now. Maybe he'd start with this miserable shack, and the van he was driving would be next on the list. With the right breeze, maybe the whole island would go up in flames and he could just walk away from the whole thing.

As a cop, you dream about being in the right place at the right time, getting a shot at a terrific case. A real whodunit complete with gunfire, all sorts of things exploding, a body washing ashore. But you never dream that when you finally get your case, all your suspects will be in the photo album of your life. What, exactly, was Albert supposed to do if he were to find out that Rickie or Jack had a piece of this? Cover for them? Arrest them? And what if the FBI got to them before he did? There wouldn't be a choice if that were the case, and this was murder. Regardless of intent, it was murder.

"Looks like the boy and a couple of his pals decided it might be fun to take the principal's car on a joyride," the Island County deputy said. "There's a note here on a possible attempted arson. One of the kids had a gallon of gasoline and some matches with him, but no charges. First offenses all around, all three boys released to their parents."

There was only one thing to do. Albert went across the street for a beer and bitched to Mo about the general state of the known universe, and even more about the unknown.

"Allow me to make an observation," Mo said, and she had the look she got when she was more fortune-teller than bartender. "The casino, the new job, the murder mystery, that's all bullshit, Albert. None of that is what's got you so turned around you don't know up from down.

"Oh pray tell, Madame. What is it that's got me spinning?"

"Not a chance. The minute you solve your problems, I lose my best customer."

Albert was rousted out of bed by dispatch, and before he had his pants on, Fitch Caster was ringing.

"It's the Parkway again. Bargain Acres is lit up and the Taco Bell is set to go next if they can't contain it. Do you realize I'm up for reelection here, Albert?"

"This is getting ridiculous. What can you tell me? Anything?"

"Yeah. I can tell you this one's big enough that a Delta Air Lines pilot reported it from his cockpit. I can tell you I've got a fuckin' security guard calling me Boss Hog and coming after my job because of all this business in Harbor Light. Now get your ass out there and find me something I can use at a press conference in the morning. If I have to come up with one more way to conceal the fact that we don't know anything, someone's going to realize we *don't* know anything."

The Drain Surgeon II, possibly the first vehicle off the assembly line after they got rid of the horses, wouldn't start. Albert grabbed a pipe wrench off the floor and banged the dash in frustration. How in hell was he supposed to save the boss's career driving this toolbox on wheels? Albert hopped out to push the van and ripped his pants, not to mention an interior abdominal wall that seemed to be located in a delicate area. He got rolling and hopped in to pop the clutch, which nearly tossed him through the windshield. But she was spitting fire now, blowing smoke and lurching into the night to serve and protect. It felt like a hernia, for sure.

He'd love to take a run past Rickie's and then past his father's place to see if Jack's truck was around and if, by chance, the engine was warm. But on a night as dark as the bottom of the ocean, the western sky was aglow and there was no time to waste. He chugged over Memorial Bridge, wondering if he'd get back on his new boat again this calendar year, and hammered toward the Parkway.

He was a night owl, Albert's mark. Loved tripping around out here half blind, slipping a hand under a blanket of fog or sneaking up on the dark to strike a match. He was in character tonight, punching in between three and four, no consideration whatever for Albert's sleeping or drinking schedule. It wasn't bad work, really. Come late and leave early, miss the rush hour traffic, no job too big or small. But did it pay?

Three or four years ago, a high school kid in Somers Point had gotten caught up in one of these direct action environmental–animal rights groups that was out to save the world from fur coats and disposable razors. He and his buddies did courageous things like set animals free from pet stores and throw paint on women in minks. It was kind of a half-assed operation, nothing like the kids who'd gone in for the likes of blowing up ski lodges in Colorado and calling the developers environmental terrorists. But there was a warrant out on this kid and Albert picked him up in Harbor Light. Caught him pouring sugar into the tanks of Wave Runners, and he had a

whole spiel about noise and water pollution and the comman-
deering of regulatory agencies by Gucci-shoed lobbyists. It
was like arresting Ralph Nader's punk kid, and this son of a
bitch flapped his gums all the way to Rag Harbor. Albert
stopped for a burger along the way and Gabby gave him a
twenty-minute lecture on the rainforest. Just yesterday Albert
had flashed on the kid as a possible suspect in the recent mad-
ness and mayhem. But the crazy bastard was up at Boston University, a graduate student in the business school, the little
hypocrite. Another dead end for Albert. His specialty of late.

He hit the end of the back bay and rode the rise up over the
Parkway, and when he got to the top, the fire leaped into view
with the full blinding force of the sun. Good god, it was an inferno, an enormous red rage. Albert felt the nuclear heat from a
distance of three hundred yards. Was it peeling the paint right
off the hood of this old crate?

Not since the *Hindenburg* went down a few paces to the
north had the sky been lit like this in Jersey. Bargain Acres
was fully involved, and this model of the modern American
marketplace was in danger of going up if they didn't contain
this thing. The Taco Bell was already cooking, and Gizmo, the
electronics superstore, was lit like the Fourth of July, big-screen
televisions exploding and digital contraptions launching foun-
tains of spark and acrid yellow clouds. A half dozen fire companies moved in blessed choreography, their hoses worming
across the puddled tarmac, and more crews were wailing off
the Parkway from Atlantic City, Hammonton, Vineland, Cape
May, Ocean City, and Stone Harbor. Three brave crews took
up a position near the gondola ride at Mama Parm's Macaronium, trying to contain the northerly advance of destruction. If

the wind kept up and the blaze jumped Tortilla Gulch, its thatched Yucatán roof an invitation to disaster, Starbucks was going to be Charbucks.

Albert drove the vast acres of heat-softened blacktop in search of Lieutenant Bob Alvin from Company Twenty-eight in Jersey Landing, which would have drawn the first alarm. A little too much chaos out here to find anyone right now, so Albert was left to scan the lot for unofficial vehicles or anything else that might provide a clue. The question a detective has to ask is, Who benefits? If this whole strip was lost, and the rebuilding of it took months if not longer, who profited?

The building trades, first and foremost, and construction had slowed to nearly a stop now that virtually every square inch of south Jersey shoreline was covered by motels, condos, strip malls, and restaurants. Unless they started building on the fairways of miniature golf courses, there was nothing left. The trade unions were worth checking into, especially since they were still tied to what was left of the mob. Who else benefited? The wheezing Main Streets that clung to life, their quaint lampposts burning low from Harbor Light to Cape May. The little apple pie throwback operations whose survival depended on the luck of the summer weather and a steady clip of pasty city folk to roll in and butter up for the beach rotisserie. Albert's father would be in his glory when the sun came up on Harbor Light. He used to sell televisions, radios, and a fair amount of electronic gadgetry until Gizmo snapped up all of that trade, and sporting goods used to be a substantial part of his inventory—he was the chief supplier of gloves, ball bats, and baseballs, and he ordered the T-shirts and sponsored a couple of Little League and soccer teams—until Summit swooped in like the Concorde, scattering the pigeons.

But if this was arson instead of, say, a short circuit in one of the eight million electronic devices plugged in at Gizmo, and if indeed this was the same hell-bent character who'd been wreaking havoc in Harbor Light proper, it struck Albert as a political statement as much as an economic play. He was reminded again of his blabbermouth collar with the rain forest lectures and the developers-as-terrorists rap. And he thought of Jack.

The most frustrating part of it was that they fished together regularly, and Albert had always maintained that you could learn everything there was to know about a person by how he fished. The type that had to fill every pause, every blissful moment of silence, you knew these people were uncomfortable in their own skin and were to be avoided at all costs. Then there was the type that had to talk to the fish, an actual conversation to lure them into the boat. You wanted to accommodate them somehow, wait till they were lost in witty repartee with Flipper, and then cut hard to the starboard side and hope for a clean ejection. The worst ones, though, the absolute worst, were the wanna-be poets who blathered about a truce with nature and the glory of fishing as a spiritual journey back to the origin of man. Give me a fucking break.

But Jack was good. He was a capable fisherman and he was invisible. He fished like he had nowhere to go, nowhere else he wanted to be. He understood it had to be that way, and that you didn't share every personal thought that bubbled up. Especially if those thoughts involved blowing up cars and bridges and setting fire to everything that threatened your quaint small-town existence.

Albert stopped out near Tortilla Gulch, the blaze a spectacular reflection on the flooded lot, and saw the shimmering illusion of his relationship with Jack. He had always seen only what he wanted to see in him. He had picked the aspects of Jack's personality most like his own, and assigned him an identity constructed solely of those things. Albert felt he had failed Jack as a friend and a mentor, and he felt afraid over the capabilities of the boy he didn't know. It might be too late to protect him now.

Lieutenant Bob Alvin came into the picture, helmeted and yellow-jacketed. He was on a two-way in the middle of the action out front of Tortilla Gulch, where it appeared the fajitas were about to sizzle like never before. You couldn't get decent Mexican around here unless you kidnapped a family of mushroom pickers and forced them to cook for you, but Albert stopped by the Gulch now and then for happy hour because they knocked a buck off a draft and threw a bean burrito and a couple of tamales out there gratis. Say good-bye to that. Mama Parm's was gone now and the Gulch was about to go up like a piñata. Alvin turned to see a hook and ladder company coming in from the Parkway and Albert caught his attention then.

"Give me a jacket and helmet and I'll pick up a hose," Albert offered.

"I've got more bodies than I can handle as it is. Look at this army out here. Have you ever seen a cookout like this in your life?"

The fire hissed and dazzled, feasting on its meal of architectural high crime. It rolled across a long line of rooftops like a great tsunami, crested and crashed, sending showers of cinder into the heavens. Albert watched in amazement as firefighters soldiered into the furnace. Windows exploded up and down the strip.

"The job's suddenly a hell of a lot more interesting with a sicko on the loose," Alvin said.

"A torch job for sure?"

"Hard to say, actually. It looks like it started small, probably at the rear of the store."

"Bargain Acres?"

"Yeah. The southwest corner."

Southwest? The hardware department.

"You sure?"

"We had a couple of men out back and that's what it looked like to them. We would have contained it if not for this freakin' wind. It really started gusting after we got here, and we didn't have a chance."

Albert saw a volunteer company out of Sea Isle take up a position in front of Starbucks and aim a stream onto the roof of Tortilla Gulch, but the fake thatched lid seemed to shed water like a duck.

"How many volunteer companies you got out here, Bob?"

"Two, but my guys know them pretty well if you're thinking the torch was either a bored volunteer or one of those perverts who goes home and whacks off."

"Everyone a suspect, Bob. You know the routine. Any witnesses at all?"

"We had one kid who was mopping the floor at Taco Bell. He smelled the smoke, came outside, and thinks he saw a car at the exit over there, but that's about two hundred yards away at three in the morning."

"No color or model?"

"Possibly an SUV, light color. Oh shit, there goes the Gulch."

The entire restaurant went up at once with a great *whooosh!* Albert was rocked back on his heels, the heat enveloping him. If it was an arsonist, he thought, he had balls. You had to give him that.

Joaquin LaRosa, who lived in the Dark Ages, was very comfortable there. He would never own an answering machine or digital watch, and was never late to open the store. He kept a pair of shoes until they wore through and then had the soles replaced, he made coffee in a percolator with a paper napkin as a filter, and he reused the grinds. Sometimes twice. And so it was no surprise that when Jack Davenport moved into Albert's old bedroom, Joaquin laid down the law with Aunt Rose. There would be no sleep-overs when Jack was home. Kids today had no self-control or sense of discretion, and there was no surprise as to the reason. A complete breakdown in parental discretion. Joaquin LaRosa realized he could not save the world alone, although there were days when he considered giving it a shot, but he would not, despite seventy-year-old urges that had neither waned nor gone wanting, be a role model for moral decay.

Aunt Rose fought this with all her might, a force as great as the summer storms that gathered off the coast and blew out windows every now and then. She respected Joaquin's old-world ways, but this was too much. She was a healthy, vibrant, frisky woman, she argued, frequently hit upon at the diner, and she would not be taken for granted. They had actually split up over this issue, finally working out a compromise in which Joaquin went to Addie's Jewel Box and bought her a diamond ring the size of a golf ball.

With Jack gone to see his girl in Philadelphia, Aunt Rose had spent the night, arisen early, and walked to the diner, as was her custom. But she was on her way back now to tell Joaquin the news. To her surprise, he wasn't there. In pink uniform and white monkey hat, Aunt Rose half ran and half walked over to the hardware store, and there he was.

"Joaquin, the maniac struck again. Burned the whole fuckin' mall out there on the Parkway," she said.

Joaquin LaRosa might have married her by now if not for the language problem. He would never get used to a woman cussing like a sailor, and he constantly scolded her over it.

"I know all about it. What do you think I'm doing here so early?" he asked, putting the final touches on a new sandwich board he was planning to set atop the blue station wagon parked in front of LaRosa's Hardware. The sign read:

FIRE SALE
10% OFF EVERYTHING

"Does that hit the mark?" he asked, a look of absolute evil in his eye.

Aunt Rose was carrying a bag with Joaquin's bacon and egg sandwich, same breakfast every day without fail, plenty of salt and pepper. He thanked her and gave her a peck on the cheek.

Of course it hit the mark, he said, happily answering his own question. It was pointed, but not insensitive. You couldn't revel in someone else's misfortunes. Not publicly, anyway. But if you were in business, you had to take what was given you and then some.

"That's gotta be months before they rebuild," Aunt Rose said.

"I'm up twenty percent since the first fire out there," Joaquin said. "This thing took out Gizmo and Summit both. I've gotta order a whole new inventory. I'm back in the electronics and sporting goods business, Rose."

"You think that bomber's through?"

Aunt Rose had secretly suspected that Joaquin was the mystery man the entire island was waiting to identify. The very possibility had, in fact, made her even friskier than usual. Harlan Wayans's death was a great pity, but she accepted that Joaquin had made an honest mistake. "I heard you get up in the middle of the night, Joaquin. What time did you get back to bed?"

"I don't know what the hell it was, Rose. Maybe four o'clock? That damned heartburn."

"Heartburn my ass," Aunt Rose said, surprising herself. She just couldn't hold back any longer. "It's you, isn't it, Joaquin?"

"I'll never tell," Joaquin LaRosa said. "Especially not with this traitor coming up the street."

Albert wanted to know more before talking to Rickie. She'd just deflect, anyway. If she thought Jack was the one, she'd cover by pointing a finger at herself again, like she already had, because what was he going to do, arrest her? He had given this a lot of thought, of course. Lots of corn mash had been invested in the project. Albert had a blunt going at all times, went to bed with one and woke up with one, and dropped hot ash everywhere without knowing he even had one going. He'd burned so many cinder points into his three uniforms it looked like he'd been hit with bird pellet, and in this van, with its shorting electrical system and the noxious fumes on those crap-clearing snakes that whipped around back there on the ribbed metal flooring, he was lucky he hadn't self-immolated.

This meditation, which did not stop with sleep, had delivered him to the conclusion that Rickie could not have participated in or endorsed any of this. Above all else, she was brutally honest, contemptuous of the deceit of others—with particular rancor for pretense of any variety—and more than happy to take ownership of her thoughts and actions. In this particular case, though, Albert suspected she was as afraid of the truth as he was. Would she have confronted Jack by now? No question. She would have taken him for a walk on the beach. She would have told him how much she loved him. How aware she was that she had not made his life particularly easy, having condemned as human waste the very man whose genes Jack carried. And then she would have asked him point-blank. And Jack, of course, would have denied everything. But that wasn't the point. Rickie would know by his answer, regardless of what he said. And then, of course, she had a job to do. She had to protect her only child. Albert had a job to do, too.

Jack didn't drive an SUV, but he drove a white pickup. It wouldn't be long before those two nimrods from the FBI got hold of the Taco Bell mop boy's statement and began feeding suspect names into a computer, matching them against vehicles. Whether they were quick enough to draw a connection, who knew? But they weren't complete goldbrickers, even if it did take two of them to do a job Albert was handling solo. They were smart enough to keep an eye on him, weren't they? He was almost certain he had a tail on him leaving the Parkway. You had to love that idea. Federal agents following Sheriff Podunk around in his neighbor's plumbing truck, hoping he'd lead them out of the dark. Albert was just praying that a tidbit he picked up from Muldoon proved to be inconsequential. Muldoon said he heard Mutt and Jeff might have caught a break from their crime lab, which had produced a lead or two on possible sources of the material that blew the bridge.

Albert checked all over town, drove up and down practically every street on the island. No sign of Jack's truck. He stopped by his father's store to see if he could dig up any information and found the old man and Aunt Rose carrying on as if they'd hit the Pick 6. Drugstore Max Phelps was up on a ladder outside his place, tightening the Harbor Light Pride banner that spanned Cannery Way between the drugstore and Mario's Barbershop. Nuba Ludwick was zigzagging around with a broomstick, reaching up to free the plastic flags that had gotten themselves all wound up. Not a minute lost here. Three firefighters were in the hospital for smoke inhalation, the damage was estimated in the millions, and it was Mardi Gras on Cannery Way. Albert's father was on a mission to find out where you went for one of those giant kliegs that shot a cone of light into the sky to promote a major event, such as the grand reopening of a fifty-year-old Main Street, and Aunt Rose said they were using lasers for that sort of thing now.

Albert managed to get a phone number for Jack's girlfriend in Philadelphia and he was headed there now. He spun off the

Atlantic City Expressway twice and then looped back on, making sure he wasn't being followed. That was all he needed. Lead the FBI straight to Jack.

The cityscape shot up hard as he approached the tolls on the Ben Franklin Bridge in Camden, great silver columns towering above the sun-dappled Delaware River. Albert would have definitely stayed—he lived here at the same age Jack was now—if not for the way it all turned sour. Young cop strapping on a holster every night and piloting through Oz, as the wiped-out postindustrial Badlands of North Philadelphia were known. He had gone to work every day thinking he could make a difference, no matter what anybody said. Gangs, drugs, abandoned houses collapsing on themselves. It didn't matter. He was there to save the world. Albert had a little old lady at Third and Indiana he used to check in with after lineup every day. Notorious drug corner. She'd tell him everything he needed to know. What crew chief was working the shift, who was standing lookout, who was carrying, what car or boarded-up house the stash was kept in.

He'd ride in like a cowboy, adrenaline pumping like hot oil, and sweep the corner. Sometimes all it did was push the gang up to Fourth and Cambria, but he had help. He'd put in a call to Sister Carol and she'd have her crew out there inside of half an hour, a dozen people, two dozen, planting themselves on that corner, pulling up lawn chairs, bringing out barbecues, holding prayer vigils, selling lemonade where moments earlier cocaine and marijuana were being peddled. Willing to fight for that corner even if it meant risking their lives. It wasn't uncommon for Albert to arrest a half dozen little gangsters out there, pluck them off the corner like it was weed abatement, and have them back on the street before he started his next shift. A year or so of that and yes, he was jaded, angry, maybe a little less fearless, too, though he wouldn't have admitted it then. That little old lady at Third and Indiana would pull back the curtain just enough to let Albert know she was there. A smile from her as she watched her grandchildren walk home from school on a clean corner was all he needed to keep him going. Back then, he went to church on Sundays with a couple other officers. They thought they were doing the Lord's work.

Albert popped over the bridge and pulled into the Roundhouse. He still had a guy in records, and he went inside to see if he could find him. He was winding around one of those long looping corridors when a familiar voice called out from behind.

"Is that one artificial hip or two? You used to have a little more bounce in your step."

"Scullion. I thought you'd be tending bar in Ireland by now."

"Give me another couple of years," said Patrick Scullion, who worked patrol in the Twenty-fourth when Albert was up there.

"You finally made lieutenant, huh?"

"They've got me in homicide. Come on back and join us, Albert. We're down three hundred positions and they're so desperate they're starting to go outside. You could start at sergeant here."

"Let me know when they start looking for captains."

About ten years ago, during one of the quietest stretches in the history of crime-fighting, Albert flirted with the idea of making a return to Philadelphia. But then he had another drink and came to his senses. He left for reasons that hadn't changed. Hadn't and wouldn't.

Jim Leonard in records pulled up the reports on Jack, and Albert held his breath while he looked over his shoulder. You wouldn't call it a smoking gun, exactly. Jack had not overpowered guards at the old Philadelphia Naval Yard and walked away with blasting caps and torpedoes to try out on his favorite targets in Harbor Light. But the file painted a picture of a young man considerably less innocent, and much more politically agitated, than Albert would have dreamed. Jack had been a busy boy the last two years. He'd been arrested for protests over a defense contract for General Electric, a sneaker contract with the athletic department at Temple University, and a plan to build a Disney amusement park of some type at Penn's Landing on the Delaware. In the last one, Jack and two comrades released five hundred laboratory mice into the chambers of the Philadelphia City Council president who had proposed demolishing the Port of History Museum to make way for a Mickey Mouse venue. The mice had been stolen from a medical research center at the University of Pennsylvania, where they were being fed a synthetic fat substitute for a burger about to be test-marketed by a national fast-food chain.

Albert ran a cross-check of the phone number his father had given him and came up with an apartment in the Powelton Village section of University City, another bad sign. Powelton was swarming with Trotskyites when Albert lived in the city.

It was the bottom left unit of a two-story brick fourplex on Thirty-eighth near Lancaster, not far from Drexel University. She answered the door with a bag over her shoulder, on her way out. Petite, brunette, way too good-looking for Jack to be spending time in Harbor Light. Albert tried talking his way in, the curiosity burning a hole in the lining of his stomach. Wondering what revolutionary paraphernalia he might find inside.

"You're his father," she said. "He's told me a lot about you."

It threw him. Albert started to correct her and then stopped himself. Jack called him his father? How long had that been going on? And did he really feel that way? Albert was flattered, confused, and angry all at once. It'd be one thing if he'd come here to watch Jack graduate with honors from Drexel and found out Jack had thought of him as a father. Unfortunately, these were not circumstances to make a parent proud. It was like going to the hospital to see your bouncing baby boy and finding out he'd set fire to the birthing center.

Laura, her name was. She said Jack had already left for Harbor Light and she was on her way to a law class at Temple.

"I just came to town to visit a mutual acquaintance and thought I might take him to lunch if he was around. I should have called last night," he said, laying a net. He couldn't read whether Laura saw that that's what it was.

"Yeah," she said. "We were here all night."

Was she covering? Did she even know?

"Where'd you say the two of you met?"

"At a march down at Penn's Landing. They were going to bulldoze a couple of small businesses to clear the way for that Disney project. Jack, me, and this guy Dave Rudnick all got arrested."

"Dave Rudnick?"

"Yeah. A friend of Jack's."

"Where's he from?"

"From here. Across the river, actually, in Gloucester. He usually comes over when Jack's here, or if we go to a march."

Laura checked her watch.

"So you're going to become a lawyer?" Albert asked.

"I thought Jack told you. I did an internship in the law office that handles Oscar Price and Senator Croydon. The office has been working on that bill about casino gambling in the district. Believe me, I did everything I could to sabotage it. I mean, to slow it down—but now that Croydon has introduced it, there's not much I can do. He's such a creep. Six south Jersey politicians go to jail for bid-rigging construction contracts on his projects, and he's just an unindicted coconspirator."

"It's a crime."

"Look, I know you'll do everything you can. Jack's got confidence in you. He said you were taking the job with Price to derail this thing from the inside."

"That what he told you?"

She said good-bye at the sidewalk and Albert went across to a convenience store for a cup of coffee. He'd give it ten or fifteen minutes, make sure she was gone, and then find a way inside the house.

The plan changed, though—everything changed—when he picked up the pay phone to check in with Georgianna. She was hysterical, and it took Albert half a minute before he could understand a word she was saying.

He finally managed to stop her blubbering, and she told him to get back to town as quickly as he could. His father had just left the hardware store in an ambulance.

Joaquin LaRosa had soldiered through a day or two of pain in his shoulder and a little bit of heartburn. Typically, he had done nothing about it. And then he was coming up the stairs from the basement with a five-pound sack of bird seed and a ten-pound bag of plant food for Mrs. Costanza when he had to stop halfway to catch his breath. At the top of the stairs, he dropped the bags and stumbled forward a few steps before falling face-first in the middle of the largest group of customers he'd seen in fifteen years.

Nuba Ludwick came running from across the street and pounded on his chest. A great debate ensued as to whether the force and weight of Nuba's considerable fist, which was the approximate size of a small picnic ham, was the appropriate treatment for an apparent heart attack victim. But whether from the medical benefits or the sheer terror of the pounding, Joaquin LaRosa responded by regaining consciousness. He was in good enough shape to argue with the paramedics, insisting that he'd be fine once he pulled himself together with a glass of water and a five-minute siesta. He couldn't walk out in the middle of a retail bonanza the likes of which he'd only dreamed about.

The doctor called it a moderate heart attack. Not only was the old man going to live, but he had now lectured his Harbor County Medical Center doctor and a half dozen nurses on the evils of a managed care system that cuts corners at every turn while insurance company executives walk home with six-million-dollar bonuses.

"For the sake of myself and the entire hospital staff, I'm going to do my best to get him out of here as soon as I can," Dr. Mark Morocco told Albert, rolling his eyes. "But your father is lucky to have gotten a warning instead of a death certificate. He's going to have to work less and eat differently, and some-one's going to have to convince him that he's not forty years old."

Sam got to the hospital at about seven o'clock and went con-siderably beyond the requisite amount of crying, worrying, and lecturing. Between the two of them, his sister and his fa-ther, Albert longed to round up the poor suffering nurses, sneak out the back door, and open a tab at Mo's. It did get to you, though. You saw the poor bastard flat on his back, white-faced and tended to, a drip going, heart monitor beeping, and you couldn't help but feel that even if he had been a bastard at times, you'd matched him every step of the way if not done him one better. This was perfect, though, wasn't it? First he makes you feel like the underachiever of the century, and then, practically on his deathbed, he makes you feel guilty for having been ticked off at him about it. Both ways, he got you.

They stayed until they were kicked out, outlasting Aunt Rose, who had brought him his favorite, a peach milk shake. The new diet would have to begin another day. Sam blubbered again when they left and Albert kissed his father on the fore-head, which surprised both his father and himself.

"Here's your chance," the old man said, winking. "That casino's a dead duck anyway. Come work at the store where you belong and we'll change the name in the window."

Albert was touched, but he wasn't stupid.

"If you and I worked together at that store, Pop, I'd be the one in that bed. Get some sleep, will you?"

Albert stopped in Somers Point for Chinese takeout and a bottle of wine and he met Sam back at their father's place on Third. She had showered and came down the stairs towel-ing her hair. She followed him into the kitchen and said she planned to stay at least a few days.

"Just until I'm sure he's fine," she said with a crack in her voice.

"He's going to be okay," Albert reassured.

The qualities that had driven them both batty and even driven them from each other at times—their father's gasbag sermonizing and his red-faced energy for every subject from the Ming dynasty to the price of bananas—seemed almost en-dearing when laid against the specter of death. Sam began to cry, her strength finally cracking, and Albert went over to give her a hug. "We've got to get him out of the store," she sobbed. "He can't handle it at his age. Especially not with all these shoppers coming back downtown because of the fire."

"Forget it. He's leaving that store in an ambulance or a hearse, that's it. He's been waiting twenty years for this kind of action on Cannery."

"Lifting sacks of manure, unloading the delivery trucks, worrying about the books month to month. It's insane."

She set up across from him at the chrome and Formica dinette. Without even thinking about it, they took the same places they had always taken as kids. How many hundreds of meals did the family have together in this room? Enough that she could still see her mother cooking at the gas range that had been there since the house was built, still smell the lasagna and the paella and the egg-and-potato tortilla pie. Albert's mother left the store early enough to get things ready, the store closed promptly at six o'clock, his father got home at exactly six-ten, and dinner was served at six-thirty, give or take a minute or two. But despite the war-camp scheduling, dinner at home was the most relaxed time in the LaRosa day. With good food in him the old man showed a generally less psychotic side. He wanted to hear all about what they were studying in school, he called their mother the best cook in the universe, and he always ordered Mom out of the kitchen after dinner while he and the kids cleaned up. Dinner was where he redeemed himself, admitting without ever saying so that his daily bluster was part performance, and that while they might occasionally fear him, they should always, always trust him.

"That's his life, Sam. The store. What else is he going to do, elope with Aunt Rose? Retire to Florida? Here, let me pour you a glass of wine and you'll come to your senses. Can you see the two of them in Palm Beach at a condo association meeting? Two weeks, and they'd kill someone with a shuffle-board stick."

"Maybe we could get Dr. Morocco to work on him."

She didn't get it. Heart attack or no, he was working. Casino or no, he was working. Oscar Price could throw up a dozen high-rise casinos on the island, stamping out every last house and place of business, and Joaquin LaRosa would be down there in the darkest shadow of the canyon, ninety-eight years old and madder than hell, selling hardware out of a pushcart.

Sam wouldn't back down. Just like her father that way. She had their father's stone-black eyes, and they were showing all the years she'd spent trying to give this family a second life. Albert noticed the crinkling skin around her eyes and the pillowing of the flesh under her chin. She hid her gray and she wore loose clothing to hide something there, too.

But she knew Albert was right. She scanned the room now, still done up in canary yellow and battleship gray, drifting on memories.

"Amazing how this place still has all the same smells," she said.

"What smells?"

"Our smells. The smell of us in this house. I ought to start going through and gathering up the things he keeps bugging me about."

"What things?" Albert asked, fingering the cork.

"The sit-down sewing machine. The sideboard. A half dozen other things."

"So why are you the one who gets all the antiques?"

"Because I'm the favorite child, don't you remember? Pop sends me these notes in the mail, because it's cheaper than phoning. *Dear Sam: Come get your mother's linens. Come get the silverware and your mother's china.* It's like postcards from the grave. Can you pass me the kung pao chicken?"

"You don't even have room for all this furniture, do you?" Albert asked, thinking that if he went ahead and moved to a condo in Atlantic City, he could use some of it.

"The sewing machine goes in the living room next to the hutch that used to be Abuela Maria's. Can you imagine the karma? That room is going to be nothing but family history. Three generations of Spanish and Italian grudges. You remember the feud between Dad and his nutball sister?"

Albert laughed like a lunatic and made a stabbing motion with his chopsticks. "No, Sam. It had slipped my mind that she tried to stab him with an ice pick at my seventh birthday party. How about Uncle Horace on the other side? He throws one pitch in the major leagues, his first and only pitch after ten years in the minors, and he beans Willie Mays in the head. Willie Mays! The whole family is misfits and sociopaths. What chance did we have?"

"Everyone but me," Sam said. "You might have been too young to remember this, but we used to have to go to Maria's for Thanksgiving when you were still in a stroller. We drive four hours to get there on a Wednesday one year, halfway to Ohio, and we're spending the whole Thanksgiving weekend there. So what happens? We're not in the house ten minutes and Abuela Maria's telling me I can't sit here, don't touch this, don't eat that. One year she said something the minute we sat down to dinner and he stands up, not a word, and herds us all out to the car. We had Thanksgiving dinner at an Arby's."

"Was that the time the mattress fell off a truck in front of us?"

Sam had her mouth full of kung pao chicken and tried not to laugh, because it might come out her nose if she did. She washed it down with a swig of water and then clanged her wineglass with her chopsticks.

"Dad thought we'd rolled right over it, but it was wedged between the wheels. We're tooling along with a Simmons

Beautyrest under there, skating down the turnpike on a giant bar of soap. Cars are pulling up alongside us and rolling down the windows. 'Hey, do you know you've got a mattress under your car?' And Dad keeps driving, like all these people are crazy. He's even cursing them out, and then we smell something burning so he pulls over and sure enough, the mattress is stuck under there good, and it's on fire."

"I still swear you guys made up that part."

"Albert, they brought out the National Forest Service. We were near some park and a crew of rangers came out, and Dad's cursing Aunt Maria in Spanish the whole time."

"It's a shame they didn't have camcorders back then."

"It's a shame they didn't have psychoanalysis back then. Maybe you wouldn't be in the shape you're in."

"And what shape is that?"

"Crazy as a loon. If you'd had any sense, you would have married Rickie."

"Rickie who?"

"Oh spare me, Albert. Are you going to tell me you haven't pined for her every minute since she dumped you?"

"First of all, she didn't dump me. I initiated it. Second of all, and for your information, I happen to be seeing someone else."

Sam might as well have left the room and sent their father in to take up her seat. She absorbed him with pity and disgust, chewing mournfully, as if suddenly even the kung pao chicken was disagreeable. As far as Sam was concerned, there was only one woman for Albert, and it was Rickie. Albert's parents, his father in particular, had cringed over his divorce, but not Sam.

She knew that that marriage was wrong from the beginning and she believed Rickie was right from the beginning. Whereas his wife indulged Albert's weaknesses and built her world around his, Rickie held over Albert the power of her own independence. She wanted him, yes, but on her terms, not his, and she elevated him in the process.

"I don't believe you," she said.

"I'm a very eligible bachelor," Albert said, grinning. "Soon to be a very eligible executive bachelor."

"You're pathetic. Don't tell me you've gone back to dating mail-order Asian women, like you did after the divorce."

"They weren't mail-order. I met both of them at the Trump Taj, as a matter of fact. They happened to be recent immigrants and needed someone to show them around a little bit."

"Show them around? Here is Albert's house, little flower. Here is Albert's bedroom. Allow Uncle Albert to take complete advantage of you, little flower."

"Are you finished?"

"Typical guy."

"Because I don't need to listen to this."

"You like to ride tall in the saddle, don't you? Big man. Strong, self-confident, independent. But if you go ten minutes without a woman to call your own and answer to your wishes, you're lost. Guys are all alike."

"Excuse me, but I think it was Rickie who started dating ten minutes after we broke up. I just met Gina. Supposed to see her tonight, as a matter of fact."

"Gina? What, you're dating a stripper?"

"Gina Fiorentino is her name."

"An Italian stripper."

"She happens to be the personnel director at Evolution. And what's the harm, Sam? I'm doing a complete remodeling job before I turn fifty. New line of work, new romance, maybe even a new town, like Atlantic City or even Vegas eventually. It's a fresh start all around."

"There are no fresh starts, Albert. There's just new opportunities to screw up. It doesn't matter where you live."

"That's cheery advice. Why don't you just pass me the knife so I can open a vein?"

"Demons travel well, Albert. They've all got frequent-flyer cards. And trust me, they know the way to Atlantic City and Las Vegas. I don't know what score you think you have to settle in Philadelphia, I really don't, and honestly, I don't mean to minimize it. But that kid's still going to be in a wheelchair wherever you live, and Rickie's still going to be the girl for you. So quit telling me you need a new boat or a new job or a new town. She's your fresh start, Albert. *Rickie.* Go sweep her up, take her to Paris or Rome, and don't come out of your room until every credit card is maxed out and the police are at the door. That's my advice."

Albert swallowed more of the wine and swilled it around contemplatively. This had turned out not to be the best vintage, really. He could usually tell for sure by the fourth glass.

"You're just like Pop, only more so," he declared. "Always got all the answers. I think you managed to pick up every one of his worst traits."

Normally he'd love to keep the match going with Sam, nice sharp volleys and an occasional overhead smash. She was generally good for a few flights of savage wit once the wine went to her head, much of it uncharacteristically pornographic, but that was always a precursor to her lying down wherever she might be and snoring like a goat. He was feeling kind of saggy, though, having started his day in the middle of the night. Racing to the hospital from Philadelphia had wrung him out, too, not knowing what kind of shape the old man was in. And then there was the small matter of a certain murder suspect who apparently thought of Albert as dear old Dad.

"So Jack called the hospital before I got there?" Albert asked.

"Yeah. Rickie got hold of him at his girlfriend's place, apparently. He wanted to come spend the night in Pop's room, but I told him the old man needed his rest, just go straight to the store tomorrow and open up. He'll be a savior, I'm sure. Pop feels lucky to have him."

She had no idea. Jack was most probably single-handedly bringing Cannery Way back to life, bungling everything along the way. Just like the well-meaning, misdirected kid that he was. First the bridge bombing turns into a murder, and now the plan to pump sales volume at LaRosa's Hardware had backfired with the old man buckling under the weight of all the work.

"I can't figure them out, myself," he said. "You'd think Jack would be flying around out there with his boots shined and his ears pinned back. You'd think he'd be chasing sex and money, making noise, turning down offers. Instead he's a pearl diver at his mother's restaurant once or twice a week and the rest of the time he's over there with Pop, renting *Harold and Maude* to Mrs. Costanza on Beta. He says he likes it in Harbor Light, but what is there here for a kid his age?"

"Have you ever gone in there and watched them together?"

"What do you mean watch them? I've been in there, yeah. But what's there to see?"

"Come on, Albert, you've got to admit Pop's a character. He gets behind that counter and he's in the pulpit. He's happy to have even an audience of one, and Jack is knocked out by it. All these proclamations we don't even hear anymore because he's said them a million times? It's all new to Jack. Last time I was here he told me Pop's the poet of the working class. If you're in Jack's generation, who do you have? Who's their role model? I see it with a lot of kids his age, clients of mine. The world scares them, Albert. They don't trust their parents — especially Jack, who only got one parent to start with — politicians don't speak for them, the mainstream media is the devil incarnate. They feel like it's all one big manipulation, a reality that's been created by advertisers and information peddlers and drummed into them their entire lives. How to dress, who to believe, what music to listen to. But it's not based on any kind of a value system, so there's this whole undercurrent of alienation out there.

"My reading of Jack is that he's totally confused. And then he meets Pop, and it doesn't matter that they're from different planets generationally. Pop's angry about some of the very things that are confusing Jack. And he cares. And he stands for something. It happens that he's about time and place, community, the politics of the economy — but for Jack it probably could be anything. It could be Rocky Road ice cream for everybody, as long as there's passion behind the cause. I think Pop's got Jack caught up in the battle to save the town from Oscar Price, if you ask me."

Albert had killed the bottle and he was up scavenging for more. If Sam kept going, he was going to need at least another bottle. None of what she said was particularly surprising, but the way she brought it all together was giving him palpitations. Should he bring her in, see if maybe she could talk him out of his own read? Not yet. Sam was of better use just tending to the old man while Albert kept up the spadework awhile longer.

"Does Pop still keep that liquor cabinet in the hall closet upstairs?" he asked.

"I think so. Bring a bottle for me, too, will you?"

The same stairs creaked in the same places as they had since Albert was a boy. He walked up almost afraid to, past the closet with the liquor cabinet. First door on the left was his room. The room Jack had taken up. He pushed in and saw nothing particularly obvious. Clothes were spun out on the floor and the bed. Shoes were lined up against one wall. Albert opened the closet and drawers. Nothing. He went over and sat on the edge of the bed and felt something at his feet. He looked down to see the edge of a magazine and pulled it out from under the bed.

Playboy. With the *a* missing.

"Are you crushing the grapes up there?" Sam called.

He shoved the magazine back under, thinking she was in the hall. His heart raced.

"Be right down," he said, grabbing a bottle of red from the cabinet.

"Here's an idea," Sam said when he got back downstairs. She was a little tipsy now from the glass and a half, or however much she had drunk. "Pop and Jack, together, as the team that blew up the bridge and burned the Parkway stores."

Albert began twisting the corkscrew with manic turns. "You're kidding, right?"

"Of course I'm kidding. Why are you suddenly so serious?"

"I didn't know I was."

"It's just that it would make sense if it weren't so implausible. Especially to think that Pop was in a bomb unit in the war."

Albert took a full swallow before asking what she was talking about.

"He was in a special unit of some type. You knew that, didn't you?"

"Well, actually, no."

"Men. I swear, you wouldn't know each other's names if women didn't introduce you."

Albert's head throbbed. No, he didn't know anything. He didn't know his father was in some kind of special bomb squad in the war. He didn't know Jack was a semimilitant protester with a carved-up *Playboy* under his bed. He didn't know anything about Joaquin's time in the army at all, which was remarkable when you considered how much the man loved playing the soundtrack of his life. There seemed to be two kinds of World War II veteran. The kind who wore American Legion caps and said the Pledge of Allegiance at every opportunity, and the kind who pushed it way back in the attic and kept the door padlocked. You would have picked Joaquin LaRosa for the former group, but the only thing Albert knew of his father's military service was that he traveled once every five years to a reunion of his division.

He wondered, if only to salve his wounded pride, how much Jack or Joaquin knew, really knew, about him.

Thank god for Gina Fiorentino. Thank god for her lush red lips and olive-skinned legs, which noodled around him and tied up snug at the small of his back. He needed a vacation, and this was it. The bed rocked. The sheets ripped. Gina Fiorentino!

Yes, he actually sang her name like an aria. Blurted out all six syllables. He was edgy, pent up, half out of his mind over the convergence of unfathomable plotlines, and needed a good scream. His father and Jack working as a team? You could take what Sam had said—"it would make sense if it weren't so implausible"—and flip-flop it. It would be implausible if it didn't make so much sense. Albert rolled onto his back and the sheets mopped the sweat off of him. Gina collapsed in a satisfied face-first sprawl, the imprint of Albert's hands on her rump like white gloves.

"You wear me out," she said through white cotton.

What Gina didn't know wouldn't hurt her. His hunger, presidential in proportion, had much to do with his angst over family and other intimates populating his list of murder suspects. But he rather liked the idea of letting her think he was an animal in the sack.

"Listen, you don't think this is a problem, do you?" he asked. "Maybe the boss has got problems with his employees getting together."

"I wouldn't worry about it, and I am the personnel director, after all. But he's out of town anyway. He and Senator Robert Croydon flew to Vegas for a couple of days."

Flew to Vegas for a couple of days? Gina seemed to have no idea how larcenous that sounded, given the quid pro quo factor. Albert was anything but naïve about political realities in

New Jersey, where the canons of law and ethics were loosely in-
terpreted and only one rule was written in stone. Profiteering
by a politician was less of a crime than failing to share the
bounty with constituents, sponsors, mentors, and all other
forms of wildlife up and down the food chain. This wasn't
even particularly brazen, as Jersey graft went. Within a week of
his introducing a bill calling for a statewide election on
gambling in Harbor Light, Croydon was on a junket to Vegas,
where he would no doubt be wined, dined, and concubined.

"I didn't know they were that close," Albert said, trying to
draw her out.

"Close enough," Gina Fiorentino said before dozing off.

Albert slept not a wink, every path obstructed. He lay still
through the night, shipwrecked on the rocks, waiting for the
tide to lift him. Albert decided to go back in time first thing
next morning. Six decades back in time.

Although it was generally understood that Georgianna and Lu
were not identical twins, it was beyond Albert's ability to dis-
cern the slightest difference between them. As they were the
same height and weight, he had suspected they shared one set
of clothes, and he could swear, as he walked into the office of
the *Beacon,* where Lu was the receptionist, that she was wearing Georgianna's Monday dress. The notion of a daily rota-
tion—Georgianna's Monday outfit becoming Lu's Tuesday
outfit—was nearly as disturbing as the fact that Lu was, at this
very moment, stuffing a Tastykake butterscotch Krimpet into
her mouth. Albert wondered if, whenever one twin wolfed a
bite, the other got a sugar rush.

"Good morning Lu," Albert said in his Officer Friendly voice. Lu had always been less discreet about her disapproval of him, and he assumed Georgianna must rush home every night and fill her with stories. "I was wondering if you could help me figure out how to take a look at your archives."

Lu looked up at him with the pained expression of the chronically overworked. "It's been an absolute madhouse around here," she said as if she were the least appreciated member of the American workforce. Just to prove her right, the phone rang, and she took the call with a tone of great distress.

The reception area was lit by two six-foot replicas of the lighthouse, same as the one on the sidewalk out front. The walls were covered with dusty award plaques and photos of Little League champs the *Beacon* had sponsored, mostly back in the days when the newspaper was a daily and competed with the *Atlantic City Press* in the smaller shore towns to the south. Framed metal plates of historic front pages also lined the walls, including the one from Hurricane Alice. The screaming headline, which ran above a six-column photo of Seventh Street under four feet of water, was **Hurricane Malice!** Albert had never noticed before, but at the bottom of that thirty-five-year-old page was a tiny ad in a pencil-lined box. LaRosa's Hardware & More. Where the difference is Service with a Smile.

"Well you go ahead and think about it," Lu said, "and the ad can run as you wish. But speaking as the runner-up in last year's diocesan essay contest, I can assure you it is grammatically unnecessary and inappropriate to use quotation marks around 'like new' regardless of the condition of the lawn mower."

Lu hung up with a sigh, deserting one imposition for another. "Follow me," she said glumly, leading Albert around the
front counter and down a dreary hall of gray fluorescence to
the *Beacon* morgue. Three walls were lined with chest-high,
liver-colored filing cabinets, and Lu opened a drawer with a
label that said APRIL '43 TO AUGUST '46. She ran her finger
along the tops of blue microfiche boxes. "This one?" she
asked, picking June and July 1944. Albert noticed that she was
wearing a Sea World bracelet. Once a year, the twins went on
vacation together. Lu always got a bracelet, Georgianna a pin.

"I'll try that one, yeah."

He expected her to load it for him, but just like her twin,
Lu could make herself clear without words. Albert fumbled
with the elephantine contraption, which looked like something
in a dental office or an X-ray lab. Lu watched him struggle to
make sense of it, a sour pucker on her face, her arms crossed
like great interlocking bratwursts. Finally she nudged him
aside, a good strong body check that would have flattened a
lesser man, and loaded the film, telling him it was the simplest
thing in the world. She showed him how to spool forward and
back through the recorded history of Harbor Light.

"Do you think you'll be able to manage on your own now?"

"I'll give it my best," Albert said.

Every Friday in those days, the back page of the *Beacon*
had a feature on a local boy either on his way into the service
or returning home from the war. Spinning through the war-
time newsreel, Albert saw that every feature on a returning
serviceman began the same way:

"A warm, Harbor Light hero's welcome to . . ."

The story sat in a slot next to the same ad every week. A cartoon of a returning serviceman whose first thought was to drop a line in the water. "Smooth, reliable power," said the header. "Kiekheafer Mercury Outboards are built to last."

Albert was getting the hang of the time machine now. One of these days he'd have to come back and revisit his glory days of high school football. He dropped in July–August 1945, fast-forwarding through the heat of that summer, which set records that still stood. The temperature hit one hundred degrees six days in a row, a lute whale had beached itself in Atlantic City, and the Sea-Fruit Cannery was calling in ice trucks from as far away as New York to keep the fish from going bad. Les Chance, of the now-defunct family-run department store that had anchored Cannery Way for seventy-five years, was quoted as saying he had sold more fans in three weeks than in the last three years. Finally Albert came to August 18, 1945, which carried the headline **No Relief in Sight.** On the back page, he found this:

A warm, Harbor Light hero's welcome to Pvt. Joaquin LaRosa, 21, who returned stateside last month after a tour of service in the United States Armed Forces!

Albert had never seen this photo. His father in field gear, helmet cocked the slightest bit, cigarette dangling. There was no conqueror's glint in his eye, no sheen of victory, moral or otherwise. Albert expected to see the war in him. Expected to see some sign of the truths you must discover when they put a helmet on your head and a rifle in your hands and they train you to kill. All he saw was a kid who'd been somewhere so far away there was no explaining it, and it made Albert want to go grab his father and shake stories out of him.

A native of the Bronx, N.Y., LaRosa is the son of Ruben and Amara LaRosa, who moved to Ocean City in 1944 to work as fishpackers at the Sea-Fruit Cannery. Private LaRosa served in the 120th engineers battalion of the 45th infantry division, whose work in Sicily during 1943 was featured in The Beacon *in dispatches from syndicated war correspondent Ernie Pyle. The 120th cleared mountain passes bombed by the Axis and restored roadways and bridges for the movement of Allied troops and munitions across Sicily and later into mainland Italy.*

Albert felt a shiver. He pulled back and stared at a blank wall, dizzy from the endless swirl of incrimination. How well did he know his own father? He imagined him kneeling on dusty mountain roads, setting charges under piles of wreckage and standing back to watch them explode. It was hard to see him there, but even harder to imagine him sneaking out to the bridge on Kip Slough and blowing Harlan Wayans to kingdom come. His father, the unerring, clear-eyed moralist. The populist preacher and conscience of the community. Impossible.

Pvt. LaRosa has joined ranks at the Sea-Fruit Cannery, where his parents continue their employment. LaRosa is the brother of Abuela LaRosa, a nurse assistant at the Veteran's Rehabilitation Hospital in Atlantic City, and lives with his parents at 43 N. 17th St. A warm, Harbor Light hero's welcome to Private LaRosa, and best of all, ladies, he's Not Yet Spoken For!

Albert hit the copy button. The machinery dished and wheeled, mechanical light flashed, and a grainy copy of ir-

refutable history came into the world. And what if it were his
father in the end, who lay in the hospital with a weak heart and
a strong constitution, keeping all the promises he'd made to
himself? No need to answer. Not now. Albert folded the paper
and slipped it into his shirt pocket. He raced for the exits and
the sun shot him a blast, white hot and blinding, and he ran
down Cannery Way on fire.

Does a motorcycle sound like a boat? Ordinarily, no. But not all boat motors sound alike. Maybe what Mo heard the night of the bridge bombing wasn't a motorcycle, but a Jet Ski. Or maybe a fifty-year-old outboard that had been rebuilt so many times, it sounded more like a Harley than a fishing boat.

Albert found Red Miller tidying the books in his trailer office at the marina, ninety-plus years old and as solidly dependable as ever. Albert had years ago suffered a recurring nightmare in which no one on Harbor Light ever died. Albert was still pinning a badge to his shirt and making the rounds at seventy-five, Red Miller was a hundred and fifteen, Albert's father was a hundred and still going on about a comeback for Cannery Way, and Nuba Ludwick weighed six hundred pounds. That might have been when Albert first thought about a career change.

Red was tapping an old adding machine, charts and logs splayed out before him, while eating a white bread sandwich of bologna and mustard. The walls of the trailer were lined with symmetrically arranged and chronologically ordered photos of fishermen and their catch, a little note under each regarding the location of the hit and the type of bait used. Red generally worked from five in the morning until five in the evening Monday through Friday and half a day Saturday, pumping gas and collecting fees for monthly berthing, visitor tie-ups, and launches. After hours, a boater could pump gas by punching in an account number, and then Red would figure up the tabs and send out monthly bills. That's what he was doing now, smearing mustard all over the keys of his adding machine.

"I need to borrow you for a few minutes if you've got the time," Albert said.

"I got nothing but time, Albert."

"If I remember, don't you keep a spare key for every boat that ties up in the marina?"

"Always have. Lot of times these guys'll come for their boat and realize they left the key at home. Old-timer's disease they call it."

"You mean Alzheimer's."

"Say what?"

"Never mind, Red. Where do you keep the keys?"

All these years in the sun had yellowed Red's hair and turned his skin the color of infield dirt. He looked at Albert with bleached blue eyes that showed a touch of hesitation.

"I suppose it's all right to tell you, you being the sheriff of Nottingham. I got them locked in a cabinet I keep down here under the desk."

"So if I needed to get on one of those Jet Skis down there, what have you got, three of them?"

"There's three in the corral and one more Jeff Andrews keeps up on his boat."

"And you've got the keys for all of them right here?"

"That's the way it works."

"How hard would it be for someone to get in here and steal some keys?"

"Not hard at all, I wouldn't guess. This ain't Fort Knox. But it never happened."

"How can you be sure?"

"That little trick you showed me. I wedge a matchstick into the doorjamb every night when I leave. It's been in there every morning when I came back."

"Well if you can do me a favor, Red, here's what I'd like you to do."

Albert went down to E Dock with Red and helped him peel the cover off a Jet Ski and launch it down the ramp and into the water.

"You'll give me the signal?" Red asked.

"I'll give you the signal," Albert said, and then he walked the seventy-five yards or so to Mo's Tavern.

Mo was sweeping peanut shells up off the planks, cigarette dangling. Albert explained the situation to her and asked if she wouldn't mind lying down on the pool table, where she was the night the bridge blew.

"Is this some kind of come-on, Albert? Because you don't need a ruse with me. I'm easy."

"Just close your eyes and tell me what you hear," Albert said, going around behind the bar and leaning out the window to give Red the signal.

Red hit the starter on the Jet Ski and revved the engine two or three times.

"Well? Sound familiar?"

Mo sat up on the pool table and stared into the darkness of that night. She was giving it her honest best.

"No," she finally said. "That's not it. I told you it was a motorcycle, not a boat."

Albert went to the window and called for Red to try another Jet Ski, but the sound was pretty much the same, and so was the result.

"Sorry," Mo said.

"Don't worry about it," Albert said. "I'll be right back."

Red Miller was waiting for him on the docks, a puzzled look on his face.

"Let me ask you something, Red. What boat would you say is the oldest out here?"

"Oldest boat?" Red scanned the marina, scratching his head.

"Bill Normandie's got that Chris-Craft that goes back."

"And the *Town Cobbler,* right? Doesn't Joe Salvatore's boat have the same old Kiekheafers it came with?"

"Sure it does. I can't remember the last time anyone took it out, though."

"All right, here's what we're going to try this time," Albert said to Red, and then he went back to Mo's, got her to lay out on the pool table again, and gave Red the signal.

The first boat Red started was Bill Normandie's, and Mo said no way. What she had heard wasn't a hoarse wet purr like that. The second boat was Albert's own. He had told Jack he could take it out when he wished, and he hadn't qualified it by saying Please don't use it to commit any felonies. In fact, the bridge blew up the night of the day Albert had taken Jack for that ride. Red revved the twin Chryslers of the Tiara Pursuit, and Mo hesitated a little on this one, but finally she said no again. Too much horsepower.

"All right, one more," Albert said, and he gave a wave for Red Miller to hit the starter on Mayor Joe Salvatore's *Town Cobbler.*

Mo's ears twitched. She opened her eyes, shut them again, then bolted up on a spring.

"Voilà!" she said.

"You're sure?"

"Positive. That's not similar to the sound I heard, Albert. It is the sound I heard."

"That's a boat, though. Not a motorcycle."

"I don't care what it is. Kind of a choppy-sounding pop and fart sort of thing. That's it."

Albert half walked and half ran back to the docks, where, as a boy, he used to fish for perch and stripers after school. And when he grew tired of that, and of watching real fishermen return from the sea with fish bigger than he was, he'd beg his father to go ask Joe Salvatore if they could borrow his boat again. That's how old the *Town Cobbler* was, and Albert knew the sound of that fifty-year-old engine so well, he was surprised he didn't put two and two together the first time Mo said she'd heard a motorcycle. She was right. Mayor Joe's boat did sound like a motorcycle. Like a tired and beat-up old chopper. But it wasn't Joe Salvatore who was on the boat that night.

Red was on hands and knees, pulling up a crab basket he baited and dropped into the muck two or three times a day. As long as he'd been working the marina, he knew right where they were.

"Did I do all right, Albert?"

"You did so well I'm going to hire you for another operation," Albert said.

"It's not like I've got anywhere else to go."

"Those logs you keep on the gas pump. How far back they go?"

"I got 'em all the way back to when we lost the harbor-master's office in the storm and they moved me into the trailer. What's that, twenty years?"

There was no reason to save the logs more than a few months, but this was the kind of guy Red was. If he found a paper clip in the parking lot, he'd save it in a jar for ten years thinking you never know, someone might come looking for it.

"And how do you keep them, by account number or by name?"

"By account number, but there's a list of who's who. You need to check something?"

Yes, he did. If the *Town Cobbler* went out that night, who-ever was piloting it would have had to fill up. Joe Salvatore was something of a miser. He'd figure out where he was going and estimate how much gas he'd need, and he often brought the boat back on fumes. Albert's father used to holler about it every time out, griping about how Joe had it figured so he'd never pay a nickel for his own gas. The medically amazing thing about Joaquin LaRosa was that it had taken this long for the coronary to hit.

They marched back up to the trailer, where Red pulled open the bottom right drawer of his desk and took out three sheets of paper covering gas charges the last three months. Albert ran his finger down the log on the latest one, stopping on the date the bridge was blown. Only one account was drawn on, which made sense. No one would have gone out in the fog that night unless they had something other than fishing in mind. Albert grabbed a scrap of paper off Red's desk and jotted down the number.

"Tell me whose account that is, Red."

Red, a medical miracle himself, had just lit a cigarette. He set it on a mound of butts in an oyster-shell ashtray and went into another drawer. "What crime in particular are you solving today?" he asked, exhaling toward the saggy, smoke-damaged ceiling of the trailer.

"One of these days I'm going to buy you a beer at Mo's and tell you the whole story," Albert said.

Red checked the account number against his records, reaching for his cigarette with yellow-tipped fingers.

"It's Joe Salvatore," he said with a puzzled expression. "Not like him to go fishing before the crack of dawn."

No, it wasn't. But of course he hadn't.

"Let me ask you something, Red. Do some of these guys have trouble remembering their account numbers when they go to pump gas?"

"A lot of them don't even bother trying to remember. Take Joe, for instance. You look inside the cockpit and he's got it taped there. I've told these guys a hundred times, anyone can get behind the wheel and pump gas on your dime. But they don't listen to old Red."

Red reached for his bologna sandwich and Albert was out the door, head down and moving fast, plotting his next move. He was halfway across the parking lot, his cowboy boots gravel-dust gray, when he knew he was being watched. He looked up to find the FBI agents peering through the window of their maroon sedan.

"You been doing some fishing?" asked the marine, who was in the passenger seat.

They'd caught him by surprise. Caught him in the act of beginning to figure things out. Had they seen the whole out-the-window business at Mo's, and if so, did they have any idea what it was about?

"I'm sorry, what are your names again?" he asked.

"I'm Dagget," said the driver. "He's Cramer."

Dagget and Cramer. Nice careers they had going. Nothing better to do than follow him around all day. How were they going to get their big promotion if all they could do was sit here playing with themselves all day, hoping the local sheriff would save their asses?

"You seem like nice guys, Jeeves and Wooster, so I'm going to give you a tip. This is a small town. People notice anything out of the ordinary. Two guys driving around in suits all day picking their noses kind of stands out. You're scaring people, okay?"

"We scaring you?" Cramer asked.

"What would I have to be afraid of?"

"Like you say, it's a small town. Not much goes unnoticed, does it?"

Joe Salvatore was behind the counter when Albert walked into the Town Cobbler, which smelled like the inside of an old shoe. Joe was cementing a heel onto a black wing tip that was locked into the teeth of a vice, his nose pointed into his work as if it were a spot-welding tool. When he had set the heel in place just so, he pounded in a half dozen brads that he plucked from his teeth, a picture of old-world craftsmanship that seemed like a scene out of Colonial Williamsburg. He didn't see Albert at first and jumped when he did.

"Albert. You shook me out of my boots."

"I didn't mean to startle you, Joe."

Joe always wore a green and red apron for his native country and he kept a pencil wedged onto his ear for etching trim lines on leather soles. He set his hammer down and spiked the volume on his hearing aid. "Listen, I've got your boots done. It worked out fine again, but you've gotten all you're going to get out of these things."

Every pair of shoes Albert ever owned had been reshod here, but there was a sign in the window saying the doors would close July 1. Joe was retiring, and there was a buzz about him around town. This brand-new true-blue Cadillac Joe was driving, tooling around town like a bug at the wheel. Where did that come from? You couldn't fix enough shoes. *Payola.* That was the whisper, and Albert at first dismissed it as typical island gossip. But he was beginning to wonder. Mayor Joe was jumping for joy before anyone else, with the possible exception of Senator Croydon, and maybe he had good reason. What was Joe's life before this? Hammer his fingers all day, then go home and eat the plate of macaroni his wife put in front of him every night. Now a man who'd counted pennies his whole life was throwing the wife into the new Caddy and cruising up and down the Parkway like the Prince of New Jersey. Dinner at the Ebbet Room in Cape May. Song and dance at Cozy Morley's show in Wildwood. Living it up like no mere town cobbler.

Joe grabbed Albert's backup pair of cowboy boots from a boxed shelf and dropped them on the counter, shined up and ready to kick.

"You can see right here where the instep is stressed to where there's nothing to work with. It looks like your arch has caved in on the left foot, the way the material pulled. You feel anything there?"

"Yeah, as a matter of fact. My left ankle's been screaming lately and my knee's not so happy, either."

"That's it. You've got a fallen arch, Albert."

"What causes that?"

Joe paused for a moment, as if he didn't know how to break the news. "Age and time, Albert. Age and time."

"That's good to know. What can I expect to fall next?"

"The price of shoe repair," Joe said with a sunny smile, pushing Albert's boots to the edge of the counter. "This one's on me for all your years of business."

Albert looked again at Joe's sign in the window and asked how it felt to walk away after nearly half a century.

"It feels fantastic," he said, his gaze already turned to a window that looked out on the good life. "What can I tell you? Forty-eight years I've been torturing myself in here. Look at this."

He held his hands out for inspection, and the only three fingernails he had left were the color of octopus ink.

"I don't know, Joe. All that spare time you'll have on your hands, what are you going to do?"

"Take a walk in the park, putter around the house, visit the grandchildren. Nothing special."

"There's always fishing, Joe. That's where I'd be. What'd you do, forget you've got a boat?"

"That old tug? Yeah, she's still tied up out there, if she hasn't sunk yet. They could put it in a museum at this point.

You know that yourself, Albert. You and your father ran the *Town Cobbler* out there often enough over the years."

"We've had a few break-ins out there, Joe. Just so you know. Some of the guys losing some fishing equipment and whatnot. I've got an eye on it now, but you might want to be careful who you loan her out to."

"There's only two other people with keys. My son-in-law, who never gets off his duff down in Cape May Courthouse. And your loco father, if he's still got the thing, but I can't imagine he'd set foot on a boat Joe Salvatore owns. Me being the big traitor. You'd think I held a minority position, the way he goes on and on and on about it. Three-quarters of this town can't wait for that casino, Albert. Why is that? I'll tell you why. Because it makes good sense all around, that's why. You caught that train early yourself."

"So that's it?"

"That's it what?"

"Keys, Joe. Keys. Your son-in-law and my pop are the only ones other than you with keys?"

"Your father's had a key practically since I bought the boat. You couldn't see over this counter back then, Albert. He helped me out with the berthing fee the first couple of years and so it was always his when he wanted to use it."

"Well just so you know. You might want to clear your things out of the boat if you've got any valuables in there."

"By the by, Albert, you hear anything new on the investigation? I heard the FBI was about to nab this lunatic."

"They're closer than you know, Joe. Nothing gets past those guys."

———

Albert locked his door and told Georgianna not to let any calls through. He rang Jim Leonard at the Philadelphia Police Department and said he needed another favor. The jacket on a kid in Gloucester, New Jersey, named Dave Rudnick.

"It's a long one," Leonard said. "Anything in particular you're looking for?"

"What's the DOB?" Albert asked.

He was roughly the same age as Jack.

"Anything that looks like vandalism, theft, terrorist threats?"

"Nothing that ambitious. I see failure to disperse, resisting, trespassing."

"Trespassing where?"

"You name it. Hold on. City Hall. Looks like a law office. Something down at Penn's Landing. Here's one at the Navy Yard."

"South Philadelphia?"

"Wait a minute. Actually I guess it's an Army Corps of Engineers supply station near the Navy Yard."

"Can you pull the file?"

"Shows here it's down at South Detectives. But I remember something about that one from the papers. Let me check the date on it. Yeah. Last November. That was when someone lifted some explosives. C4 if I remember correctly."

"C4? You sure?"

"It was in the papers at the time."

"And this kid Rudnick was charged?"

"Not with that, no. He was just charged with trespass. I don't think they ever made an arrest on the theft, but someone got away with a load of fireworks."

Albert thanked Jim Leonard and swallowed hard. He hung up the phone and Georgianna was banging at the door.

He opened up and she informed him with piqued urgency and great bosom-heaving drama that Fitch Caster was on the line, demanding to know his whereabouts. "I believe he would like an update, sir."

"Is that what he'd like? An update? Tell him I'll send him a memo. I don't have a car or a radio, George. Remind him of that for me, will you? And I'll be at Harbor County General if anything catches fire. If you need me in the next half hour or so, just call out there, ask for my father's room."

Albert punched up the radio on the way to the hospital and dialed around until he pulled in a top-of-the-hour news update on WNJX. Stuart Farmer, the security systems clown who was trying to take Fitch's job from him, pounded away. "We're talking about damage estimated at ten million dollars minimum, dozens of people out of work, and the sheriff fiddles while Harbor County burns. I don't think we could trust Fitch Caster's administration to investigate an illegal campfire, let alone handle a case of this magnitude." Fitch, God bless him, was up to the challenge. "I sincerely appreciate Mr. Farmer's concern, but a man who installs car alarms for a living might be somewhat out of his element in a case like this. I can assure you we have a team of our best people assigned to the case, and we're coordinating our efforts with those of the FBI. It wouldn't be appropriate or professional to reveal the details of an ongoing investigation, but we'll have more to say in due time. Until then, I'm a little too busy doing my job to engage in political grandstanding that doesn't serve the public interest."

Albert knew of two guys out of the detective unit that had come in, but a team of our best people? Merging onto the Parkway, he saw one of those detectives standing astride an unmarked county sedan in front of Tortilla Gulch, commiserating with a county arson investigator in a hard hat. He would rather have been left to handle it alone, but he understood the political realities, and besides, this wasn't technically part of his beat. He'd hooked up by phone with the detective squad this morning and found that the kid from Taco Bell had now been interviewed a dozen times by three agencies and still had nothing to add to his original story. He saw what looked like a white SUV from a distance, that was it. Yesterday, those two lugs from the FBI thought they'd cracked the case when they discovered a closed-circuit security monitor at the entrance to Gizmo. But the system had been disabled a half hour before the fire by someone who'd climbed onto the roof from around the back of the building and snipped the wiring.

It stood to reason that Joaquin LaRosa, despite an energy level that was off the charts for a man in his seventies, did not hop onto that roof and cat around up there with a pair of snippers. It was the work of a much younger man. Borrow a ladder from the hardware store, drop a pair of wire cutters into your pocket, and go to work. He was an industrious boy, Jack Davenport. Out to save the world, and pretty good with a match. You could replay this entire adventure and see Jack in every frame, not just the highlight reel. The night Albert came back from the town hall meeting and was certain that someone had been in his house? It had to be Jack. He'd slipped in to plot the angle of the bullet he would later fly through the front door, making sure he didn't actually plug Albert dead. It was a message, not a murder attempt. And the point of the message? Who knew? Albert hadn't entirely pieced it together yet. Same with the stunt where Jack—of course it was Jack—stole his car and plunged it into the drink for that lovely cruise down Kip Slough. Was it punishment for Albert's having leaped into the arms of the enemy? Was it simple payback for having left Jack's mother? Or was it because Jack, who had told his girlfriend he thought of Albert as his father, felt personally betrayed by him?

Albert realized that his father couldn't be Jack's accomplice. His inspiration, perhaps, but not his mentor in that way. For a while, Albert had thought it possible that old bricks and mortar, in his irrational, stubborn zeal, had put Jack up to some of this. But the very notion seemed silly now. It wasn't a flattering admission, to be dead-wrong about your own father, but he was learning that there were a lot of things he hadn't paid enough attention to. How could a son not know what his father did in the war? Very easily, as a matter of fact. That was the way of fathers and sons, the closest bond being the shared knowledge of a missed connection. It was like putting magnets together the wrong way. Science wouldn't allow it. But now the son *did* know who the father was, or at least had a very good hunch. Joaquin LaRosa wouldn't have endorsed a strafing campaign against the enemy because that wasn't the victory he was after. He wanted people to see what he saw, and to embrace his vastly superior sensibilities, without having to be clubbed over the head. He wanted his son to realize with the aid of careful self-reflection that his true purpose on earth was to work alongside his father in the hardware store. It wasn't nostalgia with him. It was knowing, with absolute clarity, that he was fighting death itself.

Albert took the elevator to the third-floor cardiac unit and marched down the yellow-tiled hallway to room 323. A nurse was taking a blood sample and Joaquin LaRosa squawked like a child at the needle prick.

"Well this doesn't surprise me one bit," said the nurse. "You're such a troublemaker, the police are here."

"How you feeling?" Albert asked after the nurse left.

"Tip-top condition. I could run circles around half the staff in this joint, but they won't let me up to visit the john, let alone go to work."

"Pop, you had a heart attack. Did you listen to anything Dr. Morocco told you? What happened to Sam, by the way?"

"I had to ask her to leave."

"What do you mean you had to ask her to leave?"

"Drove me up a tree, that woman. She came in here with a notebook full of scribbles on some cockamamie diet she dug up in one of her magazines. You're eating nuts and cabbage all day with a scrap of bird thrown in now and then. What am I, a Pilgrim? I sent her over to the hardware store to help Jack. Twenty-eight sales he had by eleven o'clock. Twenty-eight sales. I can't believe I'm missing this, Albert. I can't believe the luck. Talk to someone and see if they can't roll this bed downtown for me, will you?"

"You've got to put it out of your mind, Pop. Did you hear the doctor? I need to get you out on my boat, do a little fishing. Get you some rest and relaxation."

"Fishing? I haven't gone fishing in ten years, Albert. Not

since your mother died. You remember the way she used to do up that flounder?"

"Joe Salvatore's boat. I wonder if that thing's still running."

"I couldn't tell you myself. Why don't you ask Joe, if he's not too busy cruising around in his new Cadillac? I've still got the key, but I wouldn't set foot on it. If I were stranded on an island for forty years eating banana slugs with a stick, I wouldn't get on Joe's boat."

"Then why do you still have a key?"

"Because I never got around to giving it back, that's why. It's still right there in the nickel drawer of the cash register in case Jack wants to use it."

"Jack takes Joe's boat out?"

"That kid earns his keep, Albert. If there's a little perk thrown in now and then, what's the harm in that?"

"You sure you're making a wise investment, Pop?"

"What do you mean? In Jack?"

"I don't want to see you get hurt, that's all. It's a nice thing you've got between the two of you, but maybe you're counting on him a little too much is all I'm trying to say."

"He's a good kid, Albert."

"Yeah? You sure about that?"

"He works, that little son of a gun. Respects his elders, too, not like some of the other little deadbeats on this island."

"Well I wouldn't put his name in the window yet if I were you."

The old man searched Albert's eyes for meaning. Should Albert tell him?

It was lonely, being in the middle of it all, being the one

who suspected everyone who was close to him, and at the same time trying to protect them all. It made sense, in the end, that the one Albert was after all along was the one he knew least of all.

"That day in the store, that day you were in there making speeches, and Creed was loading up for battle, and Jack was choosing sides, I left knowing that one of you had killed Harlan Wayans."

"Harlan Wayans died in an accident, Albert. Nobody killed him."

"Ruling out yourself, who do you think did it, Pop?"

"Nobody did it, Albert. You think someone was out there trying to kill Harlan, or anyone else for that matter?"

He was the same man Albert was. Trying to protect himself from the obvious.

"Do you realize I didn't even know what you did in the war? That your only son had no idea?"

"You never asked."

"You never told."

"So what are you telling me? I'm under arrest for murder because I was with a demolition unit fifty years ago?"

"For a brief moment, I thought you might have taught Jack a trick or two. Lord knows you don't forget a thing."

"Listen, Albert. There's no bigger nut in the tree than Creed. How are you so sure he's not your man?"

"Physically impossible. His alibis check. That's how I know."

"It isn't Jack, Albert. How about his alibis? He's got alibis, too. I know him, and that boy's got a good heart. We work side by side in that store. I'd vouch for him with anybody. I'd swear on the Bible, swear on my mother's grave, swear on your mother's grave. Are you listening to me, Albert?"

The snug confines of the red vinyl booths in Peg's As You Like It diner were the preferred vantage point for watching the daily theater of bridge construction. Those were the loges. Box seats. Call Ticketmaster today. Rickie and Aunt Rose found customers idling in the parking lot when they walked over each morning to open up, and then they'd just about have to stab them with forks to get them out of those booths after a couple of hours. Instead of the usual morning and noon shifts of customers, it was a nonstop rush until closing time now, especially since some of the eateries on the Parkway had gone up in smoke.

"Here's what I don't get," Drugstore Max Phelps was saying. "How in hell do you take this old cannery and redo it to where it looks Polynesian?"

"Simple," said Jack Best, a blackjack dealer at Evolution. "You plaster over the brick, you do a thatched facade, you put palm trees everywhere. You create like an entire village and hire a few Samoans to hang around the front of the place like they live there. You build some inlets off Kip Slough and have natives paddling around out there in canoes. And your first act? Your first headliner? Don Ho."

"The Polynesians didn't use canoes," insisted Warren Smith, the pig farmer, who had been leaving daily messages with Oscar Price's office, offering to run a nightly luau at the Polynesian Princess.

"What did they use, Jet Skis?" Max Phelps asked insultingly. "Of course they used canoes. That's how they got around."

Warren waved his empty coffee cup at Aunt Rose, who had taken to wearing a grass skirt with a rather risque top she'd fashioned from coconuts, mocking the absurdity of the whole thing.

"Did the Polynesians use canoes or did they not?" Smith asked her.

"I'll tell you what they did. They took morons like you, beat them over the head with firewood, and tossed them off of cliffs. This is a chat 'n' chew, not a Salvation Army soup kitchen, and I don't see any chewing. Order some damn food if you're going to park your fat asses here all day."

Rickie was in the kitchen, settling another dispute. She'd hired a Bosnian immigrant who spoke what sounded like pig latin, confused bagels and English muffins, and responded to the regular chef's complaints with threats of physical harm.

"You think you got problems? This friggin' prostate posse is driving me out of my gord," Aunt Rose complained. "Here we go now. A thirty-minute dustup on whether the Polynesians used canoes."

"I wouldn't mind if they weren't all in the tank for the casino," Rickie said. "Do they not see the irony? The one place on the island where they can meet like this is about to be plowed under, if we don't get a last-minute reprieve."

"I don't know if they really want a casino or if they just like that they've finally got something interesting to talk about," Rose said. "Look at them. You'd think they were building the Golden Gate Bridge out there, the way these bobos sit in the booths and look out the window all day, chirping like old ladies."

Rickie looked at her watch. "He was supposed to call by now," she said.

"H. DeWhatshisname? Well it better be good news when he does."

"Don't get your hopes up. He said he's running out of walls to bang his head into. Said Oscar Price has got tentacles that reach into every courtroom, every crack and crevice."

"Every pocket."

"He says he started laying the groundwork for this thing almost three years ago."

"Right under our noses, the slimy bastard. There you go. That must be him now."

Rickie took the call in the kitchen.

"Hello."

"Rickie, it's me."

"Tell me a David and Goliath story. We can use a lift right about now."

H. Dewitt Nelson paused, a silent giveaway.

"They've upped the ante on their relocation offer," he said, but he was talking to himself.

Rickie hung up the phone and stood there a moment, listening to the endless cluck and clatter of customers. She needed some air. She needed a walk on the beach. She was at the door when Albert came up the steps.

Neither of them spoke at first.

As enraged as she was, still, about him throwing in with Oscar Dan Price, she had wanted so badly to talk to Albert. That night he came over and they sat on the swing out front, she had intended to tell him everything, because there was no one else on earth she could tell it to. Albert would have talked her down. He would have known what to do. He would have explained how she couldn't possibly have been right about Jack. She suspected not only that Jack was the bomber, his mission being to save his mother's restaurant, but that she had inspired him. How many times had she told him how proud she was of the things she'd done in her rebellious years? How many times had she encouraged him to challenge accepted truths, see the world beyond his own experience, and act on his every passion? What a fool she'd been. All she was trying to do was get him motivated, push him to where he'd figure out what he wanted to do with his life, and the whole thing had backfired. Twice now she had confronted him, or was it three times? No, he insisted. Wrong guy. What was he, crazy? Don't worry, Mom. I'm innocent.

"Where you running off to?" Albert asked.

"Nowhere in particular. It was getting claustrophobic in there."

"You'd have to leave the island to get away from it. We have to talk, Rick."

"I can't right now, Albert. I'm too busy to think straight."

"It's about Jack."

She brushed past him and down the stairs, only to turn and glare back at him, her green eyes ringed red with exhaustion and fear.

"He's my only child," she said.

"I think he's in some trouble."

"Then why don't you throw him in jail? Why don't you arrest him like you had your own father arrested? One last act of bravery before you turn in your badge and call it a career. Who knows, Albert? Arrest Jack, and maybe there'll be a bonus in it from Oscar Price."

"I'm trying to do the right thing for everybody involved, Rickie."

"You got one hell of an odd way of showing it," she said. She was halfway across the parking lot, Albert chasing after her, when a sedan pulled in and cut her off. The car came to a stop and the driver rolled down his window.

"Excuse me, ma'am, my name is Special Agent Dagget, and this here is Special Agent Cramer. We were wondering if there's a quiet place where we could talk to you for a few minutes."

Albert had cut corners here and there over the years. Every cop does because you have to. The by-the-book cop is a fiction. Do you arrest Dr. DiMitri for chasing the nurses around his office? Of course not. Do you narc out your favorite bartender for being in violation of at least a dozen building codes and not being licensed to fish out the window and serve pan-fried striper to loyal customers? No amount of suffering would be too great a penance if you did. The world was colored in gray and so you couldn't police it in black and white. Every single day on the job, you see something a rookie cop would chase, but you, with the benefit of experience, wisdom, and fallen arches, let it go because it's the sensible thing to do.

But this was no mere infraction. This was murder, arson, and a gazillion dollars' worth of damage, a high-profile case that would bear the full brunt of prosecutorial zeal. If Albert was right, this was an angry and addled kid going away to jail at twenty and coming out with a senior discount. Although Albert had taken a few liberties, he had never abandoned the principles that governed the job. If anything, he was still overcompensating for Philadelphia.

He had watched his partner stand over a woman and drive

a bullet through her skull to cover for them both, and he had said nothing. She was already gone at the time, but ballistics tests never revealed who fired the bullet that killed her. It might have been Albert. It might have been his partner. It was a shoddy review, conducted with the express purpose of quickly affirming the neat and tidy official police version of events: The husband had killed his wife, Albert and his partner had effectively put the husband down, and in the process, Albert had accidentally shot his partner in the leg and a three-year-old boy in the back.

A hundred and one times before his partner put a gun to his own head and twice as many times since, Albert had come within a hair of setting the official version straight. There was a price to pay for silence, and no greater burden than knowing too much. Was he going to make the same mistake with Jack? Was he going to tarnish the badge by sliding him out the back door just before the feds came busting through the front?

Albert headed for Memorial Bridge. Maybe there was an answer in Philadelphia.

He had had nothing at all to do with Ramon Cabrera for twelve long years after the shooting. No physical contact, at least. He thought about him, sure. How could he not? He thought about him constantly. But no calls, no visits, no inquiries. The experts said it was best that way. For both of them, it was best. But what did the experts know?

Albert's insomnia began back then. You could hide from it by day, get distracted, get tied up. But at night—and especially in sleep—you were a sitting duck. One night Albert tortured himself with it in a dream and woke up with the sheets soaked through and twined around his head, like he'd been trying to hang himself. It was the middle of summer, heat and humidity hanging like a curse and beating the hell out of everyone up and down the Jersey shore. Albert slipped down to the beach and pitched himself into the surf. For a while he let it take him where it pleased, washing him up, dragging him back. He offered no resistance. And then he thought he might just aim in the direction of the Old World and swim until he couldn't move his arms. He got about two hundred yards closer to Europe and turned around. It took no courage, no perseverance, to drown yourself. Drinking yourself to death, though, that was a test of endurance and willpower, and not just any tosser was up to the challenge.

Another night, less than a week later, the same dream woke him. Albert drove to Philadelphia and sat in the car in front of Ramon Cabrera's grandmother's house for three hours. At eight o'clock, a blue van pulled up, the side panel slid open, and a wheelchair ramp was lowered to the sidewalk. Ramon Cabrera's grandmother wheeled him down a wooden ramp and onto the elevator. The driver hit the button that lifted Ramon into the van and they were on their way.

Albert followed the van every day for a week. They picked up four broken and mangled kids each morning and delivered them to a school for the broken and mangled on Girard Avenue near Saint Joe's Prep. On the sixth day, Saturday, Albert drove to Ramon Cabrera's grandmother's house again, but this time he didn't just sit out there feeling sorry for either Ramon or himself. The grandmother answered the door and Albert said he was with the police officers' benevolent association, checking to see if there was anything the lodge could do for

Ramon. It was obvious they did not live particularly well—untended trim, unpointed brick, and windows without dressing—and the grandmother struck him as a widowed pensioner who seemed receptive to the idea of help.

But Ramon, a paraplegic, wanted none of it. He screamed from the unlit gloom of the hallway for Albert to leave and told him never to show his face in their door again, and the grandmother apologized, but what was there to do? Albert, horrified, wondered if Ramon knew. But how could he have? He left a phone number and told her to call if they reconsidered.

Three weeks later the phone rang. Exactly what kind of help was available? the grandmother wanted to know. Albert drove back to Philadelphia and had been visiting Ramon Cabrera once a month ever since for going on thirteen years. The grandmother figured out who Albert was after a few visits. She asked nothing about what had happened in the house, and Albert figured she'd already made peace with it. Albert begged her not to tell Ramon who he was, though. Ramon was likely to see this as penance, or, even worse, as charity, because, well, that's exactly what it was. The grandmother understood without Albert having to explain, and she carried the secret to her grave. When she died, Ramon had no one other than the caretakers who were paid for by his disability, and Albert upped the ante on the check he delivered every month. On one visit six or seven years ago, he drove Ramon up to Northwestern Avenue in Philadelphia, past the horse stables and out to Forbidden Path in the Wissahickon, where the Lenni Lenape Indians had once fished and hunted. He pushed him along the creek and under the canopy of hemlock, pine, white ash, and black walnut, past a grazing doe that turned and fixed its gaze on them as if they were alien curiosities. Up the path a ways, they came to a spot where grasshopper sparrows nested in the elms, a spot where Ramon liked to plunk stones into a natural pool and watch the rings radar across the surface. It was there that Ramon turned to him and asked, "You're the one who shot me, aren't you?"

The goddamned shrinks were right. He should never have made contact. Even before Ramon realized who Albert was, it was all wrong, too heavily weighted to Albert's benefit over Ramon's. What happened had happened, and there was nothing either could do for the other. Contact only recalled the incident and set up a cruel inference. The inference that the savagery of tragedy could somehow be comprehended, dealt with, mitigated by a simple act of caring. It was maudlin pablum. Utter Pollyanna bullshit. Ramon Cabrera was sentenced to a life of suffering for no good reason on earth, and the awkward friendship of the man who shot him did nothing to relieve the pain.

Yet Albert was stuck with Ramon, and Ramon with Albert. So they were trapped in a tortured coexistence built on an acute understanding of their own powerlessness. Ramon didn't pick his parents. Albert didn't know a child was in the house when he pulled the trigger with no intent beyond saving a life. Their destinies were mapped out entirely in the dark. But how many people ever see what's coming? You marry the wrong person, throw yourself into a job that doesn't suit you, stumble ahead blindly, and just when you get the courage to stick your head through to a clearing, you get clobbered by something that slipped in under the radar. Accidents. Disease. Alimony payments. A bullet in the spine. Albert thanked the

Lord Almighty for the gift of knowing you couldn't win. That was about the only thing, really—that, and a solitary day at sea—that set you free.

Albert sputtered noxiously across the penal green Walt Whitman Bridge and backfired into South Philadelphia, home of his last living uncle. Frank Cardinale, a fixer, had worked for some of the giants. Frank Rizzo. Buddy Cianfrani. Augie Sangiamino. If a constituent had a problem with something— a ticket, a booted car, a license and inspection problem— Frankie fixed it with the deft hand of a surgeon or the blunt force of a longshoreman, whatever it took. When Ramon got out of that special high school, Albert called Uncle Frankie about putting him somewhere. He got the wrong idea at first, thinking Albert wanted a ghost job for Ramon, which he was more than happy to arrange. But Albert wanted something where Ramon would actually have to show up, answer to a schedule and a boss, learn something about responsibility.

"You mean a job where someone notices if he doesn't show up? That'll take me a little longer," Uncle Frankie had said, but he eventually found him something at the Parking Authority, followed by the Port Authority, followed by Registrar of Wills. The problem was that Ramon kept blowing it. Some days he was in such a funk he didn't even call in sick. Other days he'd show up and get into it with the wrong person at work, and Uncle Frankie the fixer would have to go in and make it right.

Albert found his uncle at Shank's luncheonette on Tenth, his usual spot, with a pepper and egg sandwich and a cup of coffee with a splash of Sambuca nobody had to know about.

"I've got him another paycheck, but this is the last," Uncle Frankie said. "I've got him answering phones. You dial 686-1776, which is information, and your boy Cantinflas is going to be one of the girls taking the calls. Do me a favor, Albert. Tell him not to fuck this one up, because I've worn out my welcome in more than one place with this little *chalupa*. He starts answering the phone in Spanish, like he did at the Port Authority, and he's going to get his balls rattled like a couple of maracas."

It was a treat to cinch up family ties every now and then, wasn't it? Albert always felt a need to look into the benefits of the witness protection program after breaking bread with the Cardinale clan. He had stopped exchanging Christmas presents with most of them after the year his cousin Rocco gave him six color televisions without the original boxes. Albert's mother, who abided no amount of hustling and racketeering, and believed that even jaywalkers should spend time in the pokey before it led to something more serious, had severed ties with most of her relations and went more than thirty years without speaking to her twin brothers. But Frankie had always been one of the less-frightening relatives, and he had made a point of staying in touch with Albert and Sam, sending each of them a cheese wheel and a sheaf of lottery tickets each year for Christmas.

Albert thanked his uncle and paralleled the Delaware River on Christopher Columbus Avenue, headed north toward Center City and beyond. Ramon had moved to Spring Garden a few years ago when his late grandmother's neighborhood went to hell, but he hadn't seemed any happier or any less homebound even though it put him closer to community college, where he took a computer class and had a couple of sometime friends. It was hard to tell with Ramon, who kept fences around himself and only occasionally opened the gates. He was easy with a smile, but it was no expression of joy with him. It was a pitying, look-at-this-jerkoff kind of a smile. Part snarl, really. His tiny teeth showed, and it looked like he had a mouthful of white rice. Once in Rittenhouse Square, Albert had left Ramon alone to go get some more coffee for them, and Ramon was watching a squirrel scamper up a tree, empty cup in his hand, when a passerby dropped a quarter into it. Albert got there to see the smile, all those fish teeth in jagged rows, and then Ramon threw the quarter back at the guy.

There was nothing Albert respected more in Ramon than his inability to accept his predicament—to just take it like a good sport. He refused to be the well-adjusted crip; refused to smile for his donors so they could congratulate themselves over the goodness of their deeds. He was fucked and he knew there was no beating it. He would never get up in the morning and go for a walk. He would never be inside a woman. He would never have a holiday with family other than the other crips he met at Magee Rehab or in one of the wheelchair basketball games he so hated. That was Ramon's strength. He felt anger, not sorrow. Anger was what kept him alive.

The routine on these monthly visits had been written in stone by Ramon himself. Albert would pick him up and there wouldn't be much more than a hello or a hey out of either one of them. Then they'd go straight to either the triple-X double feature on Market Street or to Thee Doll House on Spring Garden. Albert would try to talk Ramon into something different, they'd argue about it for half an hour, and then they'd go to either the movies or the strip club. Ramon won every time.

Albert tried to at least convince him to go to a real strip joint, where the floors were dirty and the girls looked properly ambivalent about being there. These glitzy new joints, with their polished brass poles and beef-boy bouncers with headsets, had it all wrong. The girls were all Coppertone and cartwheels and every one of them looked like their life's ambition was to be an NFL cheerleader. But Ramon liked what he liked, and he had taken a particular fancy to a Doll House trixie named Hosannah. This girl had apparently taken a Wilson basketball to the plastic surgeon and said Here, about like this. No understatement with the lips, either. It looked like the doctor might have dozed off during the injection. Was it possible, Albert wondered, to get collagen injections in your brain? But you couldn't joke about this stuff with Ramon. Not regarding Hosannah, anyway, because she had been determined to prove that a wheelchair was no barrier to a good lap dance. For twenty bucks, she balanced on the arms of the wheelchair in a dazzling display, contorting herself in ways that suggested a future as a flying Wallenda. She'd always give Ramon a peck on the cheek when she climbed down. It was an obvious kick for Ramon, but there was more to it for him than getting off sexually. He looked at those women the way people viewed him. As curiosities. As poor, unfortunate souls. He was disgusted by them, felt sorry for them, fell in love with them. "Hosannah in the highest," he'd pray when they left Thee Doll House after an afternoon of debauchery, and he'd keep sniffing the tips of his fingers, which carried the spiced confection of Hosannah's essence.

Once, as a surprise for Ramon's birthday, Albert hired three of the girls to come by the house and swing from the chandeliers, and Ramon's reaction threw him for a loop. *Get them the fuck out of here!* he screamed. *I want these sluts out of my house now!* At the club, he was just another customer, one of the guys, his tongue hanging out at the sight of all that caged flesh. But in his own home, the contract was broken, and so, too, the illusion of himself as whole. He was a pathetic shut-in cripple being treated to a charity strip, and he would have none of it.

Albert double-parked on Wallace and knocked on Ramon's door. The strip club had gotten boring enough, but Albert couldn't take one more trip to the triple-X. He was usually in uniform, badge, six-shooter and all, and they'd have to trundle up to the window and ask for two tickets to *Saving Ryan's Privates* or *Forrest Hump*. And then, without fail, they'd get stares in the theater. All those greasy-faced whackers in there, guys in toupees so bad you could tell in the dark, the walking dead of municipal employment who'd marched down from City Hall on three-hour breaks. That was the crowd, and Albert and Ramon would get looks like *they* were the freaks.

Albert had an entirely different plan in mind today. He had bought the Drain Surgeon's number two van and was giving it to Ramon free and clear after a complete overhaul, new engine and all. Albert called the Magee Rehab Center, where Ramon played wheelchair basketball, and one of the staff gave him a recommendation on a garage in Jersey that modified vehicles for the handicapped. For ten grand, they were going to install a lift, rip out the driver's seat, and jack the controls around so Ramon could drive the thing with his hands, same as he did with the van that was taken away from him by some heartless stiff in the county health department. Not even Uncle Frankie could fix it this time, or maybe he'd just gotten tired of the effort. Ramon was twenty-seven. If he didn't get to where he was doing more on his own, he was going to slide into another funk like the one he was in last summer, when he wouldn't come out of the house for anything. Not for his job, not for physical therapy at Magee, not even for the porn. He just sat in the sweltering depression of his parlor watching television, and who knew where his head was?

Albert knuckled the door again, wondering what was keeping him. He wanted to run Ramon back to Jersey for a spin on the new boat, which he'd told him all about. You actually got a rise out of Ramon on the sea, a glimmer of something approximating pure unvarnished pleasure. The fishing he could do without. But the wind in his face and the salt-air wonder of a world where legs did you no particular good, that he liked.

Albert had called yesterday, so Ramon knew he was coming. The new job didn't start until next week, and basketball was yesterday. "Ramon, open up. It's Albert." Now what were the chances that in a city of one and a half million people, Jack would meet the kid Albert had shot over twenty years ago? And what were the odds that if you put these two together— Ramon at twenty-seven and sentenced to a four-wheel rickshaw for life, and Jack a healthy young buck with nothing in his way but his own shadow—that Jack would be the one headed for a fall? Jack could learn a few things from Ramon. Albert was no shrink, but if part of Jack's problem was being abandoned by his father, he had nothing on Ramon Cabrera. Jack's life was a dream compared to Ramon Cabrera's, and he was trying his damnedest to throw it away.

The next-door neighbor was on his way out and Albert asked if he'd seen Ramon around.

"Seen him? No. But he's been home. He had the TV going all night. You could hear it through the wall."

Sometimes Ramon wheeled himself to a variety store a couple of blocks away, so maybe he'd gone out for supplies. Albert parked the van at the corner and walked to the store. No Ramon. He must have gotten a late start and was still in the shower back home.

Albert walked around the block to kill time. It was a nice little neighborhood, really, kind of quiet, nothing fancy. People making lives behind painted doors and red brick. The season had really popped here, a gossamer tent greening the narrow streets, and planter box tulips and daffodils were Easter egg bright.

Albert felt a sudden wave of nausea and fought it back. He held his hand in front of his face and watched his fingers tremble. No surprise. He hadn't slept, hadn't paid his bills, he'd gone whole days without showering, without eating. He'd been going marathon distance at a sprint pace from the crack of the gun, no time to take in the scenery. It was only now beginning to dawn on him that he was in the midst of mapping out the whole voyage here and now. Romance, career, zip code. What had begun as a simple career opportunity had morphed into a test of loyalties and self-definition, and coming here, coming back, was something he had to do before figuring out the rest.

Once, when they were both half bagged, Albert almost came right out with it. The liquor had loosened his restraint, and he was aching to get it off his chest, just put it out there where he was finally free of it. He wanted to tell Ramon about his partner standing over Ramon's mother and giving her one more bullet. But he caught himself just in the nick of time, and who could say what miracle of intervention had saved him from his own selfish interests? Ramon did not need to know. He'd been subjected to enough as it was, and he simply did not need to add that image to the others he carried around in the family album. Coming so close to blurting it out scared Albert off liquor for a solid month, and he had never again imbibed when he was with Ramon. He didn't need to know, and Albert would never tell.

Albert got back to Ramon's and checked his watch. All right, this was beginning to worry him just a little. The door was locked, so he banged on it and yelled again. The last time this happened, about three years ago, Ramon had tumbled off a curb and couldn't get back into the wheelchair. Albert found him lying in a gutter three blocks from here. He was cursing himself and flailed at Albert for trying to help him up, and then he went into his Puerto Rican pride routine. Albert had darker skin than Ramon, for crying out loud, and he spoke nearly as much Spanish, too. But when he was embarrassed, Ramon had to remind Albert he didn't need anyone's help, and he acted as if Albert bore personal responsibility for the pillaging and plundering carried out by his colonist ancestors in Puerto Rico.

Albert climbed back into the van and took a few spins around the neighborhood. He went back to the store, cruised by the apothecary Ramon went to on Spring Garden, and over to the playground at the Roberto Clemente School at Eighteenth and Green, where Ramon sometimes watched a pickup game of basketball. There was no sign of him anywhere, so he stopped at a pay phone and called Magee, figuring Ramon might have forgotten about a physical therapy session or something. They hadn't seen him yet this week, and said he'd missed last week's appointment.

Albert dropped the phone. He stood there under a tree, fighting a notion at work in his gut. The last time they were together, Ramon was less forthcoming than he'd been in a while. Didn't even want to go see Hosannah at Thee Doll House. They sat and watched some bad movie together on television, a police story with too much shooting, which made Albert the cop uncomfortable but Ramon just had to watch it.

When it was over, Ramon said he could never have been a cop, couldn't imagine the pressure of split-second decisions. It was the most generous thing anyone had ever done for Albert. Ramon was telling him it was time to let it go.

Albert barreled back to Seventeenth and Wallace in the van and knocked on a next-door neighbor's door. An ancient Puerto Rican woman with a bony Chihuahua face and deep-socketed eyes answered the door. Albert started in English and realized she had no clue.

"*Yo soy un amigo de Ramon, y necessito pasar a su patio.*"

She was still suspicious of him, the uniform throwing her. It wasn't like the blue uniforms she saw around here.

"*Señora, ayúdame por favor. Yo soy policia. Tengo emergencia ahorita. Por favor, permitame entrar.*"

She stepped aside and Albert blew past her, through the house, and into the backyard, which adjoined Ramon's.

Ramon got high now and then. He never admitted it, but Albert could smell hints of reefer in the house every once in a while. In Philadelphia, you never knew what you were getting on the street. Maybe some fuckwad had peddled a bad batch of dope to Ramon and he was in there now, passed out, sick, unable to get up off the floor. It could be anything, Albert told himself. He could just be asleep.

Albert used an upturned wine barrel on the old lady's patio as a launching pad and bounded over the fence to Ramon's, tumbling on an unkept patch of grass and then quickly picking himself up. The back door had a window and Albert peered into the kitchen and hallway beyond. He banged again and called out and heard nothing. He pressed his ear to the glass and could faintly hear the television. Ramon liked playing with the remote control because it was like having a pair of legs every time you wanted to change the channel. Albert had hooked him up with a satellite dish, the whole deal, six-hundred-some channels, including a dozen porn stations from around the world. Albert would call at eleven o'clock and ask what he was doing and Ramon would say he'd pulled in an Italian station where housewives took their clothes off on TV, or a Russian news show with a topless anchor, can you fucking believe this crazy world?

And do you know what the irony was? Albert knew Ramon about as well as he knew anyone. He knew this skinny Puerto Rican kid he had shot in the back as well as he knew his father, his sister, Rickie, Jack. Ramon didn't confide in Albert; didn't tell him where he went when he retreated in place. But Albert didn't pry, that was the deal between them, a bargain struck with wordless understanding. Ramon exercised his right to his own private turmoil without apology or explanation. He suffered without shame and pitied no one more than those who pitied him. In this, he revealed himself in the most generous way.

Albert called his name once more and then unholstered his gun and smashed the window in a thousand pieces. He slipped the lock, rushed the house, and found Ramon in the shade-darkened living room, hanging from an extension cord he'd tossed up around the railing to the second floor he had never used. The television was going, a commercial for a swing-action contraption that guaranteed the perfect buttocks in three months or your money back. Ramon's face flickered blue and ghostly white. His eyes were open wide, same as they were on that night, but the terror was gone. Albert closed the lids and slumped down on the floor beside Ramon. Right where they began.

It was time.

Albert had called the funeral home and made the arrangements. He had reached one of Ramon's cousins in Puerto Rico, too. And then he had drunk himself to sleep for an hour, maybe two. Now it was time.

He drove to the hardware store at nine o'clock sharp and waited impatiently for Jack to handle two early customers who took forever digging change out of their pockets. Jack, one eye on Albert and one on his business, could tell this was it. He was tight in the shoulders and shifting like a tennis player anticipating a serve, wondering which way to lunge.

Not a bad life he'd been living. Sell a few True Value lightbulbs, torch the competition after work, and then hop into the sack with that perky little coed he was boffing. The arrogance of it was insulting. The inference that he could keep this party going for as long as he liked, playing Albert for a fool. If not for the fact that Albert, out of the goodness of his heart, had given him the benefit of the doubt from the very beginning, this day would have come much sooner. When the customers were gone, Albert hung the Closed sign in the window.

"Get your things together, Jack. You're coming with me."

"What are you talking about?"

"Don't waste time. Just get your things and let's go."

When Jack hesitated, as though he might decide to make this difficult, Albert grabbed him and yanked him toward the door.

"Get off me," Jack protested, skidding along like a reluctant pup.

Albert torqued up and gave him a jerk that sent Jack flying out the door and windmilling onto the sidewalk. A few people on the street turned around, and Albert wondered if Dagget and Cramer were watching, but he was too mad to spend much time on the thought.

"Get into the van, Jack."

"Where are we going?"

"Just do as I say and this will be easier for both of us."

They drove silently to the marina, Jack broadcasting his feelings with disgusted sighs and a good deal of staring out the window at inanimate objects. It had to be a real nightmare for Jack. Albert had never gone beyond a mild reprimand with him in all their years together, and now he was suddenly playing the ticked-off father and the strong-arm cop all in one. Jack slipped out the door before the van came to a stop and began walking back toward the store. Give me a break, thought Albert. If you're going to make a run for it, make a run for it. But spare me the sulking dramatics. Now Albert did a three-sixty scan for Dagget and Cramer. No sign of them. Then he went after Jack, grabbing for that arm again, and Jack resisted with a little more heart this time.

"The fuck you doing?" he whimpered, and you could tell right off that he was simply no good at this. You'd think he

could play a more convincing tough guy after firebombing half
the Garden State, but he was a mere boy going for some manner of unflinching political crusader, and it just wasn't there.
The posture was a little too noodly, the conviction lacking, and
you could even see some of the terror rising in him. In prison,
they took amateurs like Jack and broke them in about two
days.

"Jack, I'm going to tell you this once. You can come will-
ingly and let me explain just how bad this situation is, or I can
knock you on your ass and tell you when you wake up. Just
don't take more than ten seconds to make up your mind, because I don't think you've got that much time."

Jack was still fighting it, but the shoulders were beginning
to slump. He was no dummy. He had to be figuring that if the
jig was up—if men with badges and the personalities of bill
collectors would be knocking on his door to ask questions
from here on out—he was better off dealing with someone he
knew.

"Where am I going?" he demanded.

"You're going for a ride. It might take an hour, it might take
twenty-five to life. There's a lot to talk about, Jack, isn't there?"

The twin Chryslers caught cleanly the instant Albert hit the
starter. He revved them to a steady rhythm and then pawed the
wheel with a careful touch, gently gliding the hips of the Tiara
Pursuit free of the berth.

The more he thought about it, there wasn't much surprise
in Ramon's suicide, and even if Albert had been more attuned
to the warning signs, he would not have been able to talk
Ramon out of it. Not that that did much in the way of softening

the blow. Twice now, Albert had failed to save him, and of the five people who were in the house that night in Philadelphia, only Albert was alive today. Guilt, luck, grief, he felt all those things, but he also felt something akin to relief. A sort of borrowed peace. Ramon might have been on this boat yesterday, and now here was Jack to take his place, crippled in his own way. Another kid whose fate was in Albert's hands.

Out along the moorings, sailboats bobbed in their wake and their halyards clanged aluminum masts, cuing a wave of chimes. The sun had the whole hazy sky to play with and the winds were light, and as Albert idled for the back bay, he heard a croaking from the marshland.

"Gray tree frog," he said as if this were a habitat tour and he were the guide. "I used to hunt them in the cinnamon fern and bald cypress along the banks of the inlet." In the distance, migrating shorebirds shotgunned low across the salt marsh, out where Albert used to find diamondback turtles as a boy and take them home, only to have his father drag him back out there to set them free. "You never did help me come up with a name for this boat," Albert said to no response. "I'm tired of *Double Down.*"

They steamed out about two miles before Albert cut the engines and told Jack to drop anchor. The boat rode three-foot seas and swagged on the current, and Albert watched Jack's shadow spin across the water like a ghost. The sea swelled around them, and the salt air blew sharply across the bow, an aerosol of truth serum. They were sitting across from each other on the cushioned bench seat near the stern, a tidy little open-air confession box. Jack still hadn't looked him in the eye. He was gazing across open water, catching up on all those blown opportunities for self-reflection. That had to be the best part of being young. Very few moments of truth.

"You get a visit yesterday from those two FBI agents?"

"What two FBI agents?"

"I know you can swim. The question I'm wondering about is, how well? Because if you keep this up, we're both going to find out. I'm in no mood. Not today." Not after yesterday.

Jack shifted and groaned, reluctantly waking up to his predicament. He knew Albert well enough to know he was as stubborn as Joaquin, and that they weren't going anywhere until he got what he wanted. Jack slumped just a little more and suddenly looked even younger under that meringue of whipped red hair.

"They talked to Mom, not me."

"And?"

"She says they asked a few questions. Where I was certain nights. If she knew I got into a couple of jams in Philadelphia."

"That's all?"

"She said she tried calling you. Went over to your house and couldn't find you."

"But they haven't come to see you yet?"

Jack shook his head. "Not yet."

"I'm surprised you didn't catch the first train out of town."

"You're a cop. What would make you more suspicious—if someone hung around like everything was normal, or if they suddenly disappeared?"

Jack went into his pocket for a lighter and took a cigarette from the pack in his shirt pocket.

"They're going to come see you, Jack. If not this morning, this afternoon. Or maybe tomorrow. One of them is going to set you up and the other's going to knock you down, over and over. They're going to sweat it out of you."

"I didn't do anything. Anything they think I did, I was with your father, or in Philadelphia, so I couldn't have done it. Or I was with my mom. Depending on the day they're asking about, I was with someone who can vouch for me."

"Do me a favor and spare me, Jack, will you? Wake up and look at the world, for fuck's sake. These guys are going to bore in, look for one little slipup, and they've got you. I frankly don't think they've got enough hard evidence to fill a gnat's navel, so that's how they're going to do this. They'll sit you down, tell you what a smart kid you are, how much time you're looking at, and how they might be able to help you out in return for your cooperation. They're going to work this to where there's a puddle under your chair.

"And I don't see this registering with you. You act like we're talking about a couple of broken windows or something. Like all you did was burn a few nativity scenes or put a goofy bumper sticker on the back of my patrol car for old times' sake. This is no joke, pal. You could go to prison until you've got hair growing out of your ears."

"For what?" Jack asked, finally making eye contact with Albert. Looking at him as if he were testing innocence as a defense strategy.

"For murder. Among other things."

Jack took a drag and blew a stream of smoke that was taken by the breeze.

"But I didn't kill anyone," he said dismissively, as if he were beginning to believe his own lie.

Albert stood up and smacked the vinyl bench seat with his

hat. The boat took a swell and wobbled him, and when he got his balance he was tempted to give Jack a good backhand just to snap him out of this stupor.

"I know everything, Jack, so can we cut the crap? Or should I say, Listen to me with both ears. That ring a bell, Don Corleone? It wasn't bad. You had me chasing after gangsters for a while. But the whole thing was you, from the death threats to the Parkway torch job. The key to Joe Salvatore's boat is in the nickle drawer in the cash register at the store. You didn't happen to take it out for a ride the night the bridge blew, did you? And that lovely little postcard you left on my windshield before you drove the car into Kip Slough? Your mother's got *Time* magazine at the diner and *National Geographic* at home, and you've got *Playboy* under the bed in my old room with the *a* cut out of it. *The Los Angeles Times* threw me, but then I find out your little sweetie's looking to transfer to UCLA. My guess is she got hold of the paper to look for an apartment in L.A. How am I doing, Jack? Have I missed anything? Oh, yeah. I forgot your comrade in arms, Dave Rudnick. I know a few Philadelphia cops, Jack. I had a look at your whole jacket, and his, too. How long you think it'll take Yogi and Boo Boo from the FBI to nail down your C4 connection? You got locked up together in Philadelphia for three days last fall for trying to shut down General Electric. He got arrested last year for trespassing at an Army Corps of Engineers yard the same week someone hauled away enough plastic to blow up half of Atlantic City. Rudnick give you a crash course while you were locked up, or is all that stuff in the Trotskyite handbook, Jack? You use a cigarette delay on the bridge, too, same as when you took out Oscar Price's car?"

"It wasn't a cigarette delay," Jack said feebly. "I set a timer."

"Well whatever the hell it was, you almost took out every inch of the island."

Jack looked a little dazed by now. His freckled face was stung, as if he'd just been slapped with the surprise of his own obviousness and amateur zeal. He was younger in his shame, a boy again, the mask of adult purpose and direction peeled back.

"I'm insulted, to tell you the truth," Albert said. "You thought what, that I was some kind of rent-a-cop? Some kind of small-town hayseed?"

"I didn't think anything," Jack cried.

"Exactly. And Harlan Wayans is asleep on the hill because of it," Albert said, pointing toward the sprawling oak at the top of the cemetery.

Finally, he'd broken through. Jack's face wrenched. He looked as though he'd swallowed some of that C4 and it was about to lift him like a rocket. He rose with fists clenched, and Albert couldn't tell whether he planned to take a poke at him or leap overboard.

"I didn't kill Harlan!" he screamed, belting it loudly enough that Albert looked across the roiled surf and floating kelp wreaths to consider the possibility of his being heard. Dagget and Cramer were probably up in the lighthouse with binoculars, if they weren't out here in a sub, eyeballing them through a periscope. Once more, Jack pleaded his innocence, as if he were throwing himself on the mercy of the sea.

"You blew up the fucking bridge!" Albert roared. "That's what killed him."

"I didn't know he was up there. How was I supposed to know?" Jack protested, as if he were the one who'd gotten the short end of the deal that night. How dare Harlan get himself killed and ruin an otherwise perfect crime.

"Well maybe you should consider not blowing up bridges as a general rule, just to avoid the possibility of collateral damage. And do you have any idea what kind of jam you've got me in? I'm an officer of the law who's an accessory after the fact. An accessory to murder, no less, with the FBI rutting around in the bushes, itching to bag an island deputy for their trophy case."

"It was an accident," Jack pleaded. "You think I feel good about it? Turn me in if that's what you have to do."

"Maybe I should."

"Then go ahead. Did you never do anything by accident in your life?"

"Did you have something particular in mind, Jack?"

"Yeah. What about Ramon? Did you intend to shoot him . . . ?"

Albert sprung from his seat and lunged for Jack before he finished his sentence. Jack, who had considerably less weight to move, bolted up to meet him, his eyes big as hard-boiled eggs and his right arm spring-loaded for a roundhouse. Albert had no lightning left after training for twenty years on nothing but alcohol and tobacco, but he was quick enough to flick Jack's telegraphed swipe with his left hand and catch him with a solid counter to the jaw, putting him down like a splayed calf. It looked as though Jack might be content to stay put, but Albert picked him up by the neck, ripping his threadbare Rage Against the Machine T-shirt, and plopped him back down on the bench seat. His lip was split and he was now slumped in total defeat.

"And you don't know the first thing about Ramon or what happened in that house, so if you ever again . . ."

Jack had tears coming up now and he was starting to twitch and quiver. He tried to say something but got choked up with the dry sobs and sounded like he might swallow his tongue.

"Why, Jack? Will you tell me why you went on the war-path like this?"

"Let's just forget about it, all right? I don't even care. Just turn me in and you can be the big hero."

"I need to understand why you did it."

"There's nothing to understand."

"You're twenty years old. I understand chasing skirts and seeing the world at that age, but here you are, running a one-man army to save a hardware store and a diner in a town that's halfway to nowhere. Summit, Gizmo, Bargain Acres, Mama Parm's, that poor caterpillar jitney you blew to kingdom come. It's nice to have a hobby, Jack. Nice to get involved in the community. I can respect a guy who stands for something, even if it's anarchy. But you're throwing your life away over a casino coming to town? If you were trying to save your mom's restaurant, that's a lovely sentiment. But do you honestly think she would have wanted you going to prison so she could sell bacon and eggs for the rest of her life? She's been terrified at the thought of it being you, Jack. She's terrified."

Jack now looked as though he had a leech attached to his bottom lip, and he was working his jaw to see if anything was knocked loose in there. But the bulk of his discomfort was other than physical. He was trying to tell Albert something without saying the words, and Albert just wasn't getting it.

"Was it a thrill for you, Jack? Must have been a wild ride, eh?"

"You act like I thought the whole thing through, start to finish," Jack said, using the tail of his T-shirt to mop up the blood that sluiced down his chin.

"Well why don't you set me straight then, so I don't have to visit you in prison to get the details?"

"I just got tired of his whole attitude, man. Oscar fucking Price. The way he came in and started pushing people around. I was in the hardware store the first time he walked in with that bullshit smile, trying to cozy up to your father, and you could see right through him. He's trying to make like he's a regular guy all of a sudden, but meanwhile he's trying to buy everyone off and he's driving a one-hundred-thousand-dollar car around a town where people can't even afford car insurance."

"So you decide you're going to blow up the car."

"I didn't decide anything. It just sort of happened, and then yeah, it felt pretty good, as a matter of fact. I felt like I'd really done something, you know?"

"Yeah, it'll look terrific on your résumé."

"Well then your dad was all charged up that someone besides him cared enough to send the prick a message. He didn't even care who it was. And my mom, too. I heard her and Aunt Rose laughing about it one day at the diner."

"And the death threat? You all get a kick out of that, too?"

"I wasn't going to kill him. I just thought he should know that . . ."

"Not to Price, to me."

"It wasn't a death threat. It was, well, you shouldn't be working for him. I mean, nobody wanted you working for that asshole. Your father didn't want it, my mom didn't want it, Creed didn't want it. I left his eviction notice on your bed one night, and you still didn't get the message. I couldn't believe it, especially after you talked to my mom."

"So how do you go from threatening me and Oscar Price to bombing Bargain Acres?"

Jack hesitated. "You really want to know?"

"We don't have all day, Jack."

"I talked to Dave Rudnick, because he had some experience. And the plan, well, we were going to blow up Evolution in Atlantic City."

"You were going to blow up the casino?"

"Not the whole casino. Just like a part of it."

"Any part in particular?"

"That was the problem. We were thinking about the entrance on the Boardwalk side, where the Cro-Magnon and Neanderthal guys are. Then we thought about that whole set of slot machines on the far wall over by the Primate Pub."

"You actually went in and scoped it out?"

"Yeah. But we couldn't figure out where to do it so no one would get hurt. So we just dropped the idea."

"Then what?"

"Then I decided on Bargain Acres. They didn't have guards like the casino, and nobody would get hurt."

"But what's that got to do with Oscar Price?"

"Nothing. But it's part of the same thing. Every day at the store, your father would talk about what Harbor Light used to be like, and how it was being killed off by the Parkway stores and now the casino. My mom was saying all the same things, how all these people from other places were taking over, just kind of raping the town to make a buck. I don't even know how your father was paying me. Sometimes we'd get like five customers in an entire day. He'd sell a screwdriver and a can of paint and then reach into his wallet at the end of the day and pay me thirty or forty bucks. He had to be going broke, so that's how I got the idea. I asked Dave about trying to shut down Bargain Acres, and he said it'd be easy."

"Did Rudnick go out with you?"

"No, he just showed me how to set things up. Plus, he showed me where to go on the Internet at Laura's house, places where you can find things out. And then when I took out the whole front of the Bargain Acres, just to see your father's reaction when people started coming back downtown, that kind of kept me going."

"So now you've terrorized me and Price and saved the world from capitalism. Why the bridge?"

"To stop Price. To keep the casino out. Why else? I went up to the lighthouse one day when they were starting to build it, and I just went crazy. The way Price had all these people working for him on the taxpayer's dime, like your dad says. It was obvious he'd bought off that crook senator, too. Croydon? Your father explained all the connections for me. Nobody was going to be able to stop him otherwise, and if I bombed out the bridge, it would at least set them back a while. My mom's restaurant was going to get bulldozed, and Creed's house, and we had to do something."

" 'We?' "

"Well, me. But I didn't know Harlan was up there, I swear

it. I'd cased the bridge a few nights and I never saw him. After that, I didn't know what to do."

"You killed him, Jack."

"I know I killed him. You think I felt good about it? I fucked it up, but what was I supposed to do?"

"Give it up, for one thing. You should have stopped terrorizing the town before you killed someone else."

"I did give it up."

"And what about those two bullets through my door? That was giving it up?"

"Look, I wouldn't have done it if I thought you'd get hurt."

"Then why *did* you do it?"

"Because I was scared, that's why. To make you think it couldn't be me. That all of this was the Ianiccis and Rubios and all those other gangsters. But other than that, I didn't do anything else."

"My squad car drove itself into Kip Slough?"

"I was just pissed off that you weren't coming around even after they took out Creed's house. But I got freaked by Harlan, and with these FBI agents hanging around town, and I just gave it up."

"Except for going back to Bargain Acres to finish the job."

"No! I didn't do that, I swear to God!"

"C'mon, Jack. You expect me to believe that? I think I might have more respect if you just admitted you had to finish what you started. That you believed in it that much."

"It's the truth. I was with Laura."

"Well if you didn't do it, who did? They're about seventy-five percent sure it was arson."

"I don't know. Creed maybe? Rudnick? If you think I'm

crazy, you should meet him. I don't have any idea who did it, but torching Bargain Acres wasn't going to do me any good at that point."

"What *was* going to do you good, Jack?"

"I just wanted everything back the way it was, all right? And except for Harlan, I'm not sorry about any of it. The way it started out, I thought I could scare Oscar Price enough to make him drop the casino project, okay? When that didn't work, I thought I could make you look so incompetent at trying to catch me, you'd be the last person in the world he'd want to be in charge of security."

Albert had to work with that a while, sifting for meaning, but it was beginning to permeate the outer crust. If he was reading Jack correctly, this bomb-throwing son of the woman Albert loved was trying to steer him back to her. Look at him. Angry, frightened, still pretty much of a mystery to himself. He was more than a little scary, having inherited an appreciation of disorder and an itch for cage rattling, but he was not some Unabomber wanna-be. He was a fucked-up kid in a world of missing pieces, trying in all the worst ways to make it whole. And Albert, by Jack's measure, had let him down.

"You were trying to get me back together with your mom, weren't you?" Albert asked.

Jack turned away, having said all he was going to say, and fixed his eyes on the town he had been remaking.

Albert honestly didn't know if he could save Jack, but he knew he couldn't arrest him. He knew, too, that having crossed this line, he could never be a cop again. He instructed Jack to keep working at the store each day, and to drive to Philadelphia each night and stay at Laura's place. A set routine. If Dagget and Cramer came by, he knew nothing, he saw nothing, he had nothing to say.

Anticipating a search warrant, Albert had to help Jack cover his tracks. That meant dumping Laura's computer, which Dagget and Cramer would eventually have a look at, and it meant destroying any materials Jack might still have hanging around.

"There's nothing at my dad's house, is there?"

"No," Jack said as Albert dropped him off at the hardware store.

"There's a couple of things here, though."

"In the store, you left stuff? Tell me you're kidding."

"This is where I got some of the materials, like for the pipe bomb."

"I assumed as much, but I'm talking about obvious bomb-related materials besides that. C4. Fuses. Instructions. You weren't dumb enough to leave a beginner's manual lying around in the basement, were you?"

Jack looked at him sheepishly.

"You're killing me, Jack. We're going to be cellmates, you and I."

Albert swung by Harbor County General to check on his father and discovered, to no great surprise, that Joaquin LaRosa now had a security guard assigned full-time to his ward to keep him from escaping. His most daring attempt involved an exit from his second-floor window, sheets knotted together like he was making a prison break. Downtown Harbor Light had been mobbed, and missing out on that action had been no less uncomfortable for him than the prostate exam he had gotten this morning. He was wearing the black beret with his pajamas and doing isometrics against the wall when Albert got there.

"Rose just called," the old man said. "They're running out of time."

"I know, Pop. I know."

"This big-shot attorney Rickie hired is taking them to the cleaners, Albert. He's got the meter running at about two hundred bucks an hour, and he's coming up with a zero. The son of a bitch is trying to talk them into moving. Can you believe it? Rickie and Rose are going to relocate to the Moose Lodge about the same time the pope joins the Wildwood Elks Club."

"I didn't tell them to hire this guy, Pop."

"I don't care whether you did or didn't. There's only one person who can save that restaurant now, Albert."

Albert went into his father's room and sat on the bed, next to the phone. The events of the last twenty-four hours were liberating in the sense that he had lost all appetite for pretense, self-deception, and dread. Who was Oscar Price to hold sway over Albert's life? Albert had trembled in his presence, trying to make the right impression at every encounter. For what? He dialed the number and the surly receptionist who had spurned his advances clicked him into a holding pattern for two or three minutes, which was just enough time for Albert to harness his thoughts and sharpen his sword. Hell, two or three minutes of uninterrupted concentration were a luxury these days. He'd sacrificed a great deal of bar time for the sake of all this crime-fighting and camp counseling.

A shame, because he generally did his best thinking with a

couple of shots in him and a cloud of smoke hovering. With a couple of shots, he might even admit to knowing that Jack was right. That for a few bucks, he'd turned into someone nobody recognized. If Price weren't about to triple his salary, he'd have dropped everything to sniff around Mayor Joe and Senator Croydon, see what more he could find out about the sweetheart deals they'd cut. Albert was now fairly certain that Price knew from the first that the northern end of Harbor Light would be plowed into the slough, Rickie's restaurant included. He had had his reasons for signing on, and they went beyond money, in fairness to himself. But they didn't add up now. It was amazing, what you could talk yourself into believing. For a while, Albert even thought it was his dashing good looks and unbeatable charm that made Gina Fiorentino the easiest roll he'd ever had in his life.

The receptionist came back on now to say Price was going to be tied up indefinitely.

"Did you tell him who it was?" Albert asked.

This she clearly took as an insult, judging by the incredulous pause.

"He's tied up," Miss Sunshine repeated, real attitude this time.

Albert thought about suggesting she find herself a real job—there was no telling what it could do for her disposition— but she might already be pushing her limits in this one. As for Price, Albert didn't know what could be so important that he couldn't take thirty seconds out of his day to hear him out. It wouldn't be long before the same mechanical horse that devoured Creed's house would take a bite out of Peg's, and Price, if there were a drop of mercy in him, could save the day. How hard would it be to put the parking lot across the street instead of where the diner was? They could put it just up Kip Slough Road a ways and run shuttles, too. And Albert knew for a fact that Price had considered erecting a four-story garage on the Atlantic City side and running ferries across Kip Slough.

"Is there a message?" the receptionist honked.

Albert eyed his father, standing at the doorway in pajamas and beret.

Was there a message?

Yes, come to think of it. The message was that Albert would very, very, very much like to make one hundred, one hundred twenty-five, and one hundred fifty thousand dollars over the next three years, with more to follow. He also would very, very, very much enjoy junkets on the private jet to Las Vegas, and he could see himself ringing for flight attendants to bring another iced jumbo shrimp cocktail with those netted lemons. And he had most definitely looked forward to strutting around in a suit that said Hey, look at me, this uneducated schmo from Nowhere Island did all right for himself, didn't he? This lug has got it made, baby. He's in the clear. But the sad, unfortunate truth of the matter was that although Albert could live quite happily as a committed capitalist, he would rather sleep under Memorial Bridge and dine on nightcrawlers than work for Oscar Price in a place called the Polynesian Princess. What would his office be, a tiki hut? He wasn't even on the job yet and Price had been ordering him around like a personal attendant for weeks. Do this, go check that, get in here right away. What was it going to be like once he was on the payroll, canoeing around that monstrosity of a casino with Price yammering in his ear? But the real kick in the balls, and really, the source of his nightly torture, was that he had traded away Rickie Davenport for a sack of gold. Who was he supposed to argue with? Who was he supposed to walk on the beach with on Sunday mornings? Who else could make his pulse surge every day when he walked into the diner he'd been going to since he was in a booster seat? Getting Rickie back was no sure thing at this point. For all he knew, she was head over heels for this H. Dimwit character and that southern gentleman act he'd polished. But if he was going to have a chance, the first step was a no-brainer.

The receptionist, with an increasingly lordly tone in her voice, asked again if there was any message.

"Yes, as a matter of fact. I do have a message for Mr. Price," Albert told the receptionist. "I quit."

The gang that ordinarily watched the bridge construction like it was the entertainment of their lives was gathered on Kip Slough Road across the street from the diner when Albert pulled up in the Drain Surgeon van. Some of them had pulled lawn chairs out of their trunks, like they were setting up to watch a Fourth of July fireworks show. The entire parking lot had been cordoned off with a chain-link fence that had three lines of barbed wire strung along the top of it. A dump truck, a front loader, and a backhoe were inside the compound, and one car. Aunt Rose's pink Caddy.

Albert spotted Creed in the gallery and called him over for the color commentary.

"They gave everyone two hours to clear out or they'd have their car towed," Creed said. "Aunt Rose wouldn't budge, so they called for a tow truck."

"Where's Aunt Rose now?"

"She and Rickie went back into the diner to call that fancy lawyer."

A state vehicle with two heads inside was parked outside the padlocked gate and Albert went over to see what the deal was. Both men were on cell phones, checking in with the higher-ups in Trenton.

"Which one of you boys has the key?" Albert interrupted.

"Nobody goes in, those are my orders," said the passenger, an attorney with the state AG's office. The other guy, a hard hat, was a supervisor with state transportation.

"Well here's my order, pal. I'm going to give you Cub Scouts thirty seconds to open the gate, and then I'm going to shoot it open. So why don't you get on your little pocket phone and see what your boss has to say about that."

They managed to get hold of the one bureaucrat in Trenton who was allowed to make decisions, and he had the rare good sense to give Albert the green light. The hard hat supervisor closed the gate behind him, and when Albert heard the clean metallic click of the lock, he knew he was finally on the right side of the fence. Rickie was screaming into the phone when he walked into the diner and Aunt Rose was loading her shotgun, so it was a fairly typical day at Peg's except that no one was around to complain about the food. When Rickie got off the phone, Albert told her they needed to get together later and he'd tell her all about Jack.

And then he strode out to the bulldozer and found the keys in the ignition. He yanked them, cocked his arm as if he were aiming for the end zone, and sent them on a lovely arc in the direction of the new bridge, which stretched halfway across

Kip Slough. Now he walked back to the gate, where the lackey from the AG's office was on his cell phone reporting what he'd just seen. The transportation guy let him out, and Albert climbed into the Drain Surgeon van, telling them both to stand clear of the gate. Three or four dozen sets of eyeballs were fixed on him, and Albert didn't mean to disappoint. He cranked the van, which had perhaps single-handedly destroyed the ozone, and motored east on Kip Slough Road about a hundred yards, trailing black exhaust. He flipped a U-turn, gassed out a few more mushroom clouds of carbon, and then came roaring in, the gas pedal floored, the doors rattling, the engine scream- ing. Forty, fifty, sixty miles an hour. He had paid two hundred dollars for this tank, and he intended to get his money's worth, steering straight for the thirty-yard picket line of fence posts. The first one snapped like a twig—Albert didn't even feel it— and the rest followed in line with the racket of an airliner going down. The transmission, the front grille, and both bumpers were strewn behind him in the wreckage of downed posts and mangled fencing.

For at least another day, Peg's As You Like It was open for business.

Theresa Ianicci cooked one of her specialities at home in Harbor Light every morning, bracciole, or stuffed peppers, maybe, and then her son sent a car to bring Nonna and her Italian delicacies to Ristorante Victor in Atlantic City. The daily shuttle was a real production, handled with care and precision, as if they were transporting the crown jewels. Victor had fired a driver who took the turn a little too fast off Memorial Bridge one day, sending the top two layers of a beautiful tiramisu sliding into Nonna Ianicci's lap. She was in the kitchen of the restaurant when Albert poked his head inside, looking for Victor.

"Is that you, Albert? Come on over here and dip a piece of nice French bread into this marinara. You look like you haven't eaten in weeks."

Albert's policy with the Ianiccis, Nonna included, was to make a quick entrance and an even quicker exit whenever possible.

"You spoil me with food this good," Albert said, taking a second dip. "You and my mom, God rest her soul." They crossed themselves together, and then Albert asked if Victor was around.

"He's in the back with this fancy chef he hired. Why, I'll never know. Everything is reduction this and sun-dried that. I couldn't tell you what's on the plate half the time. Ravioli with pumpkin sauce? I get *aciada* thinking about it. Wait, I think I hear him coming."

Victor appeared along with the chef, who could tell Nonna Ianicci had been talking about him again. Albert gave a little nod indicating he'd like to chat outside, and he gave a grateful good-bye to Mrs. Ianicci.

They walked up the southern end of the Boardwalk, a two-mile strip of garish palaces built on the most basic principle of American life. That hard work was vastly overrated, and there were far quicker ways to get one up on the next guy. The Pick 6, the Publishers Clearing House sweepstakes, the dark horse, the sleeper stock, the insurance scam, the dream job that fell into your lap for no good reason, doubling your salary. Didn't everyone want to live better than they did now? Albert had jumped for joy when his number came up, an escalating six-figure salary with signing bonus to boot. That day on the island, he couldn't get over his luck. And now here he was, not one month later, giving it all back. It was pure hell, living with a conscience in the world today. The things you forfeited.

"I need to ask a few questions about Oscar Price," Albert said to Victor, who wore his usual pleated knit slacks and pressed sports shirt, loafers with no socks. Gangster casual. He was getting carried away with the tanning thing, though. He looked like eggplant.

"I thought you quit on him," Victor said.

"Even so."

"Then ask away."

"Out of curiosity, you ever hear of a personnel director he's got working for him? Italo-American girl who calls herself Gina Fiorentino."

Victor smiled ear to ear.

"Yeah, I heard you hooked up with her."

"You heard that?"

"What am I, an amateur? It's my job to know things in this town."

"Well what do you know about her?"

"She's a smart girl is what I hear."

"Meaning?"

"Meaning she doesn't have to be told what to do. If you're with Gina, maybe you forget about Rickie, right? Maybe you don't lose any sleep if Rickie loses her restaurant. Gina knows this is what the boss has in mind, so she goes after you without him having to tell her. She's aces."

"So in other words, Gina knows that sleeping with me isn't going to hurt her career."

"With you, among others."

For the briefest moment, Albert thought she was calling Naples to tell the family all about him, and now it turns out she's the town punching bag?

"Who else?"

"You don't want to know."

"Really I do."

"Her boss, for one."

Albert swallowed the wrong way and choked as if he had a cat down there. Never in a million years would he have picked

Oscar Price and Gina Fiorentino to go with each other. Price struck him as too busy counting money to remember what else there was.

"You okay there?" Victor asked.

"Fine," Albert whispered like an emphysema patient.

"So yeah, she took care of the boss, you might say. Serviced a few of the Japanese high rollers, took care of the headliners now and then. She cleaned Frank Sinatra's pipes a time or two, this girl. You're in good company, anyway."

"Maybe I'll start singing in the shower. You done, by the way? Because I should run out to Atlantic Avenue and see if I can score some penicillin."

"That's what you wanted to know? What did this girl do, Albert? She break your heart?"

"Actually it's not her I came to see you about. I wanted to know what you could tell me about the deal Price cut with Senator Croydon on the new casino. And Joe Salvatore, too."

"There you go. I forgot about him. Gina Fiorentino's fucking him, too."

"She's fucking Joe Salvatore?"

"No, Senator Croydon."

"Are you and Joe Salvatore the only ones she hasn't rolled? Is this what you're telling me?"

"What I'm telling you is that Joe Salvatore got a new car and a few bucks to throw at his wife. Croydon made out a little better. Since he put up the bill to legalize gambling in Harbor Light, six of his blood relations—either his or his wife's—have landed at Evolution."

"Six of them got jobs? Are you sure?"

"You want their names? One of them was going to be your boss when the new casino opens."

"What do you mean, one of them was going to be my boss? I was supposed to be chief of security."

"Right. But they've got a couple of positions above that in the security department. I guess Oscar Price forgot to tell you that little detail. This guy is Croydon's brother-in-law. He gets vice president for security operations, something like that."

"Vice president, he gets. Is he a cop?"

"No. He manages a tire company in Absecon. All-season radials."

Albert was aware that Victor Ianicci was no Al Capone, but he knew a few people. Would it be an imposition to ask if he could take Oscar Price on a long fishing trip? Price had fleeced him six different ways, and Albert felt like a fool. Here he'd had visions of executive rank and privilege, when in fact he would have been reporting to a tire salesman.

"Let me change the subject," Albert said. "Croydon and Price use the same law firm on certain types of business, am I right?"

"Yeah, and they're crooks, those lawyers. The law firm launders campaign contributions to Croydon."

"Well what would you make of a fifty-thousand-dollar check from the law firm to Croydon the day after the bill is introduced to the legislature? The bill to take gambling out of Atlantic City."

"How would you know about it?"

"I checked with Janelle Isola from high school. Remember her? She works at the bank in Jersey Landing."

"What would I make of it? Well first of all, Price deals in cash. Why else would anybody own a casino but to move money around without leaving a trail? I'd say he gets the fifty grand to the law firm in cash, they write a check to Croydon, and everybody keeps their mouths shut. You wanna know what I really think? I think fifty grand is light. I'd say it's the first installment. Croydon's got a lot of work ahead of him to get the legislature over to his side. Plus, he was the lead guy with getting the bridge built, the property condemned, all of that prep work."

Albert had gotten what he'd come for. He walked Victor back to the restaurant, and along the way, he felt a little guilty. Here was Victor, telling him everything he knew, and Albert was holding back on him. On Albert's suggestion, the FBI still had an eye on Victor for the bridge bombing, and Muldoon said they'd put a wire in the kitchen of Ristorante Victor. They wouldn't get him on the bridge, but loan-sharking, prostitution, money laundering, and kneecapping might keep them busy for a while. Albert almost gave Victor a heads up, but stopped himself. He was a little looser with the rules these days, but he was not quite ready to join the mob.

"Thanks," Albert said. "And tell your mom I said goodbye."

An unfamiliar unmarked step-van was parked out front of Manny's Bait Bucket when Albert pulled up to his office, but the mystery was solved the moment he got out of the car. The side panel of the cream-colored van rolled open, and Dagget and Cramer bounded out like bloodhounds.

"Nice day," Dagget said.

"Nice van," Albert snarked. "You boys got a Scout jamboree coming up this weekend?"

"We need to talk," Cramer gruffed.

"What about?"

Albert saw now that the van was a mobile office, which did not bode well. It was equipped with a computer, fax, telephone, video monitor, and a tape recorder, suggesting they expected to be doing business sometime soon. Something other than driving around in a stupor, trying to make sense of island life.

"Georgianna and I would have been happy to share our office, if you guys were looking for some work space," Albert offered as he climbed aboard.

The door rolled shut behind them with a blunt and final metallic thud, and Albert had the distinct sensation of having just stepped into a jail cell. Now the trick here was to maintain total cool, as if this were just a friendly little tailgate party among friends, and generally do whatever it took to conceal the fact that his heart had stopped pumping. He had already gone beyond obstruction of justice and accessory, and was now advancing boldly toward aiding and abetting. He could go to jail over it. But given the ordinariness of his life to this point, there was a bit of exhilaration in taking a walk on the wild side. Here he was, about to test his creative powers in an FBI interrogation. And there was, of course, an ulterior motive. Engineering a reprieve for Jack certainly couldn't hurt Albert's odds of getting a second chance from Rickie. Maybe Jack would get his wish.

Dagget and Cramer set up on either side of him, using a flipdown table as their desktop. Dagget opened a notebook and tapped it with a pen, and Cramer, the sawed-off crew cut guy, checked the batteries on the tape recorder. Something about the scene took Albert back to high school baseball, when he hit a game-winning home run against Wildwood, and Steven Genarro from the school paper wanted an interview for his story. Albert was game. He said he wanted to thank the man upstairs, first of all, and that his philosophy, after careful study, was to take it one game at a time. He said he'd been seeing the ball well, got a pitch to hit, and put a good swing on it, and that with any luck, he'd touch all the bases again later that night and be wearing Janelle Isola's panties on his head. Well sure enough, Steven Genarro put the entire quote into his story, the faculty adviser was asleep at the wheel, and Albert was suspended for three days and two games after the newspaper came out. The good news, however, was that he nailed Janelle Isola.

"This looks serious. Should I call my attorney?" Albert asked.

"Not unless you think you need one," said Dagget.

"Of course not. What can I do for you?"

"What were you doing in Philadelphia on Tuesday?"

The tape recorder was whirring and Dagget was earnestly scribbling in his notepad. They must have gone through the van with a caulking gun to seal off the smallest crack of ventilation, because it was suffocating in here.

"Let me ask you boys something," Albert said. "Are oxygen masks going to drop down from the ceiling here pretty soon?"

"You a little warm?" Cramer asked with an idiot's grin.

"I'm fine myself, but you're starting to look like a Vienna sausage. What do you say we crack the roof vent?"

Dagget ignored the request and repeated his question. What was Albert doing in Philadelphia?

"I was feeling patriotic and thought I'd go have a look at the Liberty Bell."

Dagget began writing something in his notebook.

"That's L-i-b-e-r . . ." Albert said before he was interrupted by another question.

"You didn't happen to stop by the police department, did you?"

"I do have a few old friends there. You guys know that about me, though. As close as we've become by now."

"You wouldn't happen to have been asking questions about Jack Davenport?"

"I can't remember, but I did stop by his girlfriend's place to see if he was there. Missed him."

"How about yesterday? You do anything with Davenport yesterday?"

So they *were* watching. Albert had been joking when he wondered if they were up the lighthouse with binoculars. They'd definitely zeroed in on Jack as their man, and that meant they thought Albert knew far more than he was letting on.

"Yeah. We went out on my boat for a couple hours."

"Catch any fish?"

"We struck out all around. I guess you two could identify."

"So you go fishing but you catch no fish. What's the point of that?"

"I can see you're not a fisherman yourself, but you're right. To be honest, I've been concerned about Jack. Working in that hardware store all day, helping out his mother whenever he can . . . I thought he needed some down time."

"Just how well do you really know Davenport?"

This was not sounding particularly encouraging. Albert suspected Jack would be receiving a special delivery any day now. A target letter. And they might be coming by with search warrants, too. A federal grand jury must have been convened, and Jack would be called to testify. Albert, too, probably. He could see that Cramer and Dagget were prepared to keep him here for hours, trying to catch him in a slipup. So now was the time to make the play.

"Funny you should ask that—I've been thinking myself that I don't know him all that much. What do you guys think I should know about him?"

"He likes to make political statements. Civil disobedience, vandalism. He seems to be on a career track, and all of a sudden, Harbor Light, of all places, had an opening for a sociopath."

"Look, what do you say we stop wasting each other's time? You know I'm close to Jack, and no bull, I'm worried about him. You might not believe it, but I didn't even know that my own father was in a bomb squad in the war." Dagget and Cramer looked at each other. Albert could tell there was an unspoken question: Why didn't we know that?

"But it wasn't until I took Jack out on the boat yesterday that I was sure."

Rocky and Bullwinkle hunched over their notebooks.

"I mean, I don't know much about explosives, but my old pal Mike Muldoon gave . . . Hey, you guys probably know Muldoon, don't you? He showed me how to rig up what looked like an explosive charge to the anchor."

Dagget opened his mouth, but shut it again after looking at Cramer.

"So I figured that if I told Jack to drop anchor and he was the bomber, well, you get the idea."

"What did you use?"

"It was set up to resemble a little block of plastique, about the size of a soap bar, and I had it hot-wired to the button on the electric flywheel. I had to know."

"He didn't recognize it?"

"He wouldn't have known it from saltwater taffy."

"Maybe he didn't notice it at all."

"Of course he did. He asked what the hell it was and I had to think on my feet. I told him I'd just gotten it by mail order. One of those miracle gizmos that bring the fish around."

"And he bought that?"

"He dropped anchor, to answer your question. If he knew anything about high explosives, he would have known it should have blown us to a fishing hole on the moon. But even so, I wasn't too sure about him. I've had this feeling in my gut that he didn't do the bridge, but he might have been in on some of the other stuff. So I tried to sweat him a little bit, you know? Run him into a corner, get him tripping over his own words. I tried, but I wasn't getting anywhere, so I got a little rough with him. I still haven't ruled him out for the pipe bomb in Price's car."

Dagget underlined whatever he had written.

"But I'm pretty sure we're after someone else on the bigger jobs. I think I'll know more after I talk to a guy named Dave Rudnick. Jack spent a little time in lockup with him, and that kid's got a few screws loose, from what I understand. He knows as much about explosives as I know about lures."

"We know about Rudnick," Cramer said in a tone that made Albert think they didn't know very much at all.

"Well, great, you're way ahead of me."

"Who's to say they weren't in on it together?" Dagget asked.

"Sounds like Jack isn't in this kid's league. Way too much of a pansy."

Cramer narrowed his eyes. "You expect us to believe this?"

"You can believe whatever you want. Look, you guys are under a lot of pressure and so am I. You guys are stumped and so am I. So why don't we start working together? I've got Sheriff Caster counting on me, I've got Oscar Price watching every move, I've got reporters calling on me. Then you guys come down to the bushes, a couple of big leaguers, and I'm trying to impress everyone. I would have killed for a shot at the FBI, by the way, but I barely made it out of high school, so forget college. Anyhow there I was, hell-bent on impressing the lot of you, not coming off like some small-town rube. Ordinarily an illegal left turn is the highlight of my day around here, or some old geezer flips out and waves his cane at his wife. And all of a sudden I've got murder, I've got arson, I've got mystery and drama, and here's my one shot at glory in twenty-five years of hacking. And do you know who my guy was? Jack Davenport. I was dead sure of it. But I'm playing all hunches there. Outside of the kid from Taco Bell spotting a white SUV, which could have been Jack's white pickup, and some circumstantial evidence, what is there? No witnesses, no physical evidence, no nothing. Maybe you guys have a material case against him, I don't know. Congratulations if you do. But I tried everybody and everything, and what do I have to show for it? A big zero. Nada. Zilch. You want to know what I think?"

Dagget was tapping his pen and Cramer was still recording, and Albert couldn't tell whether they believed any of this. But they were listening, anyway.

"After yesterday, I don't know where to go with it. I'm wondering if I spent so much time looking at him, I missed someone else."

"Like who?" Dagget asked.

Albert shook his head, suffering more disgrace.

"This is my turf. I grew up here. You'd think I would be able to answer that, wouldn't you? It's a public humiliation for me, but I haven't given up on it yet. I still wouldn't rule out the Ianicci crew fronting for the other casinos. Creed James still scares me a little bit. Or it could just be some sociopath who likes playing with fire, like Rudnick. Like I say, I'm stumped. Maybe it's Jack, maybe it isn't."

Cramer, who did nothing with any subtlety or class, shifted about, tipping off a proclamation. "Maybe it's you," he said.

Albert laughed, but neither one of them joined in.

"You're kidding, right?"

"You want to talk motive?" Dagget asked. "Your father's store gets a boost from the fire on the Parkway. Your girlfriend's restaurant gets a break when the bridge blows. And you've got the perfect cover. You're a cop, number one, and you're ostensibly going to work for Oscar Price, number two."

"You guys are serious?"

No answer. Albert suspected that they weren't. That they had pinned it up on the board one day along with a few other wild guesses and then shot it down. He suspected that no matter what he told them, it was still Jack in their minds, and that he, Albert, was going to have to do something bold, dangerous, and stupid to disabuse them of that notion.

About the only thing he could think of doing right now in this sweatbox, the hot breath of these two apes on him like blowtorches, was to buy some time by sending them up yet another trail. They were headhunters, essentially. Sure they wanted Jack. But they'd be just as happy if it were, say, Senator Croydon's head they brought back.

"Can I make a suggestion?" Albert asked. "There's an even bigger fish out there, believe it or not. But I've hit a wall on a lead I'm working. You guys, with your resources, your know-how, you could end up running the FBI if this one works out for you."

They were about as skeptical as any two cops could be. But helplessly interested. Albert leaned in close again. He said, "Now listen to this . . ."

Albert ducked under the Evolution facade of man ascending from apes and cut through a gaming floor that suggested the colossal failure of natural selection. They must be running a special today—an extra roll of quarters for anyone eighty pounds overweight. A South Philly kid with ears like car doors was singing "Come Fly with Me" in the Primate Pub, and two hundred people were in line for tickets to a song-and-dance revue of sitcom theme songs, starring Suzanne Somers. The proof of Oscar Price's managerial mettle was that he'd installed a moving sidewalk between the banquet buffet and the slots, and it was rush hour in the cattle chutes right now. Pure genius.

Albert cut past the clover green fields of blackjack tables, around the sober homily of croupier call-outs, and through the vast chromed cemetery of slot machine headstones. He was out of breath when he sidled up to Natural Selection for a cold beer with a double whiskey back, and here was the thing. He loved to flop in and drop a few dollars on a blackjack table now and then, loved the desperation-edged company of fellow travelers, dreamers, and sinners, even loved going home with a well-earned headache and new failures to bitch about. But the casino job would have drained the joy from the experience, especially given the cost. And it was Jack, of all people, who had helped clarify that for him. He'd expected to catch hell from his father for taking a job with Oscar Price, and maybe he had known, subconsciously, that it would push Rickie away, too. What he had not counted on was Jack feeling so let down. Through twenty-five years, a wasted marriage, and ten thousand and one nights at Mo's, Albert had kept everything that was important to him at a safe distance. Everything but the memory of gunfire in a dark room, and the eyes of a terrified little boy looking up at him. Now he had Jack's eyes on him, Rickie's son, and this time Albert wasn't so helpless.

He slugged back his refreshments and took the elevator upstairs. The receptionist was on the phone, but Albert didn't even slow down. He swept past her with a wave and said, "I'll be in a meeting if you need me." She was protesting and buzzing as Albert barged in. Price was on the phone at his desk, his eyes following Albert across the room as if Albert were a postal employee with a parachute and a live grenade. Albert went over to the sofa, his usual spot, crossed his legs, and lit himself a blunt. He was going to miss the view from up here.

The essential challenge, he reminded himself, was to send a clear message without saying much of anything. With a man of Price's psyche, you could do a far more thorough job of intimidation with what you didn't tell him. He was a details man. A micromanager. Give him something to work with, including crisis management, and his wizardry was probably unparalleled. If he hadn't already crafted his deals with Senator Croydon and Joe Salvatore to fall within arguable legal bounds, he'd get right to work removing his fingerprints, finding someone to take the fall, or calling in chits with the legions of judicial and political players whose careers he had bankrolled. That was the basic arrangement across the land, a marriage of legal extortion and political survival that governed public policy from Harbor Light to Honolulu.

In Jersey, the twist was that a bolder strain of greed often came into play, particularly when you involved a dinosaur like Senator Croydon. He was preceded in public office by his father and grandfather, both of whom ended their careers in prison, and he operated on the theory that he ought to grab all that he could before completing the Croydon trifecta.

Price abruptly ended his telephone call and peered somewhat menacingly at Albert.

"I figured it was rude, on principle, to resign over the phone. Even if it's a job you haven't started yet," Albert said as Price walked slowly across the room to join him. Price had one eye on the door, as if he were thinking of running over there and telling the receptionist to call security. Albert smiled at the irony of that.

"Have a seat," Albert suggested. "Really, this won't take long."

"If you don't mind," Price interrupted, "I don't appreciate you storm-trooping in here. I told you on more than one occasion, I believe this project will put the island on the map. As

for the details of what happens through right-of-way considerations and eminent domain proceedings, all of that is in the
hands of the state of New Jersey. I can't save someone just because you want me to."

"Well you're probably right about putting Harbor Light
on the map. And given the reach of your influence, I suspect
you'll have your Polynesian Princess before long. But I wanted
you to know I'm getting extremely tired of being harassed for
information by the FBI. I thought all they were doing was trying to figure out who our mad bomber is, but they've apparently broadened their area of interest."

Price was beginning to look somewhat less bored.

"Sheriff LaRosa, I don't speak in code, and I don't enjoy
listening to people who do," he said without moving his lips.
"Is there something specific you'd like to tell me?"

"Yes. I'd like to tell you that I'm going to count my twenty-
five-thousand-dollar signing bonus as payment for services
rendered. And I'd like to say that if a demolition crew gets
within an inch of that restaurant again, I'm going to invite the
FBI to a long lunch and tell them stories about public officials
who seem to have hit jackpots lately. I'm sorry. Am I speaking
in code again?"

Albert took the elevator back down and floated across the
casino floor. His pockets were empty, same as they always were
when he left here, but he felt like he'd rolled nothing but sev-
ens. Rare is the man lucky enough to be rescued from the grips
of his own worst instincts.

Albert gave his father an arm to hang onto and pulled him up out of the LaRosa's Hardware & More delivery wagon. Joaquin LaRosa found his feet and gave a look up and down Cannery Way. Most of the parking spaces were taken, and a dozen people were on the street. "That's the way it used to be," he said. "Once upon a time."

"Joaquin, welcome back!" Nuba Ludwick shouted from across the street. "We missed you."

"You thought I was a goner, didn't you?" the old man yelled back. "That was a little tune-up they had me in for. That's all. I'm good for fifty years or fifty thousand miles, Nuba. You watch."

He looked up and down the block for a car and asked Albert where Sam was.

"She's on her way down. She got a late start out of Long Island, but she'll be here. We're all having dinner back at the house tonight."

Albert helped his father up the curb and onto the sidewalk. "I'm telling you I'm fine, Albert. And get rid of this thing for me, will you? I told that quack at the hospital I don't need a damn cane."

"Just hold on to it, Pop, will you? It might come in handy."

"You can give it to me when you're done," Aunt Rose said. "I'd like to hook a few of my customers right up off the booth and out the door."

Joaquin took a step and then stopped when he saw Jack in the doorway of the store.

"What am I paying you for, to check the weather?" the old man asked.

Jack laughed.

"The first break I've had all day, and you're giving me a hard time."

Joaquin LaRosa held his hand out for Jack, who gave him a hug instead. The old man held tight, a grip that said a half dozen things at once.

"I love the smell of this place," the old man said when he stepped inside. "The store's in pretty good shape, too, considering the boss has been away on holiday."

"Albert came by and helped out," Jack said.

Joaquin LaRosa turned to his son.

"Tell me the truth. You quit Oscar Price?"

"I told you six times already, Pop."

"You really told the son of a bitch to shove it?" he asked, his eyes dancing.

"Don't get any ideas. I'm just here to help Jack out until you get back in shape."

"Back in shape? I'm in top condition, Albert. The ticker's stronger than ever. Hand me that feather duster and I'll give everything a once-over."

"You need your rest, Joaquin. Listen to Albert, now. He's finally making sense," Aunt Rose said.

"He's more stubborn than his old man, Rose. Thank god he got at least a little of his mother's common sense."

A customer came in asking for an electric pump for a fountain.

"Third and Maple," Joaquin LaRosa sang, and Jack led the customer toward the back of the store.

"I want you to sit down," Aunt Rose said. "The doctor said to keep off your feet for a day or two."

"Maybe I will take a breather. There's an extra hour of work in a five-minute nap, you know?"

"You see that lounge chair over there, Pop? We moved it up from the basement because that's where you're going to sit. And we're going to chain you to the damn thing if we have to. Jack and I have got you covered, all right?"

"You do a good enough job, I'll put in a word with the owner," Joaquin LaRosa said, a contented look on his round Spanish face. "Who knows when a full-time position might open up?"

Rickie Davenport used to walk home from the diner along Kip Slough Road so she could gaze out on the midafternoon sea and settle whatever desperations a day of toil had stirred. She was still an escape artist at heart, and she could slip away unsighted every day, skating like the wind across the unbordered plane of the sea.

But ever since the bridge construction began, she had to forgo these flights and chart a less upsetting route home. She took Fifth Street south to Elm today, past the gridded symmetry of century-old homes, and then she cut east toward Second. It was raining lightly and she had no umbrella, but she didn't mind. Spring colors were rioting in Harbor Light. The dogwoods in particular had exploded, creamy whites and pornographic pinks, and yellow daffodils were up like swing-band brass sections. She cried most of the way home, partly because of the color, partly because her son's fate was in the hands of federal agents, and partly because tomorrow was the day, eight years ago, that her parents were killed in the accident. When she reached her house, she had one more reason to cry. Albert was in the bench swing on her front porch in a pair of blue jeans and a denim work shirt.

"You're out of uniform," she said.

"Start of my new life."

She came up on the porch like a drenched rat, but a pretty good-looking drenched rat, and sat next to him. Albert's heart floated. With her hair wet, she looked smaller and younger. She was the girl he used to ogle in school, hypnotized by her and scared to death of her, too. The only love worth having.

"You crying?" he asked.

"No. It's the rain. So, it's official?"

"It's official. Fitch drove out from Rag Harbor about noon to introduce the new guy to Georgianna. I gave Fitch my badge, gave him my gun. And that was it. I'm a civilian."

"No ceremony? No gold wristwatch?"

"Georgianna sobbed like a child, if you can imagine that. Tears of joy, I guess. There's a banquet next month in Rag Harbor for me and two other guys retiring."

"So how does it feel?"

"How does it feel? Like I should have thought of this

earlier. Unemployment gets a bad rap, at least judging by the first three hours. But I don't know if I can handle the daily pressure of deciding on an outfit."

"So what are you going to do?"

He honestly hadn't given it much thought. Less than a month ago, it was all planned out for him. He was going to draw an executive salary, shuttle to Vegas on the private jet, moor the boat at his condo tie-up, and throw a lobster on the grill every night. But it vanished as quickly as it had appeared. That was the one thing nobody told you about the perfect life.

"For a week or two, not a thing," Albert said, improvising, or maybe it was dreaming. But that was part of the new deal. His life had fewer boundaries now, and what could be truer than whatever popped into his head at this very moment? "I'm going to stroll the beach like a castaway, go swimming before the place gets overrun with vacation strangers, help out at the hardware store until my pop gets his strength back. Then I'm going to get on a plane and go somewhere. Málaga, maybe, to see if everyone there is as loco as my father. I'm going to pluck oranges out of trees for breakfast, speak Castilian, eat fish and olives all day and drink sangria all night. Sound good to you?"

She smiled dreamily.

"I might ride horses on the beach, too, after my café con leche, but I don't want it too planned out. And after I've maxed out every credit card I can steal, I'm going to come home and run fishing excursions on the new boat until the Coast Guard discovers I'm throwing all the annoying people overboard. Maybe come September I'll figure out the rest of my life, but I'm very flexible on that."

Rickie nodded approvingly. It wasn't a particularly ambi-

tious plan, he knew, but in spirit, at least, it was a far cry from
his years-long routine of carping about a job he didn't have the
stones to quit, despite nightly efforts to summon the courage at
Mo's. If, by chance, any of this appealed to Rickie, Albert was
perfectly willing to consider including her in the trip. But he
knew her better now, and the way she looked at him and then
averted her eyes, he could tell that she still saw some of whatever it was that had driven her away. He wasn't going to push.
He wasn't going to ask a thing about H. Dimwit. This was
going to take time, and he had just bought some.

"Can we talk about Jack?" she asked.

What she really wanted to know was: What are his
chances? That's what she was asking, her voice cracked with
fear, guilt, regret. If she had been a different mother. If she had
shown him a different life. If she had made it clear that ques-
tioning authority did not mean using the *Anarchist's Cookbook*
as a recipe for life, single-handedly wiping out first-quarter
profits for legions of Bargain Acres shareholders.

When the time was right, Albert was going to offer Rickie
his own perspective on the subject. First of all, he would tell
her, no parent could take either credit or blame for the actions
of a twenty-year-old. Kids ought to move out and get their own
apartments on the cusp of puberty, if not before, because
whether they end up a brain surgeon or a bookie, it was out of
a parent's hands by then. And secondly, look at the model
Rickie had been. She worked, she made a home, she honored
her parents, she challenged all threats to her world with right-
eous indignation, forever suspicious of power and money. Jack
was all of that, and although no one could defend his excesses,
you had to appreciate a kid who was equal parts loyalist and

revolutionary. Especially if one of his causes was to hook Albert up with his mother.

"I think they know it's him, but they can't prove it yet. He's not the tidiest terrorist, though, I've got to say. I found a stash of C4—that's the plastic explosive he used on the bridge—in the basement at the hardware store."

"I'm shocked that he's that technical, among other things I'm shocked about. How did he become such an expert?"

"I've learned enough to know there's not really much to it. But the one thing you can't be in that line of work is careless. I'd call him and ask if he keeps gasoline and dynamite in plain view at his girlfriend's house in Philadelphia, but like I told you, it's a safe bet the FBI will be listening in. Sooner or later they're going to come in with search warrants and turn everything upside down. But they're sniffing up another trail right now, so they're kind of distracted. I'd say he's got about a fifty-fifty chance."

Rickie smiled bravely, her eyes filling.

"It's going to be fine," Albert said. "I've got one last trick up my sleeve that's really going to throw them. Trust me."

She shook her head as if she wished she could, showing Albert a vulnerability that was new for her. Or maybe his recognizing it was the new thing.

"My parents would have . . ."

"Your parents would have what?"

"I don't know. The daughter part, I really screwed up. And the mom part, not much better. Here's proof that your kids pay you back by turning out just like you."

Albert could have mustered a word of reassurance, but nothing that might satisfy the need. He reached for her hand instead, and the rain fell like it would never end, drenching the muscular elms and the brick-bordered flowerbeds and raising the fragrance of spring.

"Can you believe the color this year?" he asked.

Rickie leaned into him and Albert locked his arms around, breathing her in. This girl he used to spy a hundred years ago in school.

He searched every closet and drawer. No luck. It had been so long since he went swimming, Albert had no idea where his trunks were or whether they would still fit. That bathing suit went back two decades, so there was a good chance it was out of style. In fact there was a fair chance it was out of style when he used to wear it, fashion always having struck Albert as someone else's concern.

The last possibility was under the bed. Down onto the knobs of his aching knees he went, dropping an eyeball to the floor for a gander. Now this must be why people have maids come by now and then. Albert could call the Smithsonian and offer rights to an archaeological dig. The landscape was magnificent, a lunar quality to it, the dust rising in gentle slopes over long-forgotten slippers, cigarette lighters, socks, an unopened bag of Beer Nuts, and what might be an entire set of shot glasses. Everything but a swimsuit. But Albert was nothing if not resourceful, so he retrieved his khaki uniform trousers from the hamper, scrounged some scissors, and fashioned a pair of cutoffs with a black stripe down the outer seam. Perfect.

The door squeaked shut behind him as he bounded off the porch. Was there any sound as distinctive as a squeaky screen door slamming shut on a summery day? The tail of the storm curled over Harbor Light, pinwheeling seaward, and the sun blasted in behind, turning the island to steam. Albert paused to consider the For Sale sign punched into the rock garden next to the rusty anchor. One heave and he plucked it up like an ironweed, tossing it behind the rotting skiff. The A.C. condo was way out of his reach now, but who needed it? A little tweaking here and there and this bungalow wasn't a bad retreat, two blocks from the open sea. Imagine that. Albert lived two blocks from the beach, used to be a lifeguard, spent his entire childhood in the water, and had not taken a dip in years. He couldn't fall asleep without the sound of the Atlantic, couldn't imagine waking to a different scent, and yet he had not stuck a toe in the water since that sweltering night when he seriously considered a one-way swim.

Arthur Abraham was washing his new van in the driveway and gave a curious wave as Albert flip-flopped down the middle of Jib in his new bathing suit. Over the sandy bluff he marched, up the gut of the narrow, picketed path. He felt the same anticipation in his chest every time he squeezed through to the opening, and the view from the top never disappointed.

New Jersey. Who would have guessed it?

The dappled sea was endless sprawl, ever familiar and always new, and the breeze washed over the island like a salted, tropical balm. It was all a tease, of course. Summer was still only a distant possibility, and if the breeze was from Florida, the current was from Maine. If you stood here thinking about that, you were dead. You had to take it on the run, hope the shock didn't kill you, and call for help when you went from blue to purple.

Albert peeled off his T-shirt and charged on rickety legs across the seashell-littered sand and into the bracing surf, his pulse quickening and his chest filling as he dived cleanly through the briny curl of a four-foot wave. The force of it tugged at his legs and fishtailed him, and he shook with the underwater concussion of the break, the sound of the world exploding.

He swam a good hundred yards, his conditioning nonexistent but his stroke still there from his lifeguard days. He twisted onto his back and floated on the rolling sea, arms outstretched as if he were falling through time. The face of the town looked out on him, stubbornly unglamorous, resilient, and golden in the afternoon light. A month ago, he would have said it had no hold on him.

Three in the morning. Harbor Light is invisible, asleep under a cover of fog, no sound but the howl of the sea.

Three-ten. Rickie Davenport, wrenched from sleep by thoughts first of Jack and then Albert, lights a candle and watches shadows move like scattering leaves across her ceiling.

Three-twenty. Joaquin LaRosa snores the night away, Aunt Rose horned in next to him with her hand on his heart. On the nightstand is the scribbled master plan of a summer blastoff sale to beat the pants off the competition from Atlantic City to Cape May.

Three-twenty-five. Jack Davenport peers through the blinds onto the West Philadelphia street where Special Agents Dagget and Cramer are asleep in their van, parked behind Jack's truck.

Three-thirty. Four time-delay blasting caps, one set in each corner of the Sea-Fruit Cannery, ignite in nearly perfect synchronization. The twenty-megaton blast is a sonic symphony that wakes the soul of the town with the force of planets colliding. Brick and steel rocket skyward, shaking the heavens. Houses jump on their foundations. Windows are shattered in Atlantic City. Among the first to be rousted from sleep and run frightened into the street in his bedclothes, fearing enemy attack, is the originator and chief executive officer of the Polynesian Princess.

Three-thirty-five. Albert LaRosa, ex-sheriff of Harbor Light, pours himself a shot on the porch of his beach bungalow. He raises the glass, catches himself about to laugh, and downs it in one throw.

Under the direction of Joaquin LaRosa and the sponsorship of the *Harbor Light Beacon,* the entire length of Cannery Way's business strip was closed to vehicular traffic for the First Annual Demolition Days Clearance Sale and Summer Blastoff. Merchants set up sidewalk displays in front of their shops, and Peg's As You Like It diner ran a food stall in the center of the street. Down at Legion Park, where twenty-five area farmers sold produce under a circus tent, the county humane society took notes as Al Smith saddled up three of his billies for a goat-ride concession. And Elton Abramowicz, the new resident deputy, got his first taste of what he was in for when asked to mediate several disputes over a promotion offering retail discounts to anyone with a verifiable piece of Betty the Blue Crab, the Sea-Fruit mascot that came crashing down off the roof in the explosion.

By noon on Saturday, so many cars had streamed over Memorial Bridge that Abramowicz called for help with traffic control. Parking was tight at the north end of the island, where demolition crews had begun the task of removing what was left of the cannery. At two o'clock sharp, Aunt Rose was declared the Demolition Days queen in a ceremony at the Legion Park gazebo, with entertainment provided by Mario the barber on accordion. Wearing a pair of red dynamite-stick earrings she had bought at one of the crafts tables, Aunt Rose was paraded around the park in her pink Cadillac convertible, which was driven by Creed James. Aunt Rose lit firecrackers and tossed them out of the car, and a startled goat darted across the park, knocked over a display of Jersey tomatoes, and jumped head-first through the pane-glass window of Nuba's Pie Shop. At the end of his shift, Deputy Abramowicz left a message with Sheriff Fitch Caster, requesting an immediate transfer.

Special Agents Dagget and Cramer spent the bulk of their weekend in the ceiling of the capitol building in Trenton, installing a surveillance camera over the desk of seven-term state senator Robert Croydon. They had suffered the humiliation and unpleasantness of reporting to the bureau chief that their primary suspect in the series of fires and bombings was asleep in Philadelphia at the time of the Sea-Fruit explosion, and that they couldn't build a convincing case on any of the other incidents. They were ordered to immediately shift their focus to the relationship between Senator Croydon and Oscar Price, and the bureau chief ended the meeting with a throwaway comment about the difficulty Washington was having in filling two openings in the Omaha office. Meanwhile, the bureau was awaiting lab tests from the site of the cannery explosion and considering whether to reassign the case of the mystery bomber, or find a neat way to pull out altogether and lay responsibility at the feet of local authorities.

Oscar Price, for his part, had managed to cast himself as the underdog in an interview with a particularly vapid television reporter from Fox News in New York. With square-jawed optimism and American stick-to-it-ism, Price vowed to continue his uphill battle to save the island economy. Architects were drawing up plans to build from scratch on the site of the Sea-Fruit Cannery, provided state voters approved a bill to allow gambling in Harbor Light. Price was entirely unaware that his office, his home, and his new Ferrari had been bugged by Special Agents Dagget and Cramer. Nor did he know that Gina Fiorentino, whom he was still sleeping with, had been embezzling him since her first day on the job. Gina was now secretly discussing a deal with the U.S. attorney's office in which she would testify to various campaign finance irregularities involving Price, in return for consideration of a lighter sentence.

They'd taken their limits of weakfish and stripers in the channels around Brigantine, and now the Tiara Pursuit cut a wake south about a mile offshore, gunning for the horizon. The sun rode the height of its arc, and the rising interior heat drew a moderate northeasterly off the sea. This time of year, these conditions, Albert knew a spot in the shoals off Ocean City. He'd fished flounder and blue there since he was a boy, and he was headed back again, high in the cockpit, the wind in his face.

"I had no idea it was this fast," Jack said, standing off Albert's shoulder and watching over the bow as the mirrored sea slid cleanly under the hull.

"We've got the wind at our backs," Albert said.

"So how'd you come up with the name for the boat?"

"It came to me in a rare moment of clarity," Albert said as he opened it up all the way. The bow rose, and in a matter of seconds they cleared the entire length of Harbor Light, then broke for open sea, the new name painted in clean white script.

In the Clear.